MW01253454

TO REDEMPTION

Reluctant Redemption Book 3

REG QUIST

Rough Road to Redemption
by Reg Quist

Paperback Edition

CKN Christian Publishing
An Imprint of Wolfpack Publishing

6032 Wheat Penny Avenue
Las Vegas, NV 89122

Paperback ISBN: 978-1-64734-089-6
Ebook ISBN: 978-1-64734-088-9
Library of Congress Control Number: 2020943021

ROUGH ROAD
TO REDEMPTION

*To the brave men and women who,
down through the ages, have done their duty,
lived the life, and accepted the results.
Heroes all.*

CHAPTER ONE

"We got off to a late start by a day or two, Boss. But judging by the miles behind us, it just could be we've made up the most of that time. Pueblo can't be much more than just a jump and a shout away. We get a few miles further along, we'll be able to hear the steam whistle, and maybe the big brass bell, and see the black smoke blow'n from that big ol' engine, delivering your friends into town."

As usual, Trig broadcast this opinion with a grin, and a look that could mean almost anything.

Zac aimed a questioning study at the young man riding beside him, as he had done so often before.

"I'm thinking you're just a mite ahead of yourself on that, Trig. We've a ways to go yet. But then, you've been known to be a little over-optimistic from time to time."

"If you're referring to a certain young Texas lady, the less said about that the better."

"I don't recall mentioning a Texas lady. I might be referring to the weather."

"You might. But you ain't."

***

Rev. Moody Tomlinson leaned past his wife to get a better look out the smoke and grime-smeared passenger-car window.

"Sarah, my dear, I do believe those buildings we see up ahead just might be Pueblo, Colorado. Not much else to see along here, is what I've been told. First sign of civilization will be our destination. That's what the conductor said."

His totally exhausted and somewhat discouraged wife said nothing in response.

"It's been a long trip, dear. And these hard, wooden seats have done nothing much but make it seem longer. I promise you the best hotel bed we can find for this night. Then it's off to our new home."

"If we don't get lost in the wilderness or scalped by Indians before we get there."

"Now, my dear, it's not that bad. Those days are gone. Washed away and hidden in the dusts of time."

Sarah and the woman sitting opposite her, both rolled their eyes at this statement; Sarah in serious wonder at her husband's understanding of the frontier, and Nancy, her younger sister, in humorous anticipation of the trip, regardless of the seeming naivety of the good reverend.

Sarah knew her pastor husband was nowhere near as naïve as he was letting on. He was attempting to comfort her. They both understood the game. But as long as the game didn't become reality on the journey south to Las Vegas, New Mexico, the pretense would cause no harm.

The passengers could feel the train slowing for the curve that would lead them into town. The clackety clacks, as the wheels crossed the track joints, were spaced further apart as they slowed. The weary passengers sat up straighter, working the kinks out of shoulders and spines. A few stood, anticipating their relief from the smoky, stifling confines of the car.

The smiling, eager travelers that had boarded the train days ago and many miles to the east, were glum in fatigue, desperate for real rest and a hot meal. Children had finally fought their siblings to a silent standstill. Babies had cried themselves into nothing more than sad whimpering, their mothers having no solution to their discomfort.

Men and women alike, sensing the danger of expressing their feelings, were being careful with their words.

A great blast from the steam whistle was the engineer's signal that the long trip across the western flat lands was drawing to an end. The fireman gave a few energetic pulls on the lanyard that tipped the bell, as if he too, was celebrating the end of the long ride. And relief from the endless shoveling of coal.

For many of the passengers it was their first experience on the rails. But it hadn't taken many hours for the excitement of the adventure to give way to dread. With the first cinder-laden cloud of heavy grey smoke, the paying customers rushed to close the car's windows. Still, every time the carriage door was opened the smoke was there, ready to push in, filling the now suffocating interior.

Relief from the throat searing engine smoke came only when the crosswind blew it in another direction. With the unpredictable wind, relief was a sometimes thing.

"I'll assist you ladies off the train, see you to the station platform. Perhaps you can find some shade there, or maybe a bench to rest on."

Nancy laughed, interrupting the pastor.

"I can't image anything my tired bones and posterior need less than a bench to rest on."

Moody studied her for a moment, somewhat taken back by the mention of a posterior, Nancy's or anyone else's, and then proceeded with his instructions.

"I'll see to the unloading of our wagon and team. We'll have to wait our turn, but it shouldn't take long. You'll be safe enough, I'm sure, what with all the folks around.

"Zac was planning to be here, so you keep an eye out for him. The country is large. The communications are slow and unreliable. He may or may not make it here on time."

Nancy spoke again.

"You see to the team and wagon. Sarah and I will be fine. And take special care of my saddle horse. He'll be needing water and a chance to stretch his legs."

Rev. Moody took his eyes off the town ahead long enough to nod agreement to his wife's younger sister.

***

"Listen-up, Boss. I ain't heard but one or two

locomotive whistles any time in the past, but I'd be willing to bet that's exactly what that is, blow'n in from up yonder."

Trig nudged his gelding into a lope. Zac followed the example.

"We get around and beyond this rock ridge, we'll maybe see if you're correct."

"You hurt my feeling with your doubting, Boss. I hope you understand that."

Zac didn't bother responding.

Rounding the western end of the rocky ridge, Zac and Trig pulled their horses to a halt.

"Will you look at that, Boss? That there is what might be called a city. Or at the very least, a good-sized town. And there's that big old engine, puffing out foul, black, coal smoke and blowing off steam, just a hankering to finally see an end to the heavy pull from wherever it came from."

Zac took a long study of the buildings laid out before them.

"Denver's bigger, but this will do as second place. Let's get ourselves down there."

Trig smiled at his riding partner.

"From what you've told me, and the feelings I remember from the folks back home, there's no telling what trouble your overly trusting Reverend friend might get himself into. Left to himself is what I mean."

"Don't you be misjudging the Reverend."

Trig ignored Zac's last remark.

***

The arrival of a locomotive was still a novelty to

most of the town's citizens. Kids grabbed up their stick horses and galloped to the depot. People along the way waived to the engineer in the hopes of receiving a return wave. When the big steam whistle blasted, several horses pulled free of the hitch rails. Teams pulling wagons shied, making life difficult for the wagon master for a few seconds.

The clanging bell, almost dignified as it sounded out its message, was modest, but a more welcome announcement of the train's arrival.

Folks with nothing pressing in on their time began wandering towards the excitement. It wasn't long before a crowd gathered.

Among the crowd were kids with printed advertisements telling of the wonderous bargains to be had at the general merchandise store, the hotel, a particular saloon and eating house, the saddlery, the livery and horse-trading establishment, and many others. The kids were paid a penny for every printed sheet that arrived back in the merchant's hands, proving their effectiveness.

***

Among the gathering were two rough, bearded, unwashed, unwise, and slightly inebriated riders. They took in the newcomers fighting their way onto the crowded platform and smiled with unwarranted confidence.

"Ace, them there is two fine look'n ladies standing right against the shade of the station. I expect they're new to town. Look to be alone and in need. The one is nudging up to middle age but the other'n is jest com'n out'a her prime. Let's go offer our services as guides and protectors."

Without waiting for a response from his partner, the rider nudged his horse into the crowd, pushing folks aside as he thoughtlessly approached the station platform.

Ace hurried to follow.

"Don't you be getting us into no new trouble, Hammer. The sheriff still has his eye out for us after that last idea you had didn't work out so good."

Ignoring his partner's warning, the smiling Hammer rode up to the edge of the platform. He doffed his hat, allowing his unwashed hair to stick out in all directions.

"Afternoon, ladies. New to town and wondering about things, I'm guessing. Mayhap 'ol' Ace and me, we can kind of take you under our wings, so to speak. Look out fer yer welfare, you understand."

Sarah was just about to ask directions to a good hotel, but her sister pulled her away from the men.

"Sarah," she whispered, "sometimes I really wonder about you. Those men aren't here to help."

"So, ladies," laughed Hammer, "why don't you climb up here behind us? We'll ride you anywhere you're wishful of going."

He was holding his filthy hat before him like a shield, while a somewhat wiser and worried-looking Ace was cautiously edging closer.

***

Zac, newly arrived at the station, took a few seconds to assure himself that one of the ladies being addressed by the rough pair of riders was, indeed, Sarah Tomlinson, wife to the Reverend

Moody Tomlinson.

He hadn't seen the family for some years and Sarah had changed just enough to draw some doubt. And then, for her to be standing with a second lady, this one some bit younger and considerably prettier, added to his doubt.

As he was thinking this through, he saw the frantic Reverend struggling through the crowd on the platform, intent on coming to the women's rescue.

Hammer pulled his horse sideways to the platform. He leaned down and touched Sarah on the shoulder, again inviting her to mount behind him. Her scream gained the attention of everyone on the platform.

Zac was about to shout a warning to the two intruders when he heard a whirring noise from behind him. Before he could do more than glance sideways, Trig pushed his horse towards the platform, his lariat twisting into a large loop, over his head.

Several folks scrambled quickly away from the small gathering, causing Hammer to turn his horse just enough to see Trig riding down on him. His turn had put him hard against Ace.

With no shout of warning, Trig made one last whirl and released the loop. The leading edge of the bone-hard riata dropped over Hammer's head and shoulders, smacking his ear on the way past. A half second later the following side of the loop dropped over Ace, encircling the two men's arms and chests in the one large coil of rope.

Before either surprised man could react, Trig took a dally on the horn, spun his horse in a half circle and dug in with his spurs. The rope tightened, firmly grasping both men. The ruffians were yanked from their saddles, landing with a solid thump on the hard-packed depot yard.

Trig let his gelding feel the spurs again and, with a series of Rebel yells, headed for the open plain. The two men bounced along at the end of the rope, screamed in pain and rage.

Within a hundred yards of being dragged across the rocky, cactus-spread ground the men's vests and shirts were in tatters.

One of Hammer's spurs caught on the root of a low growing cactus. The spur stuck fast. The boot was ripped from Hammer's foot, nearly breaking his ankle in the process.

Ace lost his gun belt and holster. His canvas pants were reduced to cactus-needle embedded shreds.

As Trig sped forward, the two men rolled over and over, with first, Hammer taking the worst of the punishment and then rolling so that Ace was against the ground.

A large pod of prickly pear made for a tempting target. Trig eased his horse just a bit to the left. The pod exploded as the spiny pads broke off and flew in all directions. The screams of the two men could be heard back at the small station.

A large, silent crowd soon gathered. The Reverend and his wife looked on in tremulous wonder. Nancy couldn't remove her eyes from the sight, even as the receding men were half hidden in desert dust.

At two hundred yards Trig slowed his tiring horse to a lope. At three hundred yards he called 'whoa'. He unwound the lasso from the saddle horn and dropped it on the ground, leaving the two men firmly snugged together by the loop of twisted hemp. Without a backward glance he turned the gelding towards the depot, adjusted his hat, massaged the sore spot on his thigh where the lariat had been rubbing, and rode back, intent on meeting Zac's friends.

As he rode up beside Zac, he doffed his hat at the ladies.

"Sorry about all the ruction, ladies. Those two fellows won't bother you no more. As a matter pure fact, I suspect if they had taken time to think it through, they would have sent their apologies.

"Welcome to Colorado."

Rev. Moody and the ladies were speechless. The others on the platform were beginning to come out of their silent wonder. A few were smiling and nodding at Trig. The platform was becoming a hubbub of wondering chatter, with many sideways glances aimed Trig's way.

Zac studied his riding partner

"Where's your rope?"

"Felt it was time enough for me to get a new one."

CHAPTER TWO

After the crowd on the platform turned back to their own matters and the introductions and welcomes were behind them, Zac and Trig went with Moody to unload the wagon and team. The women decided to join them.

Nancy smiled at Trig.

"As exciting as all of that fine welcome was, we might be wiser to accept it as enough for the first day. We'll tag along with you men."

The engine moved the freight cars ahead one by one. When the car carrying the Moody wagon and horses came level with the built-up dirt ramp, it was only a matter of minutes before the load was standing free, and the next car was being shunted into place.

The first matter was water for the horses. Feed had been available in quantity during the confinement in the car.

Within the hour, hotel rooms had been secured, Trig had purchased a new, longer rope, and the sheriff had satisfied himself that whatever took place at the depot was well justifiable.

Standing in a rough circle on the boardwalk in front of the hotel with Zac and the others, the sheriff had said, "Those boys just can't seem to help themselves. They fall from one jagged cliff only to land on another of their own making, all the time thinking up their next foolish adventure."

Sarah steadied a worried look at the sheriff.

"I do hope they were not seriously hurt."

"I expect they'll get some rest, lay'n around pulling stickers out of their sorry hides. Might be they got a scratch or two. Some rest might give them the time they need to re-think their way of life."

He spoke with such a dry drawl that it was difficult to decide just how serious he was.

"All in all, even a ride through the cactus was better than what might have taken place, given circumstances. Another man might have just pulled iron and put a permanent end to their foolishness. Abusing women is clearly not a thing that's acceptable to folks in Colorado."

***

Nancy's eyes were bright with the newness of the events and all that was around them. She watched as the sheriff crossed the street to his office, wondering at the casualness of western law enforcement.

With the other matters dealt with, the group retired to the hotel dining room for dinner.

***

Trig's earlier actions were set aside in their minds while Zac caught up with the latest happenings in Carob, Texas. Before that information was all shared, the dinner plates were cleared away. Coffee and dessert were being laid out on the table.

Rev. Moody broke a momentary silence, turning his attention to Trig.

"Trig Mason. I seem to remember something about a Mason family. Lived to the east of Carob. Further into the pines. The old man of the family was known far and wide as Pa. Pa Mason. A couple of boys rode off to war. Don't know what became of them. A daughter married an Arkansawyer if memory serves.

"Had a son too young for the conflict. Youngest wasn't named Trig though. Don't recall his name right off. Good family.

"Now, Mason is a fairly common name so there may be no connection, but you have the sound in your voice. Must be from somewhere close by the Piney Woods. Perhaps a cousin or some such to the family I knew."

Trig had been afraid this conversation might come up. It was not that there was any shame in the family. Except for his given name, that is. He surely hoped the good Reverend didn't recall that. How his Pa had thought it would be a good idea to hang a name like that on a son was a great mystery to Trig.

"There's a few cousins and such spread around East Texas alright, but the Pa you speak of is my very own. Trig I'm known by, and Trig will do just fine."

He glared a bit at Rev. Moody hoping he would catch his meaning. The Reverend studied the young man for a moment before his lips turned up in a conspiratorial smile.

"Trig. That's a good name. Trig it is. I'll be interested to hear how you and Zac met up, but that can wait for another time. For now, I've made arrangement with the hotel for an abundance of hot water to be carried up to the bathtub. I believe the ladies will welcome that after the long trip, as I will myself, when my turn comes."

As the table guests stood to their feet Trig stopped their movements by asking, "Before you go, what can you tell me about Pa? Is he well?"

"Well. And as mysterious as always. Saw him in a private conflab at the general store just a short while ago. He nodded his recognition as I passed by but didn't speak."

Trig nodded his thanks in a duplication of his father's mannerisms.

CHAPTER THREE

With one day of rest in Pueblo and another to rig out the wagon and purchase supplies, the group was ready for the trail. Sarah and Nancy were in charge of food purchases, laying in enough for eight to ten days.

Rev. Moody purchased a trail horse. He had brought his saddle and tack with him on the long trip west. The horse would follow along with a lead from the wagon's tailgate when he wasn't being ridden. Sarah would be content riding the wagon, driving it from time to time to relieve the boredom. She had built up the wooden seat with a thickly folded quilt.

Nancy insisted on riding the gelding she brought from Texas. In a large pocket, cunningly sewn into the folds of her split riding skirt, was a Smith & Wesson #2 Army .32 Rimfire.

While the others were purchasing the items needed for the trail, Moody sauntered over to the gun shop. Within a half hour he returned with a Model 66 Winchester .44, complete with a leather scabbard, and a Colt Open Top revolver in a matching .44. There were several boxes of cartridges to accompany the weapons.

He walked to the blacksmith shop. After a couple of minutes of explanation, the blacksmith followed the pastor back to the wagon. Within fifteen minutes the scabbard was attached to the side of the wooden box, where the driver would have the Winchester close to hand. Lying under the seat on a sheep fleece bed and covered with a small piece of canvas to ward off the dust, was a 10-gauge, double-barreled shotgun, loaded and ready.

The .44 Colt was carefully placed into a small leather satchel Moody kept in the bottom of a trunk full of clothing, along with some other personal items.

Zac, forever struggling with the emotional turmoil left from the war, was not feeling especially sociable that morning. With no more than a glance to see that his riding partners were in their places, and assuming they were ready, he kicked his cavalry horse into action, heading out of town in a trot the animal could keep up for hours. He didn't bother looking back.

Trig, flashing his infectious grin, looked at the others.

"We might just as well follow along. I'd hate for him to stop to set up camp this evening and find himself alone."

Sarah said nothing, but the look on her face told of her thoughts. Nancy laughed and heeled her gelding.

Moody had decided to ride the first few miles.

"I'm thinking I'd best try this brute out while

we're still close enough to town to bring him back if he shows any orneriness."

Sarah slapped the lines on the backs of the team and quietly said, "git, you team".

The team stood in the street like statues.

Her husband, riding alongside the wagon, laughed.

"I'm not sure those nags will respond to your gentle ways, my dear."

"We are in town, Moody, with folks watching. I believe I would do best to withhold my fishwife voice for the open plains."

"As you wish, my love."

With that he removed his hat, rode up behind the near horse and gave it a slap with the pressed felt.

"Yaw. Move, you brutes."

The team lurched into their collars and headed south. Moody re-settled his hat, then lifted it again, with a grin towards his wife.

The last leg of his long-awaited trip to the new pastoral position was finally under way. After the hard bench seats and the interminable boredom of the long train trip, the thought of crossing open plains and river valleys, grasslands and cactus covered hillsides, all while enjoying God's blue skies and sunshine, and clean cool air drifting down from the Sangre de Cristo range, off to the west, was intoxicating.

Sarah smiled to herself as she watched her husband. He was like a young boy flushed with excitement at a new adventure. She just hoped and prayed that the adventure didn't turn out to be a disappointment. There was so much they didn't know about the small church in Las Vegas that had been looking for a new pastor.

The stresses of pastoring a congregation in Carob, Texas, where the war had taken such a dreadful toll, had also exacted a toll from her husband. She couldn't calculate the hours and days he had spent with grieving families, not all of them from their small church. Although the losses were heartrending in every case, the worst had been those parents who watched their sons ride off, never to be heard from again. To imagine their precious boys lying in an unmarked grave, or worse, left exposed to the weather and the varmints, had broken the spirit of many a strong man or woman. Somehow, the not knowing put a heavier slant on the loss.

Rev. Moody had carried many of those storied burdens with him, almost taking them on as his own.

His smile, and the lightness of his actions were the first break in the pressure Moody had borne for far too long. She reveled in the changes in him even though she had some private misgivings about the venture.

CHAPTER FOUR

The first night on the trail to Las Vegas was spent in a dry camp. Neither Zac nor Trig really knew the area well and the others had never been there before. During the second day's travels they arrived at a bend in a good-sized stream. As the stream bed was lying generally north to south, they followed along, straightening out the winding pathway by riding from point to point. Their second camp was tucked into a pleasant grove of trees alongside the waterway.

As both Zac and Trig were light sleepers, they decided it would be unnecessary to post a night guard.

***

Rising before dawn, Zac and Trig walked to where the horses had been corralled in a rope enclosure. The rope was down. The horses were gone. The hoof print trail led back to the north. Nothing had been heard during the night, so whoever had been responsible knew what they were doing. The two men followed the tracks for a quarter mile and then decided to return to the camp. The others would need to know what had happened.

The men walked into an awakening camp. Moody was putting a fire together. The women were not in sight. Zac figured they had gone to the brush covered bend in the stream to wash the sleep away and prepare for the day.

Moody listened to the story with upraised eyebrows.

"They're gone? How could they be gone and none of us heard a thing? Do you suppose that mule brained animal I bought in Pueblo decided to go home, and the rest followed?"

Zac answered as he gathered up his Henry and the lariat off his saddle.

"I don't hardly think that's it, Moody. That army horse of mine is steady. He wouldn't leave me unless he was driven. No, I think someone saw an opportunity and jumped on it."

Trig pulled the carbine from his saddle scabbard and slung his lariat over his shoulder.

"Best we get going. There's no telling how much walking we'll have to do."

***

When the ladies returned from their morning preparations, Zac and Trig were gone, and Moody was standing on the ridge behind the grove of trees. He explained briefly what had happened.

"Perhaps you could get some breakfast underway. For the three of us anyway. Zac and Trig are following tracks to the north. That heavy team of ours isn't about to go far, or fast, and I expect the thieves will have some difficulty forcing them along.

"I thought I saw some movement in that bush over there, perhaps a half mile away. Hard to tell from this distance but it almost looked, by color, like Zac's army horse. I'll walk over there. You keep an eye out, although I think you should be safe enough."

Zac and Trig caught up to the milling bunch of horses about two miles from camp. There was no sign of any drovers. The animals were contentedly grazing alongside the stream.

Without discussion, the two men swung away to the east to circle wide and come up behind the horses. They would try to catch one or two to ride but the least they hoped to do was drive them back to the camp where they might feel more at ease and allow themselves to be caught.

Zac glanced over at Trig.

"My gelding isn't among this bunch. That might mean he broke away and went back to camp or it may mean the thieves caught him and took him along."

Trig offered no opinion.

It took twenty minutes of quiet walking to get behind the animals. From there, a slow walk towards the herd brought the horses' heads up but none of them threatened to run. With no trouble at all Trig slipped a rope around his gelding's neck, forming a halter.

Zac did the same with Moody's animal.

They had the horses, but it had taken over an

hour, and there was no sign of other men. Zac was starting to doubt his first thoughts about their disappearance. A thief that brought the animals this far wasn't about to just turn them loose and ride away. And yet Moody's theory that his newly purchased animal had left for home didn't stand up either. The bay gelding was grazing along with the rest.

Moody walked towards where he thought he had seen movement. He went slowly and carefully, entering the bush as quietly as possible. He had no desire to scare the animal further away. It took him a while, but he finally found some fresh tracks and followed them to where Zac's gelding was grazing in a small clearing.

***

The women had the coffee on. Sarah was in the process of slicing bacon. Nancy had her hands in a bowl of buttermilk dough that would become biscuits after a time in the Dutch oven.

Sarah spoke over her shoulder to her sister.

"It's pleasant to have fresh ingredients. They won't last much more than another couple of camps before we're down to basics."

"You don't have to be worrying your pretty heads about such as that. Where we're tak'n you, you'll be happy to have anything at all. Now get up. You're coming with us and we got to be leaving. We don't have a lot of time."

The grating male voice startled the two women. As one, they whirled around, facing the intruders.

Ace and Hammer stood before them grinning,

trying their best to look proud of how well their plan was working out.

Nancy studied the men from where she was mixing the biscuits on the tailgate of the wagon. It took her a moment to place the intruders. Finally, she sorted it out.

"Why, you're the two from the depot."

"You figured that right, missy. Only thing is, we was just funn'n back then, meaning no particular harm, don't you know? But after the treatment from that friend of yours the fun is all over and forgot. Now we got serious plans for the two of you."

"Whatever plans you have just aren't going to come together the way you're figuring on. Why, you're so beat up you can hardly stand, either one of you. You need to be where you can get the help of a good doctor. Anyway, our men aren't far away. They'll be back any minute. You don't want to be here when they ride back in.

"It would be best if you were to climb on your horses and head out of here."

Hammer tried to laugh but it came out as a hacking cough. He ended up bent over, with his hands on his knees. He spit bloody saliva on the ground twice.

"Look at you. You're dying on your feet. You both need doctors."

"That's enough talk. Times a-wast'n. Climb onta them horses of ours. You don't, I'll take a beat'n to you you'll remember all your born days."

With a hand gesture, Hammer pointed at Sarah.

"Ace, you get that there one loaded and tied down. I'll see to this here one. Hurry along now."

Sarah had been slicing bacon into a pan as she

knelt by the fire. When Ace reached for her, she picked up a flaming branch and rammed it into his face, catching his shaggy beard on fire and blistering his lips. His scream would have been heard a half mile away.

Hammer moved as if to grab Nancy's arm. She had already wiped the biscuit dough off her hands, onto the apron she wore. Now she simply reached into the pocket of her split riding skirt and lifted the .32 out. Without taking any careful aim she pointed it in Hammer's general direction and pulled the trigger twice. It would be difficult to miss from that short range. Blood blossomed on his shirt front as he fell to the ground.

Ace was screaming in pain, stumbling backwards, his beard smoldering, when Moody charged over the small rise astride Zac's big gelding. He took in the situation in a flash of time. Turning the obedient animal towards Ace, with a tug on the horse's mane, he drove the three short steps required to slam the gelding's shoulder into the terrified thug. Ace was lifted off his feet and driven backwards into the water.

Moody leaped off the horse with an agility he hadn't exercised in many years. He also hadn't felt such anger or fear in many a year.

The leap landed him on top of Ace, with the two of them sinking under the water. Moody found his footing and stood up with his left hand firmly gathering up a bundle of Ace's shirt front. The overwrought pastor lifted the woman beater's head above the water and drove his right fist into the scarred face. Without thinking, running only on emotion and terror at the thought of what might have happened to his wife, he slammed the man over and over, before pushing his head under the water.

"Stop, stop. You'll kill him."

Sarah had her arms wrapped around Moody's right arm, attempting to stop the beating and the drowning. It took a few seconds of the calming voice of his wife to bring Moody back to something approaching his normal self.

With a shake of his head Moody pulled his thoughts together, nodded to his wife and dragged the unconscious Ace to the shore. He pulled the sorry attacker just far enough out of the stream to have his head and shoulders above water and dropped him there.

A thunder of hooves announced the approach of Zac and Trig. Riding bareback, with halters made from their lariats, they had left the draft team behind, charging full force towards the camp after they heard the gunshots. They slowed and swung to the ground when they saw that everything was under control.

**

With coffee mugs in hand, the travelers stood in a semi-circle looking down at the women's assailants. Moody stood in his wet clothing with one arm circling his wife's waist. Breakfast was forgotten.

Hammer had breathed his last, with a frothy, bloody dribble escaping his mouth. He had said nothing before he died.

After worming his way out of the water, Ace was lying on the ground in a fetal position, his eyes closed and his lips hard-pressed, holding back a cry of agony. His injuries had not been judged as life threatening by the men, but they were not treatable with anything they had at hand. He was badly-burned on his lips and face and he probably had broken bones from being shouldered into the water by the big horse. It was doubtful if his ribs had survived the impact with the gelding.

Moody broke the silence.

"I'm not feeling much like a pastor right at this very minute. I apologize for being a bad example to y'all."

Sarah nestled closer under his arm.

"As to being pastoral, I'll leave that to others to judge. As for being husbandly, I'll judge that. I've never been prouder of you, and I've never felt safer being with you. You have nothing to apologize for, on that matter."

Nancy forced a smile.

"You did just fine and right, Pastor. I do believe, given time, I could find scripture that demands husbands love their wives and care for them."

Moody sadly said, "Yes, but then there's also "turn the other cheek".

Nancy at first didn't know how to respond. After a moment she put her doubt behind her with a firm, emotional answer.

"In this case, Moody, "turn the other cheek" would have meant capture, beatings and rape for your wife and me. And very likely murder at the end of it. I'm not a theologian but I'm pretty sure your chosen scripture might have a different application."

Neither Zac nor Trig offered an opinion.

While the group stood in mute indecision as to what to do next, Nancy brought out her own thoughts.

"I killed a man."

The words were followed by more troubled silence.

Finally, Zac spoke.

"Good for you. I wish my Maddy had been given the opportunity to do the same when she was attacked. Good for you. Don't give it another thought. And you keep that .32 loaded and with you at all times."

With no more said, Zac flipped the dregs of his coffee onto the ground, dropped the mug into the wash water and walked away, as his troubled mind flashed back to the loss of his wife and their little girl.

Nancy made a motion as if to follow Zac, taking two steps in that direction before Trig caught her arm.

"Leave him be."

Nancy watched the disappearing man a few more seconds before turning back to the completion of the breakfast preparation. Forming the biscuits and fitting them into the Dutch oven was her first task.

***

Trig brought in the horses Hammer and Ace had staked out close by. He checked the cinches and passed the reins to Sarah. He then nodded towards Moody.

"Give me a hand here."

The two men had a struggle lifting Hammer onto his saddle, but they got it done. Trig then expertly tied him in place and went to Ace. The man was barely conscious and hurting badly.

"Can you sit a saddle? Your other choice is for me to finish drowning you so's I can tie you down like we done with Hammer."

The response was pained and barely audible.

"I'll sit."

Sarah led the horse as close as possible while the two men lifted Ace. He screamed out in agony as he was muscled into the saddle. Gripping the horn with one hand and attempting to hold his ribs in place with the other, he tried to find the position that hurt the least. With his head hanging and his eyes closed, he waited. Trig tied his feet into the stirrups.

Moody rigged lead ropes while Trig saddled his own mount. He then stepped over to the fire and lifted the lid on the Dutch oven. He was about to reach in for a biscuit when Nancy said, "Go wash your filthy hands. Bar of soap there on the tailgate."

It didn't sound like a suggestion.

The chastened young man looked at his blood-and filth-covered hands.

"When you're right, you're right."

He was back within a few minutes, waving the soap in front of Nancy.

"Done it. Now can I have a biscuit?"

He was met with a smile. The first Nancy had shown since the shooting.

Trig stuffed four biscuits into his jacket pocket and one in his mouth before he mounted his horse.

"See y'all in Las Vegas. That's all the time

assuming I'm not in jail."

The biscuit in his mouth made the words sound garbled and muffled, but no one asked him to repeat them.

CHAPTER FIVE

Zac had not returned. Moody and the two women were alone in the camp.

Moody had dug out the leather satchel holding his private things. He pushed a few items aside before laying his hand on his old gun belt and holster, along with the new Colt .44. It had been more years than he wanted to admit to since he had last strapped the leather around his waist.

Knowing it would be dried out and stiff, the pastor had carefully oiled it before leaving Carob, Texas, for the trip west.

No one in Carob had ever seen him wearing the hardware, but there were others back down the road who would remember the gear as a normal part of Moody's get-up. He had never told anyone except Sarah about those growing-up years, back on the family's ranch.

***

Time slipped past unnoticed, with all the activity

happening, and Moody hadn't given much thought to the events or how they might have impacted the women. But he needed to talk about it anyway.

"So tell me ladies. Do you wish to carry on to Las Vegas and an unknown pastoral situation, or do you wish to turn back to Pueblo and catch the train back east? I wouldn't want to force you into anything you'd rather avoid."

Sarah stood up from where she was finally preparing breakfast, placed her folded fists on her hips and gave her husband a serious look.

"Mr. Tomlinson, my dear, gentle pastor husband. I've certainly known you long enough to know you are not a quitter. And I believe Ace would testify that you are not always quite as gentle as it would appear. Nor are you someone to enter into something without giving the matter an abundance of thought. And prayer.

"Well neither am I. But, of course, you already know that. I'll admit our lives would have been just as well off without our interaction with those two despicable men, but I'm assuming that when God called you to minister in Las Vegas, He already knew the names Hammer and Ace, and He was not at all surprised at this morning's events.

"Well, I'll admit to being both surprised and frightened. But I'll ask you to remember that Nancy and I were raised on a frontier ranch. We huddled as children while our parents fought off both Mexican raiders and Comanches out to steal horses. Later, we took part in defending what was ours, loading guns for our father, and firing one from time to time ourselves. No, we are not quitters. And if need be, I could take a stand again too."

Sarah hadn't commanded so much attention nor spoken so forcefully for a long while. The words sounded powerful and determined, from this woman who had played the role of pastor's wife for so many years.

Nancy studied her sister long enough to know she had said all she intended to say. She then looked at her brother-in-law.

"It's on to Las Vegas for me. Even if you turn back, it's Las Vegas for me."

Moody had been half holding his breath and steeling himself against what the women might say. Now he blew out a mind-clearing breath and relaxed his taut shoulders.

"We'll need that breakfast. I'm thinking if we're to find the team I have some more walking to do."

***

A day and a half of steady riding had Trig pulling his weary horse to a halt in front of the sheriff's office in Pueblo. He was too tired to dismount. But the gathering of noisy townsfolk huddling around him, and the two led horses soon caught the attention of the sheriff. The office door opened and the same man who had interviewed Zac and the rest of them after the happening at the train depot, stepped out.

The crowd grew silent as the sheriff studied the situation from the raised boardwalk. It was clear he recognized the men tied onto the two led horses.

"I'd suppose, judging by the fact those two fools are tied across their saddles that I'm not going to get the opportunity to question them."

Trig was too tired to banter with the lawman.

"Not unless you have connections to the hereafter that I don't know about."

"So, what happened? Would I be correct in guessing they followed you, hoping for some kind of revenge?"

Trig turned in the saddle just enough to indicate the two dead men with his thumb.

"Drove off our horses in the night. When we went to find them, they attacked our women in camp. It didn't turn out just exactly as they planned. The one died in camp. The other died last night, along the way. I've been a day and a half in the saddle."

After a pause, he continued.

"If you don't need anything more from me, I'll leave these with you and take my mount to the livery. Need some rest my own self."

"Step down, young man. Hotel's right over there. Go get yourself some rest. Dining room should be open."

The sheriff named two men in the crowd.

"Hec, I'd like if you would take those two over to the undertaker. Bring the horses and gear and whatever's in their pockets back to Ransom's livery. And Sammy, I'd appreciate if you'd care for this man's horse."

There was no more discussion on the matter.

CHAPTER SIX

Moody decided not to trust another rope corral. After catching all the horses, he had staked them safely along the stream. He was forced to cut a couple of lariats in half to create enough ropes to get the job done.

When that task was completed, he took a seat on a rock embedded in the stream bank. He pulled off his boots, then his socks. He placed his feet into the cool water with a great sigh.

"Don't know when I last walked that many miles. My feet are so swollen I might not get my boots back on. I may have to arrive in Las Vegas, applying for a pastoral position in my bare feet."

The two women giggled and teased him about being a desk-sitting softy. It helped to ease the tension from the morning.

When Zac hadn't returned by mid-afternoon the small group decided to stay another night.

Nancy looked over the stream and the area around it.

"We're not about to find a more pleasant camp. I

just wish I could get those two men out of my mind. Them and my part in the affair."

"Time. It all takes time, Nancy," counselled the pastor.

The afternoon slowly drifted past. The women napped while Moody kept watch. They then sat by while he slept.

The women were working on supper when Zac strolled back into camp. Saying nothing about where he had been, he reached for the coffee pot. Nancy dug a mug out of the lunch box.

"I'll get that for you."

Zac thanked her and waited while Nancy poured the coffee. He then took a seat on the grass beside Moody. Nothing was said about the morning or where Zac had been.

When Moody noticed Zac studying the camp and looking over the horses, he said, "Trig rode off for Pueblo, leading two horses. At least I'm assuming he was going to Pueblo. He didn't specifically say."

Zac offered no reply.

CHAPTER SEVEN

Trig caught up with the travelers a full day out of Las Vegas.

The men were staking out the horses while the women were digging around in the food box in the back of the wagon. There was nothing left that could be considered fresh. They would make do with the remains of a side of bacon, a small sack of beans that had been soaking in a pot all day and the ever-present biscuits. There was a half can of molasses left for anyone who had a sweet tooth.

Zac had already seen the rising dust from Trig's approach, but he said nothing.

"Howdy there, folks. Thought y'all might be already in town, with a big steak and fried spuds all laid out before you on a sizzling platter, down to the hotel dining room. I must say, you're becoming a disappointment to me, Boss, lollygagging along when there must be work that needs doing somewhere. I'm thinking these eastern folks are going to go to having a poor opinion of us westerners."

Zac didn't bother turning around.

"You've been west for what, three, four months? And already you're the example to follow?"

"Well, it ain't like I applied for the position, nor nothing like that. But Pa always said when there's something to be done it's your turn to step up. He explained that with considerable energy a time or two. I kind of took it to heart."

Ignoring the bantering, both ladies offered their welcome.

Moody sauntered over and took the reins from Trig.

"I'll stake him out and rub him down for you, Trig. You grab some coffee and tell us what happened. I'm assuming you saw the sheriff."

Trig aimed a surprised look at the pastor's gun rig before he took a seat on the wagon tailgate and set his coffee mug beside him. He lifted his hat and ran his fingers through his hair. Then, as if the idea had just come to him, he laid the hat on the tailgate, hopped off and walked to the creek bank. Not worrying about wetting the knees of his canvas pants, he knelt and rolled up his sleeves. Rubbing his hands with the cool water and a small scoop of sand he scraped the day's grime away. Then, taking a deep breath and holding it, he bent over and dipped his head beneath the slowly flowing water. He scrubbed his hair vigorously and then his neck and face. Lifting his head out of the water he blew out the held breath and shook the water off, his long hair causing the water to fling in all directions.

He rose to his feet, replaced his hat, and retook his seat on the tailgate.

Zac, watching the whole show said, "I haven't

seen you quite so determined in your personal ablutions before."

"There you go again, Boss, using words I ain't never heard before. The thing is though, this fine lady over here will refuse me a biscuit or two if I hold out an unwashed hand. And I sure could make use of a biscuit."

Nancy dug into the pot of biscuits held over from breakfast and passed two to Trig with a small smile. She set the can of molasses beside him. A spoon was balanced over the top of the can.

"Just in case you feel the need for a spoonful of sweetening.

"You learned that hand washing lesson well Trig. Perhaps I should go to teaching school. I could at least see that the students were clean behind their ears, even if they couldn't read or do their sums."

***

Moody had a strong need to know what had happened in Pueblo.

"So tell us what all happened."

"Well, ol' Ace, he went on to another world before I got him to a doctor. Might be just as well, as broke up as he was.

"The sheriff wasn't much interested. Didn't ask hardly nothing at all about the happenings. I'm thinking he knew those boys pretty well. I gave him just the barest story is all. He shrugged and sent those two ol' boys off to the undertaker. I got a night's sleep and a meal or two and here I am. Nothing to it at all. Might just as well have buried them here in this soft sand and saved myself a ride."

Nancy had been carrying a worrying burden ever since the incident.

"Did the sheriff ask who had done the shooting?"

"Not a single question. As far as he knows it could have been anyone. Your name never came up."

Trig thought he might have heard a great sigh of relief escape Nancy's lips.

CHAPTER EIGHT

With the wagon and team safely boarded at the livery in Las Vegas, along with the saddle mounts, Moody and the two ladies arranged for hotel rooms, baths, and dinner.

Zac and Trig waived their farewell and pointed their mounts towards the Wayward Ranch.

Trig grinned over at his riding partner.

"That there is a mighty handsome lady the good pastor and his wife dragged along with them. Why, if I was a few years older, oh, maybe even around your age, is what I mean to say…"

Zac stopped Trig's short speech with a hard look.

"Sorry, Boss. Don't mean to intrude into your private thoughts. But she is a mighty handsome lady. Ya got to admit that. Quick with a gun too."

As he often did, the speaker tempered his words with a grin.

CHAPTER NINE

Moody rose early on his first full day in Las Vegas. The women had agreed the evening before that the next couple of days would be set aside for rest and recovery from the long series of train rides, followed by the wagon trip.

When Moody was washed and dressed, he left the room with his wife curled comfortably under their own, big homemade quilt. Although she had opened one eye watching his preparations, he suspected that she might stay there for a while.

Moody took a light breakfast at the hotel dining room before setting out to find Mr. Tracy Handley, the correspondent from the Las Vegas Community Church. Moody had exchanged two letters with the gentleman over the past couple of months, discussing the possibility of filling the pastoral duties at the popular, if small, church. Mr. Handley had advised that he was the owner and operator of the Handley General Merchandise Store. Moody figured to find the establishment easily enough if he simply walked the streets. Las Vegas was not a large town.

Sauntering slowly, taking in the sights of the new town, and admiring the offerings in the store windows, it was a full hour before he found himself standing in front of the Handley store.

After a careful perusal of the display windows, Moody pushed the door open. A larger than necessary brass bell clanged as it swung on a short chain dangling above the doorway. Moody figured it was loud enough to wake a sleeping man.

Stepping up to the counter at the rear of the store, Moody was greeted by a stern looking, grey bearded man, wearing a wide brimmed, western style hat and a large white apron that didn't do much to disguise his portly figure.

"Good morning, sir. You're up and around early today. What can I help you with?"

Moody, convinced of the importance of a first impression, had dressed and groomed himself casually, but carefully for this moment. All he could do now was smile as he approached the man behind the counter. At the same time, he was studying that man, hoping to pick up whatever signals the fellow was throwing off.

"Good morning. May I assume you to be Mr. Tracy Handley?"

"I am."

"My name, sir, is Moody Tomlinson. Rev. Moody Tomlinson. We have exchanged some correspondence."

The eyes of the storekeeper brightened noticeably as he lifted his hand from the countertop and reached for a handshake.

"Rev. Tomlinson. I am pleased to make your

acquaintance. It is an extraordinarily long ways from East Texas to this location. You have travelled far. I trust the trip went well."

"Well enough, sir. We arrived late yesterday afternoon. And of course, I wanted to meet you as soon as possible. I don't mean to take up your business hours. I simply thought to locate your store, meet you, and arrange a time when we might talk of church matters."

Tracy Handley shook his head as if to add expression to his words before saying, "No problem at all, Reverend. As you can easily see, the store is empty, save for ourselves. But I agree, we need some uninterrupted time. I have a helper coming in at noon. Would you be able to meet over lunch at the hotel? We could take whatever time is needed.

"My wife is down in Santa Fe spoiling our grandchildren, but she will be home later today. Perhaps I could suggest a dinner at our home tomorrow. I would invite one or two others from the congregation to join us."

"I'm sure we'll be available tomorrow, as we have come only for this purpose. And lunch sounds just fine. If it suited you, I would ask my wife to join us."

"By all means. Let's say 12:15 then. That will give me time to get my helper settled in."

Moody shook the man's hand again.

"Twelve-fifteen it is. I'm looking forward to it."

Moody left the store feeling positive about his first encounter with one of his possible future employers. He strolled the streets of Las Vegas, chatting with a couple of old timers sitting on wooden chairs in front of a saloon, and generally finding his way around the town.

He spotted the white painted church building situated on a somewhat raised block of land on the outskirts of the little town. He strolled over for a look. He walked all around the building and the small manse behind it, without going inside. There was time enough for that.

At 10 AM, the pastor walked back to the hotel. He was about to climb the stairs to his room when he heard his name called. Several heads turned at the sound of the female voice. Nancy was waving at him from a table in the dining room.

'Over here, Moody."

It was a constant wonder to Moody how two sisters, raised on the same frontier ranch, could be so different. Sarah was quiet almost to the point of being timid. That she had the presence of mind to protect herself with the flaming brand from the fire when Hammer and Ace threatened to accost her was totally out of character.

Nancy, on the other hand was outgoing and full of life, never embarrassed by the day's little happenings, and constantly on the lookout for another adventure. Of course, that may explain why she was single at her advanced age. She couldn't be much short of thirty, a serious challenge for a woman in the times they found themselves living in. And an equally serious challenge for any man who might think of expressing interest.

He turned and walked to the dining room. He ordered a coffee and explained about the lunch.

Nancy immediately said, "You didn't include me in that dreary affair I hope."

Moody smiled just a bit.

"I don't know that it threatens to be what we

might describe as dreary. But in any case, you are free of the task. I thought it best to keep the pastoral position and all it involves between just Sarah and myself, plus, of course, the church leaders."

Sarah turned to her sister with a question.

"What do you have in mind to do while we're in attendance with Mr. Handley, Nancy?"

"I've been looking over the town this morning. Las Vegas really does not appear to offer much to see or do. I'm thinking I'll saddle my horse and ride out to Zac's ranch. Apparently, it's not far out and it might be fun to ride in the sun for an hour or so. I'll be back by evening. That way you'll be free of my burden."

Moody was long past offering advice or even a caution to his head-strong sister-in-law. He chose to say nothing. She was in all likelihood going to follow through on her plan no matter what anyone said.

As the ladies had already completed their breakfasts, Moody simply took a sip of his coffee and then turned to Nancy.

"You are under no obligation to wait for us, Nancy. On the other hand, you are, of course, welcome to stay. If you choose to ride out to the ranch you should probably confirm the direction with the livery man. And be sure you have that pistol in your pocket."

Nancy stood and patted the unseen pocket, hidden within the pleats of her split riding skirt.

"I'm never without it and I promise to be careful."

With that she was gone. The eyes of several men turned as she made her way through the hotel lobby and out to the street.

Moody smiled at his wife.

"It's a good thing I married the older of the McCrimmon sisters. Holding down a pastoral position alongside the younger of the two would surely turn into a challenge."

Sarah had no response, but she did have a question.

"How did your walk go? Did you have trouble finding Mr. Handley?"

"Found him easily enough and talked for just a couple of minutes. We're meeting him right here for lunch. And he's invited us to his home tomorrow for dinner. He seems like a somewhat stern, but still amiable fellow."

***

Walking across the street, Nancy smiled a 'good morning' to the livery man.

"I don't wish to disturb you. You are the picture of contentment, sitting there in the sun. Your pipe adds to the picture, as well. I don't partake of tobacco myself, but many women back east have taken up the habit."

"Bad habit, but still comfort'n, young lady. There's jest someth'n about it. Cain't rightly put my finger on it but there's someth'n to ease a man's burdens. Still, best you leave it alone. You don't want to find yourself smell'n like no chimney when some young fella earns a kiss from you. No, you don't want that."

"A kiss is it? Well, that happens rarely enough. Not worth the mention. More to the point, I'm told that the Wayward Ranch is five or six miles out the east road. Is that the road I see on the north side of the hotel?"

"That's the one. What you want with the Wayward? I seen you arrive'n yesterday with Zac and that young fella. Good enough man, Zac Trimbell is, but rough, time to time. I'd trust him with my life or my daughter, if ever I was to have one, but you still need to be careful. Zac can be sudden, time to time. And somehow troubles seem to arrive at his door. I got no explanation fer that.

"Bad happen'ns out there at the Wayward, couple a month's back."

Nancy let the warning fly over her head, as she did with most warnings.

"You sit and enjoy the morning. I'll get my horse rigged out and see if I can get to the ranch without bringing more trouble to Zac and Trig."

The hostler rose to his feet.

"I'm guess'n Abbot Williams, Abe to them as what knows me, kin still recall some manners. A few of 'em at any rate. Ain't never been a woman left this here stable without I done her rigg'n-out fer her. Don't aim to start now. You take yourself a seat. I'll have your animal out here in jig time."

Within a few minutes the glistening, clean and brushed bay gelding was led out. Nancy was startled and pleased by his appearance.

The livery man couldn't help noticing Nancy's smile.

"Cleaned him up fer ya last even'n. This one, and the team, and the grey the new pastor was rid'n. Hate ta see an animal showing road dust. Brambles gathered in their tails. No ma'am. Don't care fer that atoll. Pleased ta clean 'em up a tad fer ya."

"Well, thank you. He looks great. But how do you know the gentleman I rode in with is to be the new pastor?"

"Jest knew there was one com'n an' he has the look."

Nancy smiled at the livery man as she reached for the reins.

"Has the look, has he? I'm not altogether sure Moody will appreciate that description. But I'll have fun telling him. And don't you be misjudging the new pastor. He's no tea drinking ladies' man."

"No ma'am, I saw that right off too. Saw him take in the whole town with barely more than a glance. The insides of this here dark barn too, when he brung the animals over. Careful, he was. Wary of everyth'n. And him with a holstered Colt and a 66 Winchester fixed to the side of the wagon. No, I'll not be misjudg'n the man."

***

Moody and Sarah were already seated in the dining room when Tracy Handley strolled in, holding his hat in his hand.

"I apologize, folks. I'm just a few minutes late. Got busy all of a sudden in the store."

Moody stood and shook his hand.

"Not to worry, Mr. Handley. We would never expect you to turn away from a customer. Mr. Handley, I want you to meet Sarah, my wife. Sarah, this is Mr. Tracy Handley."

Tracy was surprised when Sarah offered her hand. He cautiously reached for it and gave just a slight finger pressure as they shook. He didn't quite bow but the motion showed that he had it in mind, although in the west that formality had about run its course.

The two men took their seats just as the waitress arrived at their table. Tracy greeted her warmly.

"Good day, Emeline. I trust you are well. I want you to meet Mr. and Mrs. Tomlinson, Emeline. Reverend Tomlinson, that is. These folks just arrived after a very long trip.

The storekeeper glanced back at Moody.

"Emeline and her parents, Frank and Tabitha Bowles, are members of our little church."

"And my troublesome brother, Mr. Handley. Don't forget Toby."

She held to a shy smile to soften the words.

"No, I'm not likely to forget Toby. Good boy, although a bit energetic, shall we say. Anyway, what's on the menu today?"

**

The three diners ate their beef and potatoes mostly in silence. The custom seemed to be familiar in ranch country, in East Texas as well as in New Mexico. But the silence didn't stop them from sizing each other up as they ate.

Moody and Sarah pushed their plates away with little more than half the delicious feast eaten.

Handley cleaned up every scrap of food from his plate and then sopped up the remaining brown gravy with a last slice of bread.

Moody couldn't help thinking that the man had earned every inch of his waistline.

When Emeline had cleared the table, she brought

more coffee for the men and a cup of tea for Sarah. Handley wiped his lips and hands with the table napkin and looked over at the new pastor.

"Now, sir. I'm sure you have questions. Where should we start?"

CHAPTER TEN

Riding into the Wayward Ranch yard, fresh from the long trip home from Pueblo, Zac and Trig pulled their horses to a stop, surprised to see two heavily loaded wagons in front of the Gonzales' cabin. There were a dozen or so unfamiliar horses in the corral. Several people were milling about the yard. Everyone seemed to be ignoring the new arrivals.

Trig looked over at Zac with an unasked question, but Zac offered no explanation.

They dismounted and tied their horses to the outside of the corral after letting them take their fill of water.

Amado Gonzales came trotting from the barn to greet them.

"Welcome home, *Señor* Zac. Welcome Mr. Trig. Much has happened since you went away."

Zac turned and studied the yard.

"Well, I can see that Amado. Perhaps you should tell me what it is that brought all this activity, and who these people are."

"Oh, *señor*, it is good that my cousins have come. Here they are safe. Not be kill. *Mi Madre,* she has been much worry. *El gran ranchero blanco,* the big rancher. The man who kill *mi padre.* He is take much land from my people.

"He steal the sheep and the cows, too. He shoot some of our people, he and his riders. These, my cousins and one uncle. They are the last of my family. For many years we have the land. The *Gobierno,* the big men in Mexico City, they give the land to the people to have forever. But the ranchers, they say no, we take the land for ourselves..."

Zac waved his hand for Amado to stop.

"Yes, I know all of that. But what do these people hope to do here, on the Wayward?"

"I think, señor, they hope to be no more kill."

"Well, Amado, we will deal with this another time. Right now, we need to care for our horses and get some food and rest."

He turned back to his big gelding, but Amado jumped ahead of him.

"No, *señor.* I will care for the horses. *Mi Madre*, she is make food. I will tell her you are home. She bring food to your house for you and *señor* Trig. *Rápidamente,* she will bring food. We talk more after you eat and rest. Tomorrow, we talk more. *Mañana.*"

The young man smiled, happy with his plan, and led the two geldings into the shade of the barn.

Trig, who had remained silent during the discussion grinned at Zac.

"Well, it looks like you're going to have some visitors for a while."

Zac hunched his shoulders and headed to the

house with no further words.

As the two tired men approached the big adobe house, they saw movement and then a swirl of color under the *ramada*.

"Out. Out," said a female voice. "*Ve con tu mamá.*"

With a giggle and a flash of grinning faces, two little boys and one girl in a bright yellow and white dress scurried from the patio. Behind them stood an exceptionally pretty young lady, all summery in a white dress with a billowing skirt trimmed with light blue pleats, smiling at the two men. As they approached, she spoke in excellent English.

"Welcome home, Sirs. I hope you don't mind that we have been enjoying the shade of your *ramada*. The children were getting under their mothers' feet. I thought to bring them here to give the women a break from the noise and activity.

"I am Consuela. I am a cousin to Amado."

Zac and Trig were both speechless. Zac because he was still trying to sort out his thoughts on having a yard full of visitors. Trig, because the beauty of the young lady held him nearly tongue-tied.

"Come, gentlemen. Take a seat. There is cool lemonade here. I will fetch some more glasses from the house."

As Consuela stepped towards the yard, heading for the old bunk house, Zac said, "There are glasses here in this house. You wanted to, you could step through that door and pick some off the shelf over the counter. Bring one for yourself. Perhaps you can make more sense of what's happening than Amado did."

Zac and Trig pulled the two big, white-painted, wicker rocking chairs up to the small table that was kept on the patio. Trig walked to the end of the patio and dragged up a wooden kitchen chair. When Consuela returned, she set the drinking glasses on the table and stepped towards the wooden chair.

Trig quickly said, "No, I'll take that one. You'll be more comfortable in the rocker."

The young lady smiled shyly.

"Thank you, sir."

Some of the terracotta floor tiles were of uneven thickness, causing the chair to tip a bit from leg to leg as Trig took his seat.

With the cool drinks poured, Zac said, "So, Consuela. First, perhaps you can explain how you know the language so well. Then outline what has taken place up north.

"I can understand most of what Amado says, with his struggling English and my bit of poor Spanish. But you talk nothing at all like that."

"I learned in the mission school. Up north. In Denver. My parents understood that we would not always have the whole territory to ourselves. That others would come. Strong people. People who wanted the land.

"Although they believed our place on the Pérez land grant was forever, they also believed it was important that we learn to live together, the Anglos and us. We would one day have Anglo neighbors.

"They were also convinced that the newly arriving Anglos would not be interested in learning the Beautiful Language. Life for my people is difficult enough. With the language barrier it is very nearly impossible.

"So, my two brothers and I were sent off to school. I missed my family, but we had our summers at home.

"Now, I'm happy they sent me. What they foresaw has come to pass, and even more. There is still much land that seems empty until a person learns the culture. Most of it is held in old Spanish and Mexican land grants. Even though those that first received the grants are gone to their graves, *La Gente*, the people, have always thought of it as their own. But the Anglo, he sees it as being there for the taking."

Trig commented, "It sounds like your parents were wise in their decisions."

"My parents were wise in their thinking but not in their ways. They prepared my brothers and I to live beside the Anglo, but not to think like him. The Anglo never rests. He does not think of *mañana*. He does not plan for the *fiesta*. He does not know how to enjoy his life. What he wants is more. All the time more, without really enjoying what he already has.

"While *La Gente* were simply living their lives, happy with all that God had given them, planning the *fiesta* or enjoying the *siesta*, the Anglo, he was making plans for the land. And so we are here. Here on your ranch with our wagons and with the ones who did not die. We are here with nothing but our lives. Other *Pérez*, other families, have gone their own way, but all have left the land.

"Amado and his family lived where the Anglo wished to settle. His family was the first to be pushed off their land. Amado's father, my uncle, tried to fight, to hold the land. He is now in his grave and Amado and Alejandra are here.

"More of us lived further west, into the hills.

Now the Anglo, he has come there too. We fight, a few at least. But our weapons are old, and it is not the way of most of us.

"So now the Anglo, he has our land, our sheep, our cattle and our graves. And he has his sheriffs and his army and his courts.

"Even though there are many of us, we are not able to compete with, or even fight the Anglo. Our cultures are very different. I fear he will have his way. I don't know what is to become of us."

Zac and Trig studied the young lady for a few seconds and then sat silently.

CHAPTER ELEVEN

After a bath, a good meal and a night's rest, Zac figured he was up to facing the problems and questions his visitors brought along with them. After breakfast, Zac briefly told Trig what he knew about Amado's family and the situation they had escaped from at much cost, including the life of Amado's father.

Trig, showing his more serious side asked, "So what are the options? If they stay on the Wayward or somewhere around here, there is the problem of them making a living and a life for themselves. It sounds, from what Consuela said, that they have nothing. It don't seem hardly right that a big rancher should push them off their land and steal their herds, as well. That don't seem right, no how."

"No. It's not right. We will have to talk with Consuela more to find out the details. How big were those herds? She said that some resisted, but I wonder how hard. Did the people try to fight, or did they take a few shots and then run for their lives?

"And how big, really is this rancher? A man with

a gun and a crew backing him can seem mighty big, when, in reality, he's just an ordinary man with an opinion, and lot of push in him.

"You're right though. Keeping the animals was a mean thing to do. And against any law I've ever heard of."

They sat silently, sipping coffee, for a full minute.

"We have to talk with Consuela again."

***

Before anything else was done, Zac and Trig went for their horses. Amado had done a good job of brushing them down. He then turned them out to graze in the big horse trap that Zac had fenced in a couple of years before. Both animals came at the call of their riders.

A thorough examination of the geldings showed that Trig's needed two shoes tightened and one probably needed replacing. While the blacksmithing tools were available in the shed on the Wayward, it wasn't worth firing up the forge for that little job. He would ride into town later and let the blacksmith take on the task.

When the two men walked back to the gate Consuela was standing there watching the horses. The same three toddlers were laughing and running around, secure in their belief that they were safe with Consuela minding them.

"Good morning to both of you. I trust you slept well. Your horses look fine after your long ride."

"Good morning, Consuela," responded Trig. "You're looking fine yourself."

Trig seemed to get away with saying things that

others might be criticized for. His innocent grin paved the way for his comments.

Consuela might have blushed. Trig couldn't be sure. Standing in full sunlight her face shone, in any case.

Zac asked, "Do you have time to tell us more about the situation?"

"I have nothing but time. My mother and my aunt won't let me anywhere near the kitchen."

With a radiant smile she added, "They say my time for that work will come soon enough. Mind you, my mother never said that until after she had taught me the spices and how to use them. Of course, she showed me the few desert herbs that have useful properties. And then there was the flat bread to learn and the roasting of the lamb and grinding of corn and the onions and the chilis."

Trig nearly tripped over his tongue as he responded, "All good information for a young lady, I'm sure."

While the two young people laughed together, Zac left them several steps behind as he made his way back to the *ramada*.

***

They were deep into the discussion of the situation to the north, where the Mexican families' herds were now grazing on land claimed by the Anglo rancher, when Nancy rode into the yard. Barely glancing at the barn, the corral and at the activity around the old adobe bunkhouse, she rode her horse up to the tie rail outside the picket fence that fronted the big house.

Zac and Trig rose to their feet, showing their surprise at her arrival.

"I believe it's customary on western ranches to offer coffee and perhaps a small bite of something to passing strangers."

Nancy was enjoying the surprise the men were still struggling with. Zac especially couldn't find any words for a few moments. He finally remembered his manners.

"If we're holding with western tradition, I'll have to suggest you take a load off. In other words, good morning. Please step down and come to the *ramada*. What brings you to the Wayward? I thought you would be weary of riding the country after the trip from Pueblo."

As he was talking, Zac was walking towards Nancy and her gelding. He took the reins from her and secured the animal to the hitch rail and then held his hand out to help her to the ground. Of course, she needed no assistance but they both pretended otherwise.

Stepping to the ground, nudged close to Zac by the sideways shuffle of her horse, she placed her hand on his chest to prevent their further touching. Zac stepped back as if he was stung by a wasp. Nancy smiled and chuckled a bit while she slid sideways. She lifted her hat off and hung it on the saddle horn. She then turned in a slow circle to take in the yard and buildings of the Wayward Ranch.

"So, this is the Wayward? It's a beautiful spot. Enough open space for corrals and some pasture. A nice grove of pines behind the barn and another alongside the house. A few acres of level land for the headquarters but then surrounded by grass and cactus covered hills. Some low mountains behind. No neighbors close by to bother a person.

"I liked the way the trail wound through the hills on my ride here. The hills are lovely and picturesque, but I must say, for a ranch girl from south Texas, where the grass is green and plentiful, these hills look a bit barren. And yet they support ranches. You'll have to explain that to me sometime."

"Sometime. But right now, come to the *ramada* and meet Consuela."

The two women shook hands while eyeing each other up as possible contenders. Contending for exactly what, neither could have explained. But it seemed to be the way of women. Especially beautiful women who were in the habit of commanding whatever attention was available.

Nancy took a seat in the rocker that Zac had abandoned.

"I didn't know there were so many people making their homes on the Wayward. Somehow, I thought of it as a bachelor's retreat, although you did tell me of a mother and son who cared for the place when you were gone."

Zac sighed and hunched his shoulders.

"The ranch was as you have just said until a few days ago. I'm as surprised as anyone, seeing all the people and activity. But Consuela has just been telling us about the happening up north, where many Mexican families were recently driven off their land-grant homes. There was fighting and some were killed. Stock was stolen. So these folks you see here, except for Amado and his mother are all new to the Wayward.

"We were just trying to talk it through a bit when

you rode up."

As he was talking, Amado trotted from the barn. He waited until he saw Zac nod in his direction before untying Nancy's gelding.

"I will look to the care of the pretty lady's horse."

He turned his back while Nancy laughed, and the others smiled. He might have hunched his shoulders at the sound, it was difficult to tell.

The four people sitting around the table were silent for a few moments. They wouldn't have admitted it, but they needed that time to kind of size each other up, to take the measure of one another.

Nancy had only known Zac on the trail. He had been a somewhat reclusive and quiet man, but competent as a leader of their small gathering. Now, they were on his ranch, his home, where his will, and his alone, would determine events. She wasn't quite sure what to expect.

The continuously smiling Trig had also proven to be competent and careful around the camp and on the trail. Apparently, he was a long-term guest on the Wayward.

Consuela was an unknown quantity to Nancy. The startlingly pretty girl would draw attention wherever she went, but Nancy was comfortable with that. The considerably younger Consuela posed no threat to her. But still…

It usually paid dividends to remain aware.

Consuela broke the brief silence.

"I will make more coffee. I believe this pot is nearly emptied."

Zac waited while she picked up the pot and walked into the kitchen before looking over at

Nancy.

"You shouldn't be riding the trails alone. I'm happy to see you and have you as a guest on the Wayward. But when you're ready to go back to town, I'll ride along."

He wasn't scolding. In fact, Nancy was touched by the evident care in his voice.

Trig offered an alternative.

"Zac's right Nancy. There's considerable unrest with all the changes in the country. Lots of strangers riding about. I'm going in later to have my horse shod. I'd be happy to ride along with you."

CHAPTER TWELVE

As the hotel dining room lunch dragged on, the discussion of church matters took second place. With Moody, Sarah and Tracy simply getting to know one another, the subject turned to the past years.

"So, Pastor Moody. I sense that you have not always been in the ministry."

He let the sentence rest there, like a man holding his breath, allowing the pastor to respond. Or not.

Moody paused, thinking of his reply.

"Texas is, after all, still a young state. Many of the settlers came for the free land. My family was no different. My aging grandparents led the family west from Kentucky, over forty years ago. My grandparents, my own parents, recently married at the time, and a collection of aunts, uncles, and cousins. They applied for all the land they could lay hold of, bidding on plots adjacent to one another. Together, they held a sizable block of real estate. That was down near the gulf but not right on it. There was still some interaction with Mexican bandits and, of course there were some home-grown troublemakers, as well. And then we can't forget the Comanche.

"But the family, working together, managed to hold onto it all, even after the war. They did not all survive the various challenges, from rough horses to the civil war, and some smaller battles much closer to home. Still, there's enough of the family left to keep the home fires burning. I took an active part in the ranch, but my heart was calling me elsewhere, although I wasn't sure where. I loved the ranch and all it offered, but it didn't satisfy my soul. I wasn't sure what would satisfy until I attended a series of outdoor meetings held by a fella who travelled the country back before the war.

"I'd been to meetings before, of course. Mostly held by the shouting kind of preacher who offered as much emotion as they did scriptural facts. But this man was different. He was quiet and sincere. Modest in his ways. He mixed easily with the community between meetings, visiting ranches and farms, as well as town folks. When he rode into the ranch yard the day after I first attended the meetings, I was struck by his caring and his willingness to help and get involved.

"The morning of his first visit he worked side by side with my father, birthing a foal. And he showed that he knew as much as my father did, and more. But his modesty was such that he seemed to feel no need for praise or thanks. I took another long look at the teachings I had been raised with and decided that this was the kind of man my grandfather had been talking about all along.

"Although Grandfather was gone by that time, I

have often thought how much the two men would have enjoyed knowing each other.

"By the time a week of meetings was over I had found my direction in life. I have never to this day questioned my decision. And Sarah, a ranch girl through and through, has followed and supported me every step of the way."

Tracy smiled at the two visitors.

"Quite a story. I'm happy it worked out for you. It sounds like you've enjoyed a happy and fulfilled life."

"Well, overall happy, I suppose. Although the recent war placed a lot of heartache at our doorstep, as it did for everyone involved. And fulfilled, I'd say, in the sense that following the pattern God laid down in scripture and striving to bring the message of His love to those we meet, is fulfilling.

"To lay it all out before you, and to answer the question that is obviously needing to be asked, no, we have no children. That is the one part of life's fulfillment that has eluded us. But we have learned to be content in whatever place we find ourselves to be."

There was more silence as Emeline refilled the men's coffee mugs. Sarah held her hand over her teacup and shook her head as Emeline reached to refill it.

After taking a couple of sips of fresh coffee, then nervously shuffling his feet, and reaching for his hat, Tracy said, "Folks, I apologize, but I must get back to the store. It has been a pleasure meeting you both. We will look forward to our dinner tomorrow evening. Are you sure you can find the house from the directions I provided?"

Moody stood and picked up his own hat.

"We'll be fine, Tracy. We'll plan on six in the afternoon."

CHAPTER THIRTEEN

Alejandra spread a lunch of cold flatbread, goat cheese and sliced beef, along with some garden vegetables sliced into bite sized portions. It was pleasant under the shade of the *ramada*. Zac, Trig and the two ladies took the lunch leisurely. Consuela was getting over her nervousness in Nancy's presence and Trig had somehow gotten control of his awe of Consuela's beauty. Zac appeared to be immune to it all.

Finally, after an hour of idle chatter that forced Zac to stretch his crumbling patience, he brought the conversation back to the reason the Wayward yard was abuzz with activity.

"Consuela, do you know where the other families have run off to?"

"Some, I do. Others, I am not so sure. Most have gone to relatives who can take them in until they know what is going to happen."

"And what is the name of the big rancher that has chased the people off the land and stolen their stock?"

Consuela showed her first sign of difficulty with the English language.

"His name is, I think, Pattikin. Perhaps it is something different. It sounded difficult to my ears."

Nancy threw out a couple of names that might be more accurate, without Consuela showing any sign of recognition.

Finally Trig said, "Knew a family back east named Patriquin."

Consuela rewarded Trig with a radiant smile.

"That sounds like what he said, but I can't be sure."

"Close enough," answered Zac.

"Do you know how many men he has or where he makes his headquarters?"

"There is no real town close to there. Just a small trading post started years ago by Mr. Manco. There is also a blacksmith working out of Manco's small barn. He keeps a few horses for sale to people who pass by.

"For *La Gente*, the needs are simple. We purchase little from the trading post. Sometimes, maybe a shirt or a pair of pants, or a coat for the winter. Our gardens and our flocks and our cows give us most of what we need. But over the years Mr. Manco has somehow sold enough to satisfy his desires, so he has stayed. In a small part of his building he has a table and some chairs, where he sells drinks.

"He has always been a good friend to his Mexican neighbors. He also sells our wool after the shearing. I think that is where he makes most of his money.

"The rancher makes his home somewhere north of the trading post. Not too far, I think. He might be using one of *La familia's Haciendas*. He and his men seem to be often around Mr. Manco's store."

Zac thought about this before saying, "I need to go to town."

He glanced up in time to see Amado walking between the barn and the adobe bunkhouse. An ear jarring whistle escaped Zac's curled lips. Amado turned immediately and began trotting to the *ramada*.

"I'd like if you'd saddle our horses, Amado; Trig and myself and the lady."

Consuela glanced up at her cousin.

"I will ride with these people to town, Amado. Perhaps you could find a horse for me."

Without a word the young man was gone on his errand.

***

Zac escorted Nancy to the hotel. He stepped out of the saddle and then stood cautiously by while Nancy dismounted.

"You be sure to tell Moody that you're back. He'll be concerned And again, I warn you about riding the country unattended. My advice is, 'just don't do it'."

"Why Mr. Trimbell, how you fuss. A girl could almost convince herself that you care about more than simply her safety."

Zac paused, lifted his eyes to the clouds floating along the horizon and let out a held breath. He was no longer amazed when simple words or circumstances brought back old memories. Horrible memories. Memories of suffering and dying and unpunished crimes, and love torn from his life.

Was he, in fact, saying something more to Nancy than his simple words indicated? Did he even have the freedom to do that?

In the midst of the whirl of agonizing memories of his lost wife and daughter, did he dare think of another. Did his dreadful loneliness justify that kind of betrayal of his wife? Or was it not betrayal, but some feeble excuse for not moving forward with his life?

Perhaps the time for another interest would come, but not yet. Not while the pain and depressions were apt to overtake him at any moment, all out of their own volition, with no control from himself. No, this was not the time.

Holding out his hand for her reins he said, "I'll take your animal over to Abbot's barn."

Sensing that she had perhaps pushed Zac too far, Nancy made no more teasing statements.

"Thank you. And thank you for your advice. I know you're correct. I shall be very careful."

As Zac was leading the horse across the street Nancy called out, "When might we see you again?"

"We'll see what happens."

Not at all happy with the answer, Nancy turned and headed for the boardwalk, raising little puffs of grey dust from the front street of Las Vegas.

Trig, followed by Consuela, rode to the livery, arriving just before Zac led the two horses up to the door.

"Afternoon, Abe. Got a little shoeing matter here if you might have the time."

Abbot turned his eyes away from the arriving

Zac and took the reins from Trig.

"Give me an hour."

Trig opened the gate to the small corral and led Consuela's gelding in, after loosening the girth and removing the bridle.

Zac slapped his big army mount on the rump while it trotted into the corral on its own. He then led Nancy's horse into the dim interior of the barn, tying it in a stall.

Zac looked over at Trig and Consuela.

"I'm going to talk with Link, over at the sheriff's office. Come along if you wish."

CHAPTER FOURTEEN

"Link, you'll remember Trig. And this is Consuela. She and some others of her family have come down from up north."

"Heard something about that. Heard too, that you got the new preacher safely to town."

"Well, since you heard about those things, perhaps you've also heard something about a rancher named Patriquin. Holds out around a small trading post run by a fella named Manco."

The sheriff took several seconds to think about the names.

"Never heard of Patriquin. Manco rings a familiar bell. Never been up there my own self. Not much law in that area and I don't get paid by the good citizens of Las Vegas to patrol the entire north half of the territory.

"You might get more information if you were to talk with Abe over to the livery. Seems he knows more than most, what with travelers dropping by with time to talk."

Trig stood, chuckling a bit.

"We'd best go for coffee right now. Maybe a piece of pie. Got Abe shooing a horse. Wouldn't want to interrupt a man at his work."

***

An hour later the trio approached the livery. Abe was again sitting in his favorite chair, with the front legs off the ground and the back resting against the weathered, wooden wall.

"Howdy there, youngsters. Got yer shooin' done."

He pointed with the stem of his pipe.

"Take a look if'n yer want'n to. He's with that bunch in the corral."

Trig turned his head towards the corral and then swiveled back with a grin.

"I'm not sure I want to be the first to question your work, Abe. Think I'll just let 'er go."

"You wouldn't be the first, not by a long shot."

"Well, still, I'm happy if you say I should be. What do I owe you?"

As Trig dug in his pocket for the coins to pay for the shoeing, Zac broke in and turned the conversation with, "We need to talk to you, Abe. And I want you to meet Consuela. She and her family were run off their land up north a ways. Fella named Patriquin, or some such a title. Seems he argued the land was open to whoever claimed it. That the land grants had been set aside. Do you have any information on that?"

Abe sat silently while he knocked the dottle out of his burned and scarred pipe bowl. He seemed to need time to think. Finally, he stood and motioned towards the dim interior of the barn.

"Let's get out of this afternoon sun. Cooler inside. Not so many eyes on us there either."

Once inside the barn he led them into the small office. Zac and Trig stood while Abe and Consuela took the only available chairs. Abe got up and closed the door before he started talking.

"Those old grants are funny things. Troublesome. Confusing too. They were considered to be legal; worked mostly alright under the old system. Most of them took in more land than could ever be used by one ranch or one family so no one much worried about it. They were mostly just lines on a map that no one had any real knowledge of. Some of the grants overlap others. A lot of that country still ain't been seen by any but Indians, and not often by them.

"Most grants held groups of families, and still the land wasn't all used, or even explored. Does that sound like how your family used the land, young lady?"

Consuela nodded and hesitated before saying, "Yes, there is much land. Not all of it grows good grass. Some is very rough. Rocks and hills. Only the sheep or the goats can find a bit of something to keep them alive among such rocks. The cows, they stay to the lower lands where it is flatter, with more grass. We never knew the real boundaries of the grant.

"The old ones, those that are now gone from this earth, they told their sons where the boundaries were and who had given the grant. They were marked out by hilltops, canyons, anything that would last over time. But after so many years…?

"We only know the land is ours, given by the

Gobierno as a gift to Grandfather *Pérez*. For many years, *La familia's* have been on the land. We lived and we were content."

"Does the area have a name? Any village up there?"

"None that I know of. The only name people mention sometimes is Manco. Mr. Manco runs a small trading post beside our land."

Abe grinned at the sound of Manco's name, but he said nothing.

***

After a time of silence, Abe filled his pipe again as he looked from one face to another, finally settling on Zac.

"You intend to take this trouble onto yourself, Zac?"

"It was kind of brought to me. Fifteen or twenty people camped out at the Wayward. I haven't met them all or counted them. Consuela is here with us because she went to school and learned our language. The rest are going to have to either get their land and herds back or make a start somewhere new. Them and the others that scattered around to the south."

Abe looked surprised. Clutching a burning match but not holding it towards the tobacco he thought back over Zac's words.

"Are you say'n this Patriquin run these folks off without they took their animals with them?"

"That's seems to be the situation."

Abe completed the lighting of his pipe and blew a puff of sweet-smelling tobacco smoke into the air.

"Strange I ain't heard of that. Maybe too recent for news to get down this way."

The older man studied his visitors as he thought through what to say. Finally, he spoke directly to Zac.

"Manco's a fair and honest man. He'd not take sides against the Mexes. Know him from years back. We rode together. Worked a couple of the same ranches back in the earlier days. Mexes and Anglos working together. Didn't know what had become of him. Went north is all I knew. If he's allowing this Patriquin fella to hang around the post, it's because he don't have much choice.

"If you were to take a notion to ride up that way, you talk to Manco. He'll level with you once he knows who you are. You tell him hello from me. Ask him whatever became of Scarlett. He won't answer the question nor tell you anything about the lady, but he'll know you been talk'n to me. Ain't nobody but him and me know that story."

Zac seemed to remain silent longer than usual, almost as if he was tired of the chase, weary of the problems that came his way. Finally, having made his decision, he spoke, looking at the floor, as if the others weren't present.

"I'll take a ride. Too noisy around the Wayward anyway."

Trig laughed at the statement.

"Not by yourself, you ain't."

CHAPTER FIFTEEN

After a day of looking over the town, the time for the dinner with Tracy Handley and his wife came. Moody and Sarah again dressed well, but casually. Las Vegas showed no signs of valuing starched shirts or women's crinoline stuffed dresses. Carob, East Texas had been much the same.

As the Handley home was less than one quarter mile from the hotel, they decided to walk the distance.

Tracy Handley was holding down a wicker chair on his front verandah, visiting with two men. They all rose to their feet as Moody and Sarah turned into the yard.

"Welcome, Moody. Welcome, Sarah. Please come in. There's cool lemonade here if you wish to refresh yourselves after your walk.

"And please, I wish you to meet Kyle Webster and Troy Archer. Their wives are inside giving helpful advice to Anita. I'm sure the dinner will be especially noteworthy with their beneficial input. You will meet them in a bit."

Moody was surprised at the change in the grocer's demeanor. There was a lightness to him that hadn't shown itself at their earlier meeting.

After handshakes all around, they took their seats. Handley poured glasses of lemonade while the men asked about the trip from East Texas. It seemed to take no time at all for the newness of the meeting to wear itself off, although Moody sensed just a bit of rigidity remaining in Webster.

Moody decided to take control of the conversation.

"And what keeps you men in Las Vegas? Are you in business, such as Mr. Handley here, or are you ranchers?"

The two men glanced at one another to see who would speak first. Finally, Troy Archer said, "I have a small spread south of town. We run a few range cattle, but our main enterprise is dairy: milk, cream, butter. My hired hand and I milk twenty head. Bertha, my wife, helps with the separating and the churning of butter. The kids are old enough to help too, although we take their schooling as being of first importance."

Sarah asked, "Do you deliver your milk door to door in town? There was a family back in Carob that did that. Their deliveries were always welcomed, but my, dairying looked like a lot of work to me."

Troy chuckled and rubbed his face with his rough hand.

"Well, I'd agree it's a lot of work. And Bertha would bless you for saying so. But it's all I know, and we make a decent living at it. So, we remain thankful."

Moody turned his eyes towards Kyle Webster, opening the way for his input.

"I have the saddlery and gun shop. Which reminds me, Rev. Tomlinson, I'm told that you arrived in town armed. Now, obviously, I am not against men, or women either, for that matter, owning and being familiar with weapons. But it would seem to be a bit out of character for our new minister, if indeed the board should decide to hire you, to be a man of violence or potential violence."

The silence on the veranda was total. The challenge, coming so early in the meeting was completely unexpected. Unknown to Kyle Webster, who had his back turned to the door, the three women who had been in the kitchen were standing in the doorway listening. It had been their intent to join the group for a cool drink before the dinner was served.

From where they were sitting, both Moody and Sarah had seen the ladies arrive. Everyone was holding silent, wondering what the new minister's response would be. Finally, he spoke.

"I have always felt it best to be prepared to care for myself. You might recall that God called on a young man with a weapon, a simple sling, to defeat the warrior put forth by the Philistines. You might also recall that the young David, after he was chosen king, was a man of war. And God blessed him in that.

"Moses, Joshua, many of the prophets, they were all men who wore arms and used them. 'Be strong and courageous'. That was God's admonition to Joshua. I believe he would have us do no less in our day. We live in a land that is not altogether settled or safe. Perhaps the world will never be altogether safe.

"I have a wife to protect. That is one of the callings of a man, a husband.

"On the trip here from Pueblo, our camp was put upon by a pair of hoodlums, while the men were away seeking our wandering horses. Both of those men ended up dead. No, I didn't shoot them, but one I knocked down with my horse and then was in danger of beating him to death or drowning him in the stream we were fighting in. Sarah stopped me before I completed what might have been.

"Later, I felt bad about my actions. In fact, I quoted scripture. 'Turn the other cheek' had come to my mind. Sarah's sister, Nancy, brought me to my senses by reminding me that if these men had succeeded in capturing the two ladies, as was their stated intent, it would have meant beatings, rape and probably murder at the end of the ordeal."

There was an audible gasp from the women.

"No, Mr. Webster, I am not a man of willful violence. But I am a man determined to live with honor among my fellow citizens. And to live with honor means to act the man, by the conditions that are set before us.

"If that is a stumbling block to you or the board, it is best we know that now."

The men weren't quite ready for such a forceful challenge, but they rallied quickly, assisted by the ladies.

A tall, statuesque woman wiped her hands in her apron and stepped across the veranda floor, holding her cleaned hand out to Sarah.

"I am Anita Handley, Mrs. Tomlinson. Welcome

to our home. What a dreadful experience you and your sister went through. I'm happy that you are here, unscathed and healthy.

"I must say, after hearing that sordid story, I am very glad your husband was up to the challenge presented on the trail, and that he was successful in protecting you and your sister.

"These other ladies are Bertha Archer, there on the left, and Marie Webster."

Turning to Kyle Webster with a boldness uncharacteristic of most women, she added, "Kyle. I hope if the time ever comes that you or Marie or any of your family are threatened with physical violence, that you will be both prepared and able to come to their defense.

"And at the risk of shocking you, I will tell you that neither Tracy nor I ever leave our home without carrying a weapon. I am quite a good shot, I might add."

Leaving no opportunity for rebuttal, she said, "Now, if you're ready, let's go see how badly I've burned the roast."

Kyle Webster was quiet and contemplative during the evening meal.

CHAPTER SIXTEEN

After discussing his thoughts with Consuela, Zac went looking for her brother, Ademar.

"My brothers are both as fluent in English as I am," Consuela had told Zac, "but perhaps not nearly as open to talk. Ademar is a man that likes his privacy and respects the privacy of others.

"He will ride with you. I know without asking. He is very angry about losing our homes and our herds. It was in him to stay and fight but with some of our people already dead, and against so many who were better armed and ready to kill, fighting any more would have been foolish. He will be ready to go back."

Zac had trouble finding Ademar when he wished to ask him to ride north. The young man was finally located in a grouping of brush beside a small stream, about one-half mile from Zac's home.

There he was attending to his own laundry. When Zac rode up, Ademar stood from his kneeling position by the water, a wet shirt in his hand. The bushes beside him were draped with canvas pants, cotton shirts, worn out socks and two pairs of Long Johns.

"We have not yet met. I'm Zac. I believe you will be Ademar."

The young man simply nodded.

Zac stepped down from the grey gelding he had chosen for the short ride. The two men shook hands and Zac sat down on the grassy hillside.

"This is a fine place to be when one has private matters to deal with. I've always liked it here. I come often to think, and sometimes to pray, as I watch the stream flow along its meandering path."

Ademar hesitated before saying, "The women are busy. Anyway, I like to care for myself. It has been good for me up until now."

Zac smiled and agreed.

"I'm kind of like that my own self. Do most things for myself. Usually like being off, away from the noise of others."

"And yet you have come to me."

There was a question left in the short statement.

"Yes. We ride north, Trig and me. Up to where you called home. And to where your herds now graze on land a rancher has claimed for his own. I am wondering if you would want to ride with us."

Ademar was slow answering while he carefully wrung the water from the sleeve of a red shirt.

"That is why I do the washing of clothes. Consuela said you would go. I was thinking you might ask."

"Are there others nearby that you could bring with you?"

"There are some who wish to fight. They would ride.

"There are others, the old ones, who would not be much for the fight but would come to drive the animals away. They would ride too, these men, with their dogs."

"Can you have them here in two days, with food for themselves and perhaps a bit to share?"

"They will be here."

"Can they be ready to ride at first light the day after tomorrow?"

"We will be waiting beside the corral when the sun first shows itself on that morning."

With no further words Zac stepped into the saddle.

***

Consuela stayed on the Wayward with Alejandra, while Zac, Trig, Ademar, and Amado, along with seven men armed for fighting, and six more who were along to care for the herds, rode north. Four sheep dogs sometimes ran along with the horses and sometimes rode behind the saddles of their owners. Amado refused to stay behind. He was young but these men had killed his father.

With a Winchester carbine loaned by Zac, he would go and do what must be done.

***

Three long days of riding later, the direction and the destination chosen by Ademar, the three lead riders made camp a half mile south of the trading post.

"We will visit the Manco *mañana*. For now, we

need rest and food."

Before long, they were joined by the trailing group.

After a cold supper and coffee, made over a small, almost smokeless fire, and settled carefully out of sight behind a sheltering rock, the riders set out guards before rolling in their blankets. Zac and Trig joined two Mexicans on the dawn guard.

The sun was just beginning to warm the land the next morning when Zac, Trig and Ademar trotted up the dusty trail and dismounted in front of Manco's trading post. The others waited behind, in whatever shade they could find, but within sight of the small trading post. Amado waited with the older men. His time was not yet.

***

Manco's door was simply a light piece of canvas, flapping in the wind. Zac pushed it aside with the barrel of the Henry. Glancing in, he could see little in the dim interior. Quickly, but carefully, he stepped inside and immediately took a step to the left. Trig followed, sliding to the right.

Ademar hollered from the doorway.

"Manco, you are here?"

"I'm here. No one but me. I saw you rid'n up. Step in and rest yourselves. Cooler inside."

Zac and Trig could both see the tall, gaunt man now that their eyes were growing used to the dimness. They stepped forward, with Ademar just one step behind.

The trading post owner glanced at Zac and Trig, without recognition. He then took a slower look and said, "*Hola*, Ademar. Wasn't sure I'd be see'n you up this way again. Tell me about *La familia*. Are you all safely to the south?"

"Most. Not all. Some will never leave this place. They will sleep under the grass forever."

"Bad business, Ademar. I never seen the like. Don't hardly know what can be done without holding a near war. And that ain't the way of the *La Gente*. Who are your friends?"

"This one is known as Zac. He has a *rancho* by Las Vegas. The Wayward it is called. My family is there because my aunt and my cousin have lived there for more than one year. This other man is Trig."

"And do you trust these men, Ademar?"

When Ademar was slow to answer, Trig thought to address the question himself, knowing that Zac had no liking for matters of the sort.

"Fella named Abe. Runs a livery down at Las Vegas. Friend to Zac and the Wayward. Shoed my horse a few days ago. Said you were a trustworthy man. Is that still true now that you have different customers for your post?"

It was a response designed to show that trust was required in both directions.

Manco showed his dislike for the question. He was about to come back with a bitter response when Trig grinned and said, "By the way. Ol' Abe, he said to tell you he's been wondering whatever became of Scarlett."

Manco slammed his hand down on the countertop and spoke with a raised voice.

"Scarlett is it? Why that old reprobate. I've a good mind to saddle up and ride down there. Needs shooting, that old man does."

Trig laughed and held out his hand. Slowly, Manco grew a small grin and finally completed the handshake.

"Set yourselves down fellas. I've got nothing cool to drink but I always have coffee. Like it myself."

There were four chairs around the much scarred, homemade table. Zac and Trig grabbed the two that faced the doorway. Ademar slid into the one facing the back of the building, where he knew there was another door, leading from Manco's sleeping quarters to the outside. There was an outhouse, a small barn, a hand-dug, open air cistern and a couple of sheds in the back yard. The sometimes blacksmith and horse trader was evidently off on some other business. There was no sign of him.

Manco laid out four clean crockery mugs before returning with the coffee pot. He set the hot metal pot on a brightly decorated Mexican terra cotta tile in the center of the table. He then sat in the last chair, fully understanding how the others had placed themselves.

"Help yourselves. Got no milk nor sweetener."

The four men carefully studied each other for a full minute as they sipped the surprisingly good coffee. Trig broke the silence.

"Now, that's a good cup of coffee."

"It's the water. Come across this little freshwater spring some years back when I was travelling through. Just a seep really. It was a few feet of green grass, mak'n a path outa the rocks that I noticed first. Enough of a runoff so's my horse would suck a bit of water from the wet grass. Followed the trickle back into that rocky growth you can see out back.

Nicest little flow of fresh water bubbl'n up outa the ground you could ever hope to find. Took a look around the country and decided to stay right here.

"Hired a couple of Mexes to build this adobe and here I am. And here I'll stay. I don't need nor want much in life. Content to let the days pass, with a memory or two poking its head up from time to time.

"Dug a small cistern on that runoff. Lined it with rocks. Just enough water for me and a couple of horses that I almost never ride. Got a dog too. Good dog. Got him from the Mexes. Too old and crippled up for herding sheep but still a good animal. Hides up there in the shade of the rocks and watches. I knew you was com'n well before I first seen you. No need to face the door neither. Dog will let us know if we got company com'n."

Zac, in his usual no-nonsense manner, got right to the point.

"Mr. Manco…"

"No Mr. needed, Just Manco. That's all."

"Alright Manco. You asked if we could be trusted. I'm not insulted nor concerned by the question. It's a good question, whether it's asked out loud or not. So I'll tell you that you can relax on that matter. I believe that if Abe was here, he would confirm that.

"But as Trig just said, there's a whole new situation up here, with new men seemingly in charge. Can Ademar's folks still trust you?"

"Noticed you didn't ask about yourself trusting me."

Manco cringed just a bit at Zac's stare.

"If I find I can't trust you, you'll not have to worry about saving for your old age.

"Now, tell us what's going on, as far as you've seen."

CHAPTER SEVENTEEN

Shocked by Zac's unsmiling words, Manco nervously cleared his throat to continue his story, aware that the words were not an empty threat. He hesitated, asking himself how much he could say before his own safety would be challenged. What if these men rode back south and never returned? He would be left with Patriquin and his bunch.

But Ademar and the other riders were here now. The threat was now. He decided to speak.

"Marcus Patriquin. Likes to be called Sarg. Rode in here with a handful of longhorns and five, maybe six riders. Little over a year ago, that was. A new rider shows up, time to time. Never seen them all at once. Could be more back there in those hills.

"Rode in here like somebody come. Sitt'n his saddle like a king, or a count, or some such a thing.

"First thing he done was pull up outside that there door and holler for me to come out. I did as he said, but I took my own sweet time about it.

"Never much took to gett'n orders. Didn't like it as a kid. Didn't like it in the army. Cost me a rid'n job or two along the way. Surely not going to let anyone order me around now. But I was alone and not figur'n on dy'n right that very day.

"I belted on my Colt, which I don't usually wear, from having no need. I pushed that canvas aside and stood to where I could see him, but he wouldn't see nothing but maybe a bit of shadow, in the darkness of the adobe. I stood there and just looked at him. Waiting.

"He didn't like that much at all. Kind of set the limits of our relationship though, which is what I wanted.

"First thing he does, he ups and says, "My name is Marcus Patriquin. I'm usually known as Sarg. I'll be taking over this land. There's to be no animals but mine eating this grass. And you, Trader, you sell to only me and my ranch hands. You ever sell to the Mexes again I'll tear this shack down around your ears. That understood?"

His three listeners were silent, staring at him, the coffee forgotten.

"Well, sir, he spoke his piece and rode off, four hands follow'n him. I let the curtain drop and went back to what I was doing. But I'll admit to doing some thinking."

"Who did the Mexes trade with after that?"

Manco looked at Trig, who had asked the question.

"Snuck in here a few times, mostly at night or just before dawn. Otherwise, I don't know. Maybe rode to Pueblo. Long ride though. Ademar could tell you, if it matters.

"Land right around here was held by Gonzales. He tried to fight Patriquin off, but he had little chance. Him and one son are buried up the draw a ways. His widow, Alejandra, she rode south with nothing but her only living boy and a few clothes.

"Ademar and the others, they were off to the west and a bit south, into the rougher hills. Patriquin left them alone till just recently."

Zac turned to Ademar.

"That about size it up, Ademar?"

"Where we buy or sell our wool matters to no one but ourselves. But you may wonder why *La Gente* didn't come when first my uncle Gonzales needed help. But we were two days' ride away. One day to come for us and another to ride back. Some came when the news was brought to us. When we came, my uncle and cousin, they were in their graves. Amado and his *madre*, *mi tia*, my aunt, were gone with their wagon and their poor horse. There was nothing we could do. Soon, it will be different."

Zac looked at the young man, wondering what he meant by the last statement.

Sure there was nothing more to learn from the trader, Zac stood and looked at the man.

"This won't be the final end to this mess. The courts will have to deal with the land grants and the ownership coming from their decisions. That's beyond our control or interest. But I expect the matter with this rancher will be dealt with in the next couple of days. Don't you be doing anything foolish in the meantime."

As Zac turned to the door the trader gave him a hard look. Glancing back, he was startled to see Trig grinning at him.

Manco stood in the doorway, watching the three riders turn their horses to the north. A growl and then frantic barking from the dog caused him to turn around. Seven heavily armed men were riding down from the shaded hill to the south. All wore the traditional, wide brimmed *sombrero*. None of the men looked his way as they rode past.

As the riders swept by the trading post, he thought he had never seen a tougher looking group of men. Or men more determined. Or perhaps it was that they were finally getting angry.

Riding at a steady pace, the seven men stayed a respectful distance behind Zac and Trig and Ademar.

CHAPTER EIGHTEEN

Trig heard the hoofbeats in the distance, behind them. He turned in the saddle, counting only the armed riders, the fighting men. The older men, the shepherds and herdsmen were not in sight. When he turned again, a few minutes later, the seven riders were not to be seen. He studied the rough hills to the east but saw nothing.

Ademar noticed the puzzled look on Trig's face.

"Do not worry, my friend, they will be with us when the time is right."

Trig had questions but he held his peace.

***

Two miles north of the trading post, and close to the Gonzales adobe, Ademar pointed out the rising dust approaching from the north. That much dust, moving that fast, would mean riders.

Only a small cluster of trees and brush, dominated by a large half-dead poplar, prevented the two groups from seeing each other. Ademar immediately moved to the east, close upon the rocky up-thrust. Zac immediately recognized the purpose of the move and appreciated the leadership of the young Mexican. They pulled their animals to a restful walk and continued slowly north.

It was a wait of only a few minutes before horsemen rode into sight. Zac had never seen Patriquin, but he knew the man on the rangy bay at the head of the riders could be no one else. He was sitting tall in the saddle, looking like he owned the world, just as Manco had described him. He was followed by five tough looking riders.

Patriquin's surprise was total when Zac, Trig and Ademar rode just a few feet out from the shading rocks. Ademar called for him to pull up. With a cruel jerk of the reins Patriquin turned his horse towards the three riders and stopped, his eyes firmly planted on Ademar and his *sombrero.*

His men immediately spread out, dividing themselves, three to the north and two to the south, but all close to the rocks. They couldn't help noticing that both Ademar and Trig held their carbines across their saddles, Trig's pointing to the left and Ademar's, the weapon in his left hand, pointing to the right. They didn't seem to be aware of Zac's Henry, hanging from his right hand, tucked closely along his leg.

"You're on my land," Patriquin barked, "No Mexes wanted, nor welcome. Nor any Mex lovers either. You've got just one minute to turn those crowbait animals around and get gone."

Zac was about to speak when Ademar again took the lead. Shifting his carbine and holding it steady along his thighs, pointed at the rider closest to him, but with his eyes still on the leader, he answered, "No, *señor*, this time it will be different than before."

Patriquin couldn't have been angrier, or more surprised.

"You filthy Mex. I'll have your hide stretched on the barn wall. Now take these other two and get gone."

He was fairly spitting in rage.

Ademar could hear the rustle of footsteps in the rocks behind him and the clunk of iron shoes on grass covered rock. He didn't have to turn around to know what was happening. Patriquin leaned back in his saddle when he saw seven more big-hatted men descend from the rocks. Two were horseback, five were on foot. One more, a much younger man who seemed somehow familiar sat his horse slightly off to the side, a hateful look on his face as he studied Patriquin and one of the cowboys.

The rancher turned and looked at his riders, but they had their eyes glued to the many weapons pointed their way. Each one sensed that to move or reach for a Colt, was to die.

Not able to hold back any longer, his anger and need for revenge burning up inside him, Amado pushed his way past the older men. He lifted the carbine, borrowed from Zac back at the Wayward, to his shoulder, pointing it at one of the cowboys.

"That one. That one will see no more days on this earth. That one, I see him kill *mi padre*. Shot him, like the coward he is, when *mi padre* was already wounded and lying on the ground. Today I will pay this man for that."

Zac leaned from his horse and gently laid his

hand on the young man's shoulder, slowing him for a moment, while yet, supporting him.

With ten weapons pointed their way, none of Patriquin's men moved. If they had noticed that Trig and Ademar had their weapons trained their way they said nothing. Their eyes were firmly fixed on the seven men who had descended from the rocks.

The rider singled out by Amado fidgeted nervously, moving in the saddle until his gelding began fidgeting too. The rider next to him spoke out of the side of his mouth.

"Sit still you fool. We might get out of this yet if you don't do anything stupid."

Zac looked the situation over carefully, looking for weaknesses in their position. Satisfied, he glanced sideways at Ademar and nodded, as if to say, 'your lead'.

Ademar indicated Patriquin with a lift of his chin.

"Now you will step off your horse."

"I'll be danged if I will."

No one was expecting what happened next. Without a word, Zac lifted his Henry to waist height. Quicker than a man could tell about it seven shots rang out. Zac's cavalry horse stood like a rock. The first shot took Patriquin's hat off his head. The next two were so close to his horse's front hooves that the animal snorted, backed up and reared, his feet well off the ground. Patriquin tumbled to the side, shouting in fear and anger. He reached with his arms to soften the landing but Zac's next .44 plowed dirt on the spot his hands were reaching for.

With the land stealer crumbling into a ball on the ground, Zac put three more shots into the dirt in front of Patriquin's face. His terrified scream startled the already uneasy horse. The animal whirled and ran off, his head and ears up, the stirrups flapping.

A few other riders, cowboys and Mexicans alike, barely managed to hold their mounts steady.

Although the shots had quit coming, the echoes were still reverberating off the rocky hillsides and the air was full of the foul-smelling, sulfurous powder smoke. Patriquin rolled himself into an even tighter ball, covering his head with his hands.

Zac's action was so unexpected and took so little time, that no one else had moved or reached for a weapon.

With the thunder of the shots rolling away across the grassland, Ademar spoke again.

"Now, Mr. land stealer, you are off your horse. You see how easy that was. It is also easy to kill you. But now you will stand up and pretend you are a man in front of these others. These ones who would help you steal land and herds. You will stand up now."

Patriquin, attempting to regain some of his confidence, slowly stood, wiping dust from his face. While he was struggling to his feet, one of the men behind Amado had lifted his raw hide riata, forming a loop. He stepped his horse a bit to the side to gain clear throwing space and with a single flip of the braided leather, Patriquin had the loop around his arms and chest. His defiant yell was drowned out by the clattering of steel shod hooves on the rocky ground. Patriquin was again lifted off his feet and thrown to the ground. The roper's horse stopped and stood steady, holding some strain on the lariat, while two other Mexican riders dismounted. Within seconds Patriquin was thoroughly bound, hand and foot. He lay on the ground in sullen terror.

No matter what happened from this day forward Patriquin was finished as a rancher and a leader of men. His terror filled screams had ended his reign on the frontier. No man would ever follow him again.

CHAPTER NINETEEN

Zac spoke to the frightened riders.

"You men, step to the ground. Unloose your gun belts and drop them. Move into a group here in front of me. Leave your horses where they are. And don't you start thinking that any of you has a choice in the matter. I'm not a real patient man. I'd like it if you could move quickly."

Sullenly, the wary cowboys stepped from their mounts. One by one the belts and weapons hit the dirt. Slowly, they moved away from the rocks and gathered in one place. Patriquin watched the actions with disgust at his men, and with obvious fear in his eyes.

"Now, Amado, call your man forward."

Amado stepped his horse up beside Zac and pointed at the man he had singled out before.

"Now you will come here, *hombre muerto caminando*. We have some business to do, you and me. We do this business with a rope and a tree. Or we use the bullet. You have a choice *hombre*. What you wish, eh?"

Zac and Trig, both, looked at the still grieving young man with admiration for his determination and purpose. It was as if they were watching him mature as he spoke. Just a few days before, back on the Wayward, he had been running ranch errands, cleaning stalls, and helping his mother. Today he was doing a man's work and doing it well.

The newness and the seriousness of the situation had Amado quaking inside with fear and expectation. A man's life was at stake. Amado recognized that as no small thing. But not far away from where they stood were two graves, his *Padre* and his *hermano*, his brother. He would do what he had come to do.

His hope was that his slightly trembling voice wouldn't give him away, or the shaking of his hands.

When the rider failed to draw closer, Trig took two steps, leaned from his saddle, grabbed the man by the collar and flung him to the ground at Amado's feet. The Mexican riders that had tied up Patriquin stepped up and did the same with the guilty man.

Zac spoke to the Mexicans.

"Untie Patriquin's feet. We'll be wanting him to do some walking."

When the two condemned men were standing, Zac turned to Amado and Ademar. Without a word he pointed to the line of brush and the half-dead cottonwood. There was no need to explain his meaning.

The Mexican men ran quickly through the opening in the rocks and mounted their horses. Again, without need for words, they surrounded Patriquin's riders and ushered them towards the woods. Two Mexicans rounded up a couple of horses and led them along.

It took no time at all to reach the tree and for the two condemned men to be hoisted onto the saddles of the led horses. With no formality or the tying of special slip knots, the men's own lariats were snugged over their heads and under their chins. With the hemp thrown over a limb and tied off to the bole of the tree, all was in readiness. A loop was left in the rope to allow for a short drop.

Patriquin looked with disdain at his riders.

"A fine lot of men you are. Took you on to ride for the brand and there you stand like a bunch of schoolgirls. Cowards, the lot of you."

One of the riders quickly answered.

"I ain't never considered myself as being real smart, Sarg, but I can sure enough count. Ain't a likely prospect going against odds like this here, this morning. Anyway, I ain't never done noth'n worth hang'n for. Unless being stupid enough to follow an empty shirt like you is a hanging offence."

Patriquin turned his face away with no more words.

***

Standing beside the base of the tree Zac spoke to the other Patriquin riders.

"I expect you men are just as guilty as these two. It's unfortunate that we have no way to prove anything. But when you take a good look at what's to come here, you're staring at your own futures if you ever team up with another man like this.

"Now, you watch. If you turn your head away or

close your eyes, you'll find yourself hanging from another limb. Take this morning as a lesson. Then gather up your horses and get out of here. And I mean out of here by a long way. Don't ever come back. And you warn anyone you run into that has designs on this land, it's not going to be healthy for anyone troubling these families again."

With that he nodded to Ademar and Amado.

Those two, removing their big *sombreros*, used them to whap the rumps of the horses. With a collective gasp from the watchers, the men were lifted from the saddles and dropped to the ends of the ropes. The result was in no way pretty, but it was clearly effective. It was all over in a matter of seconds.

With the hanged men swinging before him Amado lurched, tried to swallow, and then ran to the off side of the tree. He could be heard throwing up. No one commented. No one said anything at all, but every eye was on the slowly swinging, twisting horror.

After a full minute Zac spoke again to the Patriquin riders.

"How many other riders did Patriquin have and where will we find them?"

The cowboy who had proclaimed his innocence before, offered the information. All was silence for a slow count of ten. Then Zac motioned to the grassland with a sweep of his hand.

The Patriquin riders didn't have to be told twice. It took but a few minutes to round up their horses and pick up their weapons, but soon they were mounted and out of sight, heading north.

Trig walked over to the tree. Unceremoniously

he sliced through the ropes. With the weight of the bodies, the ropes sang over the limb and fell limply on the ground beside the dead men. Taking a freedom upon himself he said to the Mexican group, pointing out no one in particular.

"Drag them over to the hillside and cover them and the ropes with rocks. They deserve that much decency, at least."

CHAPTER TWENTY

An hour later, the silent, thoughtful group rode into the yard of what, up until one year before, had been the Gonzalas *hacienda*. After the events of the morning it no longer seemed quite so important. The fight was about the land and the stolen animals, not an old adobe.

During their ride, the shepherds and herdsmen had caught up.

Amado pulled his horse to a halt as they entered the yard. He swept his hat from his head and, with thankful reverence, crossed himself, as he had been taught. He brushed unbidden tears away before nudging his horse back into action, approaching the small adobe.

Stepping inside he was satisfied that the cowboys had at least respected the space enough to keep it reasonably well swept out, although there were dirty dishes from their last meal. Silently he thought, '*Mi Madre* would not be happy. But at least it is so that she could make it clean again. I don't know what she will decide. Maybe so she will decide to not come back.'

***

Zac took a seat under a shading bush. He was ready to go home. Home to the Wayward, where he would have peace. And the freedom to sit under his own *ramada* reading a book. Or roam the quiet hills. And sleep in his own bed.

Yes, he needed to go home.

As usual, after an incident like the one that morning, his emotions were stretched nearly to the breaking point. He hated the violence but knew of no way, or any place that it could be avoided. He also knew that if he sat in the shade much longer the unwanted memories would come. The fighting. The war. The cannons. The screams of the dying. The pathetic whinnying of the wounded horses. They would all be pouring from his damaged memory if he didn't control them.

A couple of the Mexes were putting food together. As soon as he had eaten, he would turn his horse back to the south.

***

With the provisions they found in the adobe a lunch was put together. The riders were all excitement, several speaking at once although it didn't sound like anyone was really listening.

Zac and Trig dished up a small plate of food each and took a seat, back in the shady spot beside the small house. Neither could follow the language well enough to make out the rapid-fire Spanish.

Ademar joined them there, standing just a short distance away.

"It was a grim task but good, just the same. The land does not need men like those that were here."

After a silent moment he asked Zac, "Do you ride home now?"

"Yes, I don't think you need us anymore. Your men now know that they can stand up for themselves. You can find your herds. Your flocks. Bring back your families. I'm sure you can also find the Patriquin herd. I think you can call them your own without anyone bothering you."

"There will be other Patriquin riders. You look where we were told they could be found. But be careful. Don't start a fight. You can stand up for yourselves better if you don't make enemies."

Ademar shuffled his feet for a moment but finally sorted out what he wanted to say.

"We are much grateful to you men. Thank you.

"I will stay here now. Perhaps you could tell Consuela and our people that it is now good to come home. We need to get the people back here to keep the land safe from others who might come.

"You must take Amado home with you. He is young. His *madre* will be needing him. I think it best if she doesn't know about the hanging."

He turned and was about to leave when Zac stopped him.

"I'm happy you got the land back, Ademar. But you need to understand. Patriquin didn't really amount to much. He was mostly all talk. With a truly big rancher and a tougher crew it would not be easy. These thousands of acres of unused grass are like an open invitation. You must watch who is coming.

"Don't look to start trouble but be ready to hang on to what is yours.

"Even then, I'm afraid there will be many big fights. But the fights will be with lawyers and courts. You cannot win that fight with guns.

"The people, *la gente*, will not hold the land unless you can prove in court that the old grant is true. You might need to find some of the grandfathers, perhaps one who sits in the sun in Santa Fe, who will remember."

***

Amado did not willingly ride, but by evening he and Zac and Trig were many miles south, on the trail that would take them back to the Wayward.

CHAPTER TWENTY-ONE

On a spit of land nestled between two hillsides, and divided roughly in half by a flowing stream, Abner Sallow farmed the deep soil, deposited over the centuries, by that very same stream.

In New Mexico, close by Las Vegas, a territory known more for rangeland and rough, semi-desert scrub, this small patch of growing soil was an anomaly. Abner had been following the stream when he first saw the fifty acres. The land had been heavily grazed. Except for a narrow strip along the waterway, the soil was dried out and cracked. Portions of the stream bank had crumbled under the weight of grazing cattle. The native grasses were being crowded out by weeds and small cactus.

The land was of little value.

But the farmer in Abner liked what he saw. He walked the land, garden spade in hand. In several places he turned up what remained of the sod and examined the soil beneath. He was impressed by both the tangle of remaining roots as well as the depth of the topsoil. He walked to each corner of the misshaped parcel and studied the slopes. He climbed the low hills surrounding it to get a view from on high. He judged the sunlight hours and when the land would be in the shadow of the hillsides.

He stood at the highest point of the land, along the stream, and held his arms out from his sides, forming a 'T', one arm away from the plot of land, the other pointed towards the far boundary.

Carefully, hoping not to be influenced by the land itself, he held his arms at what he hoped was close to level. Using this measure, as he sighted down his arm, noting where his fingers pointed on the hillside, he saw a distinct drop in elevation. Not a big drop, but enough, reaching its lowest level at the furthest point. He judged that irrigation was not only possible, but the diversion of water would not be all that difficult. The slope, both downstream on the small watercourse, as well as side to side on the property, formed a shallow bowl, a natural receptacle for gravity irrigation.

He closed his eyes and imagined acres of saleable produce. Corn. Perhaps an acre of oats for his horses, a bit of hay, a few acres of grazing. Potatoes, carrots, and many other crops. Peppers. He would have to learn how to cultivate peppers, a crop he had never grown.

With the heat and sunshine of New Mexico, plus the flowing water, there was no end to what an energetic man could produce.

He pictured a small but pleasant home at the higher end of the property, with barn, chicken coop and the other necessary outbuildings.

He closed his eyes and imagined he and Bertha

building together. Building for the long term, the two of them and the child that would be gracing their home in the next few months. He could hardly wait to return to town with the news. Bertha would be as pleased and excited as he was. Now first he had to convince the rancher who owned the land to part with that small corner.

***

Toby Drummond, owner of the GG Ranch, known locally as the Double G, lifted his foot to the bottom corral rail. He laid one elbow on the top rail and nudged his hat upward with the other thumb.

"What you're telling me, young fella, is that you want to buy that odd shaped piece down there to the south end of the ranch. And only about fifty acres. Why, that ain't hardly enough to raise a single critter on. Wouldn't scarcely graze that wagon team of yours."

He pointed over his shoulder at the team Abner had pulled into the shade of the barn.

Smiling indulgently at his visitor the rancher said, "Don't know what you've got in mind, but I'll tell you what. I'm not about to miss the use of that little bit of grazed-out land. The community needs newcomers. So you just go right ahead. Do as you wish. My men will hold our cattle away. You do what you want with it, and God bless. I'm thinking you're going to need His blessing to accomplish anything down there."

Abner was caught off balance at the offer. It took a moment to gather his thoughts. Finally, he looked the rancher eye to eye and answered.

"That's a generous offer, Mr. Drummond, but I can't accept it. My plans are for the long term. I'll need title to the land to bring both myself and my wife the comfort we need to do the work we have in mind. Will you sell me the land and guarantee not to divert the creek?"

There was another long pause as the rancher studied his visitor, as if he was trying to guess what he had in mind. But, no matter really. The land held little value to the GG.

"Do you have one hundred dollars?"

"Yes, I have. Not with me, but yes."

"Alright, son, we'll mark off the land and I'll give you title. You bring me the hundred next time you're out this way."

After another 'thank you', and a firm handshake, Abner climbed aboard his wagon and turned the team for town. Somehow, he managed to hold back his smile until he cleared the big gate posts of the GG.

As he drove, he thought of what had to be done. Building a fence would be the start. Drummond said his men would hold the cattle apart from that piece of land, but he couldn't take the chance. A few loose cattle could destroy a season's crops in an hour. He wasn't going to let that happen. So, a fence was first.

He had brought a plow and a set of harrows west with him. Opening the soil to the sunshine would be his first task after the fencing. It was late in the year to hope for a saleable crop. He might get a few fast-growing vegetables off that could be taken to town for sale. That and a bit of a kitchen garden he and Bertha would need.

Could he do all the work and still get a house built before cold weather returned? They could manage with the tent for the summer. When the baby's time was closer, he would move Bertha back into town until the birth was safely behind them.

Abner and Bertha were a long way from wealthy but, on the other hand, they weren't poor. With gifts from both of their families before they ventured out to New Mexico, they had enough to keep the wolf from the door until the next growing season.

Abner would start his enquiries about building an adobe first thing. Although he knew nothing at all about adobe, with the help of men experienced in that local building style, they would for sure be out of the weather by fall.

***

Interestingly, almost right from the start, his best customer was the Double G ranch.

Abner was digging a small load of his first year's late produce for a trip to town. He looked up when he heard a buggy's approach and walked to the fence gate. He had met no one but Drummond himself when he first visited the GG. It was only when he was able to see the brand on the buggy horse that he figured out who his visitors might be.

A man he had never seen before was driving the buggy, with a well-dressed lady holding down a place on the spring seat beside him. Riding alongside, sitting atop a tall, almost pure white gelding, rode a girl. Young, but not a child.

The girl was hatless, with her long blonde hair flowing in the wind. She wouldn't be considered beautiful, but she was certainly attractive enough. Idly, Abner had guessed her age at perhaps fourteen or fifteen. He couldn't help noticing there was a prominent trail of freckles over the top of her nose and across both cheeks.

***

"Good morning. Welcome. Won't you step down and come into the shade? My wife has some lemonade chilling in the well if you'd enjoy a cool drink. I'm Abner Sallow."

"Good morning to you, Mr. Sallow. I'm Trudy Drummond. This is Clive, GG cook, and my daughter, Honey. We heard about the wonderful things you've started over here. It's late in the year but we've come to see if you have anything available that might brighten up the menu at the ranch."

That had been the first of many produce purchases for the GG.

***

Now, fifteen months later, Clive again pulled the buggy up beside the yard fence and stepped down. He tied the single horse off to the fence and turned to help Mrs. Drummond.

Before the lady could step down, Abner came from around the small tool shed. Like most people in the new west, Abner was practiced at hiding his hurts and his problems. 'Stand on your own two feet', was the word of the age. And so, Abner hid his heartbreak and greeted the visitors. There was no smile in his welcome. He hadn't smiled in months.

But there was sincere pleasure at the thought of another customer coming to his garden.

"I thought I heard buggy wheels. Welcome. Again. It's always good to see you, Mrs. Drummond."

He glanced at the cook and the rider on the white horse.

"Clive. Honey. Welcome."

Abner waited while Mrs. Drummond took a slow, wondering look across the small farm.

"Why, Mr. Sallow. With Clive and Honey doing the buying, it's been some time since I've been here. What marvels you have created."

Clive simply nodded at Abner, but Honey swung off her horse and smiled.

"May I hold your precious little girl, Abner, while mother and Clive make their choices?"

"She's always happy to see you, Honey. You know where she is."

Honey walked into the shade of the tool shed. There, raised well above ground level to protect the baby from snakes, Abner had constructed a crib of sorts, with a cloth awning over it to hold out the heat of the sun. It was built on small skids, like a sled, so he could move it as he worked through his crops.

Mrs. Drummond followed her daughter to where the baby was resting. She watched as Honey picked the little girl up and snuggled her. The baby gurgled with a smile of familiarity and reached out with one hand. Honey clasped the hand and kissed it.

"You go do your buying, Mother. I'll be right here when you're ready to go home."

Abner was watching from a short distance away.

Gertie Drummond turned to him with a sad, small smile.

"What a beautiful little girl. You have been through a hard time, Mr. Sallow. I have not been here for some while, but I want you to know that I have been praying for you and the baby. Please know too that if you ever need help, we are available to you."

Abner nodded his silent thanks.

***

Four years later, the farm was producing abundant crops. Whatever concerns Abner and Bertha originally had about making a living were well set aside.

Abner was working dawn to dusk, only partly because of his love of the land. The greatest driving force keeping him awake and working, was the need to forget. The need to be busy. To keep from thinking too much. The need to heal from the loss of Bertha.

So, the father and his precious four-year old daughter put in long, lonely days together. The father worked in his fields. The daughter played in the dirt of the yard, and then took her rests in the light, wooden enclosure Abner had built. As he worked, he dragged the enclosure around the farm, keeping his beautiful little girl close and safe.

But the days were long and lonely. Abner never left the farm except to sell his produce or to purchase the few items his farm, his chickens and his milk cow didn't supply. He was often lonely. But he had made no friends. Nor had anyone in this cattle-minded community made any serious attempt to get to know him.

He and Bertha had attended the Community Church a few times when they first arrived. But no solid connections were made. It was almost as if there was something suspicious about a family earning its keep in anything but the cattle or sheep industries.

There had been other troubles too. A few of the young troublemakers from town had harassed his animals. Once, they had broken into the yard and had ridden their horses through the fields, causing much damage. Abner could see no solution, so he simply made the necessary repairs and continued on, doing what he had come to do.

***

Absorbed with hoeing and pulling weeds, Abner would have missed the rider approaching if the dog hadn't barked. He straightened from his hunched-over position and looked towards the buildings. A broad-shouldered man riding a bay gelding was just pulling his animal to a halt at the hitch rail beside the yard gate. Spotting Abner in the distance, the man waved and shouted.

"May I step down? I'd like to visit a minute if you can spare the time."

Seeing no threat, Abner, saving his voice, simply pointed at the hitch rail, leaned on his hoe, and waited. The visitor would have to come to him. He wasn't about to walk away, leaving his little girl behind.

Coming within arm's length before he spoke,

the visitor held out his hand.

"Good morning, Mr. Sallow. I'm Moody Tomlinson. I've recently been appointed pastor of the Community Church. I've looked forward to meeting you."

With grave suspicion, the farmer completed the handshake.

"Abner Sallow."

He made no further comment, simply waiting for the pastor to state his purpose for the visit.

"And who is this little person?"

Abner stepped the few feet to the safety enclosure, rolled back the shading piece of canvas draped over the top, and picked up the little girl. Of course, the girl was perfectly capable of walking, but Abner concerned himself with the few snakes that had made their presence known over the years. Anyway, both the child and Abner enjoyed a tight hug from time to time.

"This is Summer. She and I farm this land together."

There was no smile or any other discernable look to Abner's face, except, perhaps suspicion.

"Beautiful child. I'm sure you enjoy each other's company during the workday."

Moody took the time to look all around the small holding. The wagon team was grazing in the furthest corner of the property, back where the land almost came to a point, making it impossible to drag plow or harrows efficiently. Where the land widened out, there was an already harvested hay meadow. A considerable amount of dried grass was stacked a short distance from the barn.

Closer to where the two men stood, the corn

held precedence, immediately past the potato patch. From there to where they stood was an orderly arrangement of fields, all fed from the array of hand-dug irrigation ditches, fanning out like the tiny ribs inside a poplar leaf. The flow of water was controlled by a series of crude, but effective gates.

All in all, it was an impressive piece of work for one man to have accomplished.

Moody turned back to Abner.

"I stand in awe, Mr. Sallow. Toby Drummond described what this land looked like when you purchased it from him. The change is wonderful. What you have accomplished is simply wonderful."

"Thank you for that, I suppose. It's good to have one's work recognized. But not everyone approves of me, my work, or my life.

"So, what brings you out here today?"

Moody noticed the lack of any sign of welcome, or offer of friendship, but he didn't let that bother him. He had seen too much of life to get upset by a slow start when meeting a new man.

"Well, Mr. Sallow..."

"Abner. Abner will do just fine."

"Alright, Abner. Thank you for that. And, of course, I'm Moody. I don't live by the offered titles.

"The thing is, Abner, I've been trying to meet the parishioners one on one. I've worked through those that I see on Sunday morning. Of course, many of them live in town and are easily accessible.

"Yours and your wife's names are on the register from some time back. I made an enquiry about yourself and some others that no longer attend. That information was helpful, but I thought we might both benefit from a short visit. At least let you know that there is a new presence in the pulpit on Sunday mornings. And a new face for more personal contacts. Whether that is an improvement or not, I will leave for others to decide.

"I was told the shortened story of your arriving in town, of your identifying the potential of this piece of land and of the tragedy that fell on your life, and the life of that beautiful little girl.

"You probably already know that the Drummond family hold you in high regard. It was Mrs. Drummond who spoke to me about you.

"I hoped it wouldn't do any harm to meet you and put a face to your name, and perhaps put a new face to your thoughts of the Community Church."

"No harm done, Pastor, but now I have work to do."

Moody accepted the dismissal with good grace. He didn't offer to shake hands again, but he did offer his friendship.

"Thanks for taking this time with me. I've enjoyed meeting you. I'd like to come again if you don't object too strongly. I might even come and help you sack up some potatoes when the time comes."

"We'll see."

"OK. I hope the next time you bring produce to town you'll drop past the house and let my wife know. She'd like to get her hands on some. I was led to believe that you sell eggs as well. Is that true?"

"Vegetables and eggs. On a rare occasion, a pound or two of butter."

"Thank you, Abner. I'll keep you in my prayers."

By the time Moody was untying his horse, the child was back in the wooden enclosure and Abner was hoeing weeds.

CHAPTER TWENTY-TWO

Zac and Trig were working together in the big corral, attempting to iron some of the kinks out of a wild horse they had caught and brought to the Wayward. The animal was one of the four trapped after two difficult and frustrating weeks of riding and walking over rough terrain a few miles west of the Wayward. After a more careful look at the animals, two were turned loose again, judged to be unlikely to ever be of much value. But they had high hopes for the black stallion they were working with. The men had agreed that the animal was four to five years old.

Although the big black was nervous and shied away in fright every time Zac attempted to walk down the catch rope, he showed no real threat to the men.

One of the animals they turned loose had rolled his eyes back, alternating between charging the men with bared teeth, and rising on his hind legs, pawing the air as he attempted to strike Zac down. After a couple of attempts to calm the animal, Trig had climbed aboard a saddled horse. Zac shook the lariat off and opened the corral gate. When the rebel animal charged to freedom, Trig had ridden behind to drive him well away from the Wayward property.

If either of the two remaining animals showed sufficient promise, they would be branded and gelded. That was no simple task with an adult horse. The men had no intention of attempting it until they had put the horse through some workouts.

None of it was easy, but a good ranch horse was worth the effort.

Their work was interrupted by a hail from an approaching rider. Zac tied the wild horse off to a corral rail. He and Trig both made their way to the gate.

The visitor tore into the yard, still kicking his heals on an exhausted, froth covered animal's flanks. A rider Zac knew only by sight, not by name, was terribly wrought up about something.

The nameless boy often hung around the livery barn, having decided that he had enough school learning for that particular day. Why he didn't leave school altogether was a mystery. It was doubtful if his education was going to ever lead him away from the ranching life.

But as the kid had yet to learn, no rancher would tolerate the abuse of his riding stock. His current ride would have him seeking another job. And perhaps a life lesson from the rancher.

As the rider came closer, he yanked the horse's head up cruelly, pulling him to a sliding stop.

He spoke excitedly over the stamping and huffing of his exhausted horse.

"Hello, Mr. Trimbell. Got a message fer ya."

"Well, slow down and tell me what it is."

"Bad news, Mr. Trimbell, real bad news. Mr. Link Spangler. You know who I mean? The sheriff?"

The young man stopped and gasped for breath. Zac was becoming impatient.

"Yes, yes. What about Link?"

"Well, sir. The sheriff. He's dead, sir."

The shock to Zac and Trig could hardly have been more pronounced. The two men stared wordlessly at the messenger.

It was Trig who shook off the shock first.

"What can you tell us? What happened?"

"I don't know nothing more than what I just told you. Except that Abe, that's Mr. Abbot, him from the livery, he said I should ride as fast as ever I could. Ride to fetch you, Mr. Trimbell. Mr. Abbot said as how it would sure be good if y'all could come to town just as soon as ever you can."

"Thank you, son. You'd best get off and walk that animal some to cool him down. Water trough's over by the barn. And you slow-walk him back to the livery."

Zac looked at Trig. Neither man had anything to say. Silently they went to their already saddled horses and mounted. Zac rode over to the big, open door of the barn. As was his custom, he whistled through curved lips. Amado ran to the door in answer to the familiar whistle, still holding a manure fork. He had been cleaning stalls. When Zac explained the situation, the young man crossed himself, his eyes wide in surprise.

"Tell your mother we'll be gone for the day. We'll eat in town."

Amado silently nodded.

Zac spoke once more to the young messenger.

"You mind now. You walk that animal back to town. Don't raise him to more than a slow walk. And don't you ever again run an animal like that. I'm pretty sure that's not what Abe meant for you do."

"Yes sir. I understand, sir."

***

When the men from the Wayward neared Las Vegas they could see three or four knots of people deep in discussion on the boardwalks. Another cluster of men was gathered in front of the sheriff's office. Zac pointed his animal that way.

Abe pulled away from the gathering to welcome Zac and Trig, taking a hold of the bridle on Zac's horse.

"What happened, Abe?"

"Well, sir, it's the craziest thing. Link, he was just sett'n there in that chair, where he was apt to set, enjoying the shade, when these two riders came loping along, raising a good deal of dust and scaring folks and buggy teams along the way. Didn't seem to care one way or another what was happening around them. Knocked poor Phoebe down, spread her shopping all over the road. Never once stopped nor said 'sorry'.

"Strangers, they were. No longer young. Grizzled and dirty. Armed like they was going to war. Hard look'n, if'n ya take my meaning.

"Link, he leaned forward in his chair and called out to the men.

"Slow down there, men," he says.

"That's what he hollered. I seen and heard it all from over where I was tak'n a bit of a rest in my own tipped back chair.

"When Link hollered out, that there old man, say'n neither yes, no, nor howdy, he yanks his animal to a halt, reaches for his holstered Colt and lets fly with three, four shots. Hard to tell how many, they came so fast. One of them shots took Link in his off shoulder. But he still managed to pull his own weapon. Another shot took Link in the gut. Worse place a man can take lead.

"But by that time, Ol' Link, he got off a shot or two his own self. Took that first man right out of his saddle. Laid him on the ground. Deader'n any man was ever dead.

"The gun fire got everyone's attention. Doors flew open all along the street, with folks running every which way. Kyle Webster, he comes a runn'n outa'n his gun shop dragg'n that ten gauge Greener of his.

"That second old man, he was giv'n his horse the spurs, lean'n over the animal's neck, look'n to git somewhere's else and hop'n ta git there in a hurry, I guess. He didn't make it.

"Kyle, he lifted that ol' Greener to his shoulder and let 'er fly. One barrel and then t'other. Kilt 'em both. The man and the horse, too. Darndest thing you ever did see.

"Kyle, he lasted no more than jest a couple a minutes. Time I ran over there his eyes was glass'n over. He tried once to set up. Barely got his one shoulder off'n the ground, then flopped back down and was gone.

"Doc, he come a runn'n, but there was no help'n any of them, Kyle, nor either of them grizzled fellas. Like I said, craziest thing I ever did see."

***

Zac and Trig slowly walked their horses to a hitch rail and tied off. They had no real idea what to do. Finally, Zac led the pair over to the livery.

"Abe. Can you tell me where they took Link's body to?"

"Them other two, they was took away by ol' Tubbs, down to his undertak'n shop. Doc opined that Link shouldn't be mixed up with them two, so he had the boys carry him over to doc's office. Tubbs can deal with him there."

With a great sigh of sorrow and defeat, Zac spoke to Trig, without looking his way.

"I'll go over to the church, see if I can track down Moody. Come along if you're wishing to."

***

Fifteen minutes later, the two men were sitting around the kitchen table with Moody. Sarah was pouring coffee while Nancy cut generous slices of chocolate cake.

Moody faced Zac with a grim look on his face.

"I've been to Doc's as well as over to where Tubbs works. Before you rode in. Sad affair. Needless. Dumb. Three lives snuffed out over nothing much at all. I know Link was a friend of yours. I only met him a couple of times, but I liked him. Always seemed quiet and competent. I'm really sorry about the whole mess."

Trig turned his head towards Zac.

"I don't recall anyone ever saying. Was Link a married man?"

Zac was slow to answer, lost in his own thoughts. Finally, he raised his head enough to say, "Long ago. I never met the lady. That was all before my time. Died in childbirth, her, and the baby both, is what I'm told. Link would never talk about it, so that's second hand from Doc."

Trig had another question for Moody.

"Any identification on those two men?"

"I don't know. Tubbs will have to tell us when he's finished his work."

***

Sarah sat down beside her husband, with a cup of tea and just a tiny slice of cake.

Nancy brought a cup of coffee to the table, taking a seat beside Zac. She had no cake. Wrapping Zac's hand with a firm grip of her fingers she said, "I'm so sorry about your friend. I'm sure we'll never understand why these things happen or what those other two were thinking. Sometimes we just have to have faith and believe that God is in control, even when we can't see it."

Zac pulled his hand away. He stood, lifted his hat from the peg by the door, and left the house. Moody pushed his chair back, as if to follow. Trig and Nancy spoke almost on top of each other.

"Leave him be."

Moody slowly re-took his seat and buried his face in his hands. No one said a word for a while. Finally Trig also stood.

"Thank you all."

The cake was left uneaten on the table.

CHAPTER TWENTY-THREE

Life on the Wayward Ranch was quiet, its owner reflective and often unseen. The sheriff was buried the day after the shooting, along with the two oldsters who had started the ruckus.

At first, the consensus in Las Vegas was that the two shooters should simply be dumped in a hole and forgotten about. Pastor Moody swayed the feelings, in spite of his newness to the town.

"No. we'll not be doing that. We'll not be doubling their foolishness with foolishness of our own. They'll have as decent a burial as we can put together, given the circumstances."

With some reluctance the town fathers agreed to cover Tubbs' small cost for two wooden caskets. Only a few people stood around the coffins as Moody officiated at the burial. Beside Moody stood the Catholic Priest. Moody had made a special effort to speak to the man, saying, "We know nothing at all about those men. They could have been Protestant or Catholic or not much of anything at all. But it would be a respectful thing if you would join me in the burial."

Many a questioning eye was cast from the townspeople as the two men of God walked slowly behind Tubbs' old wagon hearse.

Later that afternoon, most of the town, men, women, and kids, alike, plus many from the surrounding area, gathered in the small cemetery as Link was laid to rest. Zac and Nancy stood together as Moody again spoke comforting words to a hurting community.

The priest, knowing that Link had been a sometimes attender of the Community Church, was present, but he stood back several feet.

Zac didn't really notice when Nancy twined her fingers through his own, holding his hand throughout the service. Trig stood off to the side, with only Consuela to accompany him.

When the service was completed, Zac silently mounted his horse and rode home. Back to the Wayward. Trig and Consuela lingered, visiting with Moody and the others.

Without saying a word to anyone but Alejandra, Zac threw a few supplies aboard his big Cavalry horse and rode out, picking up the dim trail that started behind the house. The trail led to the far hills, after dipping through a couple of dry washes, and circling around several cactus covered slopes.

Alejandra crossed herself as she watched this good man ride away.

Zac had nowhere special in mind as he rode. After losing another good friend, another name to add to a list that was already far too long, he just needed to be away. To be quiet. To think. Or maybe not to think. Maybe to hold his mind blank.

Perhaps he would pray, even though he usually felt that his prayers simply drifted away on the never-ending wind.

He had no desire to talk with anyone. Few would understand.

Perhaps another old soldier would understand.

Someone who had felt the ground shake as the cannons roared.

Someone who had held a buddy, as the man closed his eyes in death.

Someone who lived in daily terror, but who rode into battle after battle anyway.

Someone who had wrapped his head in his arms. Weeping. Praying. Pleading for it all to stop.

Perhaps someone like that would understand.

But in the end, it would just be a sharing of misery. And what good would come of that?

No, he needed to be alone for a day or two.

***

Moody was somewhat familiar with Zac's emotional letdowns. But, except for Trig, and at an earlier time, Lem and Phoebe, he had managed to keep the problem isolated from anyone else. He knew some wondered at his moods and his frequent quiet times. He was content to let them wonder.

There were few people that Zac trusted fully enough to share things with. Moody was one of them. The two men had talked long on the ride down from Pueblo.

One day he had said, "It's not at all like it was, Moody. The last time you and I talked, when you led me to the graves of my family, in that little church yard, I hardly knew up from down. Somedays I wanted to cry and then I wanted to scream. Many days I wanted to hunt down the killers that destroyed my family. But I had no descriptions, nowhere to even begin the hunt.

"The next day I would think, 'let it go', knowing the men would eventually come to their own bitter ends.

"Coming west was a spur of the moment decision, with no real planning put into it. So was hooking up with Lem and Phoebe. Lem is a tower of strength, and although she was a slave for most of her life, Phoebe somehow has extraordinary insights into people. I'm not sure I'd have held it together if it wasn't for those two.

"Now, my situation is largely improved. The ground doesn't fall from under my feet nearly as often as it did. I'm thankful for that.

"I still hear the cannon in the nights, but not often. I still dream of dead and dying soldiers, but again, not often. My biggest fear is seeing and hearing my wife and my little girl in that burning cabin, screaming my name, and begging for help. When that happens, I'm tempted to just let go. To let it all go. To go to sleep and never wake up.

"Then, I'll get off by myself for a while. A day or two, or sometimes even just a few hours, and life seems worthwhile again."

Moody was silent as the horses plodded along, giving his friend time to say more if he desired. When that didn't happen, Moody wondered if his timing was right or if he should wait. Finally, he decided to be bold.

"Do you remember my question as you were

riding away, Zac?"

Zac nodded but was still slow to answer.

"I remember. Every day I remember."

So much time went past that Moody thought the conversation was ended. But finally, Zac said, "Is it still well with my soul?

"That's a hard question, Moody. It's not simple to answer. I have no doubts about God being who He says He is. But after the sights and terror and human misery on the battlefield, and then what happened to my family, I admit to having some doubts about how we understand God.

"In battle, both sides were crying out to the same God. My parents, my wife and my little girl were all believers. Struck down by dreadful men. I don't understand any of that, Moody. I have to admit that I don't understand."

As Moody had no simple answers the men rode on in silence.

CHAPTER TWENTY-FOUR

Abe sent the same young man out to the Wayward again.

"You take the message to Zac that he's wanted in town. But there's no special rush. Don't you be riding that horse half to death again. You hear me?"

"I hear you."

As the day had worked itself into midafternoon before the message was received, Zac waited until the following morning to saddle up. Trig and Consuela rode along with him again. The two young people had been spending a lot of time together, although neither had spoken about their true feelings, if such feelings even existed.

Since most of the Mexican families had returned to their land, Consuela had no real company, and little to do. With her parents in their graves and one brother taking over whatever was left of the herd and the flock, she felt no particular responsibility to the family or the ranch. And she had no desire at all for that remote, lonely life again. She and Francisco, her quiet, studious brother, had stayed on the Wayward.

Francisco was seldom seen. He was a man of books and solitude. Even back on the home *rancho* he had shown no interest in the land or the animals.

Zac had given him free access to his own small library and, on a couple of occasions, brought a book or two from town, when one became available in one of the stores. They were always used, traded for some small bit of merchandise, and often badly abused. But the young man read every word, often twice over.

On the few times that Francisco rode to town, he was welcomed at the church, where Moody, like Zac before him, had given the young man access to the many books he hauled halfway across the country.

***

Zac arrived in town and pulled up at the livery, calling out to Abe. The liveryman hollered, "Back here."

Zac and Trig tied off and sauntered into the barn.

Consuela wanted time to search out a new dress at Reid's store, so the men were alone.

"What's happening, Abe?"

"The city fathers, that is, Pop Hennessey, the mayor of this here metropolis, wants to see you. I saw him just a short bit ago at his ranch supply store. I'm guessing maybe you could find him there."

With a quizzical look but no comment, Zac turned and headed across the street. Trig walked beside him.

The men had to wait for the mayor to deal with two customers before they could speak in some confidence.

"Good morning, Zac. Good of you to come in. The council wants me to talk with you about the loss of our sheriff and the hiring of another man."

He stopped talking just long enough to take a deep breath and gather his words. Surreptitiously he slid a badge from behind a stack of merchandise, into the middle of the counter, holding his hand over it.

"Well, the truth of it is, we'd like to offer you the job. It's between elections and we have the right to appoint someone until the next election. And we've all agreed that you're the man we need. So, there it is. All you have to do is pick up this shiny badge and the position's all yours."

The mayor's face alternated between a hopeful expression and one of doubt. Knowing Zac's independent nature, he had not been anywhere near as sure as a couple of the other town councilors that he would take the job.

Zac didn't even have to think it through.

"I suppose I'm grateful that you place that trust in me, Pop. But I'm thinking you already know my answer. Thank the other men for me but you'll have to look for someone else."

Zac turned to go but Pop Hennessey called him back.

"I tried to tell them what your answer would be, Zac, but they weren't really listening. They did, however, suggest that if you said no, we'd make the same offer to your friend here. Do you see yourself wearing this badge, Trig?"

Trig came close to laughing as his first response. Zac turned a steady eye on him and said, "You've been wondering what to do with yourself. This might be something to do until you figure that out."

Trig stumbled for words before saying, "Give me a couple of hours, sir. I'll be back, one way or the other."

With that he turned and left the store. Zac was only moments behind him. Wordlessly, Trig led the way to Reid's store. Zac waited outside as Trig went in. He was out in less than a minute with Consuela walking beside him.

"What is the rush, Trig? I was not finished my shopping yet."

"You can go back. Right now, we're going for coffee and a talk."

Consuela had never heard him being so abrupt. It was as if Trig didn't realize how out of character his response had been.

Settling into the small café they took their seats and ordered coffee. When the waitress brought the big enameled pot and three mugs, Trig said, "Got any pie?"

"Just a few pieces of apple left from last evening. Or you can wait until the fresh ones come out of the oven. Be, maybe a half hour."

"How be you bring us three of those ready pieces."

Consuela giggled a bit and laid her hand on top of Trig's.

"I have never eaten pie in the middle of the morning."

"Then, this will be good practice."

Realizing that Trig was not in a joking mood,

Consuela said no more, simply waiting for someone to tell her why they were there.

The pie was eaten in silence, with Trig and Consuela studying each other. Zac offered no advice. But internally, he was smiling as he watched Trig rummage his way through his conflicting thoughts.

Finally, Consuela pushed her empty pie plate away and looked at Trig.

"So now I have eaten pie in the middle of the morning. It is time for you to tell me why we are here and what is upsetting you."

Trig tried to choose his words carefully.

"I'm not upset. Not at all. Unless it's with myself. Zac turned down the Sheriff job, as any thinking person would have expected.

"Then it was offered to me. I have never once thought of myself as a law man.

"I need to do something with my time, and my life. I can't go on eating Zac's groceries and not producing something. I have some few coins left from before, but they won't last forever..."

As if the idea of money had awakened another part of Trig's mind he laughed lightly.

"I never once thought to ask about pay. I'm assuming that at least a few coins would be exchanged once in a while."

Zac nodded, happy to be having this discussion with Trig, and not about himself.

"I'm pretty sure you can plan on making a living wage. Just so long as you don't want to live too high."

There really wasn't much discussion, although there were enough silent moments to allow for it.

Trig fiddled with his pie fork, clanking it against the empty porcelain pie plate until Consuelo finally lifted the fork from his hand and carried it, and the plate, into the small kitchen. She smiled as she returned to her seat.

"Better you include Zac and me in your thoughts, or I am returning to the store. There is a nice dress there. If it fits it would save me from having to sew, which I am not very good at doing."

Zac picked up his hat and adjusted it on his head, as if he was fixing to leave.

Trig raised his eyes from the table and let out a great sigh.

"Give me some advice here, Zac."

"Nope. I've said all I plan to say."

Consuela glanced over at Zac with a question.

"And what is it that you said?"

"I just said that he was going to have to do something with himself and this might give him an income until he figures out his next move."

Trig picked up Consuela's hand and massaged it with his fingers.

"And what do you say?"

"I say it is something to do. Maybe you will do it for a little while and maybe for a long time, but it is at least something. And I will move to town and cook for you and keep a cabin clean and welcoming for you."

The two men were startled into silence at the statement, glancing first at each other, and then at the woman.

When Trig managed to breathe again, he turned enough to look directly into Consuela's eyes. Even after all the time together he still somehow shrunk up inside at the sight of her beauty.

Collecting his thoughts a bit, he asked, "What exactly are you saying? You can't live with me. We would have to be married to do that."

Consuela's smile was radiant.

"Well, of course, I already know that. But there is you and there is me. And I think you kind of like me, no? And your friend Moody is a man of God, is he not? He can do the marriages, yes? So? Where is the problem?"

Zac roared in laughter, causing both the cook and the waitress to sneak a look at their only customers. He re-fitted his hat and stood.

"I'll go see what's happening over to the livery. You don't need me here."

He laughed again as he was pulling the café door closed behind himself. He hadn't laughed like that since before the war. As strange as it was, it somehow felt good.

CHAPTER TWENTY-FIVE

Zac and Francisco were settled into the same shelter of brush and stream that Adamar had been doing his laundry in, a few weeks before. As it had been with Adamar, Zac was forced to hunt for the quiet, elusive brother. But finally, the two men were face to face.

Francisco, wondering why Zac had come, simply waited.

Zac squirmed a bit to find a more comfortable position before saying, "Francisco, I've been thinking that your people, your *La Gente*, need you. You're intelligent. You're well read. You're a thinker. And you will never make a rancher. I think this might be the time life has prepared you for."

Francisco still said nothing. Between these two often silent men, it almost became a contest to see who would speak. Finally, Zac continued with his thoughts.

"It is good that your family and the others have their herds and land back. But as I told Adamar when we were with him after the ranch was recovered, when all the chips were down, Marcus Patriquin was a small man. Him and his crew both. But there will soon come bigger, stronger men, with bigger herds and more riders to back them. The land is too plentiful. The grass is too rich. It cannot stay empty forever.

"There will come many more *gringos. La Gente* will not be able to stop them. There are not enough of you and you don't have the herds to justify the grass claimed. *La familia* will lose the land again unless someone can prove that the old land grants are valid. That will require a lawyer and a lot of work. And much time. I think you are the one to start that work."

Francisco studied Zac with a steady eye for perhaps a slow count of twenty. Clearly, he was considering this new thought.

"I don't know what you are thinking, or how I would do this thing. I know nothing about the grants except what I heard spoken in my family for all of my years. Many times, I heard the story of how the grandfather's grandfather was gifted much land. It was a gift of tribute for some brave thing done for Mexico, done long, long ago. The *Gobierno*, the government in Mexico City, they wished to thank the grandfather.

"Our family has lived on the land all these years. Sometimes many of us. Sometimes not so many."

Zac nodded in understanding, but one important piece was missing.

"Does your family have any old papers? Perhaps a map? Anything that would help a lawyer take the claim to a court?"

"I know of nothing like that. We just all know

where the boundaries are. We have always known."

***

Zac tossed a few pebbles into the small stream. He needed to phrase his thoughts carefully.

The Mexican peoples had been on the land for generations. Although mostly a welcoming people, they had never really learned to trust the *Gringo*, the foreigner. The few times they were confronted with *Gringo* laws and courts had not been happy times. And yet it was *Gringo* law that would make the decision on the land grants. That process hadn't really started yet, but it would soon have to, if the *La Gente* hoped to save even a bit of their lands. Without the grants being ruled as valid, Zac held out little hope for Francisco's people, but he would do what he could to help.

***

"Tomorrow, Francisco, we go to town for the wedding. You and I will go early. Amado and Alejandra will come later with your mother. You and I will visit Mr. Abraham Howells. He's a lawyer in town. I've only met him a couple of times, but he seems like a good man. He helped me get the proper title to this land when I bought it. We will ask him if he would work on the land grants and let you work with him. You might find that working with the law is the correct place for you to be. Perhaps, with some study, you could also become a lawyer.

"We would finish up our talking and be ready for the wedding and the small fandango after. Does that sound alright to you?"

The normally neutral faced Francisco showed his first smile.

"I think I would like that. I will be ready early in the morning. We will talk with this lawyer."

***

Abraham Howells looked up from his desk when the street door opened. At the sight of Zac and Francisco he pushed his chair back and stood, a big smile on his face.

"Why, Zac, it's good to see you again."

The two men shook hands before Zac nodded towards Francisco.

"Abraham, I'd like if you would shake with Francisco. This young man has been staying on the Wayward for a while. It's his families' land that was recovered up north last month. And it is his sister Consuela who is to be married to my friend Trig, later in the day.

"Francisco is a man of books. He has read everything on the Wayward and most of what is on the shelves in the church. He studied at the mission school. His English is good. And we have a proposition for you."

The lawyer gave the young Mexican a smile and a firm handshake.

"If Zac recommends you, Francisco, that's enough for me. I'm pleased to meet you. Come, both of you, take a seat and tell me your story."

***

After a full hour of first listening and then asking

questions, Abraham smiled and nodded.

"We are all aware of the difficulty with the land grants, of course, although the details are sketchy, to say the least. I have not heard of any challenges reaching our courts. Someone will have to start that process moving. Perhaps you are the one for that, Francisco.

"Mind you, we are not yet a state, so our court decisions might not be seen as final. And if the final decision is left up to Washington there is no telling how it could get twisted around. But I agree. It is time to step forward.

"Now, I hate to bring this up, but I'm afraid reality leaves me no choice. I have a wife and four children. A lawyer in this small town barely pays the bills many months. If I am to put considerable time into this effort, some funding will have to come from somewhere. Do you or the family have any money for this, Francisco?"

Before Francisco could answer, Zac reached into his shirt pocket and lifted out a folded piece of paper. He unfolded it and laid it on the lawyer's desk.

"This might cover the first part of the work."

Abraham reached forward and picked up the paper. He glanced at it, turned away and then took a longer look. He studied Zac as he tried to formulate a response. He looked again at Francisco and then back to Zac. He laid the paper back on the desktop, studying it some more. What he was looking at was a check for a considerable amount of money. The amount made the lawyer shake his head in wonder. Finally, he found some words.

"If this is for real, my friend, there is sufficient

funding here to cover income and expenses for both myself and Francisco for the next year. Perhaps longer."

"It's for real. Take it to the bank. They'll honor it."

"Someday, Zac, you and I have to have a long talk. I'm thinking you might have an interesting history and a story to tell. I have long been chronicling the happenings of the West in general and New Mexico in particular. I started back in university and continued during the war. I kept a daily diary, at least as best I could, between battles. Some future generations might be interested in our history.

"I have heard the rumors about you owning a gold mine up in Colorado, but I never put much stock in that. Looking at the check I'm thinking there may be something to it."

Zac made no response while Francisco's eyes darted between the two men.

Zac finally stood.

"Come on, Francisco, we have to go to a wedding. Then we'll find somewhere for you to live."

CHAPTER TWENTY-SIX

The wedding was like most frontier weddings; well attended and brief. In a small frontier town, there was little entertainment. The townsfolk were likely to grab any opportunity for a break in the daily routine of their lives.

The bride was radiant in a white dress and veil, with her arms loaded down with flowers gathered from the gardens of several church members. Briefly Trig wondered where the white dress came from, but when Pastor Moody began to talk, he did his best to take his eyes off the surroundings and focus on the ceremony. He was still in a bit of shock about how the entire matter had come to be.

Francisco stood a step or two behind the bride, taking the place of their father, ready to say, 'Her mother and brother and I do', when Moody asked who was giving the bride to be wed.

A cousin from a ranch a few miles south had been driven in to stand up with Consuela. Zac, dressed in the only suit he owned, along with a dress shirt, complete with a string tie, stood beside Trig.

***

When Moody was talking with the bride and groom before the ceremony the subject of churches and beliefs had to be addressed. Moody looked at the beautiful young lady and asked, "Consuela, what is your background or training in matters of belief? Although it is common for Mexican folks to be of the Catholic faith, I know that is not totally universal. Are you comfortable with being married in the Community Church?

"I was familiar with Trig's family from back in Texas, so I know something of his background. But I believe you two would do well to start out your married life with agreement on this important matter."

Consuela answered, "I would guess that back before my parents' time our family would have been Catholic. But we lived far from others. Only *La familia* were there. We never saw a priest. Before we moved here a while ago, I had only been to Las Vegas one time when I was very little. I don't really remember much about that trip.

"When my father decided that his children needed to learn to speak English, he took us to a mission school in Denver. The school was run by the Methodist Church. I came to love the people and their teaching. I am comfortable with having you say the words over us."

***

With all the preparations and questions behind them, the wedding moved forward with only a two day wait after the discussion in the café. The Community Church ladies took over and soon the matter was out of the bride and groom's hands. They only had to prepare themselves and be present at the appointed time.

***

Standing at the small altar, Trig held Consuela's hand and responded at the proper time.

Moody had to smilingly prod Trig twice to get the expected response from him. Consuela, on the other hand was a statue of decorum and self-control.

When the service ended with the new couple being announced as husband and wife, Trig was lost in wonder. He knew he should walk his bride out of the church but somehow his feet wouldn't move.

When someone suggested that he should kiss the bride, his face enflamed with embarrassment. Finally, he turned towards Consuela with a small smile. She lifted her veil and placed her hand at the base of his neck. Gently she pulled his head down until their lips could meet. To a rousing cheer from the onlookers, the deed was done.

***

Everyone moved outside where the church folks had set up tables. Although there were a few chairs, most people stood in small groups after they had found a cool drink and a snack. Visiting time was rare enough in this hard-working frontier town, and not to be wasted.

The weather was ideal. The snacks were consumed and then the full meal was laid out. Still, most guests continued to stand.

***

As the evening began to ascend, a small group of musicians formed a circle off to one side and tuned up their instruments. Within a few minutes, a squawk from a fiddle, joined quickly by a guitar and then by a Mexican cradling a *Guitarrón*, an exceptionally large guitar, signaled the start of the dancing.

Zac thought he had found a somewhat hidden spot along the edge of the crowd where he could be present without anyone really noticing him. He didn't make it. He hadn't taken more than a dozen steps when Nancy slipped her hand into his and said, "I'd love to dance."

CHAPTER TWENTY-SEVEN

Moody was comfortably settled into the pastor's role at the Community Church. The problem was that he didn't see the pastor's role as being comfortably settled. He was of the belief that too many pastors settled in comfortably, avoiding the trials and problems of the church folks and the town in general.

He made daily rounds of the town, meeting and visiting with businesspeople, ranchers in town for supplies, and anyone having time for a coffee or a brief visit. He spent many hours riding to local ranches, helping where he could, visiting when there was time.

He chuckled at the thought that he might become known as a fixture on the chairs in front of the general store.

Ever since the lunch with Tracy Handley, where they had met Emeline Bowles, Moody had thought often of Emeline's brother Toby. Emeline had labeled him as 'troublesome'.

The two of them had never met and that

intrigued Moody, as well. Clearly, the young man was not in the habit of attending church.

He would not like to have his plan labeled as a scheme, but he had to admit it fit the criteria.

On a bright warm summer morning, after his home and church duties were cared for, Moody made his way to the sheriff's office for a visit with Trig. As there were no pressing law matters that needed attending to, the two men sought the chairs. Several businesses in town, as well as the sheriff's office had chairs in front. The chairs were popular and well used, mostly by the men, although Nancy was occasionally seen visiting with another woman, in front of the millinery shop.

The sheriff's office fell into the shade under the roofed-over portion of the boardwalk. Trig and Moody, enjoying the shade and a break from other duties sprawled side by side, their booted feet extended halfway across the boardwalk. From where they were seated Moody had a clear view of the main business side of the street.

Trig and Moody visited about everything and nothing until the pastor spotted a young man headed towards Bowles men's wear store. Judging by the familiarity of his approach to the store, it could be only Toby Bowles.

Moody waited a diplomatic amount of time before excusing himself from Trig. It was time to press his plan. Some might call it a scheme, but Moody insisted, in the privacy of his own mind that is was really just a plan.

Walking as casually as he knew how, Moody made his way to the Bowles store. Pushing the door open, he stepped inside with a genuine smile.

He liked the Bowles family. Of course, it was his professional duty to like all of his parishioners, so it was imperative that he keep his personal preferences to himself. He had long practice at this.

"Good morning, Pastor."

The voice came from behind the big wooden counter at the back of the store.

"Good morning, Frank. Great day. Since Trig and I have solved all the law problems in our town, during the past half hour, it came to me that this would be a good day for fishing. I'd truly enjoy a few hours on the water. I thought I'd come and get some advice from you. I'm told there's a pretty good fishing stream not too far to the east of town. I haven't seen the stream. I've never been past Abner Sallow's place. I'm hoping to pick up some directions or advice from you. What can you tell me?"

"Well, Pastor, I can tell you a couple of things. The first would be that I'd love to be going with you. The second would be that I'm pretty sure that's not going to happen. The third might be that Toby loves to fish and he knows all the right spots. We've fished them together often enough."

With that he turned his head towards the canvas curtain separating the store from the small warehouse area in the rear.

"Toby. Get yourself out here if you want to go fishing."

Smiling at Moody, the father nodded in understanding.

The curtain parted and a boy of fifteen years, just growing into the first signs of a man's body, emerged. Moody liked him immediately. Toby held a steady look from a pleasantly tanned face, studying Moody and then his father. He left whatever questions he had, unasked.

"Toby, I don't know that you've met Pastor Tomlinson yet. The pastor has taken an urge to go fishing. He needs some advice and directions. I could probably manage on my own for the day if you cared to act as a fishing guide."

Moody stepped a bit closer to the counter and reached across for a handshake.

"Good morning, Toby. I am indeed the pastor, but my name is Moody. I'm pleased to meet you."

Toby silently completed the handshake.

"Your father indicates that you're a fisherman, Toby. I don't get out too often and haven't been to the water at all since arriving in Las Vegas. But I'm sure wanting to try my skills on this beautiful day. How would you like to take me under your wing for a few hours? Show me the ropes, kinda?

"My Sarah would put a lunch together for us and we could ride out and see how they're biting."

Toby, still holding his silence, looked at his father. That wise man chuckled a bit and said, "Of course, if you prefer to stay here and mind the store, you could do that, and I'll go fishing."

"No, I'll go. I just need to go home and get my tackle. I'll ride by the church."

Even with the unsmiling and suspicious Toby being careful with his words, Moody took the commitment as a good start. And perhaps the start of a valuable friendship.

CHAPTER TWENTY-EIGHT

Just one short week after the wedding Trig was settling into the sheriff's position. He had no real idea what the job was or what the city fathers expected of him. He decided that probably it would all become clear over time. He made his first task the sorting out of the many papers in the desk drawers, along with several boxes of assorted arrest records, wanted posters and miscellaneous junk left behind by Link, and, probably, by the last couple of sheriffs before Link.

After the burial, Tubbs had gathered the bits and pieces of plunder from the two shooters' pockets. He placed it into separate paper bags and folded the tops over, so nothing would get lost. He had stowed them on a shelf in the sheriff's office before the wedding. Trig hadn't noticed them for the first few days. Now, opening them and spreading the contents into two piles on his desk he started wondering about what might have been in the saddle bags. He left the office and stepped over to the livery.

"Abe! You here?"

The door to the inner office opened and Abe called, "In here. Just made some coffee. Come join me."

Trig had watched Abe making coffee before this.

"Thanks, but I haven't got the time. I'm wondering what became of those killers' saddles?"

"In the tack room, first on the right as you go in. Horse is in the corral if you want to check him out."

"Thanks, Abe. For now, I just want the saddle bags."

"Help yourself. Saved 'em for ya."

***

Back in the office Trig carefully sorted the mess out so that one pile didn't run into the other. Between the emptied-out paper sacks and the saddle bags, there was everything from scraps of paper to a pocketknife each, a couple of letters and some bits and pieces of camp food. A couple of sacks of ammunition to fit both their handguns and their carbines, about rounded out the pile. If either man had a change of clothing it must be rolled up in the bedroll. He would look at them later.

Trig figured the men must have planned on purchasing more supplies, which might have explained their reason for entering Las Vegas.

Of course, that didn't explain their belligerent actions on the front street. The actions that had cost them both their lives.

Along with the saddle bags and bedrolls, one rider had carried a large canvas panier that contained the camp cookware and a few other odds and ends.

Someone had hung the two sets of handguns on a peg in the office. Each belt carried a large camp knife, hung on the side of the belt opposite the holster. Trig figured it would have been Tubbs again who salvaged the hardware. One handgun had been picked off the dust of the street and replaced in the holster. Trig would get around to cleaning the weapons as soon as he could. Their carbines were still on the saddles.

Trig sorted everything out, coming to the conclusion that there was nothing there of any interest to the law but the letters. And it was doubtful if they would lead anywhere.

The letters did, however provide a name for each of the men. The one who started the shooting was Galen Victor. The man shot down by Kyle Webster called himself True Baxter. There was no guessing what their birth names were.

Trig used his arm to scrape everything but the ammunition and the two pocketknives into a box, after he emptied trash from the box into a burning barrel behind the small jail. He placed the box and its contents, along with the saddle bags into a small closet in the office. It might be needed later if there was ever an enquiry.

He took a wet rag and washed the desktop and then sat down to read the two letters.

***

For the first few days after accepting the sheriff's position Trig spent most of his time kicking himself for having made that decision. He chose not to put the badge on, but he did carry it in his pocket, out of sight. Finally, with a need to finish what he promised to do, he settled in, resigned to his current situation.

***

Consuela thought everything was wonderful; the job, the steady income Trig had finally thought to ask about, the little cabin they managed to rent, the excitement of shopping for their own foodstuffs, the purchase of new sheets and covers for the bed, even the work of cleaning out the cabin she found to be to her liking. And she had enjoyed the first few days of marriage as they stayed in the hotel while they were fixing up the cabin.

She was particularly pleased with her choice of husband. The small risks his sheriff's job entailed didn't really bother her at all. She had great faith in Trig and in the future ahead of them.

***

Trig sat staring at the letters and re-reading the two names, wondering how he could discover who these two were. Or should he even bother? He could simply leave the matter as a done and done mystery, buried and forgotten about. But somehow, that seemed to leave too many questions needing answers. Finally, he thought of the box-full of old wanted posters.

He leaped to his feet and pushed a couple of other boxes of junk out of the way so he could access the one he wanted. He lifted the box onto a chair and propped the folded top flaps back. Lifting out a handful of posters he sat down to read. Most of the writeups were old. Few had anything resembling an actual photograph. The pencil sketches were of little help.

Still, he carefully scanned each one, realizing the wanted men had almost certainly changed their names, often making multiple changes whenever it proved to be convenient. He would rely more on the descriptions. He read one poster after another, flipping the rejected ones into a second pile, upside down, so as not to become confused. After the first hour he walked across the street and bought a large cup of coffee, carrying it back to the office. The coffee pot and mugs that sat on a wooden shelf would need some attention before he would risk their use. In any case it was too hot out to tolerate a fire in the stove just to make coffee.

He was about halfway through the stack of posters when he found one that had two names, two sketches and two descriptions on it. He sat up straighter and started to read. The more he read the more convinced he became. The names were different, but the description matched perfectly, from the little Trig had been told.

He hadn't seen the men until after they were laid out in Tubbs' back room. By that time, Tubbs had cleaned them up and combed their hair, something the men seldom did for themselves, judging by appearances. He needed an opinion from someone who had witnessed the event and who could judge the men's actions and attitudes.

Taking the poster, he headed back to the livery.

"Abe", he called into the dimness. "Where you

at?"

"Out back. Come on through."

"Look what I found, Abe. Take a read and see if this rings a memory of those two shooters."

Abe was a slow reader, but he leaned his back against a corral railing, propped the hay fork he had been working with against the corral, turned so the sun would light the page, and started in. Trig shifted from one foot to the other as his patience was tested. He was tempted to offer to read the document aloud while Abe listened, but he finally chose to wait.

Abe dropped the poster to his side and looked up at the new sheriff.

"Son, I do believe your first test as sheriff is headed in the right direction. If these aren't the men I'd be surprised."

Without further discussion Trig thanked Abe and took the poster from him. Heading across the street, he made his way to Tubbs' shop. He found him building another coffin.

As he had done with Abe, he asked Tubbs to read the descriptions and give his opinion. It took the undertaker only a minute to read and then raise his eyes to Trig.

"That's them. Well done, Sheriff. Can't be anyone but them. The descriptions fit exactly, right down to the bullet wound on the upper leg of that bigger fella."

The two men smiled at each other as Tubbs passed the poster back.

***

The next stop was the telegraph station. Once inside,

Trig wondered why he hadn't asked about covering his job expenses. He decided he would pay for the telegram and then clear the question up with Pop Hennessey. This would be his first experience with telegraphs. With a grin he approached the operator.

"I'm afraid I'm going to need your help. I know just nothing at all about sending a wire. If I tell you what I want will you write it out for me and send it?"

"Of course, Sheriff Mason. Happy to. But you might wish to see what I do so's the next time you can do it yourself."

The title of sheriff caused Trig to back up and take a deep breath, at least in his mind.

"I ain't been the sheriff but for a few days. I'm not sure how you even knew about it. Still kind of takes me by surprise."

The operator laughed and reached for a paper form before saying, "You'll find that I see most folks through this office sooner or later. There's few things that don't end up in a wire of some sort. Eventually. Anyway, your name was all over town within hours of you taking the job."

The operator leaned over the counter with the paper turned a bit sideways so Trig could watch as he wrote.

"Tell me who this is addressed to and then tell me what you want to say."

"Send it to Judge McKiver, San Antonio. Texas. That's the name at the bottom of this poster. I'm guessing that's where the wire should go."

The operator wrote that down and then lifted his head, waiting. When Trig didn't respond, he smiled and said, "You're going to have to tell me what to write."

"Oh, sure. Well, I want to tell him that two men answering the description on a wanted poster were killed in this town. The men called themselves Galen Victor and True Baxter. They match the description on a poster for Julius Snider and Toby McMaster. Tell him that I'm wondering if he has further information."

When the operator finished writing he turned the page all the way around. Trig read it and looked up at the man.

"You'll see I put the word, 'stop' between subjects. That takes the place of a period in writing. It separates the thoughts.

"The company charges by the word so you always keep it shortened. Just the bare information usually allows the receiving party to figure it out. The other thing to remember is that everyone along the line will be able to read this. You need to be careful you don't give out any secrets."

Trig read the message again and figured it was fine the way it was.

"That looks good to me. How much do I owe you?"

***

By the time Trig was walking back to the office Consuela was approaching from the other direction. She had promised to stay away until lunch time. Trig glanced up at the sun and then down the sidewalk towards his new bride. They would go for lunch and then he would ask her if she'd like to clean up the coffee pot and mugs for him.

***

Trig found that waiting for the return telegram was demanding as much of his limited patience as anything he had ever done. He decided to visit Mayor Pop Hennessey to discuss the shooters' property, the horse and the two saddles. He would also find out about expenses while he was there.

CHAPTER TWENTY-NINE

Pastor Moody wasn't a desk riding man. He spent just enough time indoors to prepare for the Sunday service. Then he started looking further afield for what he called his 'real work'. He strolled the town, visiting with folks he met. He talked with everyone who could take the time to chat. He occasionally laid down a couple of ten cent pieces to pay the price of coffee while he listened to some visiting rancher's story.

Moody amazed Abe at the livery one day by showing up in work clothes and old boots to help clean the barn. The two men scraped and shoveled for a couple of hours and when they were finished the place looked sparkling, in livery stable terms at least.

After washing hands and faces with a bucket of water from the town well, and a bar of soap that threatened to loosen the skin on Moody's hands, the two men took seats along the shady side of the barn.

Abe disappeared into the small office that

doubled as his sleeping quarters. He reappeared a short while later with a cup of coffee for each of them. Abe leaned his chair back onto its hind legs, totally contented, ready to share a windy or two.

Moody took a sip of coffee and gasped. Shudders ran through him as he swallowed. He knew that if he gagged or spit out the dreadful, tar-like substance, Abe might be insulted. He somehow downed the entire cup, but he smilingly refused seconds.

Abe told his tall tales and Moody laughed at all the appropriate places. Moody told a bit about the war years in East Texas and more about their trip west, a happier subject. The afternoon ended with Moody walking home, where he built a fire in the big stove and heated water for a bath.

The following day he again put on work clothes. He saddled the gelding and rode out to visit with Abner Sallow on his small farm. Toby jumped at the chance to ride along with him. Their fishing venture had only produced one small fish which they threw back into the water. More importantly, it sparked the beginning of a man to man friendship.

Arriving at the farm, Moody rode down the fence line until he was adjacent to where Abner was working.

"Good morning, Abner. I've got a couple of hours to spare. Brought a friend along with me. I'm hoping you have another weed hoe I can get the use of."

Abner stopped working and leaned on the hoe. His questioning look soon turned into a welcoming smile. The days on the small farm grew long, with few folks ever coming his way. Moody had become a welcome visitor.

"Put your animals in the corral. Water and shade there."

With that he turned back to his work. Summer, his little girl was pulling weeds beside him, as he cautioned her on what was a weed and what was a saleable plant. The task was made easier with the lateness of the season. Most of the crop was well into its maturity and would be picked soon.

***

During the previous weeks, Moody had asked some questions of the church leadership. He went first to Tracy Handley who was clearly the main spokesman for the leadership board.

"Tracy, I need you to be completely honest with me on my promise that your words will go no further."

The two men were out for a private evening stroll. Moody had walked to the Handley home after dinner and called Tracy out for the walk.

"That sounds ominous, Moody. But ask away. I'll promise to tell you anything I know for sure. I'm pretty reluctant to repeat rumors."

"Fair enough. What I want to know is what seems to have driven Abner Sallow from our fellowship. He appears to be a friendly enough man. He's made me welcome a couple of times now but he's clearly uninterested in re-joining us at our worship services. He won't say anything specific and I haven't really pushed, but I'm sensing that perhaps things were said or done that deeply offended him."

Moody left the question unasked, but it was clear enough anyway.

The two men were silent for a full minute. In that time, they reached the schoolhouse. Taking a seat on a bench beside the small wooden structure, Tracy leaned forward with his elbows on his knees. He rubbed his forehead with his hands. A bit more time passed before the man spoke. He didn't look at Moody.

"It wasn't a time that brought any glory onto the saints. Nor did it bring any glory to the Lord. Foolishness and pride and stubbornness. All of that plus a serious lack of sensitivity to the man's feelings. And all done by a couple of otherwise good ladies. Ladies who really meant well but who refused to see the harm they were doing. That we all, including the leadership team, and the pastor at that time, stood back and allowed it to happen is a matter of considerable shame to me.

"Two or three of us tried later to mend fences but to no avail.

"You know that he lost his wife. Bertha was a lovely lady. A good wife, a good mother, and a good neighbor. As Abner tells the story, when she took sick neither she nor Abner thought much about it. Folks come down with colds and sniffles all the time. The baby was only a couple of months old. Bertha was still able to care for her but each day she became a bit weaker.

"Abner had the farm to look after. He was spending long hours on the land. Then he had the responsibility of caring for Bertha and making the meals. It was only a few days. Not long at all. But one evening Abner came into the house and found Bertha unconscious. He thought she was just sleeping so he cleaned up and looked after the baby, before starting to put a meal together. When Bertha didn't seem to want to wake up on her own, he tried to waken her. The baby needed feeding and Bertha had to eat herself.

"She wouldn't wake up. That's when Abner knew he needed help. They're only a few miles from town, but how could he ride for the doctor and leave Bertha unconscious and the baby crying in her crib? He fretted in indecision for a while and then decided to water down some cow's milk for the baby. The child didn't like it, but he forced a bit down her throat. She settled down and finally went to sleep.

"Abner climbed onto one of his team horses bareback and whipped the poor beast all the way into town and to the doctor's office. Nearly killed the animal. By the time the doctor got out to the farm Bertha was gone. It was all very tragic. Abner blamed himself for not getting the doctor sooner, but Doc told him it wouldn't have helped anyway. Pneumonia kills a lot of people and, really, Bertha was as good as gone as soon as she got sick.

"We lack a lot of things on this frontier. Good medical assistance is one of them."

***

With that information secreted in his mind, Moody picked up a hoe and joined Abner in the garden. They talked of this and that as they worked but they both avoided the topic that most interested Moody. Toby pulled weeds by hand, and cared for the child, as the men hoed.

It wasn't so much that Moody wanted Abner

back in the fellowship, although he wanted that too. The larger interest was to see the young farmer find peace in his unchangeable situation, and purpose in his future. Still Moody waited his time, knowing that all things eventually come to a head.

***

In a canvas sack tied to the saddle horn Moody had brought enough lunch for the two men as well as Toby and Summer, with enough extra to last the bachelor two or three days. When Sarah was putting the food together, she added a small bag of cookies and a few peppermint candies and one orange. She printed Summer's name on the outside of the paper sack and sent it along. Moody placed the lunch on the shelf inside the well cribbing to keep it cool.

Toby and the two men washed up and took seats under the small ramada the workers had included in the building of the adobe. Moody laid the canvas sack on the outdoor table Abner had built and lunch was spread out. Moody said grace and the three adults ate in silence.

At the end of the lunch hour, Abner passed the paper sack to Summer. She smiled widely, opened the top and looked in wonder.

"Daddy, look. Can I keep it, Daddy?"

Abner laughed.

"Yes, look at the name on the paper. You and I have been practicing letters. Can you read your name? Well, perhaps not. But you will soon."

Running his finger along the printing on the paper he slowly spelled out S-u-m-m-e-r.

"I guess it must be yours. That's your name."

A bit later in the afternoon Moody lifted his head from the hoeing.

"I've got to leave you my friend. Judging by the sun, I'm in danger of being late for another appointment."

"I can't thank you enough, Pastor. You've been a big help. And thank you too, Toby. I believe you've made a friend of Summer. And myself too, of course. Come anytime. And not just to work."

***

In late morning, two days later Abner heard wagon wheels on the dirt trail. Glancing up from his work, he was startled to see several men on horseback and two buckboard wagons. The grinning faces of several kids poked over the sides of the wagons.

The visitors tied off their horses and went to help the women down from the wagons. Nancy was horseback, preferring a saddle to a wagon seat.

Riding beside Nancy were Moody and Sarah. Everyone was in work clothing.

Abner stood in the gardens, staring out at the commotion. Summer started to run towards where the kids were gathering but Abner called her back.

Most of the visitors were from the Community Church but a few non-attending townsfolk had joined in. Among the group were Trig and Consuela. Toby rode with them, having identified Trig as a friend and a man to look up to. That gave him two adults, Trig and Moody, to admire, besides his father.

Without waiting for an invitation, the men

started lugging old sawhorses and miscellaneous lengths of lumber into the house yard. The women followed with baskets and boxes of food. Someone spread a cloth over the rough boards and almost as quickly as a person could tell about it, lunch was spread out.

Sarah Tomlinson made her way towards the garden. When she was within hearing distance she said, "Good morning, Mr. Sallow. Come join us for lunch. We've come to help you get those potatoes out of the ground."

Again, the little girl was running, this time towards Sarah. She saw so few visitors that she couldn't hold back her excitement. Abner didn't call her back this time.

Sarah spoke to Abner again. He was now close enough that she didn't have to raise her voice.

"May I take your lovely daughter's hand?"

Summer glanced back once at her father before smilingly lifting her hand to Sarah. Together they walked to the house with Abner just a few paces behind.

Abner found himself without words, and no one else made an issue of the visit.

Arriving just a bit late was Honey Drummond. She swung off her horse as Abner took the reins. Abner, as always was struck by her kindness and her poise. She was more pleasant looking than beautiful. Her smile had captivated Abner from the very first, originally as a fourteen-year-old child needing adult protection but lately as an adult herself, one that brought out altogether different feelings from the young widower.

Over the years, as she had been doing the vegetable shopping for the GG Ranch, she had grown tall, slim, and strong. Her self-confidence had also grown. And, perhaps best of all, she had proven to be a great female influence on the young Summer. The child had almost come to treat Honey as her mother.

It took all of Abner's willpower to hide his growing feelings.

At the sight of Honey, Summer lifted her hand from Sarah's and ran to this young lady she had known all her life. Honey swept her into her arms and twirled her around. Laughing and giggling, they joined the group for lunch.

By late afternoon, the potatoes were sacked and in the root cellar. The shovels and digging forks were back in the wagons and the workers had all washed the evidence of their toils from hands and faces.

The ladies had uncovered and dished out several pies and a selection of cookies. Fresh coffee was boiled and ready.

The children had included Summer in their games. The little girl had played and laughed and smiled through the entire afternoon.

As they gathered for the pie and coffee, Moody said, "Well, Abner my friend, we're about done up here. But that pie looks good enough to say grace over."

Accompanied by a few chuckles, the pastor proceeded to ask the Lord's blessing on Abner, Summer, the farm, and the food.

A few people were shuffling towards the table when a woman's voice called out, stopping everyone where they stood.

"If you don't mind, I have something that needs to be said. And it needs to be said where you can all hear."

Miriam Grand stood there looking at Abner. Penelope Hopper was a few feet to her right. The wait of only a few seconds seemed like hours, as people feared what was coming. Finally, Miriam spoke.

"Abner, I owe you a sincere apology, and I need to ask for your forgiveness. And lest you think that anyone has put me up to this, may I assure you that is not the case. No one has mentioned my dreadful tirades against you, back when you lost your dear Bertha.

"I had managed to convince myself that a man alone could not raise a child, and certainly not a baby. But what a beautiful little girl your daughter is.

"I was wrong and totally out of order Abner. Again, I ask your forgiveness. You have raised a lovely little girl. And now, when it is far too late, I realize I should have been here offering to help instead of trying to take your baby away from you. I was wrong and I'm embarrassed and I'm more sorry than I can tell."

Before Abner or anyone else could say anything, Penelope Hopper stepped away from her husband.

"Abner, I had no idea that Miriam was going to say anything. I almost didn't come today. I feared that you might be terribly angry at me still. You have every right to be. Miriam didn't act alone back when the baby was so young, and you were recently widowed. Everything Miriam has said applies to me as well. I too, seek your forgiveness."

Abner stood there speechless. His lips worked and he fidgeted with his hands. He looked at the ground and then at the sky. Finally, he simply nodded and walked away, with a simple, "Thank you all for your help."

CHAPTER THIRTY

Pop Hennessey shouldered the sheriff's office door open and stepped in. In one hand he held a small sack of ground coffee and a couple of cans of evaporated milk, along with a cloth bag of sugar. In the other he held an envelope.

"Morning, Sheriff. Figured the town should supply you with a bit of coffee and some fix'ns. Once anyway. Just to get you going on the job. After this you can make your own purchases. Can't have our sheriff falling asleep on the job for the need of coffee."

That Trig had been sheriff for a couple of weeks already didn't seem to have any impact on the mayor's thinking.

Pop lifted his eyes to the three iron barred cells he could see through the open doorway behind Trig. There were two battered and bruised men sleeping on the bunks in one cell.

With a grin he said, "Heard you brought in your first two prisoners last evening. Heard they was in a tackling mood. First they tackled the rotgut Ol'

Buck sells over to the Dusty Trail Saloon. Then when the rotgut got sufficient control of their common sense, they wandered out into the setting sun and right away tackled the wrong two women. That's the story making the rounds anyway. Heard then that when you called them off, they made their next mistake. Figuring there was twice as many of them as there was of sheriffs, they tackled you.

"I must say, they look pretty pitiful lay'n there on them hard bunks. Got a few bruises and such they may not remember how they got. How's my story? That about what happened?"

Trig really didn't want to talk about it, so his hesitation took up the next thirty seconds as he fiddled with something on his desk, with his sore and battered and skinned-up hands. Finally, remembering that he had been sheriff for only a short while and that he was talking to the mayor, he figured there was no escaping.

"Seems they figured two of the prettiest ladies in town might enjoy their company. When that didn't turn out just exactly right, they started to down-talk them. Tried to manhandle them. I came along right at that time and didn't care for what I saw. Didn't care for it by a long shot.

"I told them to lay off. Told them they were under arrest. They turned their energies on me, the both of them. One managed to fling a fist my way but he missed by a country mile, com'n close to fall'n down in the process. They left me with no choice. With them lobbing their arms in all directions, foul language com'n from their mouths and the ladies standing right there, I set in to get them under control. I guess I done that alright, but I'm hoping neither one has any permanent damage. Won't really know until they get up and wash the blood off their faces. They've been sleeping pretty much ever since I dragged them in here."

Pop laughed with glee and said, "Way I heard it you set right in. Smote them hip and thigh, is what's being said around town. Didn't let up until they were both lay'n on the boardwalk, bleeding and groaning. Then you commenced to drag them, one at a time across the street to the jail. I do believe, boy, you could run for sheriff for the rest of your life if you keep that up."

Without waiting for another comment, the mayor offered the envelop to Trig.

"Picked this up along with one of my own, over to the telegraph office. Thought I might just as well bring it along."

Before Trig could look at what was in the envelope, the office door was pushed open again. A determined looking Nancy led the way, holding the door for Consuela, who was loaded down with a savory smelling picnic basket over one folded arm and a steaming coffee pot in the other hand. She quickly stepped to the desk and set the articles down.

Trig and the mayor looked on with questioning expressions. Trig had never once thought about his wife cooking up their personal supplies and feeding the prisoners.

Consuela glanced at the cells but said nothing. Nancy had walked right into the back room. Consuela finally followed her. The girls stood there looking at the two pathetic men sprawled on the bunks.

Nancy glanced back once to see if Trig was going to interfere. When that didn't happen, she pulled the small revolver from the pocket of her split skirt, reversed her hold, grabbing it on the barrel, and proceeded to hammer the steel bars with the butt. The two men jarred into consciousness, one falling off the bunk, landing on the filthy floor. The second man rose to his feet in one confused, uncontrolled motion.

Trig leaped to his feet but was too slow to stop what came next.

Giving the prisoners no time to orient themselves or ask any questions, Nancy again reversed the gun and fired a single shot against the adobe wall on the far side of the little space. The standing man dove to the floor, joining his drinking buddy. Both men covered their heads with their wrapped arms.

Consuela also produced a small revolver. Casually pointing it at the floor between the two men she pulled the trigger twice.

The lead from Nancy's shot had scattered adobe dust through the small cell, while Consuela's shots ricocheted off the terra cotta floor tiles with terrifying 'whangs' before imbedding themselves in the back wall, again scattering dust and small bits of adobe throughout the room.

Trig was about to reach for the women's guns, but there was no need. Nancy dropped hers down along her leg, turned and walked back into the office. Consuela held her weapon at the ready as if the men might jump to their feet and somehow arm themselves.

Trig clearly had no idea what to do. But he relaxed when his wife dropped the pistol into the skirt pocket, under her red and white checked apron.

When the echo of the shots dropped away the two men rose to their knees and then their feet. They were battered and bloody and dazed looking. Clearly, the effect of the bad liquor was a long way from being worked out of their systems.

Consuela looked at the two men with disgust and pity. Disgust with what they had attempted the evening before, but with pity at what the two young men had allowed themselves to become.

Trig finally found his voice, although the entire action hadn't taken more than a few seconds.

"No more. No more, either of you women. Put those guns away and keep them put away. We're not going to go to shooting every drunk in town. Now, stop it!"

The mayor was watching the whole episode with good humor and admiration for the feisty women, when the outside door burst open again, showing Abe standing there with a double barrel Greener at the ready. Pop burst into wholehearted laughter, waving Abe off at the same time.

"It's alright, Abe. Everything's alright. Might just as well wave off those folks behind you. It's all over. No harm done."

Trig got his wits about him enough to ask the women what they were trying to do. Consuela was the one to answer. She stepped towards the cells again before speaking.

"I brought the breakfast for these men. Maybe good to eat before I shoot them again. Is that not so?"

In her excitement Consuela was reverting just a

bit to her Mexican accent and way of speaking.

Nancy joined Consuela and the two women faced the prisoners again. Nancy took over the speaking.

"Boys, you're fortunate the sheriff came along last evening. You need to understand a couple of things though. Consuela here is the sheriff's wife. I'll leave you to guess what all that means.

"Neither of us welcomes the likes of you two anywhere near us. And we are both armed at all times. If the sheriff hadn't come along, you would both be dead.

"It's been a few weeks since I shot a man. Who knows, I might miss, being out of practice and all. But you shouldn't count on that. Now, thank Consuela for the breakfast. And don't even think of coming anywhere near either of us ever again. Is that understood?"

Neither man said anything. But they were clearly frightened half to death. One of them aimed a pleading glance towards Trig.

The women turned and left the building. As they were passing the desk Consuela said, "Their breakfast will get cold."

Again, Pop Hennessey burst into laughter. Abe joined him with a grin and a chuckle, but Trig looked like he didn't know what to do.

The mayor watched the women disappear down the boardwalk and then turned to Trig, with a grin splitting his face.

"Sheriff. As a long-confirmed bachelor, I'm not one to give married folks advice. But if I was you, I'd maybe ride slow and sit loose in the saddle. For your own health and wellbeing, is what I mean."

Trig finally looked at the two prisoners and asked, "Do you want some food?"

One prisoner leaned a bit so he could see past the inner door, studying as much of the office as he could. In a quavering voice, forced through a scratchy throat he asked, "Are they gone?"

Trig answered the question.

"They're gone, but you do anything stupid and I'll shoot you myself. Now, do you want to eat?"

"I want to eat, Sheriff, but I'm thinking I need to know what's to become of us first."

Trig, still totally green at the job, turned to the mayor. The question was asked with his eyes only.

The mayor gave Trig a choice.

"Keep them until we find a judge and they can be sent to prison. Or, because they didn't actually get to do what they had in mind, you could fine them for being stupid. Fine them for whatever they have in their pockets and let them go, with a warning to go back to the ranch and stay there."

Trig hadn't stripped more than the men's weapons from them when he put them in the cell. He didn't examine their pockets. Turning away from the mayor and back to the cell he questioned, "You got any money left that you didn't waste on rotgut?"

Both men dove into their pockets, pulling out the few coins they hadn't already spent.

"Got a bit left."

Trig again glanced at the mayor but when he got no advice, silent or spoken, he turned back to the men.

"You count out ten dollars for me. You owe me a new shirt. The rest will be for the town coffers."

Trig hated to touch the filthy coins the man passed over, but he finally added it up to the ten he had asked for.

"Alright you can go, provided you leave town right now. Go back to the ranch and stay there until you know how civilized folks act."

"I'd take that breakfast the lady offered if you'd let me go out back first so's I can take care of business and wash up some."

Within a half hour, Trig was alone in the small office wondering what he had gotten himself into.

CHAPTER THIRTY-ONE

When everything had calmed down, after Trig escorted the men to the livery and saw them ride out of town, he poured water into the basin on the sheriff's office washstand. He rolled up his sleeves and scrubbed the results of the morning's activities from his battered skin. His knuckles were the worst. He tolerated the pain as he gave them a thorough wash. With that done he sat down at his desk and opened the telegram envelope.

"Julius Snider stop Toby McMaster stop proper names stop one thousand reward each stop part of war raiders gang stop partners Hec Blanco aka Red stop Luthor Aitken aka Boss stop last known El Paso stop rewards stop raided Carob Texas counties stop"

McIver

***

Trig read and reread the short message. There was a wealth of information contained in the few words. There was also more than one challenge or potential challenge. And there was a world of trouble if he didn't handle this correctly. He tried to think of what his friend Zac would do if he heard of this.

He had no idea how to claim the rewards for the two men taken down in Las Vegas, or where the money would go when, or if, it was ever received. He guessed it would go to the town. He would ask the mayor the next time he saw him, but for this one morning he had seen all he wanted to see of the mayor, and just about anyone else.

Holding the lengthy telegram in his hands he wondered. Carob, Texas. Is it possible? His mind went immediately to Zac. Zac and the black couple his friend had talked so much about, Lem and Phoebe. Their lives were all turned upside down by raiders. Their lives, and a lot of others as well. Was it possible? What should he do? And what would Zac do with the information?

Trig didn't know all the details of Zac's struggle for peace in his mind. He had seen enough on their times together to know that Zac sometimes struggled mightily. But he didn't even come close to understanding it. Would this information be a help to Zac, or would it be the opposite?

He sat staring out the open door without really seeing anything, trying to figure out what to do. His mind went back over the ride to the gold country after the stolen cattle. He expanded his thoughts to include the ride down south, where they finally brought an end, of sorts to the rustler gang.

He sorted through his memories of Zac's periods of silence. Hour upon hour the big man was sometimes withdrawn and uncommunicative. Then there were his disappearances, the latest being on their ride home from Pueblo while escorting Moody...

Moody! He needed to talk to the pastor. Of course. Why did it take so long to think of that?

Easing the telegram back into the envelope he folded it once and stuffed it into his shirt pocket. And that reminded him that he had to buy a new shirt. The one torn in the fight had been put into the stove early that morning. Consuela had carefully picked it up with two fingers, held it as far from her as her arms allowed, lifted the lid on the stove and dropped it in. Then she carefully washed her hands. Trig had watched the entire episode without comment.

He closed the office door and started to walk towards the church. On his way he stopped by the livery. Abe was at his normal stand, on a tipped back chair in the shade of the livery wall.

"Abe. I need to thank you for running to my rescue this morning. There was no real danger unless it was from ricocheting bullets. You couldn't know that of course. I'm almighty glad neither you nor I had to use our weapons. But I thank you for being there."

Abe received the thanks stoically, simply nodding.

"Another thing I've meant to ask you about since I believe you know just about everyone in town. Do you know anyone I can hire to clean out the office, especially the cells? They're pretty bad. Mattresses need cleaning. Floor. Well, pretty much everything."

Abe was quick with an answer.

"Mrs. Perez does some cleanup work around town. She'd be happy to make a few extra dollars. I'll send the kid to fetch her."

"Thanks, Abe."

***

At Trig's knock on the back door of the church Moody hollered, "It's open."

Trig stepped into the small office and found the pastor sitting behind a cluttered desk, pencil in hand and a written-on sheet of paper before him. His study Bible was propped open on his left.

"Hey, Sheriff. I heard there was some excitement this morning." Moody couldn't hide his grin.

Moody's response was, "The less said the better, I'm thinking. Anyway, no harm done in the end.

"How is the new job suiting you so far, Trig? Do you think it's something you might come to enjoy?"

Trig pulled a wooden chair over to the desk and sat down. As he was pulling the envelope from his pocket he replied, "Enjoy might not be just exactly the right word. Everyone knows I have no idea what I'm doing. I guess there's not really much to it until something goes wrong. And then it probably goes so wrong, or so fast, like with Link, that there's not much time to think anyway. We'll give it a bit of time. See what happens."

He placed the envelope in front of Moody with a nod of his head.

"Appreciate if you'd take a read of that."

Moody leaned back in his chair and read the wire, glanced up at Trig and then read the wire again. Laying it onto his desk among all the clutter, he bent over it and rested his forehead on his hand, reading the wire one more time, more slowly this time.

His reading was slow enough that Trig imagined the educated man reading each individual word while attempting to tie the words and his memory of his time in Carob, and his current thoughts, all together.

Moody had ministered in Carob all through the war and for a few years after. Although he had not seen the raiders, nor been directly impacted by them, he was very much involved with the aftermath. While Zac was still away at war, he had buried Zac's family in the church yard cemetery and led the service as they were committed to the Lord. There were others, too, that he had done the same for. One of his reasons for coming west was to attempt to put the bitter memories of war and its aftermath behind him and his wife.

Tens of thousands of others had come west for the same reason. Now, here it was, all the bitter memories, in the form of a simple telegram, pulling it all back into the present like an unwelcome plague. A troubled sigh escaped his lips, but he didn't yet lift his head.

"I had great hopes that this wouldn't happen. I wanted the matter to die, just like the gang's victims are dead. Bringing something back to life, well, I just don't see what good it can do. If it leads to a vengeance trail, I really don't see any benefit to anyone."

His every thought turned to Zac. Without mentioning his name, he continued.

"Some days I get the feeling that he's healing, getting over the past. He's a strong man. Maybe the strongest man I've ever known, both physically and mentally. But somehow the war took something out of him. Hurt him deeply. Of course, it hurt many men just as deeply. And then his family…

"I just don't know what this will do to him."

Trig waited a cautious few moments before saying, "You're speaking of Zac, of course."

"Yes, Zac. My old friend Isaac. My, how I wish he was still the old Isaac. You never knew a kinder, harder working man, more in love with family and life, than Isaac."

Trig didn't know exactly how to respond but since he, too, was from East Texas, he had some slight knowledge of the Trimbell family, mostly from his father's telling.

"Some days I see signs of the old Zac. Or Isaac, as you knew him. At home on the Wayward, he seems contented and at peace. Many days it would be difficult to believe that he was troubled about anything at all."

Moody finally raised his head, looking with sadness at Trig.

"Yes, I know. But then something happens. Something he feels he has to offer his help on. Seems he can't bring himself to turn away from anyone's need. Some examples I've seen. Others I've only heard about. More stress. Another relapse into memory. Another healing. I pray every day that it will end well for him."

There was silence in the small room as each man thought his own thoughts. Finally, the pastor brought the obvious truth out into the open.

"You have to show him this. For two reasons. First, it would be unkind to keep it away from him. There is every likelihood that the two men buried up on the hill, and these men, these two in El Paso, if they are still alive, that is, are the murderers of his family. Second, and more practically, there are no secrets in a town such as this. Once the telegraph agent saw the wire, it was destined to become public information. So, my advice? Get someone to sit in the sheriff's office, and ride out to the Wayward."

Moody refolded the telegram and put it back into the envelope. Passing it back to Trig he said, "You have no choice."

***

With troubling thoughts, Trig walked back to his office. He arrived just as a lady, burdened down with a mop and a bucket full of rags, was stepping onto the boardwalk in front of the sheriff's office.

"Good morning. I'm assuming you're Mrs. Perez."

At her nod, he smiled and welcomed her. He opened the door and the two of them entered.

"It hasn't seen a broom or mop for some time. The cells smell like something bad was buried back there and dug back up again. I wouldn't really blame you if you turned around and went back home."

Mrs. Perez set her bucket down. Stepping to the cells she took a careful look around and then walked back to Trig.

"Better there are no prisoners. I will clean it good for you. I will put the mattresses outside where you can burn them.

"I will need five dollars. Will you pay me, or do I have to fight again with the mayor?"

It crossed Trig's mind to enquire what had happened between Mrs. Perez and the mayor, but he let it go. Sliding the coins taken from the prisoners earlier in the morning across the desk, he said, "Here's ten in coins. They're as filthy as the cell floor. You might want to drop them into a jug of water for a while before you handle them, but they're yours. And thank you.

"I'm going to be away for a couple of hours. If anyone comes in, or any bad guys ride into town, you tell them to just wait. I'll deal with them later."

Mrs. Perez returned a big smile.

"I'll tell them. I hope perhaps your wife does not do any more shooting today."

Her grin couldn't get any broader.

Trig hunched his shoulders and left without a response. But he had the feeling that some incidents in life were going to be difficult to live down.

CHAPTER THIRTY-TWO

It was only a slow hour's ride to the Wayward Ranch. Trig had done it in less time but for this trip there was no hurry. Not being anxious to share the telegram with his friend, Trig half hoped he would find that Zac had ridden off somewhere and wasn't available. But that was not to be.

Entering the Wayward yard, he saw Zac in the corral, putting some finishing touches on the stallion the two of them had been working with when the kid arrived with the news about Link.

"Morn'n, Boss. let's you and me go have us a sit down."

Without waiting for a reply, Trig rode to the house, dismounted and tied off. He was always appreciative of the location of Zac's hitch rails. They were placed on the shady side wherever possible.

Trig strolled to the ramada, pulled the white, wicker chair up to the small table and sat down. Zac finished what he had been doing with the horse before he turned it loose and walked to the house.

"What's up, Sheriff?"

"I'm not totally comfortable with that title yet, Boss, but for this errand I guess it fits."

With no further words he slipped the envelope from his pocket, slid the wire out and placed it before Zac.

"Take a read of that, my friend."

Zac, like Moody, earlier in the morning, read the document and then read it again. Squirming a bit to find a more comfortable position, he read it yet again, even more slowly this time."

Trig figured he had better supply some background.

"I went through the old wanted posters stashed in the office. Came up with one that matched those two hard cases that shot up Sheriff Link. Sent a wire off to enquire about them. This is the answering wire. Just came in this morning."

Zac laid the document on the table and looked at it in silence for an uncomfortably long time. He then got up and without a word walked around the corner of the house and was gone from sight.

Trig sat in wait for all of fifteen minutes. When Zac didn't reappear, he finally said to himself, 'well, he knows where to find me'.

He tightened the cinch, mounted, and rode back to town.

***

Trig had rearranged the thoroughly scrubbed office so that he could see out the window from his office chair.

It was a full two days after his trip to the Wayward that he watched Zac ride up and dismount in front.

Trig went out to meet him.

"Judging by the load on that horse and the fact you're towing another, I'm guessing you're going somewhere."

Zac brushed some dust off his pants and studied the new sheriff before he spoke.

"Wasn't going to. Thought it all through. Finally figured I had to. I don't really need to do it for myself. At least I don't think I do. And yet..."

"Why then?" asked Trig, after the silence had dragged on for five seconds.

Zac spoke very slowly, as if he was carefully weighing each word.

"Someone murdered my wife and little girl. My folks. Burned our homes. Burned up my family along with the buildings. Weren't happy to just steal our horses and cattle. They had to steal our futures. Take away our happiness. Kill our chances for love.

"Stood at an altar one time. Stood there beside my Maddy. Vowed before God to care for her. Included our little Minnie in that vow when she arrived on the scene. Vowed the same for my folks as they aged.

"I wasn't able to keep that vow. My country got first dibs on my service and loyalty. I never saw that coming, wasn't prepared for it...

"Then when the country was finished with me, I had no way at all to know who did the killing and burning. And I had no way at all to track them or find them. Although it broke my heart to do it, I let it go. At least as much as I found the strength for. That's when Lem and Phoebe and I pointed the wagon to the west. Although Lem and Phoebe's lives were spared, they lost everything else.

"I believe I would have given up and simply died off if it hadn't been for those good people.

"Terrible lot of hurt and harm done by such as those raiders.

"I can't change the war. I did my duty and then some. The men whose screams I still hear in the night are no longer my responsibility. They never were really my responsibility. I was never an officer or in command.

"But when my little girl screams for her Daddy, I just can't ignore the cry. Night after night I hear my Maddy shrieking in pain and fear, calling out my name as the fire … The fire… The fire…"

Zac closed his eyes and was silent.

Trig had known but a few of these details. As the words spilling from Zac soaked into his heart, Trig's eyes were opened to the horrid truth of Zac's experiences. He took on a whole new insight into the struggles his friend lived with daily.

There was a long pause as Zac finally opened his eyes and stared off into the clouds, getting control of himself.

"My God, Trig. I just can't let it go. I can't. I don't believe God would want me to let it go.

"Men like that should not be running loose on the land. There's no telling how much more harm they'll do before they're brought down. Or how much they've already done over the years since the war, like those two did to Link. The best I can promise is what I've already promised myself and God. If I find these men, I won't punish them myself. We're becoming a land of law and order. I'll abide by that as long as humanly possible. That's the only promise I can make."

Trig stood silently, not having a single word of comfort or advice to offer.

***

Abe saw the two men talking and wandered over. Not wishing to interrupt, he stood a few feet off. Zac noticed him and nodded.

"Abe, I've got some miles to ride. I'd like it if you'd check these animals over for shoes. Let me know if you spot anything else to worry me."

With that, he turned towards the general store. Abe and Trig looked wordlessly at each other for a short while. Abe finally asked, "He heading to El Paso?"

"Seems like."

"Long trail. Near enough three hundred miles I'm thinking."

"I guess. Never been there my own self."

"Going alone?"

Trig didn't answer. His mind and eyes were focused on the general store.

Abe took the horses and led them to his livery shop.

***

When Zac finished buying his camp supplies, he walked with burdened arms back to the sheriff's office. Laying his purchases on the boardwalk he said, "Abe got the animals?"

"Yes. I'm figuring he'll soon be done unless he has to replace some shoes"

The two friends stared at each other, saying nothing, until Trig cleared his throat.

"Zac, I'm going with you. I'll go right now and quit this job and be ready in a short hour."

"No, you won't. You just got married and you have a good job. A responsible job. You stay here and look after that lovely bride of yours. And I mean, you take care of her! You hear me?

"This is my ride."

The look Zac pointed at Trig was something he had never seen before. Everything about caring for loved ones was wrapped up in that look.

"Abraham Howells, down to the lawyer's office has a letter from me. From before. Gives him instructions on what to do with the Wayward, and the rest, should I not return.

"I don't want to discuss this with Moody. I'd appreciate if you'd wait as long as you can before telling him."

Trig signaled his agreement with his typical nod.

"Zac, I've been sorry ever since that wire came in that I ever looked at those old wanted posters. If my doing that were to lead to you being harmed in any way, I'll never forgive myself. You ride easy. You hear?"

Finally resigned to the situation, Trig turned and said, "Wait just a moment."

He walked into the office and returned with a sheet of paper.

"I copied that wire. Wrote down all those names for you. It's a lot to remember. This might help. You take care my friend. I'll look for your return. Send a wire if you have news.

"Abe says El Paso is the most of a three-hundred-mile ride. You keep an eye out. There's bound to be a man or two along that lonesome trail who's best left alone."

***

Abe was soon leading the two horses along the short walk from the livery.

"Fit as a fiddle, Zac. But that's a hard trail. Long too. You check those shoes often. You should be alright."

Trig helped Zac load the pack animal. He and Abe shook hands with Zac and wished him good hunting. They stood on the street until their friend disappeared around a corner and down the trail. As usual, Zac held the reins with one hand while the Henry hung at the ready, alongside his right leg, gripped with strong fingers.

Zac didn't notice, but Nancy was holding down a chair in front of the millinery shop. She watched every step Zac's horses took until he was out of sight. Then, silently, she tipped her head down and prayed.

CHAPTER THIRTY-THREE

A few days became a week. A week became ten days. And Zac rode on.

There were many drifters across the west, men who were just riding on, to where, most of them didn't know, or much care. But Zac wasn't drifting. He had a purpose. Perhaps a deadly purpose, although he hoped the dying, if there was to be dying, would happen to the raiders and not to himself.

The land was sun-struck, arid and mostly barren. Water was scarce and difficult to find. Although sparse grass grew among the rocks and semi-desert brush, cactus, and shrubs, to Zac's eyes it was a long way from good cattle country. He knew that some were attempting to ranch, but he could see little promise to the effort.

He also knew the land would soon enough fill up with hopeful men and women. Men to whom the mere ownership of land was the culmination of a dream. Land ownership meant freedom. Of a sort at least. If nothing else, it was the freedom to prosper or fail by your own efforts.

As he rode, careful study of the land showed a bit of grass here and there, under and around the other desert growth, most of which had a spine or a sticker on it. Zac figured a cow critter could survive, provided it could find water somewhere close by, but it would take many acres of land to fill the needs of a nursing cow and calf.

By Texas standards, or the plains country of Colorado, the parts of the west he was most familiar with, this was poor ranching country. It was also poor compared to those lands to the west of Santa Fe, out where he and Trig had chased rustlers and stolen cattle for the WO, the Lazee, the J-J and the Lazy-A. In defined pockets, distributed among the hills, each of those ranches were settled on fair grass.

***

Zac's thoughts grew grimmer as he rode. He found himself picturing Maddy's beautiful face or hearing Minnie's childish giggle. Without warning, those images were overtaken by gun shots, men's wicked laughter and flames.

He would shake those images from his head, only to have thoughts and memories of his parents take their place. If he managed to push those mind pictures aside, he was again horrified by the image of four grey headstones lined up in the cemetery beside the church in Carob. Headstones that represented all he had loved in life.

Over the past few years, he had found hard work and busyness to be at least a temporary release for his troubled mind. But the hours sitting the saddle left his mind too much freedom. His thoughts threatened to overwhelm him.

He had to struggle with all the internal strength and resolve he could muster, just to hold off the blackness.

Down the long and unfamiliar trail south, he saw few people. In places, he followed established pathways. From time to time he happened on a wagon or coach road. He could step up his pace and cover distance at those times.

At other times, when the trails seemed to be leading him away from his goal, he cut off and rode over the barren, cactus-dotted land. But always he rode south, skirting brush-covered hillsides, keeping a safe rifle distance from cover, not knowing who might be standing in wait of an unwary traveler. He reluctantly bypassed the sand hills, regretting the extra time it took to swing around, but knowing that to venture into the sand could easily cost his life.

He asked directions at two struggling, remote ranches.

He purchased a side of bacon and a cut of smoked beef from another ranch. As he was finding a safe place to stow the meat, under the protective cover on the pack horse, the rancher's wife approached carrying a small paper carton containing six eggs, a rare treasure on the frontier. She had carefully placed each egg into a small nest of dry grass, protecting them from the harsh treatment they would receive as Zac rode out.

Zac held the small packet in thanks. His offer to pay was graciously refused. The woman simply said, "Travel well. Be careful," and returned to her rough-built stone and stick shelter.

For all but two nights, he camped alone.

Not far north of El Paso, two trails merged into one. Zac couldn't politely avoid the rider heading south, along the other trail.

He held back just enough to allow the stranger to reach the junction of the two trails before him. The fellow lifted his hat to Zac, dismounted and loosed the cinch. He then poured some water into his hat from his canteen and gave his horse a bit of relief from the heat of the blazing sun.

Zac rode within fifty feet of the stranger and dismounted, still holding the Henry in his right hand. He would not loosen the cinch until he was satisfied about the intentions of the other man. He stayed on the off side of the big cavalry gelding, studying the stranger across the top of the saddle.

"Howdy. Hot as blazes, ain't it? Hoping to find some water along here before long. Known as Joshua. Joshua Fairley.

"Named this here four-footed friend of mine Rocky. That's on account of I dealt him away from a tame Blackfoot up in the shadow of the Rockies. Up into the Porcupine Hills. Now that's a beautiful country. Grass? Why man there ain't no end to the grass. And green. So green and lovely it comes near to hurting the eyes in wonder. Makes a man want to just sit and look at it. Soaking it in.

"Flowing rivers about everywhere a man could want one. You ever see it? Naw, I'd guess not. Long ride from here."

The stranger didn't seem to require any response to his talk.

"Now I've had some folks, them that don't know horses, say that's a lot of handle for this no-account looking gelding. But this here is a lot more horse than he shows right off. Likes to keep his real worth hidden, you might say. But when the chips are all laid down... Well, you know what I mean. That gelding of yours looks to be of the same type, although he appears to hold his flesh a bit better. Deserve the very best, the both of them, if you were to ask me.

"Just gave him the last of my water. Got none for myself. Sure hope to find something soon. I believe I'd welcome a scum covered mosquito swamp right about now. You headed for El Paso?"

Zac, never really a talker, didn't answer for a short while. During the silence, the other man went around the horse checking legs and feet.

To a casual watcher it might appear that the talker was careless, taking his eyes off the stranger while he fussed over his horse. But Zac noted with appreciation, that the man had him in his peripheral sight the whole time.

Joshua pulled a pocketknife out of his pants pocket and pried a small pebble from one hind hoof. The big black gelding waited until Joshua let go of the foot before kicking out, as a way of showing his thanks. The young man anticipated the move and managed to avoid the iron shod hoof.

Joshua walked three steps towards Zac.

"I'll move along by myself then, fella, if that would make you a happier man. Don't mean to intrude. Don't mean no harm neither. A visiting kind of fella, I am. Oh, I'll visit hours on end with ol' Rocky here if it comes to that. Prefer to visit with someone that once in a while visits back though. But I can see you're wishing to be alone, so I'll move on. Can't be far now to El Paso. Could be we'll run into each other there. Ride safe, my friend."

***

Joshua turned his horse so he could attend to it while still keeping an eye on Zac. He flipped the saddle stirrup and fender over the seat and bent to tighten the cinch. Zac thought he heard him humming as he worked. Otherwise the day was silent.

The horse turned and tried to nip his owner on the shoulder. Again, the move was anticipated and avoided.

As Joshua was lifting his foot into the stirrup Zac called out, "Got an extra canteen here."

Joshua set his foot back on the dusty trail and smiled through cracked lips.

"Thanks, Friend. That sure does sound like music to these ears."

With a smile he covered the distance between Zac and himself. When he was within a few feet, Zac reached under the canvas tarpaulin on the pack horse and lifted the canteen free. Over the back of the gelding, he tossed the full container to Joshua.

"Like to keep it under the cover. Might stay a bit cooler."

Joshua caught the water bottle in midair, pulled the stopper and tipped it to his mouth. Almost like a single movement. Although he could have drunk the whole half gallon, he remembered his trail etiquette, satisfying himself with just a single swallow. He recorked the canteen and passed it back.

"Take another. I'll have enough."

Tipping the canteen towards Zac, to express his thanks, the thirsty man took two more swallows.

"Probably could've made out, but this sure makes the day smile."

This time Zac accepted the returned water bottle, stowing it again under the shading cover.

Zac nodded his head towards a solid growth of desert brush on the side of the trail.

"Getting late in the day. That westering sun sure can pack a wallop. Some shade over there and a bit of graze. Might give the animals a break, and ourselves too. Move on a ways as the sun settles down."

Joshua glanced back and nodded in approval.

"I heartily approve of that thought my traveling friend. I'm in no particular hurry. And as far as I can figure it, ol' Rocky, he ain't got no appointments to keep neither."

All three horses were turned loose to graze, and the men squatted on their heels in the shade. Zac finally tipped his hat back on his head a bit and, without glancing at the other man, said, "Zac. Short for Isaac. Seems we might have both had folks that put stock in those old Bible names."

"Happy to meet you, Zac. Folks picked that name for me from the Bible, for sure. They thought of ol' Joshua as a hero of some sort. And I guess he was.

"I do believe my folks might have memorized most every name in the Bible. Memorized a good bit of the rest of it too. Pa, he used his Bible, the only book he ever owned, to teach Ma the English.

Took some time, but Ma, she picked it up real well. Picked up her belief in the God of the Bible too, so you might say the whole thing served a double purpose.

"Memorized some myself. Never saw no harm in it and a good bit of help, time to time. No sir, never saw no harm at all."

Zac didn't enquire further about Joshua's family and neither man offered a handshake. They both seemed to enjoy the silence and the shade. Neither one sat down, finding the squatting position a relief from the hours in the saddle.

Waiting while the worst heat of the blazing sun passed them by, Zac squatted in satisfying solitude. The much more outgoing and restless Joshua passed the time fidgeting and tossing pebbles at unobtrusive ants.

Two hours later, Zac smoothly rose to his feet, staggered just a bit, and then straightened up. He had been favoring his wounded hip for the past few days. He felt no need to talk of it.

Wordlessly the men went to their horses and readied them again for the trail. This time, Zac took a single mouthful of water for himself and, as Joshua had done earlier, poured water into his hat for each horse. He kept the horses between himself and his companion, although he had sensed nothing threatening in the man.

The two men mounted and started south. With no further questioning, they rode together. Showing his understanding of Zac's wishes, Joshua kept his silence.

A few miles down the trail Joshua pulled his horse to a sudden halt. Zac did the same. Joshua smiled over at Zac.

"Is that sound really what I think it is?"

"Only one way to find out."

Joshua stepped to the ground and passed his reins to Zac.

"I'll go take a look."

The young man disappeared behind a bush that neither of them could have named. He then scrambled down a boulder strewn slope. On the trail above there was silence. Zac studied the surroundings while he waited, watching for threats.

In just a couple of minutes a smiling Joshua walked back onto the trail. Picking up the reins, he started leading Rocky forward.

"Short downward path just ahead. Nicest little fresh-water pool you ever did see, down in a shaded hollow. Small stream tumbling over some rocks, ending in a noisy falls. A bit of a scramble for the horses, but it's not far. They can manage."

CHAPTER THIRTY-FOUR

The two travelers made camp in the stream-watered hollow and settled in for the night. Where they built their fire was clearly a well-used spot. The ring of rocks was flame blackened and the shallow dug-out pit was nearly full of ashes.

There was little talk, but Zac had a question that had been troubling him as they rode along.

"You're traveling pretty light, Joshua. Makes me wonder at all the truck on the back of that pack horse of mine."

Joshua was delighted to have his camp companion begin a conversation. There had been more silence than he liked. It was true that in his home country, out of a trap line, he had been much alone. But the silence wore on him, just the same.

He could stay on the story of camp supplies the rest of the way to El Paso if Zac didn't stop him.

"Raised on a fur trading post. Hudson Bay. Up yonder a ways. Well, actually a far ways. Fort Victoria it's called. On the North Saskatchewan river. Pa was the trader. Out from Scotland. Barely out of short pants when he was set aboard a sailing ship. Never saw his home or kin again. Came by canoe across the Great Lakes, up a couple of other lakes and then up the river chain, all the way west. To fur hunting country.

"He kicked around the forts for a few years, working for the Company, learning the trade, and studying the Indians. Took some considerable years before the company made him Factor. That's the chief trader on a trading post.

"Hudson Bay, they don't send out trappers. They're a trading company. Indians do the trapping, like they always have. Only now they use steel traps provided by the company. They bring their furs to the fort. Trade for things they can't make for themselves.

"Pa learned to trap a bit as he made friends with a few Indians. Far as that goes, the Indians up there were pretty much friendly. Hudson Bay treats them pretty good so there's little trouble. Mostly Cree, but some Beaver, Chipewyan, a few others. A group of Blackfoot now and then but they're constantly at war with the Cree, so they pretty much stayed to their home country, south a ways.

"Ma, she's a Cree. She's the one taught me to trap. Back when I wasn't much more than a skirt-hanging kid. Her and a couple of her brothers. Of course, I just did it for fun. And to learn. The furs went to the men for trading. I couldn't keep any of them but Ma, she held a few back. Not for trading but for clothing.

"Made my winter parka and moccasins from my own hides. Trapping is done in the cold of winter. I needed that parka and moccasins. Fur mittens too.

"Anyway, on the trapline a man only has what he can carry himself. Mostly that means metal traps, furs already taken and just enough grub to get by. And maybe a blanket. Taught me to be self-sufficient, if nothing else. Learned to eat off what the land laid before me. Beaver tail was the best. Or ptarmigan, when I could spot one. Good eating. Snow white, they are. Hard to spot in a country covered in snow.

"On a longer trapping trip, a man might pull a sled or toboggan, taking along some supplies, but I never was out for long enough to need that.

"I must admit though, this country around here is a sight different from the bush I was raised in. Pickens ain't nearly so good here. Up there? Forest for a thousand miles, I suppose. And water everywhere a man might care to find it. Small game to eat never about everywhere. Fish in all the streams.

"Been a few days here with small rations but I've managed. I would say I managed. Expect I can make do somehow."

***

The two men made up their own meals with Zac warming up a liberal slice of the smoked beef to go along with some bacon, and Joshua eating the cold remains of his lunch rabbit.

"Man can starve on rabbit. I like it though. I've eaten a lot of 'em. But you need a bit of bear or a cut of fat moose to go along with it. A body needs some fat."

Zac grinned at the man. He was starting to

follow Joshua's talk, even when he seemed to begin in the middle of a sentence.

"Dip your rabbit in some of this bacon grease if that would make it slide down easier."

"Thanks. I'll do that."

***

The men put out the fire with a pot of water and moved their camp away from the stream. They had no desire to keep others, either man or animal from the life-saving water. In any case, they'd sleep better behind some shelter.

Joshua waited until almost full dark before slipping out of his clothes. With his boots set aside, he pulled on a pair of moccasins from his small pack. He grinned in Zac's direction, although he could no longer see him.

"Going to take a bath. Won't be long."

"That's almighty cold water down there."

"Well, you're right, far as that goes. But tomorrow will go easier with a little less grime on my hide. Back home it was common to rub ourselves down with snow, then warm up by the fire."

Joshua heard his first real laugh from Zac.

"First snowbank we come to you can show me how it's done."

***

Before first light the next morning Joshua was at the stream. He had four nice trout lying on the grass. He gutted them out and laid them on rocks surrounding the fire Zac had made.

"Get that pan out, my traveling friend, and a bit of that bacon grease. Not too much. Don't want to lose the taste of these trout. Two each. That's a good start for any day."

While they were eating, Joshua looked over at Zac with a grin.

"Heard someone at the water in the dark of the night."

"Eat your fish."

Joshua answered with a hardy laugh.

***

Two days later they rode into El Paso.

CHAPTER THIRTY-FIVE

Together they rode the length of what appeared to be El Paso's main street. Zac wondered if his companion just might twist his head from his neck with his looking around, swiveling one way and then the other.

Zac wasn't exactly sure what he was hoping to see or where to begin his hunt. He had thought about the problem, off and on, during the long ride. His thoughts now were interrupted by Joshua saying, "Looks like there just might be more Mexican folks than there are whites."

"That bother you?"

"Don't bother me at all. They're folks just like the rest of us. I saw a good bunch up Santa Fe way. And I'll remind you that I'm half Cree. I was raised among men and kids whose family tree would look like a beaver tail stew, with anything laid to hand thrown in. Only the women were what you might call 'pure bred', and they were Cree or of some other native tribe. Just a few white women showing up here and there. Tough country on white women, but a few have stuck it out.

"Given time those white women and their children will build a nation.

"Still, you have to admit that these Mexicans are some different from the whites. Know how to dress fancy if nothing else. Some of the girls can really turn a man's head."

***

Zac turned to a tie rail in front of a hotel. He stepped down, tied off and stretched mightily.

Joshua watched Zac stretch and stomp his feet to gain some circulation.

"Noticed you limping a bit at our last stop. Favoring your one side. You alright?"

"Alright. Nothing to concern either of us."

Zac turned towards the building behind him.

"Don't expect this is the best El Paso has to offer but it might serve. I'll give it a night anyway."

Joshua stepped down and tied off beside him.

"I'm game. Need to find some grub pretty soon too."

The two men took rooms and managed to find a chili joint close by. They ate well if a bit plain. Joshua pushed his plate away and grinned.

"Never had much for spices back up north. Mostly just a few herbs the women picked from under the covering growth. This pretty much caught me by surprise with my first taste. That was some weeks ago. Kind of grows on a man."

Zac was tired. Too tired to respond to Joshua. Fatigue frightened him. He knew it was often the door that led to a dark place. He was in the habit of working hard and long, but he made a habit of stopping while there was still something of his stamina left. His solution to the fatigue was to push back from the table, rise to his feet, pick up his Henry, and say, "Like to go for a walk before bed."

Joshua stood to his feet beside Zac.

"You go ahead. I spotted a couple of chairs out front of the hotel. Think I'll just set by for a while. Done a lot of that, time to time, back at the fort."

***

With Zac now needing to get to the business that called him south, he pondered on what to tell Joshua. They were sitting over breakfast the next norming. Joshua forced the conversation.

"What's your plan now, partner?"

A lot of men, treasuring their privacy, would have bristled at the question. He figured Joshua still had a bit to learn about the culture and habits of the land he was riding through.

Zac hesitated for a while before following his thoughts from the night before. He liked Joshua and had come to more or less trust the man. But he could see no reason for him to get involved in something as personal to Zac as this manhunt.

On other ventures Trig had followed along and had turned out to be a big help, especially in the matter of tracking or finding old, weather-worn trails. But Trig was different in that he already had a connection to Claire Maddison, the woman at the center of that matter. Joshua had no such connection to the raiders of Carob, Texas .

Zac doublechecked those sitting in the small

café. Deciding he could speak softly enough to hold his secret he said, "We'll probably be saying 'adios' here, Joshua. I've business of my own to deal with. Business that could take me almost anywhere. Could become a shooting matter. No need for you to know the details. It's enough if I tell you it's honorable on my part. Or at least as honorable as a serious crime can be.

"If you stay in El Paso, we may bump into each other again."

With that Zac offered for the first time to shake hands.

Joshua didn't extend his own hand. Instead he said, "Nope. You gave me water when I had none. We rode the same trail, shared the same campsites. I'll be hanging around. I kind of like that chair in front of the hotel. Good view of all that's going on. We'll hold that farewell handshake for just now.

"You go about your business for a day or two. See if you can locate your man, or men, whichever it is. I'll set by. We may decide to go our separate ways, but not yet for a while. You go. Do what you have to do. But first, you give me a bit of an idea what you're looking for. I'll keep my eyes open. Could be a help."

Zac studied his new friend for a long time. Trust did not come easily to Zac. Especially in a matter as deeply personal as the one that brought him to El Paso. He finally made a decision.

"I'll tell you this much. And this is based on weeks' old information so it may have all changed by now.

"I need to track down a couple of rough men. Raiders and rebels during the war. Murderers.

Thieves. The word that came my way is that there are two of them traveling together. But there could be more.

"They're dangerous. They were in here in El Paso a month ago. Could be almost anywhere by now. You see or hear anything, you let me know. Don't do anything on your own."

Joshua simply nodded and said, "I'll stand by."

CHAPTER THIRTY-SIX

Zac's first stop was at a lawyer's office. He saw the lawyer's street-sign as he walked towards the livery where they had left their horses. He waited a few minutes for the lawyer to deal with another matter and then was invited into the back office. He started into his question without much preamble.

"I'm Isaac Trimbell. Las Vegas. Formerly from Carob, Texas. That's way back east. I'm interested in one piece of information only. And I would like to keep my enquiry in confidence. At least for now. Do you mind if I ask you a question? It involves someone in your town, and I need an honest answer from an honest man. I can pay for your services."

The lawyer studied Zac with fierce eyes. His look might have made another man squirm. It had no effect at all on Zac. Perhaps a half minute went past. Finally, the lawyer let out his breath, lifted his elbows off the desk and leaned back in his chair. He steepled his fingers under his chin and studied Zac intently for another ten seconds.

With no more preamble than Zac had used, he

answered, "I claim to be an honest man. I'd shoot any man who argued to the contrary. As to your question, I'd have to know what it is before I could promise to answer. I will, however, guarantee absolute discretion."

Zac's stare was every bit as intense as the lawyer's.

"It's a simple question. Is the sheriff honest and trustworthy?"

The lawyer broke into a full belly laugh.

"Young man. I'm pleased to be able to say that after a rather sad series of questionable sheriffs, the man the town now employs would, I believe, arrest his own mother if he caught her shoplifting. If you have sensitive matters to deal with, I believe you can do it with confidence. Is that all you need?"

"One further thing. Do you happen to know if there's a Federal Marshal in town?"

"They tend to move around. I believe the last one headed back east a while ago."

"Thank you. What do I owe you?"

"Get out of my office."

The lawyer said this with a bit of a grin.

***

Zac walked around until he found the sheriff's office and entered. A rough looking man, a man with face wrinkles too deep for someone his age, was sitting behind the desk with his hand close to a Colt revolver lying there. A second man was standing against the wall, a carbine hooked through the crook of his elbow. In his other hand he held a cup of coffee. His intent stare cautioned Zac against any form of threat to the sheriff or himself.

"Morning, Sheriff. Sign out here says Huey Branson. That you, Sheriff, or is that an old sign?"

"That's me. Who needs to know and what do you want? And if you don't park that Henry beside the door and leave it there, you're going to be in no condition to want anything at all. Lay the revolver on the desk here."

Zac turned and leaned the weapon against the wall beneath a couple of long duster coats hanging from pegs. He turned back around and laid the handgun down, within easy reach of the sheriff before saying, "Sorry, Sheriff. Been carrying the Henry since '63. Sometimes forget I've got it. Feel a bit naked without it."

He lifted his chin towards the man with the carbine.

"No insult meant fella, but I have confidential matters to lay before the sheriff. I'm unarmed and the sheriff is at no risk. Do you mind?"

The sheriff studied Zac carefully, pulled the handgun closer and said, "Just stay nearby, Daniel."

When Zac was alone, he pulled a ladder-back chair away from the wall, turned it backwards and sat, laying his arms comfortably across the back. Tipping his hat up with two fingers, he faced the sheriff.

"I'm Zac Trimbell. Las Vegas. Originally from Carob, Texas. Just rode in here last evening. I've made an enquiry this morning. I'm told you're an honest man. It's an honest man I need to talk with because I'm talking about life or death. This matter can't be talked about outside this office. Can't have no news getting around. Could be my death. Could be someone else's."

The sheriff studied Zac intently but said nothing at all. Zac took that as permission to continue.

He reached into his shirt pocket and pulled out the paper Trig had given him.

"This is the copy of a wire received almost two weeks ago up in Las Vegas. I'd like if you would read it and tell me what you might know."

The sheriff lifted the paper and read it. It only took a few seconds. He kind of slumped down in his chair.

"I saw them. This wire is probably based on an enquiry I sent east when those men showed up. But there were three of them, not just the two. The third one showed up a couple of days after the first two. They hung around for about a week. I didn't like their looks, but I had nothing to justify questioning them. I sent a wire east, to the Rangers, with their descriptions. Got a wire back a few days later with these same names. It was too late. They had ridden out by then.

"I never heard these names before receiving the wire. Most likely they were your men. One was called Luthor, for sure. My deputy heard him called that down at the saloon.

"What all are they wanted for and how are you involved in this? Are you a bounty hunter?"

Zac explained the story in shortened form, telling only about the loss of his family, leaving out the hurt done to the rest of the community. While the sheriff took in every word. Zac closed with a simple statement.

"I need to find these men, Sheriff. I promise not to do vigilante justice unless they get me backed into a corner. If it's possible, I'll turn them over to

Federal law. I need to do this. These men shouldn't be running loose."

Zac gave the sheriff time to respond. When that didn't happen, he continued.

"There's another reason too. A deeply personal reason. I'll tell you so you have the full story. Or as much as you need anyway.

"You might think less of me after the telling, but I'll have to take that chance."

As the sheriff remained silent, Zac stirred up his courage to tell about the sleepless nights. He was not in the custom of exposing his innermost feeling and problems, but he needed this man's help.

When the short tale was ended Zac said, "I may never be able to turn off the war dreams. But I might put a stop to the others. Maybe let my little girl rest. Maybe show my wife I've done whatever I could for her.

"Maybe they'll stop crying out to me in the night. Maybe I can hope to get a night's sleep somewhere in the future."

The sheriff rubbed his face with work toughened hands and looked at Zac. He spoke quietly.

"Do you still hear the cannon?'

The two men studied each other, not even asking or carrying what color uniform the other wore. There was no need for Zac to answer. The answer was written in the silence between the two men.

The sheriff said, "Probably two thirds of the men down in those saloons at night still hear the cannon. They try to hide it with loud laughter and rotgut whisky. But that doesn't fix anything. A lot of lives still being ruined by that old war. The war probably caused more problems than it fixed.

"I've heard men screaming in the night from those cells back there. Hear them right through that closed door. Sometimes I want to scream with them. Sometimes I want to shoot them, just to bring them some peace. You need say no more, Zac. I get the picture."

Again, there was silence, broken only when the lawman said, "My deputy was kind of following those boys around. Heard them talking down to the chili house. Talked about going further west. Arizona, he thought. Although they could have turned back up into New Mexico. All I know is I was glad when we saw the last of them. It could be that the Federals wired a warning off to the west. Tombstone or Fort Huachuca maybe. I wouldn't know about that.

"If you follow them, I advise you use every caution. And don't be over worried about Federal law. Those men are not going to let themselves be taken. You shoot them if you get the chance. Shoot them dead. They'd do it for you if they got you in their sights. We're talking in confidence here, Zac. I know you won't repeat what I just said."

There was nothing left to discuss, so Zac stood and holstered his Colt. He tucked the Henry into the crook of his arm and was about to leave. The sheriff stopped him.

"Zac, if you find their trail heading somewhere else in Texas, come back and I'll deputize you. Can't do it for New Mexico or Arizona. Good hunting, my new friend, and good luck."

Zac nodded his thanks.

CHAPTER THIRTY-SEVEN

Zac walked back over to the hotel and spoke to Joshua.

"I'll be riding out now. I got the information I need. You stay here and enjoy the sun. I wish you well in your adventure. And watch what you get involved in with those pretty, Mexican girls. Not everything is what it may seem. There's always someone watching over them."

Joshua grinned at Zac.

"Why, those girls are like candy for my sun-strained eyes. But that's all they are. I witnessed enough on the trapping frontier to know trouble when I see it. But none of that is to the point, is it? What are your plans? Could be they'll fit with mine.

"I may have failed to mention it, but I originally set out to see the wide Pacific Ocean. Saw a picture or two in a book one time. Set out to see the real thing. Pa, he talks endlessly about sailing the ocean as a lad. Of course, that was a different body of water. But I figure an ocean is an ocean and I'm bound to see one. Maybe take off my boots and wade in, just to know I'd done it. Might even dip up a taste of the saltwater.

"I kind of got sidetracked back north a way. Wanted to feast my eyes on those snow-capped mountains for a while longer. I had no intention of riding to Mexico. Now that I've done that, I'm off to the ocean again. If that's the same direction you're heading, I'll still side you."

Zac studied the grinning young man.

"Get your horse."

Zac checked out of the hotel after getting his small pack from the room. Most of his truck he had left at the livery. He then went to the closest general store and purchased a stock of trail supplies. He would let Joshua scout around for rabbits if that's how he wanted it.

Carrying his supplies in a cloth sugar sack, he headed for the livery. Walking in, he was surprised to see both his horses rigged out and standing ready, beside Joshua's Rocky.

Joshua greeted him with a grin.

"Ready when you are, partner."

"Are you going to check out of the hotel or buy supplies?"

"Already done both while you was gabbing with the sheriff. Didn't want to cause you any delay."

Zac checked the cinches on both horses, stowed his provisions, and led the animals into the sunshine.

Both men mounted. When Zac kicked his horse into a northerly direction, Joshua called out, "Just a few more minutes here, Zac. I'm bound to lay foot into Mexico. Even if it's just across that bridge."

Zac had a questioning look on his face, but he turned his horses and followed. They trotted their animals south, slowing when they came to the crowded bridge. It appeared as if half of El Paso was either going to Mexico or coming back. Within a few minutes they were on the south side of the Rio Grande. They rode another two hundred yards before turning back. Joshua grinned at Zac.

"There's not ever been one person, up to home, man nor woman, either one, that's ever been to Mexico. None I ever heard tell of anyway. Oh, they come from about every other old-world country and half of the north part of the continent, but not from Mexico.

"Come to story-telling time around the campfire I'll have a thing or two to offer. I can tell of the miles ridden. The spicy foods. The high hills and the deep canyons. The men I've met on the trail and the search for food, along the way. And now I can honestly say I've been to Mexico and they won't know if I'm talking true or making up stories. I'll not have to tell anyone that I only rode in a short quarter mile. It's still Mexico."

Zac looked at Joshua's grin and thought of Trig. Both young men were clearly prepared to enjoy simply being alive. He wondered if he had ever been that young. Had he ever simply enjoyed life. The memories were dull and indistinct.

"You ready to go now?"

"I was ready to go a half hour ago."

Joshua laughed and heeled his horse.

***

As they rode out of town Zac explained, "We're

not far from the Texas border. We follow the river up here for a while and then we're back in New Mexico. I intend to ask a few questions along the way, as opportunity allows. The best information I was able to get was that my men are heading into Arizona. That's quite a bit further west. If I find information that questions that, I'll do what has to be done."

Joshua didn't seem to mind where they were heading as long as it was west, towards the blue waters of the Pacific.

CHAPTER THIRTY-EIGHT

Following the old Butterfield Stage trail, in just one long day of riding, the two men crossed from Texas into New Mexico. There was little along the way to attract a traveler, or anyone else, for that matter. Zac figured the rebels would have ridden right on through.

The next evening, they rode into a dusty and desolate stage station. Except for the stage stop, there was no sign of settlement. Nor could he see any purpose that would attract a settler. It was bleak country, from any point of view.

After caring for their mounts, they walked to the stage depot and entered. With no thought required, Zac pointed the way with the Henry. Stepping inside just a single stride before coming to a halt while he examined the room, he relaxed and spoke to the woman setting tables for dinner.

"Can you feed two more?"

"It's catch as catch can, fella. First come, and all that. I never know who might be on the road. Or how many. You're here, so I'll feed you. Go wash up.

Basin's by the door. Take a seat. No menu. Just beef and beans and potatoes, as long as they last. Lots of bread. Baked this morning, me and Tiny."

Perhaps the biggest woman Zac had ever seen stepped from behind the wall separating the small kitchen from the eating area. She was all of six feet if she was an inch. As slim as a woman of her size could be. Broad in shoulders and hips. Hands as big as most men. Looked strong as a man too. Zac figured it would take a determined man to woo her into marriage.

"You call me, Rose?"

"No Tiny, just talk'n to the travelers here. Nothing to fuss over."

Zac and Joshua took seats at the end of the one long serving table. Zac sat so he could face the front entry. Joshua walked around the end of the table and sat facing the kitchen door. Zac smiled in approval.

Rose called out from the kitchen, "Coffee's on the stove. Come get it. I ain't got the time to do every little thing for you."

Joshua laughed and responded, "Sounds about like home. Do you want me to come peel potatoes for you too?"

There was no response from the kitchen.

A few minutes later Rose arrived with two bowls and one platter of sliced beef.

"You might want to leave something for the others."

"Yes, ma'am," laughed Joshua.

Zac was more serious, posing a question.

"Rose, we're kind of keeping an eye out for three riders. Hard cases. Might have come this way. Only name we know is Luthor. Have you seen anyone like that?"

"You bounty hunters?"

"No, ma'am, were working with the law."

The statement wouldn't stand up to a close examination, but it was near enough.

Rose looked both men over carefully.

"Seen some rough ones come through here, time to time. Mostly don't worry about them. Feed them and hope they'll just go about their business. But those three! Wouldn't want those three to come back. I couldn't see one single thing I liked about any of them.

"You tell anyone that we talked it could get real bad for my man and I. Tiny too."

"I'm good at keeping a secret, Rose."

The woman looked all around, as if there might be someone sneaking in to listen, but they were alone.

"Four, five days ago. Didn't hear no names. Stomped in here and demanded we feed them. Tiny, she took offense at their demanding. She was well along towards setting them to rights. I dragged her back into the kitchen and told her to stay there. Those boys had me scared clear through. I don't mind admitting to that.

"Warmed them up some lunch fixin's and sent them on their way. Didn't offer to pay and I didn't make an issue of it. Those boys are going to cause some hurt if they haven't already. You be careful if you should find them."

"Thanks, Rose, we'll be careful. Did you see which way they went?"

"Stood right there on that front stoop and

watched till they were out of sight. Hoping my man wouldn't ride in about that time. Took the trail west. I expect they're following the stage line, feeding at the stops along the way."

***

Three days of careful riding later the two hunters rode into San Simon stage stop. They had been following the stage trail figuring that's where their prey would be riding. There had been no sign of the men. The trail was strewn with hundreds of tracks. There was no hope of identifying or following any particular track.

Joshua was fascinated by the country and the landscape, leading him to form an opinion.

"Well, I don't see much value to any of this unless there's something to mine under all that sun blistered rock and cactus. It's a far cry from the forests and rivers I grew up in. No snakes back home, neither. Some we've seen along here make me question laying out my blankets, come nighttime.

"That tall cactus now, that's new to me. Didn't see anything like that down through New Mexico."

Zac answered, "I've never seen it before either. Heard about it though. Some folks back north were telling me about it. Said it mostly grew in Arizona, and not all of Arizona either. Called the saguaro. That's the first we've seen. You might call it the first saguaro."

Joshua laughed.

"That's only the first 'cause we're heading west. If we were to be heading east, it would be the last. 'The last saguaro'. Almost sounds like the title to a poem."

Zac, still not having fully figured out his traveling companion, shook his head at Joshua's grin, before completing what he was saying.

"Saguaro. Mexican name. Spelled with a g, so I'm told, although I've never seen it written right out. But you pronounce the g like a w and you'll be pretty close to right. Don't ask me to explain that.

"You could ride back and ask one of those pretty Mexican girls you were admiring. They're bound to know the language."

Joshua, soaking in this information, didn't figure the suggestion needed a response.

**

They had been careful with their questions along the way, but they quickly saw that from San Simon there were trails leading off in several directions. They were going to have to make a decision. To make the correct decision they would need some information.

After putting their horses in the small livery corral, they carried their saddles and packs into the shelter of the stable. A bored but talkative stable hand greeted them. Zac was too tired to have patience with the man's chatter, but Joshua fit right in.

Winking at Zac, where the stable hand couldn't see, Joshua said, "Why don't you go arrange for some dinner for us, Zac? I'll just straighten these packs up a bit and be along in a few minutes."

Zac nodded in understanding and left the two men to their chatter.

A half hour later Joshua washed up at the basin set by the door and entered the stage stop. He took a seat beside an off-duty stage driver and reached for the platter of meat.

After dinner and coffee on the veranda, while they discussed whatever was on their minds, with the driver, and a couple of others, they made their way to the stable to get their bedrolls.

Spreading their beds on the bit of hay in the small loft, Joshua quietly said, "Found out our men took the south road. Apparently, it leads down to some mining country. Two, three small settlements down that way, and a bunch of mines. Biggest town is called Tombstone. Doesn't sound like a town with much promise. A name like that. Probably be gone by the end of summer."

***

Sensing they were closing in on their quarry, the man-hunters rode even more warily. With the rebels taking to a side trail they were figuring the trio weren't in any particular rush. They might have friends in the area. If they had left some bloodshed behind them somewhere along the way, they may have gone to ground. Provided they could find adequate shelter. Or, they might have moved right along, heading for that town called Tombstone. Sounded like a place where they might fit in.

It was doubtful if they were looking to find employment. That didn't match with their pattern.

The narrow stage road led them through miles of cactus covered slopes, enclosing shallow, dry valleys. A couple of times they were led through

rough, rocky passages, hacked, or blown out of the low, jagged rocks that formed barriers, mostly on a south-east to north-west axis.

Nowhere did they see a settlement or a ranch house, although, here and there were a few head of scrawny cattle. Again, Zac studied the ground and wondered why anyone would bother.

They arrived in an adobe and rock-built settlement called Turquoise. By first glance, Zac figured the place was no more than maybe one year settled. They managed to find a woman-cooked meal of chili and flatbread, but still chose to make camp out among the cactus, at the edge of town.

Returning to the small eating house for breakfast, they drank coffee, sitting back in their chairs until all the other customers had paid and left.

When the woman came to clear away the dishes Joshua said, with a smile, "Looking to meet up with a couple of friends. Three, to be exact. They left out of San Simon a bit before us. We thought they might pull up and wait but no luck on that. We're wondering if they came this way or we somehow got off their trail. Any chance you had three fellas in here the past two, three days? Travelers? Friend's named Luthor. Other two are known as Red and Boss. That's not the names their mamas gave them but that's what they answer to now."

The woman took the dishes to the small kitchen and returned with the coffee pot.

"Mister. You're either real green to the country or you think I am. If you even knew those men, it's not because they're your friends. Picked you out last evening as hunters. Wary as coyotes lay'n alongside the chicken coop wait'n fer a chance.

That's you two.

"You want some advice, I'd say you need to practice look'n less interested in folks. Saw you study'n every man that came in here. Same thing this morn'n. You might just as well wear a sign around your neck."

The café lady ignored Joshua's grin.

"Yes, your men were here. Three days ago, it was. I fed them. And happy to see them go. Heard them say they was heading to Tombstone.

"You want my advice? Let them be. Soon or late, they'll run afoul of the law. Folks don't fool around down there in Tombstone. I could see right off that we wouldn't be invit'n those fellas to stay and teach Sunday School. They'll do something dumb or talk rough to the wrong man and end up in boot hill, they stay around Tombstone.

"You let them be. Give it some time. Things usually sort themselves out."

Zac put his coffee cup down and stood to his feet.

"That's good advice, Ma'am. Thank you. What do we owe you for the meals?"

Riding side by side out of Turquoise, Zac came as close as he ever did to smiling. Nodding at Joshua he said, "You made a good start. Have to admire you for that. But as to returning home and entertaining the folks with tall tale from your trip, I'd say you need to practice up some. That old gal saw through you before you had hardly said a word."

Joshua leaned back in the saddle and shrugged.

"Back home, what with the Indians, the bitter winter weather, and the thousands of miles with no folks around anywhere, we need each other.

Depend on each other. Our lives could well depend on the next fella. The truth becomes important.

"If an Indian thinks you're stringing him along, he'll never trust you again. What I'm talking about is when you're out on the trap line.

"Around the campfire, at the end of the trail, with everyone safe and settled in, it's a different matter. The white man is no match for the Indians at story telling time once you're all settled in and safe.

"Still, I take your meaning. I thought I was doing right well back there until she took me down a peg."

He then had a good laugh at himself.

CHAPTER THIRTY-NINE

Riding into Tombstone, Zac and Joshua were surprised by the multitudes of people, and the activity of the town. It was a much larger and more alive town than the name implied.

They rode easy in the saddle, their toes barely touching the stirrups. There was no reason to think the fugitives would recognize either Zac or Joshua, or even know about them. but caution was still called for.

On the first street corner they came to, as they neared the center of town, the crowd of milling people must have numbered at least fifty. All were gesturing and talking over one another.

Joshua studied the activity, turned to Zac, and asked, "What do you suppose got these folks so riled up?"

Zac didn't answer, contenting himself with a shake of his head. Joshua flagged down an older, bowlegged, and big-hatted man crossing the street.

"What's all the excitement about?"

"I take it you wasn't here. Well, there's been

three fellas caus'n up a stir, these past three, four days. Didn't recognize the town for what it is, I'm guessing.

"Rode roughshod over some folks in the sa-loon. Laughed at them as they set down their drinks and made for the swing'n doors. Tore a dance hall all to pieces. Drove decent folks out of the ho-tel. Finally made a sure enough mistake.

"Went to troubling Miss Molly, down by the the-a-ter. It's on the boardwalk outside the the-a-ter that I'm talk'n about. Miss Molly, she was having none of it. Neither were them hard rock mining boys stand'n by. Tore inta them fellers with a fare-thee-well.

"Them fellas, they rode in from the east, just like y'all seem to have done. If'n you're friends of those boys you'd be best to turn around and hightail it for the far country. Those fellas jest ain't going' ta win no pop-u-lar-ity contests. Not here in Tombstone, they ain't.

"It's the two that's still alive I'm talk'n bout. Well I guess you'd call them alive. Pretty near tore apart though.

"Smart mouthed a couple a hard rock miners, com'n ta Molly's de-fence. Shouldna' never a done that. Them miners, why they tore inta those boys like a rabid catamount lion might. Fellas looked like a half a mountain had fallen on 'em when them boys was done.

"Broke up a few chairs and a winder 'r two over there to the the-a-ter.

"Sheriff's got two a 'em stretched out on bunks down to the town jail. Ain't much chance 'a them ever se'en the light a day agin. Them miners, them and the sheriff, well, ain't none 'a them in a forgiv'n mood.

"Miss Molly, she sings like a nightingale and dances to set yer heart ta dreaming of the girl ya left back ta home. Decent woman too. And there ain't many of that type out here.

"I predict a short future for them two rowdies.

"N'other, one. He tried to run. Stoled a horse from right in front of the pool hall. Got near to the edge of town afor ol' Buffalo Wylie got his Sharp's Big .50 a-limbered up an' pointed in the right direction. Blew that there fella right out'n the saddle, no more spine left than a rattler's got.

"Shot twice, ol' Buffalo done. Didn't really have to. No need for it. The horse never done no wrong that I could see. But ol' Buffalo, he maybe don't do much, one day ta t'other, jest kinda sett'n in the sun mostly, but what he does do, he sets out ta go all the way with. Kilt the horse with the second shot. Ain't no real explanation fer that. Jest did 'er on general principles, you might say.

"Fella that owns the horse is right upset.

"Then to make a full deal out'n it, the City fathers, who watched the whole thing, they say the fella's got ta drag his own dead horse off'n the street.

"Sure do beat all, what ya kin see, ya keeps yer eyes open, whil'st yer in Tombstone. Ain't no other town like 'er."

With that, the talker cackled like a hundred- and fifty-pound laying hen and completed his walk across the street.

Zac and Joshua rode to a nearby rail and tied off. Stepping onto the shaded boardwalk they made their way to the gathered talkers. Zac eyed the crowd until he found a man with a badge on his shirt. He pushed his way through the mob.

"Sheriff," he called, over the noise of the talkers, "need to talk with you."

The sheriff looked his way, his eyes immediately taking in the Henry.

"Down there."

He pointed along the sidewalk, away from the crowd.

"You first. And you keep that Henry pointed at the ground!"

Once away from the crowd, Zac silently pulled the copy of the wire from his shirt pocket. Without explanation, he held the wire out to the sheriff. The lawman studied Zac for a moment before holding the paper up to read it. Zac and Joshua watched the man's lips move as he worked out the message. He seemed to pause and then look back at Zac.

"You think these are the men we have in jail?"

"Pretty good possibility. Did you empty their pockets or find a name anywhere?"

"We haven't gone that far yet. I have a deputy out looking through the stables for their horses. Might have something in their packs. What's your interest?"

Zac hesitated, reluctant to tell anyone else about his background. Joshua came to the rescue.

"Those men terrorized a small town back east, during the late war, as it says in that wire. Zac, here, that's his hometown."

With no more questions, the sheriff nodded at Zac and said, "Let's stroll down to the jail. I'll take a look at whatever they're carrying with them."

***

Zac was about to follow the sheriff into the jailhouse when Joshua stepped in front of him.

"You don't want to do that, my friend. The last thing you need is another nightmare, seeing faces in the dark of night."

Zac was about to push past Joshua, but a light hand on his chest caused him to pause and study his new friend. Joshua held his eye with an intense look.

Joshua hesitated, wondering if he could say more. Finally, he spoke gently.

"Do you think I don't hear you groaning and thrashing around in the night. And one night, you screamed enough to half scare the daylights out of me. You don't want any more images roaming around in your mind. Let it go."

The two men held their eye contact until Zac finally let his shoulders slump. He turned to the side and with two long steps almost fell into one of the barrel armchairs on the boardwalk.

Joshua, still speaking gently, said, "You set by. I'll get their names if names there be."

He was gone several minutes, minutes that seemed to cover all of eternity to Zac. Minutes that gave Zac time to think. But was he really thinking or just rambling in his mind?

Was it even possible that his living nightmare could be coming to an end? Are these the men? Or, at least what was left of the gang? He was still sorely tempted to rise and go inside, but something held him back. Joshua's words, for sure. But something else too. Did he really want to see the faces of the last men his terrified wife saw on this earth? His lovely daughter? His father? His mother?

During the nighttime horrors of the years since the war he saw no faces on the raiders. The men were little more than a blur. Perhaps it was best to leave it at that.

Zac's family went to their graves with those evil faces embedded on their souls. Did he want that for himself? What would that help?

Over the years, even with the good friends he had made, not even Moody, his pastor friend, had ever suggested that he simply get over the matter. How could a man just get over such a loss? He was thankful that no one had ever suggested anything of the sort. He couldn't get over it. But could he heal? Could his soul find some kind of rest?

"Is it still well with your soul?" That had been Moody's question to Zac as he rode out of Carob and into a new life. It was still the question that lay heavy on his heart. It lay heavy because deep down inside, he knew the answer. He also knew that adding stress to his already stressed-out soul would not help.

He would leave it to Joshua. A simple answer would be made to satisfy.

Allowing his mind to relax, as much as it ever did, at least, he seemed to doze, or dream or wander in his mind. At the first sound that came to his ears he came back from wherever he had been.

***

At the end of the interminable wait, Joshua and the sheriff walked out together. Zac remained seated, looking at the two men.

"Red and Boss, branded right onto their shell

belts," was all Joshua said.

The sheriff added, "Red died while we stood there. I can't see the other lasting much longer. I expect he's all broke up inside. Those miners weren't offering any mercy. Set to it with a will and a passion. If he comes around, he still faces the gallows if I can get confirmation of your wire."

As he passed the paper back to Zac, he said, "I copied out the wire. I'll get a message off right away to Ranger Headquarters."

Still taking control, Joshua asked, "Will you relay that confirmation to the sheriff in Las Vegas once this is all settled? The sheriff in El Paso too? Let them know if Boss lives or if he died. That would end the matter and tie a bow on it."

"I'll be sure to do that."

Joshua thanked the man and said to Zac, "C'mon my friend, we have miles to cover."

As if in a dream. Zac stood and walked with Joshua to where their horses were tied.

CHAPTER FORTY

Instead of turning around to point back the way they had entered Tombstone, Joshua took the lead and headed west. Zac looked around the little town, hoping to hold it in his memory, knowing he would never be back. They rode side by side until they reached the end of the town road, leaving the business district behind them, facing only scattered shacks strewn about the desert, and entered into the trail through the wasteland.

Zac pulled to a stop and spoke to Joshua.

"I'll be riding back now Joshua. Just came this far to see the town. I have no idea how far it is to that ocean you're longing to see or how to get there. But this trail is heading north-west so I guess that should do you, for a while anyway. For myself, I'll be riding home, by the quickest way I can find. So, this will be goodbye. I wish you well. I've enjoyed your company."

He lifted his hand for a handshake, but Joshua just smiled, leaving his folded hands gripping the top of the saddle horn, again refusing the signal of friendship.

"I got some directions from the sheriff. Seems we're only a few days' ride from a much bigger town. Tucson, he called it. From there apparently you can ride north and get back to your home country on a different trail. He talked of low mountains, green grass and tall trees. And he mentioned something called a rim. Some kind of a rise of land. I don't remember the name. Sounded strange to my ears. Says it's pretty country all up through there. A bit steep in places but good riding just the same. That's what he said, anyway.

"I'm not overly fond of this desert riding. The thought of grass and green trees is kind of calling out to me.

"That ocean follows all along the coast, maybe a thousand miles or more. So I figure I've got lots of opportunity to continue on west after going north a ways. What say we stay together for a while yet? Get out of this desert country. Head for those green hills. There'll be folks here and there that can point us the way."

Wordlessly, wondering if there was more to it than Joshua was letting on, Zac nudged the gelding into motion and headed for Tucson.

***

The two travelers camped out in near silence, the first night after Tombstone. Zac, reflecting on the day's events, was clearly not in a talking mood. Joshua recognized the situation and respected it.

***

Earlier that day, while sitting on the chair in front of the sheriff's office, Zac had felt as if the very life was draining out of him. Although settled first in Idaho Springs and lately in Las Vegas, in a part of his mind he was back in East Texas. In his nighttime visions he had been chasing these men for years. The chase was unrelenting, waking him at night. Driving him through the misery of nightmare after nightmare. And all the time, not even knowing who he was chasing.

Could the hunt really have come to an end? Were these the right men. Or did they merely represent all such men. And yet, they were known to have been in Carob, his hometown. The chances were good.

He felt almost hollow inside. And weak. Like a great letdown after a long, all-out effort. He had felt that way a few times after a fierce day of battle. It was not an enjoyable emotion.

But had he ever felt this weak before? Weak almost to the point of collapse? He knew his body was still strong. The weakness was an internal matter. Something out of his control, even if he could muster the will to control anything.

He was still wise enough to know that much was wrong in his soul. But were there still a few things that were right?

Was there still hope? Hope for him? Was it possible that his life would find meaning? More than simply going through the motions. Living and moving only because he was drawing breath. Not much caring, one way or another. Could he find real meaning? Peace? At least a form of contentment?

The sheriff in El Paso talked of the men

cluttering the saloons. The men who still heard the cannon. The lost men who hid their despair behind loud laughter and strong drink. That was not for him, not for Zac Trimbell.

With this recent chapter in the drama put behind him, was there, perhaps, new light for his soul? Could at least this piece of his battle be considered as over? Complete? Could he somehow forget it and move on? Could his long struggle with nightmares and lengthy silences, where he couldn't bring himself to speak, or make a decision, or even to really think, be coming to an end? Could the blackness that so often came unbidden, somehow be turned into light? Did he dare to hope for the light of God in his life again? Or had that light been there all along, unseen or unrecognized by him?

He had felt this way, and thought these thoughts so often, that he had come to understand he must simply be still. To wait it out.

It was as if these thoughts had a life of their own. He wasn't consciously putting the thoughts into words. They were acting on their own, one thought, one memory, climbing onto the coattails of the last, all clamoring to be heard.

At times over the years, good friends and hard work had seen him through, keeping his mind occupied. But this was of a different order. For all the years since his loss, the knowledge that the killers of his loved ones had escaped punishment and that he was helpless to do anything about it, had been a terrible burden to bear. Could it be possible that this, like the nightmares, was really coming to an end?

The end of the matter should be bringing him

peace, if not contentment. Maybe it would, later. He would think of that another time. But right then, that was not where his mind was taking him.

It was true that the end had not been brought by his own efforts. But did that matter? Or was having it ended enough by itself? Did it help that he was here, in Tombstone, at the conclusion of the matter, when it all came to an end? Was there meaning behind his long ride?

His world, and his rational thoughts were at the breaking point. Reality was a dream world, floating off into the distance.

Although hoping for an end to his years-long quest for the raiders, he still felt the weight of the past pressing him down. Was his mind fighting one last battle before the names of the raiders were made known?

He gripped the arms of the sheriff's chair like a drowning man. Afraid to move. Out of control. He couldn't shoot his way out of this battle. There were different weapons required for this war.

He remembered reading about battles that did not involve flesh and blood. He couldn't remember exactly where that was written or exactly what the weapons for those battles were. In fact, he didn't fully remember or understand any of it. He did remember hearing about those unseen weapons during long forgotten sermons. But it all seemed so long ago. So vague.

To his almost paralyzed mind, and completely beyond his control, the chair was suddenly floating above a black hole. He had the certain knowledge that if he moved, he and the chair both, would fall. Fall into the deep blackness. Fall to where? He had no idea, and it terrified him.

His mind whirled with unidentified emotions. He didn't see his wife and daughter or hear their screams. This wasn't about them. It wasn't about the cannon or the rifle shots or the many battles he had fought. This was all about him. Somehow, he recognized that he was in a battle for his life, for his very soul.

But who was he battling? Was he battling some other, inner part of himself or was there something deeply spiritual about it? Something harmful and sinister and evil? And if he somehow won this battle, would that put an end to it?

'Is it still well with your soul?' Moody's question haunted him. Had haunted him for years. But he couldn't think. Couldn't figure it out.

The chair still hovered over the darkness. He could feel the evil. He could smell the brimstone. He had smelled it often enough on the battlefield. The burning sulfur. The stink of the grey-black smoke.

But this was different. There was something subtle about this. There were no roaring cannons. There was no small-arms fire. There was only the blackness. The sinister unknown. The silent menace. And the terror. And, still, the brimstone.

And so, he hung on to the chair. Afraid to move. And time passed. How much time? He had no idea. It seemed like ages. Was he even counting time as he had always known it? Or was he in some other realm?

Were there people around him? Rushing past? Looking at him and wondering? Visiting on the sidewalk? He had no idea. There was just him and the terror. And the threatening blackness.

At the first sound of Joshua's voice it was like he awoke. But he wasn't really asleep. It was as if he had been somewhere else. Where? How? He didn't know. But at the sound of the voice he was back.

He realized how tightly he was gripping the chair arms. Slowly, very carefully he moved, wiggled just a bit, testing the firmness of the earth, still in a sitting position. The chair remained secure. The boardwalk didn't open below him. The darkness was gone. His mind cleared. But he was exhausted almost beyond description. Exhausted deep into his soul.

Gradually Joshua's words started sinking in.

Joshua seemed to be doing alright. He was talking to the sheriff. Zac would leave it to Joshua.

***

Three days of pokey riding brought them to the edge of Tucson. The town, rapidly becoming a city, was huddled in the center of a huge flatland. The entire area was cactus strewn, but still showed a decent growth of grass. There were more cattle here than there had been further east and south. Scrawny, inbred looking, horned animals, but still cattle.

The high-country valley was ringed by mountains. Not large. Not like the Rockies, but mountains, none the less. Zac figured the higher elevation flat lands might be good cattle country, but he had no desire to ride up and look it over. He had become anxious to get home.

The flat-fronted adobe and brick buildings

hadn't taken on the appearance of most frontier towns. This was an old town, much older than the typical town in the newly settling west. The entire town held a distinctly Mexican flavor. There were few boardwalks and little interest in roofing over the ones that did exist. Rain was clearly a seldom-seen novelty. Snow would be unknown.

Zac and Joshua checked into a hotel, staying for two days. They rested and let the horses rest. All three animals were re-shod. Both men took in a stock of traveling supplies, and on the third morning they headed north. There were trails leading in many directions, mostly to mining sites, but the sheriff confirmed the directions received from the liveryman, so they saddled up and moved out at a good pace.

The travelers spent two days exploring and absorbing the Mogollon Rim country with its rocky terrain, its deep gorges, it's running stream and its pine forests.

Continuing north, they rode into high, flat country, a few pines dotted among the low growing cactus and the grass. Further north they entered the true pine forests. With the trees spread comfortably apart, there was ample grass for grazing. They started seeing more cattle. Better, more carefully bred animals.

Purely guessing at their location, Zac turned to the east. It wasn't long before they started to see Lazy-E cattle. Zac smiled at the sight and at the thought that they were nearing the home range of his old friend, Major Bartholomeus Gantry.

Without going into the details of the matter that brought the Major back into his life, Zac explained a bit to Joshua. He spoke with some enthusiasm, first because he would enjoy seeing the Major again and, secondly, it probably meant they had chosen the road that would take Zac back to territory he knew, and home.

A few miles further east they were spotted by two cowboys. Raising their hats as a peaceful greeting, Zac and Joshua rode slowly forward. The two cowboys split apart and rode closer, one on each side of Zac and Joshua. Zac turned his horse to keep the Henry within useful range of one rider. He left the other rider to Joshua.

The cowboy who seemed to have taken the lead pulled to a stop and hollered out, "Lazee range, boys. You got business here?"

Zac asked, "The Major at home?"

"You know the Major?"

"Sure as I know myself. Names Zac Trimbell. He was with a few of us on a rustling matter not too long ago."

"Heard of you. Come along. It's not far to the ranch."

Within an hour the two travelers were seated in the shade at the Lazy-E headquarters. The Major had greeting Zac with true warmth. Zac wasn't sure how it was all supposed work between a soldier and his old commanding officer but the Major scoffed at any distance between them.

Zac looked over the wide acreage surrounding the Lazee.

"Well, Major, you said two things about this ranch, back on the Wishart place, the A, they call it. You said it was a beautiful, well grassed spot. And you said it was a bit on the remote side. I'd say you were correct on both counts."

They spent a single night on the Lazee before heading further east. Along the way they called into the J-J Connected and the Lazy-A, receiving a welcome at both places.

Begging the need to get home, Zac didn't tarry at either ranch. He explained just enough to Joshua to satisfy the young man's questions.

Albuquerque followed a short day of riding from the Lazy-A. A quick, 'hello', with Pat, at the Albuquerque livery and they were riding towards the WO ranch. Walter and Anna brought them up to date on ranch matters and Claire's marriage to Leonard, and their return to the Lincoln County Ranch.

Three days later they rode into Las Vegas.

CHAPTER FORTY-ONE

Nancy and Consuela were the first to see the two men ride into town. The girls were hidden in the shade of the overhang in front of the hotel dining room. Neither of the men took note of their presence.

Zac turned his horse towards the sheriff's office. He dismounted and tied the animal off. Joshua followed his moves. Stamping their feet on the boardwalk to get the blood circulating after the hours in the saddle, made enough noise to bring Trig to the door.

"You keep making all that noise, stranger, and I'm going to have to arrest you."

"Could you trust him into my custody, officer?"

The men turned to see Nancy stepping up onto the boardwalk showing a big smile. Consuela was a step or two behind.

Everyone laughed and Trig grabbed Zac's hand in a friendly greeting. When Zac freed his hand, Nancy unabashedly gave him a hug, squeezing until Zac was distinctly uncomfortable. Consuela stepped up beside her husband and smiled at the goings-on. Joshua stood a couple of feet away, waiting for an introduction.

As Joshua was being introduced, Abe wandered over from his livery. That required another round of greetings and introductions.

Abe, always first, a lover of good horseflesh, pointed with his chin.

"I'm seein' many a mile on those animals. How be if I was to take and rub them down some. Maybe find a bit of liniment to soothe what ails them?"

Zac said, "Appreciate it. Maybe take a good look at those shoes too. We've covered some distance since they were hammered on. I'll be wanting to get out to the Wayward just as soon as we finish saying 'hello' so if you had the time perhaps you..."

He was interrupted by Abe.

"Figured as much. Leave it to me. You go for lunch and they'll be ready for you."

As Abe led all three animals off, Nancy asked, "Did you men have anything to eat since breakfast?"

Answering her own question, she said, "I'm betting not. I'm also betting you might have chewed on some jerky for breakfast, along with a sip of slough water. Of course, that will either make you strong or kill you.

"Well, come along. Consuela and I were just going for lunch at the café. Come and join us. Someone has to look after your welfare since you do such a questionable job of it yourselves."

It sounded like Nancy was including both men in her analysis. Joshua wondered how he had managed to get included in her assumptions.

Nancy's smile took in both men as she suggested,

"But first, you might want to use the sheriff's facilities to wash up a bit."

Zac decided his hunger overrode the concern about Nancy's demanding ways and her fetish about cleanliness. It wouldn't hurt to scrub off the worst of the trail leavings.

Together they walked across the road and entered the hotel dining room. Trig, not having any immediate law matters weighing him down, decided to join them.

It took only a minute or two to place their food orders with Emeline, who seemed to be working every time Zac entered the dining room. Nancy squirmed in impatience and anticipation as the orders were being taken and the coffee cups filled.

Emeline had no sooner taken a step away from the table when Nancy looked from Zac to Joshua and back again.

"So. You've been gone for weeks and you arrive home with this young stranger. I couldn't begin to guess where all you've been. So speak. I want to hear it all."

Trig pushed himself into the conversation before Zac could answer.

"I guess where you've been would be interesting to know but what I want to hear first is, is it ended?

"Got a wire from Tombstone telling of finding the men. Said they were all dead. But no details. I'm thinking you wouldn't be home if it wasn't wrapped up."

Zac hesitated so long that Nancy and Trig both, were starting to show their impatience. Finally, Joshua glanced at Zac.

Knowing how the matter was so deeply personal

and potentially hurtful to Zac, he asked, "Do you mind if I tell the shortened story, Zac?"

Zac simply nodded his agreement. With that, he stared off into the distance, behind Trig, not really seeing the café walls or ceiling, but seeing the face of his lovely wife and his smiling little girl, and knowing he had done all that he could do. He hadn't been the one to catch the men, but he was there at the end.

Perhaps Joshua was practiced at telling long tall tales around the campfires on the trapline, but with the matter of the hunted men, he shortened the story to the bare essentials. In the short telling he explained how he and Zac had met, and where he was from.

The table was silent when Joshua was finished, every eye was on Zac. What had been excitement at the idea of hearing about an adventure had turned into relief for Trig, already fitting firmly into the law keeper's role. He found a satisfaction in knowing an open file could now be closed.

For Nancy, she found her heart warmed at the thought that this man she admired so much might have finally realized the completion of such a bitter matter. She was without words. Her only real response was to gently place her hand on top of Zac's and offer him a small smile.

Consuela's only comment was, "You have ridden many miles. I'm happy you are home safely."

There was little chatter during the meal. When he was finished, Zac laid down his fork, pushed his plate forward just a bit, and stood. He set some coins on the table, reached for his hat, and looked at Nancy, who was also standing by this time.

"Nancy, I'd appreciate if you'd tell Moody I'd like some of his time. Best we talk out at the ranch. Tomorrow or the next day would be fine. Whatever suits his other responsibilities."

"I'll do that. I'll come with him too if that's alright."

"You're welcome any time, but I'll be wanting some alone time with Moody. You could perhaps talk Amado into showing you and Joshua some of the back country."

Nancy slowly started to understand. She smiled and nodded her acceptance.

Walking across the street towards the livery, Zac said, "Lots of room out at the Wayward, Joshua. You're welcome."

With no further words the two traveling men mounted the horses Abe had cared for and rode from town.

CHAPTER FORTY-TWO

Zac slept almost around the clock. He hadn't fully realized his fatigue until he had let down, after completing the big dinner set before him by Alejandra Gonzales. He took his seat on the big mohair, wing-back chair. There was no fire needed in the rock fireplace, on this warm evening. He leaned back, comfortable in the enveloping chair and placed his feet on the ammunition box that made its home there.

The need to sleep hit him with the exhalation of his first breath. With that realization of his exhaustion he sat up and looked over at Joshua.

"No sense me falling asleep here when what I should be doing is going to bed. You do as you like. Make yourself to home. I'll see you in the morning."

With that he was gone.

***

The hour hand on the big wind-up clock on his bedtable was nearing the six when Zac awoke. That was late for him. The light peeking through a slit between the shutters on his window brought him upright and fully awake, ashamed that the sun was up before him.

He pulled on some clothes and stepped into his boots. His hat hung from a wooden peg beside the kitchen door. No one ever wore a hat inside his house. That was a practice forced on the family by his manners-aware mother.

A trip outside, and a good wash-up on the back stoop, a futile try at combing his long hair, and he was ready for breakfast.

On his way through the kitchen he had walked past Alejandra Gonzales without speaking. Now, re-entering the house, he smelled the preparation of breakfast with appreciation.

"Good morning, Alejandra. I'm late. Sorry for holding up your morning. Have you seen our guest?"

"Mr. Joshua is at the barn with Amado. Amado, he milk the cow. Mr. Joshua went to the horses, I am thinking."

Zac poured himself a cup of coffee and took his customary seat at the table. Before long, the two men from the barn walked in, Amado carrying a pail of milk and Joshua entering with a smiling 'good morning'. They sat and joined him for breakfast.

***

At mid-morning Nancy and Moody rode into the yard. It was Moody's first visit to the Wayward.

Zac couldn't avoid a quick hug from Nancy

before he received a hearty handshake from Moody. Another handshake and a smiling welcome followed the introduction of Joshua. Zac then introduced Moody to Alejandra and Amado.

With the introductions complete, Zac led Moody into the shade of the ramada. Nancy and Joshua followed Amado to the corral, where he already had two saddled horses ready, with a third awaiting Nancy's rigging.

"These are good steady animals. We will let your horses rest while we ride the hills."

Alejandra cleaned up the kitchen and placed a fresh pot of coffee on the back of the stove to keep warm. She had already been told the men needed to talk. They wanted no interruptions.

Moody and Zac were soon alone.

Sitting on opposite sides of the table, in the big, wicker chairs, the two men studied each other. Moody knew Zac had a story to tell and Zac knew the time had come. But neither man was sure how to begin.

It might have been easier if Zac was facing a stranger. But he and Moody went back many years and knew a lot about each other. It was difficult to share intimate matters with someone so close.

Zac let the silence continue for a full minute before saying, "Thanks for coming. I knew you would want to know what happened and what my part in it might have been. To tell you that, and perhaps some of my thoughts, I believed it best to be here where no one will interrupt us. I also need to tell you what happened in Tombstone."

"You have a lovely place here, Zac. I can easily see why you like to be at home. I'm happy I had the chance to come.

"Nancy repeated what she had been told at lunch yesterday, so I have a brief understanding. If you want to fill in some gaps about your travels and meeting Joshua, I'd be pleased to hear them. If not, that's alright too."

Zac fidgeted some while he stirred up his courage. Facing battle with the Henry in his hand he was nearly fearless. Facing his old pastor friend with his ammunition being words; words and feelings, he was not sure where to start or where to end. But he started anyway.

"First, I guess I have to apologize for leaving town without telling you what was going on. I knew you would try to talk me into leaving it alone and I knew I couldn't do that. I asked Trig to fill you in on the wanted posters and the telegraph wires after I was gone. I hoped you could understand why I had it to do."

Zac gave Moody an opportunity to speak. Into the following silence he carried on with his story.

"You know that I eventually caught up to the men. I was too late to do anything myself though. They had been in El Paso but had left a couple of days before we got there. By that time, though, the sheriff had started the wires burning to Ranger headquarters and, eventually to the judge that sent the wire to Trig, in Las Vegas.

"Joshua and I, we traced them, stage stop to stage stop, all the way to Tombstone, always just a bit behind.

"It seems that as soon as they arrived at what they must have seen as a rip roaring, anything goes frontier town, they started right in bullying their way around the local populace. They got away with that for a day or two but then they went too far, and a few hard rock miners set out to teach them manners.

"One man was already dead when we arrived in Tombstone and the other two were in jail, badly beaten. In fact, one of those two died shortly after we got there.

"One thing Joshua didn't tell the group at lunch yesterday was that he put a stop to my going in to see the two men in the jail.

"Joshua is young and he's from a significantly different life, working traplines, living with Indians and having an Indian mother, and all that. But he's a very perceptive young man. Seems they might grow them up young in that life.

"I hadn't told him much at all about why I was on the hunt. Still, he somehow knew that seeing the faces of the murderers would not be helpful to me.

"I finally agreed. He went into the jail with the sheriff while I took a seat on the boardwalk.

"I don't hardly know how to tell you this, Moody, but all the long ride home I knew I would have to. You've earned an explanation, being patient with me and being my friend over a lot of years."

Zac spoke slowly, at times, choosing his words with care.

"I've sensed something deeply spiritual about my journey since the war, but I have been unable to sort it all out."

The two men sat silently while Zac confirmed in his own mind, what he wanted to say. Moody said nothing, giving way to Zac, as he prepared to tell his story.

Finally, nodding as if he had made a decision, Zac raised his eyes from the table and looked fully into Moody's face, as if seeking permission again to share his troubling story. He saw compassion and the confirmation of his needed friendship.

He leaned forward, placing his crossed arms on the tabletop, prepared to begin the tale.

***

"There's much to this story that I don't understand and some that still scares me.

"Moody, sitting in that chair, outside the Tombstone sheriff's office, with the murderers of my family less than fifty feet away, as quick as a flash, and with no will of my own, my mind started re-working all my worst nightmares. All the things I've been living with since the war, and since the murders. One scene leaped into prominence only to be pushed aside by another that was scrambling for first place. All tumbling through my mind in some weird random order, faster than a man can think, each one worse and more horrifying than the last.

"Then, it's like I was suddenly somewhere else. Somewhere in another world. Another sphere. I wouldn't have any idea what to call it. The chair I sat on was on a boardwalk in Tombstone. I don't know where I was.

"I hope to never experience anything like that, ever again. What I saw, and felt, terrified me. It still does.

"I'd been through incidents of that nature a number of times, visions, almost, that were similar, although nowhere near so clear, as if I was looking through a smoke-smeared window.

"But this one was different from the others. Greater, somehow. Clearer. Much more intense. This time it all seemed to go further, deeper."

Zac slowed his talk even more, hesitating just a bit a few times, with a voice, and a few hand gestures, that emphasized the deep meaning of his experience.

When Zac glanced back up at Moody, he realized that his friend was studying his hands. Zac glanced down and was shocked to see that his hands were now balled into iron hard fists, as if he were ready to do battle. The veins and muscles of his hands and forearms were bulging and pulsing, as the emotion of what he knew he had to share was tensing his entire body.

He took a shallow breath as he attempted to relax. In a quiet, questioning voice, as if still doubting what the pastor's reaction would be, he started into the heart of the story.

"It was like the chair was suspended over a hole in the earth, a void, an opening so black that there was no light at all. As if the hole sucked up all the surrounding light and let nothing back out. I can't tell you how large the hole was. It just was. That's all. And there was nothing else.

"I gripped the chair's arms with a desperate fear, knowing that if I just moved, even wiggled on the chair, I would fall into the pit myself.

"There was a great tugging on my spirit. As if there was a battle for my soul. But I was outside the battle, having no real part in it.

"Most people would scoff at this. But, Moody, as

sure as we're sitting here, I tell you the truth.

"I saw hell. Or at least a small portion of it. And I recognized the terror of it.

"I smelled it and felt it too. The brimstone. The burning sulfur, like it was back then, on the battlefield, with the cannon belching out burned gun powder along with their great iron balls. The foul smoke raking my nostrils. The clinging evil. I heard nothing at all. But the silence almost made it worse.

"If I stop and allow myself, I can see it and feel it and smell it, even now. Nothing in my wildest dreams can compare to that. None of my fears has ever approached the despair that entered my heart as I looked down into that bottomless pit.

"It was as if I was in some other way of counting time. Joshua only left me alone for a few minutes but in the vision, I was gone for hours. Ages.

"I didn't come back until Joshua spoke, and then touched my shoulder. And when I came back, I was exhausted, totally spent. The sting of brimstone was still in my nostrils. The smoke was still stinging my eyes. Grasping, evil, cloying fingers were trying to pull me back. But there were some other, more powerful hands holding me up.

"Again, with no thought or effort of mine, the boardwalk was back. People were again walking past. The horses were still at the rail. And Joshua and the sheriff were standing there looking at me.

"I'm not ashamed to tell you, Moody, I was terrified. I never want to experience anything like that again."

The telling alone, was beginning to exhaust Zac, as if he had been living the experience again.

***

The two men sat in companionable, wondering silence. Zac looked at the tabletop. Moody never took his eyes off his friend.

***

Moody knew he had to choose his words as carefully as he had ever chosen words. Zac, of course, was correct. There was no doubt that he had been through a deeply spiritual battle. Moody knew these battles were common. But few, if any, ever witnessed the conflict like Zac had. Generally, these battles raged in that other sphere that Zac had mentioned. The sphere that was spoken of in Scripture but that few, if any, ever saw or experienced.

The battle for mankind's souls was as old as humanity and as common as night and day, but almost never seen or witnessed.

Zac's struggle was not only years in the making, it had also been years reaching its peak. Now that a peak, a summit, of some sort had been attained, Zac needed a solid foundation on which to move forward.

As the man's pastor, what could he say? Did any of his theological studies prepare him for this. He knew they hadn't. Not directly, at least.

But still, no matter the challenge, and there was a wide variety of challenges that could be experienced, the answer was always the same; God is real. Unfortunately, so is the enemy of mankind.

***

Moody shifted in his chair and crossed his legs. Taking a deep breath, he started.

"Zac. In a way I envy you. You have seen and felt something of the eternal. As penetratingly awful as that was, and is, it should leave you with no doubt that there is a spiritual realm that is more real than this earthly domain.

"I think I can safely say that you would acknowledge the reality of the enemy of our souls. The fact that you were dragged that far down, and yet were pulled back, should be evidence enough that the supremacy and love of God is greater than the power of the evil one."

Zac lifted his eyes just a bit and said, "Your words have come close to haunting me these past years, Moody. Your question, 'is it still well with your soul'? Those words have entered my mind so many times I couldn't begin to count them.

"The vision and the brimstone didn't answer the question, except that it did confirm for me that I still have a soul. I guess that's something."

Moody chuckled just a bit.

"Oh, it confirms much more than that, my friend. Do you think God would fight for you unless it's true that you not only have a soul, but that your soul is much loved and worth fighting for?"

Zac took a moment to put an answer together. All he could think to say was, "I never thought about it like that."

***

Again, the silence was long. Feeling they may benefit from a short break, Moody stood.

"Apparently there's a pot of coffee on the stove. I'll get it."

***

With their mugs filled with the steaming brew, now getting stronger and a bit bitter, after sitting on the stove for so long, Moody spoke again. The break had given him time to think and to silently pray for answers.

"Isaac. Zac is a good enough name I suppose, but I will always think of you as my old friend Isaac.

"You have been through a long struggle. Years long. I'm only guessing here, but I have thought all these years that the war and the horror you came home to, affected you differently than it might have affected others.

"Some, of course would have given in to anger and revenge. Others would have gone into denial and tried to live a normal life, fooling only themselves, and too often crashing in the end. Some would have drunk themselves into the grave. Some would have turned from God in bitter defeat.

"But, although I know the questions run deep in your heart, you didn't quit. Not really, you didn't. You haven't shied away at the thought of God.

"I can't hope to know the full mind of God, Isaac, but I'm prepared to believe your experience in Tombstone could be the summit of your pain. If you will give full credit and thanks to God for keeping you from that pit, I feel safe in saying that He wants to heal you, heal your mind and your soul. Give you the peace that only He can give.

"I would never be so shallow as to brush

everything in this world off as being God's will. I've seen too much pain and hurt, and just plain evil for that. But I do believe this. I believe that God sees and knows.

"Every healed wound leaves a scar, Isaac. We expect too much if we believe we will somehow get through this life without some scars.

"To hope to get back to the freedom and innocence of youth is too much. That's not real life.

"But the mistake so many make is to concentrate on the scars. And that's not real life either. God probably won't heal all the scars, but He still offers a new, worthwhile life to those who love Him and trust Him.

"God is well aware of the hurts and heartaches of His people. He advises in Scripture that we should weep with those who weep. Why would we ever think that He does any less. God must hurt deeply when His people are hurt.

"Does God weep like we do? Well, Jesus did.

"You will never get over the hurts from losing your family, my friend. But you can surely have and enjoy a fresh start. I'm not implying that life will go back to what it was. There's been too much water under the bridge for that. But I believe you can have and enjoy peace. Know that you did your part in the war, and the horrors were out of your control. Know that you loved your family and they loved you in return."

Moody stopped and took a deep breath, along with a sip of coffee. Zac didn't seem to have anything to say.

"I've done a bit of reading, Isaac. I had trouble finding information, but I finally tracked down a book. A medical book. It appears that what happened to you in battle has been common through the ages and through all the old wars. Many of the ancient records hold tales of strange things impacting men's lives during and after battle. There have been several names for it over the years. Many medical people are now calling it 'soldier's heart'. A few are calling it 'battle fatigue'. But no matter what it's called, it appears to happen when a sensitive man has reached the limits of the horror his mind and soul can endure.

"The mind seems to protect itself in various ways. In your case, with the murders and the challenge to your faith, on top of the battle experiences, it clearly appears to have become a spiritual battle. Hopefully, the last major battle in this personal war of yours was fought on your behalf in Tombstone."

***

Zac seemed to have nothing to add, as more silent moments went past before Moody finally, carefully spoke again.

"Isaac, as your friend and your pastor, I believe it's time we got on our knees."

CHAPTER FORTY-THREE

Without waiting for lunch, Pastor Moody saddled up and rode home, with the promise from Zac that he would come to town soon.

Zac took a bit of the lunch prepared by Alejandra before putting some light trail supplies into a saddle bag and hanging two canteens from the horn. He tied a bedroll behind the saddle.

Walking to the Gonzales home, he said, "I'm going off for a day or two. I'd like if you would ask Amado and Joshua to escort Nancy back to town. And tell Joshua to make himself to home."

With that, he stepped into the saddle, rode around his adobe house, and disappeared into the scrub brush, cactus, and pine tree covered hills.

He desired time alone. Truly alone. With no one telling him he needed to eat, or bringing him coffee, interrupting his thinking or his praying. Moody had left him with much to think through. He couldn't do that without the silence of the hills.

Ten miles in back of his ranch he pulled up at the sheltered spot he had in mind. A trickle of water made the canteens unnecessary. But in the desert or even in this semi-desert, he took no chances.

He gathered broken branches, some pine bark and a couple of sun-dried pine knots for the small fire he would light later, in the cool of the evening. After carefully checking for snakes, he dropped his bedroll on top of a gathering of old needles and dead grass, about the softest bed he could hope to find in this rocky country. He lay his saddle close by, with the Henry near to hand. Although hoping not to need it, he kept his belt and holster snug around his waist, with the .44 Colt easy to grasp.

He turned the big cavalry horse loose. He was in the habit of staking out the animal when they were on the trail, but on the home ranch he wouldn't wander beyond a whistle's call.

He then took a long, careful look around the country. It was only a matter of a few steps for him to reach the crest of the low hill he was on. Even from that summit he could see no one, either close by or in the distance.

Convinced he was truly alone, and likely to stay that way, he sat on his bedroll, leaned his back against the pine trunk and reached into the saddle bag for the Bible he had been carrying for years. Bent from wear, a bit torn and water stained, with just a few pages coming loose, it was still his favorite book, although he had a couple of newer Bibles on the shelves at the ranch.

That was not to imply that he opened it very often. Still, over the years, he would have felt uncomfortable without having it near. Now, with the intent of fulfilling his promise to Moody and his more important promise to God, he wondered how much he would remember from the readings of his former years, even back into childhood. Memory is a tricky thing. Would his stand the test?

***

A much nearer memory was only a couple of hours old.

As Moody was readying for the ride back to town he had looked intently into Zac's troubled eyes.

"This is your redemption time, Isaac. Don't miss it."

***

Now, sitting under the pine, he opened the book randomly before laying it across his legs. Intent and serious, he thought, or perhaps it was a prayer, "Lord, it's been a while."

Zac sat silently with his eyes closed, weary to the bone with the struggles of the years. So much wanting it to end. How many times had he wished for the night visions to cease, to let him sleep and live in peace? The wishing probably wasn't really praying. Or, at least not, 'God, meet me or I die', kind of praying.

He remembered the thought from months before, while searching for rustled cattle, when the visions came upon him. "I wish I knew how to pray. To really pray."

Well, why not. Could he not pray? What was stopping him? Perhaps it was the fear of his prayers not being answered. That he was doomed to live this struggling life until the end. But did that even make sense?

Perhaps he was so wound up inside that he couldn't let go.

With his Bible open on his lap, and let the thoughts tumble through his mind, hoping God would speak to him, or at least bring him a peace that would offset the terror of the vision in Tombstone. He and Moody, on their knees, had made a start. Now it would be between Zac and God, alone.

After a few minutes, his thoughts, seemingly with no conscious efforts of his own, were becoming lighter, happier. His memories, of contented times. The first since he rode off to war.

Cautiously, he welcomed the change. A full letting go would perhaps follow later.

There would never be a single good thing about the devastation of war. Or his part in it. But he had somehow survived. That was surely something to be thankful for.

He realized that he was now remembering his wife as he had first known her. His lovely Maddy, with the pleasantly calm, radiantly happy face. Like it had been the day of their wedding. He hadn't dreamt of that Maddy for many a year.

Since his return to Carob his troubled mind couldn't seem to get past visualizing his beautiful Maddy, terrified, screaming, as she was pushed into the burning cabin. Nothing had brought him closer to breaking down over the years, than those terrified screams, which awoke him night after night, unless it was the thought of their little baby Minnie.

As much as he hated that image of the last moments of his wife's life, he literally curled up inside when his beautiful little girl was added to the picture. The image was horror upon horror.

Of course, he hadn't been there. He didn't really know. The imagery was a product of his own mind. There was no report from any onlooker. Perhaps that was not how it was at all.

But the cabin was burned and Maddy and Minnie were dead and buried. Those were the facts, no matter how it happened.

If he could somehow get past those mental images of Maddy, possibly he could spend the rest of his life gladly remembering her smile, and the glint in her eyes as they stood before the altar. And the love of his little girl, who was so young when he put on the uniform.

A very real sorrow came from the thought that he had so little time with his daughter, and that she wouldn't remember him. Did God have a plan to cover that? He could only hope so.

He continued silently sitting until he finally had the urge to lift the book.

Although he had read much as an adult, before the war, he somehow flashed back to his father reading at the big family table, with the kerosene lamp trembling and flickering as a bit of winter's wind slid past the cabin door. Although his mother and sister were clearing up the dishes, working from a pan of hot water sitting on the big cast iron stove, they knew to be as silent as possible. They were listening too.

His two brothers, sitting on the other side of the table would often lay their chins on their folded arms, intently watching their father, and listening to the old stories that he somehow made alive with suspense and interest.

His father was in the habit of turning the book to one of the boys, showing them the portion he was about to read, and inviting them to start the reading off, including chapter and verse.

When the dishes were dried and put away, he repeated the process with his daughter.

Psalm 33 was one of his father's best loved portions.

"It's a happy Psalm," he would say, "A victorious song to almighty God."

"Isaac, look at verse 20. You've read it before. What does it promise?"

In a quiet, hesitant voice, young Isaac would sound out the words, his finger sliding across the page as he read, ending up with, *"Our soul waiteth for the LORD: he is our help and our shield."*

Now, nearing three decades after those family times, Zac, sitting under the partial shelter of the scraggly pine, felt his heart open wide in memory and reflection.

"Oh, Pa, you tried so hard. You taught your family. You taught us how to live. You taught your sons to be men. You didn't deserve the treatment that ended your life. Still, I can't believe anything but that you went into eternity with those very words on your lips."

"Our soul waiteth for the LORD: he is our help and our shield."

After a time of thinking about his parents, Zac uncharacteristically chuckled a bit.

"But you always brought us back to Psalm 30, Pa. Why, we even tried singing a few times when you read *'Sing praises to the Lord'.*

"It's a wonder birds didn't fall from the sky when they heard us singing. Ma could sing a bit, but I doubt there was ever a Trimbell put on this earth that could carry a tune, although many of us tried. I still try, time to time. I expect the crows to join me with their off-tune cawing."

In his pleasure of remembering those evenings around the old kitchen table, he turned to Psalm 30. He read the entire Psalm and then read it again. On the third reading he was pulled up sharply at Verse 2.

"O LORD my God, I cried unto thee, and thou hast healed me".

A shudder went through him. A realization. A wonder.

As thankful as he was for the help of Phoebe and the others, good people all, faithful friends. As grateful as he was for his escape into alternating hard work and quiet times. As much as he had experienced some good days, he realized there were far more that were not so good. But all the time it was God he was missing.

Contrary to what the Psalm said, in his anger, his devastating hurts, his great loss, he had ridden off, searching for a new place, a new way. But although there were many new places, he had found no new way.

"O LORD my God, I cried unto thee, and thou hast healed me".

"Lord, I haven't cried out to you. Not in that way, I haven't. I've asked You 'why' ten thousand times, but there has been no answer. Maybe You allowed me to go through those hard times to bring me back to You. Back, in a different way. Perhaps a deeper way. A way with no more doubts attached. Perhaps I don't need to know why.

"If that's the case Lord, I'm crying out to You now. It's time enough, and more. I'm no longer crying out for my family or the soldiers I killed and others that I watched die, I'm calling out to you for myself."

Zac paused as he felt a trickle slowly form in his eye and gently roll down his cheek. Crying had never been something he did much of. But as he sat, with the book open on his lap, and his mind repeating, *"O LORD my God, I cried unto thee, and thou hast healed me"*, the trickle of tears became a flood. The flood brought on a heartbreaking cry, a sobbing, turning into a soul wrenching, renewing wailing, a release, sometimes silent, sometimes audible.

In a flash of time he wondered if it was possible that God would use his tears to wash his eyes, the eyes of his heart. So that he could see. Truly see.

He was no longer focused on his loss of family, as devastating and important as that was, he was now focused on his years-long separation from the God he had once loved so dearly. He wanted to come back. He needed to come home. Between sobs he whispered that to God.

Whether because of a touch from God or simply from some renewed strength within himself, he couldn't have said, but a glow of warmth and acceptance overtook him, flowed through him.

He continued to sit, sobbing, cleansing, hoping, praying.

Was this the combat-toughened cavalry soldier who survived battle after battle?

Was this the man who picked up after the war and led his friends west, fighting when there was fighting to be done, facing those who would oppose them, but still, always moving west?

Was this the man who had done battle for friends who were threatened by their adversaries? Was this the man who fought as if he didn't care?

Well, he didn't much care. Didn't much care if he lived or died. Had no real reason to care. Had nothing particular to live for. Only carried on day after day because that was how God had put the human form together – with an almost unquenchable, unconscious desire to survive, to keep on living.

Yes, this was the man. Yet really not the same man. Not quite the same man.

This was the broken, deeply hurt man who had again met God. The God who had promised, *"I will restore health to you, and your wounds I will heal, declares the Lord".*

Was God in the process of healing him, restoring his health,

as he had promised in this verse to heal the land of Israel?

And what about the other promise, *"He will wipe away every tear from their eyes".*

Was that promise for Zac too? For Isaac Trimbell, soldier, husband, father? Now a childless widower?

Could he really have the tears dried up, those shed and those still held within him? Could those tears be somehow wiped away?

What about the dreadful memories? The visions in the night?

He had so many questions. But perhaps it was

enough for now.

He would take his rest and pray for a peaceful night, alone here in the high-up hills.

As he thought about readying his small camp for a night's rest his mind flashed back to that old kitchen table again, and Psalm 30. How many times had he read, as a child, *"weeping may endure for a night, but joy cometh in the morning"*?

CHAPTER FORTY-FOUR

Zac rode back into the Wayward Ranch yard in late morning on the third day of his hilltop retreat. He rode directly to the small barn, dismounted, and led the big gelding into a stall. He was just unsaddling when Amado and Joshua hollered their hellos from the door.

He turned and nodded at them. As he lifted the saddle off to carry it to the tack room, he asked, "Did you get Nancy back to town safely?"

"No," Joshua said seriously, "We couldn't do that."

Zac was walking away so he didn't see the grin forming on the visitors' lips.

"And why couldn't you do that? Seems simple enough."

"Well, it's simple enough, when you just out and say it like that. But that doesn't account for the fact that the lady refused to go."

That got Zac's attention.

Still cradling the big saddle, balanced over his right shoulder, the bedroll obscuring a part of his face, he stopped and turned.

"What exactly does that mean?"

Joshua was now grinning from ear to ear. Amado wasn't exactly sure how to approach the subject, so he stayed quiet, leaving the discussion between these two *Americanos*.

"Well, she hasn't exactly said. But making a surmise, based on the evidence before us, I'd say she stayed on, thinking she could bring you some comfort in your declining years. Or perhaps even before that time comes upon you."

Zac had no idea what that meant or what to say in return, so he continued to the tack room. He emerged a minute later with his bedroll over his shoulder and the Henry hanging from his right hand.

Wordlessly, he took only a quick glance at the two grinning men as he left the barn and headed for the ranch house. Reaching the ramada, he carefully laid the Henry on the table and turned back towards the Gonzales house. Behind that little house, the former ranch bunk house, a rope was strung from two poles. He unrolled his bedroll, shook each blanket out carefully and flipped them over the rope. The canvas cover that he used for a ground sheet followed. He then brushed them as carefully as he could with his bare hands, removing as much desert debris as possible.

"Welcome home."

Zac turned his head at the voice he recognized as Nancy's, but he remained on the far side of the ground sheet.

"Good to be back. Good to have you here too, but it makes me wonder. Don't you have something in town that needs doing? I'm surprised you can escape the tight reign of responsibilities you've taken upon yourself in town."

Zac remained hidden behind the hanging ground sheet so Nancy couldn't see the look on his face. She had no way of judging the seriousness of his comment. But she had never let little things like that bother her. So she simply walked the remaining distance to the clothesline and began picking dry grass and desert burrs from the blankets. It was as if they were talking through the hanging blankets, neither having seen the other yet.

"I'm thinking you need to let me wash these up for you."

That brought Zac from the other side, peering around the ground sheet to where he could see Nancy.

"Now, why in the world would you want to do that? I've usually done for myself, except for what Alejandra has done since she arrived here."

"Oh, I could do lots of things for you. And no, to respond to your previous comment, I am not loaded down with responsibilities in town. Of course, you already knew that. I am what you might call a reluctant lady of leisure. Bored silly would be the other way of explaining my situation. Even sweating over a steaming laundry tub sounds exciting compared to my normal days.

"Of course, if we were to simply forget this old bedroll, there might be other things we could do. Like take a walk together or even carry a picnic lunch up to that little creek meadow you told me about. Who knows, we might find something worth talking about."

The silence from Zac's side of the hanging

blankets was profound. He wasn't at all sure he knew how to react to this outspoken woman.

He finally quit picking desert trash off the bedding and stepped again, to where the two could look face to face.

"That sounds a little ambitious for right now. I've been three days up yonder. Got some washing up to do. Perhaps you would settle for a lunch under the ramada for this one day."

"Lunch under the ramada sounds wonderful. You go and do whatever you have to do. I'll see Alejandra about putting some food together."

"Take your time. I'll need a few minutes."

***

Zac hung his saddlebags on the peg by the door and then built up the fire that was still left from the breakfast preparation. It would take too long to heat the water in the reservoir, so he put on a small pot of shaving water over the fire before going to his bedroom. A short while later, with a bundle of clean clothing wrapped in a towel he re-entered the kitchen. The water was not fully heated, but it would do for a fast shave.

Five minutes later, with just one small nick on his chin, which had mostly quit bleeding, he removed his riding boots and pulled on a pair of ankle-high moccasins for the walk to the creek.

It was generally understood on the Wayward, that when a towel or other clothing was hanging from the brush above the only deep pool on the small stream, someone was bathing. Of course, neither Joshua nor Nancy would know that, but he stripped off, waded into the three-foot-deep water, and hoped for the best.

**

Zac and Nancy were sitting together over lunch, each in a big wicker chair, and both feeling somewhat uneasy, wondering where this was all headed. Zac found that he was hungry after almost three days on the mountainside, making do with his own meager cooking efforts. He had always enjoyed Alejandra's cooking, but he tasted something a little different this time. Perhaps in the choice of spices. He spoke for the first time since taking his seat.

"Do I taste a touch of Nancy in here? I don't know what it is but it's good."

Nancy was pleased that he had noticed. With a smile she responded, "It's not easy to help Alejandra. The first time I ventured into the kitchen I thought she might take the broom to me. But after tasting a cup of my coffee, she kind of relaxed.

"I had the chance to explain to her that on the home ranch the crew ate with the family. Whatever women were there at the time, all shared in the cooking. It had to be good and it had to be plentiful. The men worked hard. The women did too. Everyone ate just as hard as they worked. We went through a fearful mound of stored potatoes, turnips, corn, and such, on top of the beef we killed and butchered ourselves.

"Of course, the smoke-house fire was never allowed to go out. The same small fire pit had embers smoldering in it for years, with the wonderful smell of burning desert wood curling around the hanging meat.

"We kept a dozen or so hogs on feed and butchered them ourselves. We didn't bother with a sow. It was easier, and less messy to buy a few eight-week-old weaners from a neighbor. We raised them on good feed and let them run loose in a fenced, grass pasture of their own.

"Without smoked and cured ham and bacon we couldn't have kept a crew.

"It was a lot of work, but kind of fun too. Especially when Sarah and I were growing up, and Mother was teaching us to cook. The ranch hands teased us unmercifully, and we loved it. Loved the attention. Of course, as we were breaking towards maturity sometimes the teasing changed into something more serious. With mother's guidance and Father's threats, we were able to keep it all under control.

"And then Moody rode over one day and caught Dad alone in the barn.

"I don't know if they talked about the weather or the passage of time or the price of beef. But they must have sooner or later got around to talking about Sarah.

"I have no idea what all was said but I do know that it wasn't long after that we had a wedding and one less cook to help with the work."

***

The noon lunch dragged on into midafternoon before Zac pushed the dregs of his last cup of coffee aside. They had somehow found enough to talk about while still avoiding the subject that was clearly on both their minds.

"We'd better get you back to town. I'll have Amado saddle your horse."

CHAPTER FORTY-FIVE

Within a week, Joshua was beginning to fidget. He had been to town a couple of times, mostly visiting with Trig at the sheriff's office or Abe, at the stables. But he spent most of his time on the Wayward.

He had been riding the grasslands and the deserts of the west for more months than his original plan had called for. And he still hadn't seen an ocean.

With fall not too far off and the heat of summer fading into cooler days and chilly nights, his mind went to his north-country home and its early winters.

During the warmer months Zac had used the table under the ramada almost exclusively for his meals. He and Joshua were sitting there when Zac brought up the travels of his young guest.

"Joshua, you're a good companion and welcome here for as long as you wish. Still, I remember your plans. You're not going to see any ocean from New Mexico. Do you have new plans now?"

"You're reading my mind. I've been thinking that winter comes early and stays late back home. the men will be looking to their traps and the women will be laying the winter's food supplies aside. The hunters will have brought in a moose or two and probably a couple of elk, by this time.

"Some of the meat is cut and preserved in brine, using big stoneware crocks or oak barrels.

"Of course, for generations, my people have dried meat and pounded it into pemmican, mixing it with fresh berries and herbs found in the forests. Of course, in the old days, we ate mostly buffalo. But, there's not many left. The few still alive are watched over by the People, to keep them alive, hoping to build up a small herd, over time.

"We'll freeze some meat too as soon as winter snows are on the ground."

The young man had a wistful look on his face.

"I'm enjoying all these travels, but I miss the family and the activity of the trading fort. So you're right. I need to be heading north again. But first, west. That is, if I'm ever going to see that ocean."

Zac didn't want to discourage Joshua, but he had to say something, so at least there would be no misunderstanding.

"That's a lot of miles of travel you're talking about. Are you sure you can do all that and still get home before winter?"

"I've asked myself that same question. In our culture, travelers are often gone for long periods. Even a year or two occasionally. The voyageurs' canoe trip west in the spring and back east, down the river and lake chain in the fall, on the York boats, took months. It's part of who we are.

"If I get held up along the way by the weather, I'll winter over somewhere and go home come spring.

"Anyway, I'm a bit of a jump ahead of you. I was in town yesterday. Trig and I got to talking about the same thing. He was asking about the north country. I'm afraid I cost the good folks of Las Vegas a couple of hours of their sheriff's time. I guess everyone likes to talk about their home and I'm no different.

"We went across the street for lunch and when we came out, a string of wagons was pulling in from the south. Santa Fe, I believe.

"Trig asked where they were heading to.

"Denver," a fella on a big, black horse hollered back.

"Have to find one more driver before we can pull out."

"Well," says Trig. "Here's your man."

"He points at me and the freight man looks me over like he might be buying a horse. I was tempted to lift my foot so's he could check it out or show him my teeth. Anyway. I've got a job driving freight to Denver. Where I'll go from there, I don't know. I'll figure that out later."

"When do you leave?"

"First light, tomorrow morning."

***

In the dimness of the pre-dawn, Joshua quietly closed the kitchen door behind him and headed to the barn to saddle his horse. He had no intention of waking the ranch. His goodbyes had been said the evening before.

Nearing the barn, where the outside lantern was casting its feeble glow, he could see two horses tied to the corral. One was his own, saddle and pack in place. The other was Zac's big cavalry gelding. He heard shuffling and light talk from the stable.

Stepping into the doorway, he saw Zac approaching with his saddle. Amado was walking beside him, assuring the rancher that he understood the day's orders.

When Zac looked up and saw Joshua in the lantern light he asked, "You had breakfast?"

"I came out the side door. Wasn't near the kitchen. Didn't want to wake the house."

"Well, turn yourself around and get back there. If you were to somehow escape the Wayward without Alejandra seeing to your welfare, she's be liable to give me a tongue lashing. Or saddle up herself and come after you.

"I'll just tie this rigging on and be right in. Amado will join us. I'll be riding to town with you. I've got some things to do there."

With a sturdy breakfast and the second set of goodbyes behind Joshua, he and Zac stepped into their saddles, and headed out the trail. Away from the dim light from the house and the slight shadowing from the barn lantern, the trail was coal black. There was no way to safely ride at more than a trot. Even then the men were trusting more to their horses than their own eyesight.

They arrived in town in time to hear the last of the grumbling, half asleep drovers threatening the team animals into their places. Dawn was just breaking. The store fronts were dimly visible. The only lights in town were in the hotel and the café, where the men had taken their breakfasts.

The trail boss, sitting high in his saddle, was

shouting last minute orders, as his confused horse was turning in circles, not sure what his rider was asking of him. The boss saw Joshua riding up and shouted, "Throw your gear on that wagon. That'll be yours for this trip. Your swamper has the harnessing done. Up to you to see it's done properly. That's your job from here on out. Run your riding animal in with the spares. The drover will care for him."

His horse turned another full circle while he hollered out to the crew, "Now let's get a move on. We've miles to cover."

Joshua checked the animals and the rigging before quickly approaching Zac for the last time.

With a firm handshake the two men silently said their goodbyes. All the necessary words had already been spoken. Joshua held Zac's hand just a bit longer than Zac was comfortable with, but finally he nodded, turned the hand loose and walked to the wagon. With an overhand wave from the trail boss and overriding shouts from the drivers, the teams dug in and the wagons headed north.

The remuda and the chuck wagon were well out in front, clear of the rising dust.

Joshua turned his head in time to see Trig join Zac. The two men stood there until the train turned east, and out onto the trail.

CHAPTER FORTY-SIX

Zac rode the three blocks to where Abraham Howells had his law office. Seeing no light in the windows, he rode back to the café. A quick glance into the small interior showed no sign of the lawyer. But the hotel dining room was just beginning to come to life. There he found the lawyer, seated with Francisco, a book open between the two of them.

The lawyer was pointing something out to the young man as he talked quietly, in an attempt to keep their discussion private.

Francisco was listening intently, his eyes following the moving finger, and then looking back up at the lawyer.

Lawyer Howells, with his back to Zac, didn't see him coming. Francisco smiled and said something to Howells, indicating with a point of his chin.

Abraham turned and looked over his shoulder. He closed the book and held his hand out to Zac.

"Morning, Zac. Come join us."

"You look pretty intense with your conversation. I don't want to disturb you."

"Lawyers are paid to look intense. That's how we justify out exorbitant fees."

"Well, you've got a good early start on those fees, this morning."

With everyone grinning and relaxed about the intrusion, Zac pulled a chair back and sat down beside Francisco.

Abraham slid the book out of the way and leaned his elbows on the table.

"We were just discussing a possible approach to the grant issue. We're nowhere near finished but we're making headway. Putting some pieces together if nothing else. Francisco had a productive visit in Santa Fe. He managed to locate three old timers who had some information. One had a hand-drawn map, signed by some military man. Of course, there are many grants and what holds true for one may not hold true for another, but it's a start. What's happening with you?"

Zac, essentially a private man, gave only the briefest rundown on his activities.

The lawyer and his protégé were served their breakfasts while Zac simply had coffee. Between bites of bacon and eggs, the lawyer explained some of the details of their enquiry and approach. Zac didn't understand all the legal jargon, but he listened carefully.

"So, what's next?"

"Next is a long ride for Francisco. He needs to ride north again to tell the others that they can feel confident about holding the land and that we are working hard to make it official. He also thought of one old man who lives off by himself, just him, his missus, and a bunch of goats. Francisco says he's older than the hills. He may have some information. Someone has to go and find out. That someone is Francisco."

Zac was troubled with the information.

"He can't ride up there alone. There's no way that would be safe. Amado will want to go with him, but we need to find a couple of others too. I can't go this time. There's too much happening here. But I'll try to find someone. You stay here, Francisco, until I get back. I'll ride to the ranch and have a talk with Amado and his mother."

***

Zac left the two at the dining room and rode to the little church. That was his real reason for riding to town.

It was still early. Zac found Moody at the breakfast table. Zac wasn't sure how much more coffee he could drink but he accepted one more cup. Sipping the coffee, he waited for Moody and Sarah to finish eating. When the plates were cleared from the table Moody looked at his friend and asked, "Do you want to go to the office in the church building or are you alright here?"

"We're fine right here. Won't hurt for Sarah to hear what I have to say."

Sarah had placed the dishes into the big pan of water heating on the stove. Moody looked from Zac to Sarah before saying, "Come sit back down, Sarah."

In silence the pastor and his wife waited for their friend to take the lead. It took a while, with Zac fidgeting and rolling his hat around in his hands.

Finally, he cleared his throat and looked at Moody.

"The thing is Moody. The problem is. Or was, at least. That I've become pretty independent over the years. I learned in the army that, even with the backing of the boys around me, getting my job done and looking to my own safety was up to me alone. Oh, we were a fighting unit, don't think we weren't. When we rode into battle, we were one, undivided fighting machine. But that fighting machine was made up of a whole bunch of individuals. And each of those individuals wished to survive, to live.

"Doing for myself has been a difficult habit to admit and face."

The pause of ten seconds seemed much longer.

"After you left the Wayward, I put some fixings together and rode into the hills by myself. I stayed the most of three days. I was as scared as I've ever been, not really knowing what to do or what to expect.

"I knew I had to somehow talk with God. And let Him talk with me. As you said to me, that was my time. I didn't want to miss it.

"I read my Bible. I started remembering happier days. I thought of Dad teaching me some of his favorite verses, especially in the Psalms. I even laughed at a couple of the memories.

"For the first time in years, I was able to picture Maddy herself, smiling and facing me at our wedding. I purposely blocked out the burning cabin and her screams of terror.

"I'm not sure I would tell this to anyone else. I cried. I don't think I've cried since I was a kid. But I couldn't stop. And then I didn't want to stop. I don't really know what it might mean to wash my soul of hurts and heartaches. You said something like that, Moody, although I don't remember your exact words.

"The thing is, I guess I could say it took almost six years. And then three days alone in the back country, for me to give up."

There was another pause.

"I don't know where those words came from just now. Give up. I haven't thought of it that way before. But maybe that's what it was. And what it took."

Zac filled the silence with another sip of coffee.

"You helped me to understand, Moody, that to hope for everything to completely go away, for life to be fresh and clean, like I always thought it would be, was unrealistic. Or for it to be as if the horrible things had never been. That wasn't going to happen.

"That's a part of what I gave up. It wasn't until the morning of the third day, after staring at the campfire most of the night, that I finally figured it out. And accepted it. That was like a burden lifted."

"I finally decided that, while what I have isn't perfect, and it sure wasn't the original plan, it isn't bad. It's enough."

There was wondering silence around the little table for a long time, with no one seemingly knowing what to say. Both Moody and Sarah understood that much more had happened on that hillside, but those details were for Zac alone.

Finally, Zac stood and lifted his hat from the chair beside him. Wordlessly, the other two stood as well.

Moody put his hand on Zac's shoulder and

smiled at him.

"You're going to be fine, Zac. It's like you crossed some kind of a threshold. A bridge. Now give it time for the Lord to work. He has His own timing, but when he's done, you'll find that He's thorough.

"My only piece of further advice is, when the old memories haunt you, don't suffer your bad days alone. Don't crawl back inside yourself. Our door is always open, and you have other friends. Don't be afraid to lean once in a while."

Sarah spoke for the first time.

"I don't know how much you will want to tell Nancy, but it might be good if you would tell her a bit anyway."

Zac figured there was a message hidden in Sarah's words, but he didn't pursue the thought.

CHAPTER FORTY-SEVEN

Back at the Wayward, Zac talked with Alejandra and Amado together. He explained why Francisco was riding north and that he wanted two or three tough, well-armed men to ride with him. He didn't mention Amado, but he knew the young man would have his own say.

"Another thing, Alejandra, I don't want you to be here on the Wayward by yourself. I can't always be here so I would like you to either move into town until Amado returns or find someone who will come here to be with you. Perhaps one of your family. A cousin, an aunt."

Alejandra was quick to answer.

"Amado, he will not be left behind. This I know. He will ride north with the others."

She looked at her son.

"Amado, you go now. This day still. You go find Martina. You know where she is. She is to come to this place. You tell her.

"Her two sons, Mario, he who is oldest. Damián, the youngest. You bring them. Their brother is needed with the sheep. These boys know the fight. They not be afraid. You go now."

Since that decision was taken out of Zac's hands he simply rose and walked to his own house.

***

Mid-morning the next day, Amado and two well-armed, tough, and determined young men rode into the yard. At first glance they could have been cowboys from any ranch in Texas or beyond. They dressed and wore their belt guns like any cow man might have. They had tossed their tradition, large, decorative sombreros in favor of the newer and popular, pressed felt, Stetson style hats.

They were accompanying a lady driving a squeaking and worn-out buggy. She might have been forty years old or she may have been fifty. It was impossible to tell.

The men stopped at the corral and loosened their cinches before taking the animals to water. The woman drove the buggy to the front of Alejandra's small adobe.

She stepped down and passed the reins of the buggy animal to Amado, who had come on the run.

The two women greeted each other with loud, happy voices, and hugs. Whereas Alejandra was tending towards plumpness, her five-foot stature hiding the strength of the woman, Martina was taller by several inches and slim. Her face and body held strong vestiges of the beauty of her youth. She looked equally competent as her sons. Her every movement announced that if her boys couldn't deal with the matter, she might saddle up and care for it herself.

Zac was close enough to hear their talk. But, as was usual, the Spanish came so fast, with the two women seeming to speak at the same time, that he was unable to make out more than a word or two. But the greeting was happy so that was good enough for him. The important thing was that Alejandra would no longer be alone. Zac would be free to do what must be done.

He wandered over to the corral. Introductions were made while hands were shaken, and sharp eyes scrutinized each other. Zac was pleased with Alejandra's choice of riding partners for Francisco and Amado. These looked like men who would tolerate no foolishness. Both spoke English enough to make themselves understood.

Mario, the oldest, tall, and slim, like his mother, stood with his carbine cradled in the crook of his arm, not laying it down, even on the home ranch. Around his waist he wore a belt with the loops stuffed with shells. The much-battered holster held a handgun of some sort. All Zac could see was the top of the badly worn wooden grips. Judging by the looks of the man, he needed no advice on weapons.

Damián, the younger brother was shorter and a bit heavier, but tough looking. He bore a deep scar across his chin. A fall from a horse? A knife fight? There was no telling and Zac wouldn't ask. Somehow, Damián had acquired newer weapons than his older brother carried. Again, Zac thought it would be a waste of time to offer suggestions about weapons.

Damián had a freshly rolled cigarette hanging from the corner of his lips. Zac was about to speak when Amado made it unnecessary.

"We will move from the barn, from the hay, for when the men wish to smoke the cigarette."

Zac merely nodded and turned away.

Considering these men, and others Zac had met, made him wonder about things again, as he had on the first ride north, when Marcus Patriquin was captured and hung, and the land re-claimed. Why had not these men gathered together to protect their land, their ranches and their families? A dozen men like this, working together would be able to stand off any encroaching rancher.

But there had been many times in history where good men, standing as individuals were pushed aside, where all of them together could have stood firmly. Perhaps it was the lack of a leader. Someone, it seemed, had to provide the gathering point, a place where a line was drawn, and the challenge laid down, or accepted.

And then there was the matter of culture. There was a wide gulf in understand or appreciating the other's way of life.

Consuela, who seemed to see more clearly than most, had talked of that: *"The Anglo never rests. He does not think of mañana. He does not plan for the fiesta. He does not know how to enjoy his life. What he wants is more. All the time more, without really enjoying what he already has."*

Perhaps there was danger in too much contentment.

Well, it was all out of Zac's hands and mostly too late anyway. The ranchers were threatening to take over the vast grass lands. It was only if the families stayed together until somehow the grants could be confirmed, that there was much hope for the original families.

That made Francisco's, and lawyer Abraham Howell's work important. Of course, there may be others working on the grants, as well, but Zac knew nothing of that.

***

It was later in the afternoon, when it was confirmed that the women were settled and doing fine, that Zac went to the men again. He found them sitting in the shade of the barn, chewing grass stems. He addressed them together.

"Men, if it suits you, we will ride to town in the morning. Francisco is ready to go. He waits for your coming. If you will care for your animals today and see to your personal needs, we will ride after breakfast."

There was a general murmur of acceptance and a couple of nodded heads, but no actual words spoken. He addressed Amado.

"Amado, when we get to town you take the men to the general store. Get what trail supplies you need. Put it on the ranch account."

"*Si*, Mr. Zac. We will be ready, and we will do as you say."

***

It was mid-morning the following day when Zac, crossing the street from the stable to the small café, heard his name shouted.

He had just bid the last farewell to the young

302 | REG QUIST

men who were riding north that morning. As he watched them push their mounts into a slow lope, his mind was torn. On the one hand he was perfectly content on the Wayward. Sometimes.

At other times he missed the types of adventures the men were riding on.

He almost missed the shout. With the men mounted and gone, he was preoccupied with thoughts of Nancy. What to tell her? Certainly not everything. And then, why tell her anything at all? Was she somehow important to his life? Well, was she? He had much to consider. But was he even close to considering such things? Was it not too soon? And was she the one? And was she even interested?

There were a few shoppers on the boardwalks and three men were visiting in front of the barber shop. Except for one rancher working on a broken wagon beside the livery stable, there was no traffic on the street. The town was quiet enough for the shout to be clearly heard.

"Zac. Zac Trimbell. I've come for you. And now I've got you. Turn around and take your medicine."

Several heads turned at the shout. People on the boardwalk stopped and stared. Zac slowed his walk and looked over his shoulder. The turn put the bright, morning sun fully into his face.

He saw three men standing, side by side in the street. Their faces were shadowed by their wide hat brims. But he could see enough to know the men were armed and appeared to be serious about whatever they were attempting. He stopped walking and, shifting his feet, turned towards the men. Only the shouting man had his Colt in his hand. The other men's weapons were still holstered.

"You talking to me?"

"That I am. You took money from me and now I've come for it. Come for your life too if you don't quickly come up with the cash. Can't abide you breathing the same air any longer. You need to be somewhere different. Like in a grave. I need to see the end of you. I've waited months for this chance and now I've got you."

The voice and the bit of face Zac could see confirmed the man's identity.

"Zaborski. You were in the Georgetown jail the last I heard of you. You and those others standing there with you. Don't rightly recall their names. I can't believe you were turned loose. I suspect some of your rustler friends might have broke you out."

"Naw. I'm innocent," Zaborski replied with a laugh. "Sheriff Billy, he apologized for the inconvenience, and let me go. Can't hold an innocent man. But I still want my money back."

"I believe none of that, Zaborski. And the money wasn't yours. It was rustler's money. It went back to the rancher you stole it from. I don't need your money. So now you've come here to be re-captured. Or perhaps to die. If you're foolish enough to start a gunfight on this street, you may get lead into me, but you'll get enough, and more, yourself."

Without seeming to really move, Zac had the Henry, still hanging at arm's length, tipped up and pointed at Zaborski.

***

"Stand down, all of you. Any shootings to be done this morning, I guess I'll be the one doing it. Stand down, I say."

The shout came from the boardwalk in front of the sheriff's office. Everyone glanced that way. Trig, with his shiny sheriff's badge pinned prominently to his shirt, was stepping quickly down the dusty street. He hadn't lifted a weapon yet.

"No one move. One of you men move it'll be the last move you ever make. Now stand still."

The men stood as if mesmerized, the audacious actions of the sheriff, walking against three guns, leaving them wondering.

The two men with Zaborski, clearly showing signs that being there, on that sunny Las Vegas street wasn't really to their liking, shuffled their feet, as if they might take out running.

Step by step they watched the sheriff approaching.

Zaborski shouted out, "I'll shoot you, Sheriff. I'll shoot you and Zac Trimbell both, you come any closer."

Trig stopped walking and grinned at the gunman. His fists resting on his hips.

"I don't think so. I don't think so at all. These other two cowards are out of it. You can see that clearly enough.

"You're alone, Zaborski. And you have no idea at all the damage Zac can do with that Henry. I ain't too much of a slouch with a Colt my own self.

"Of course, I have to own up to missing a shot once. Mind you, that was a while ago.

"Naw, you ain't doing any shooting on this sunny morning. Again, I say, stand down and lower that weapon."

Trig walked to the first gunman and lifted his Colt from the holster. He did the same with the other. He held eye contact with the men the entire time. Neither man spoke nor made any threatening moves.

"All right, you two."

He pointed with his left hand.

"You walk over there to the sheriff's office. You go and sit in a cell. Take which ever one suits you. I'll be along shortly to lock you in."

Strangely, the two men, after glancing at Zaborski and then at Zac and Trig, and then at the men lining the boardwalk, most of them armed, looked at each other and wordlessly made a decision. Turning to the sheriff's office they trudged, one after the other, towards the jail.

Someone on the boardwalk broke into loud laughter. The hilarity became general along the walkway. Zac thought he saw the would-be gunmen hunch their shoulders, as if they could feel the laughter.

Trig stepped up beside Zaborski. He still held the weapon in Zac's general direction but seemed to have forgotten that he had it.

Trig thrust out his hand.

"Turn that weapon around. Lay the butt on my hand. Carefully. Put it in my hand. Do it now."

His voice alone commanded respect.

Trig had stayed to the side of Zaborski. He had no intention of coming between the gunman and Zac.

Zaborski, scrambling for one last vestige of dignity, hesitated, tempted. The hesitation lasted no more than a few seconds. In weighing the choice between jail or a grave, very clearly, he decided that life was worth living.

Carefully and slowly he turned the weapon and lay it on Trig's hand.

"Good decision. Now, let's get you all locked up. I'll send off a couple of wires. Find out how is it that you come to be free."

Laughter again broke out while the two men made their way to the jail.

Abe walked to the jailhouse door, carefully watching the entire operation. Nestled in the crook of his arm was a Sharps Big .50. The weapon could take down a man in the next county, but Abe appeared to be perfectly at ease with it.

Trig noticed the big weapon as he was stepping up onto the boardwalk.

"A Sharps, Abe? I've seen you with a double 10 gauge. But a Sharps? You fire that thing off in town, you'll stampede every horse from here to wherever. Chickens will quit lay'n. Cows won't milk for a month. Liable to take the wall out of whatever building you hit. How many other weapons you got hid away?"

"Never you mind, young fella. You see me raise this Big .50 to my shooting eye you just get out of the way. This old piece of wood and iron could tell some tales, I want you to know. We've not always spent our time shoeing other folk's horses, young man. You try to remember that. Now, never you mind me. You just go lock up your prisoners. I'll stand by whilst you get 'er done."

Trig shook his head and grinned.

The whole matter in the street had lasted but a couple of minutes. Zac wasn't sure he had taken a breath the entire time.

After seeing Trig enter the jailhouse, with

Zaborski ahead of him, and with Abe watching over the operation, he relaxed and resumed his walk towards the café. He glanced up to see Nancy and Consuela. Nancy was just tucking her pistol back into the skirt pocket. He couldn't see if Consuela was armed or not.

He tipped his hat towards the ladies.

Consuela spoke quickly.

"My husband. He is very brave, no? But smart? I'm not so sure. Me? I would have shot those men and made them dead."

Zac felt it was best to leave the matter between Trig and this fiery wife of his.

"Well, I could use a coffee and a minute or two of quiet. Will you ladies join me?"

Wordlessly they turned towards the café and fell into step with Zac.

After a short visit with the ladies, Zac left them to their other activities. He had no intentions of speaking to Nancy in front of Consuela, or anyone else.

***

Zac walked across the street to the small jail. Trig had the men secured in two cells, with Zaborski in a cell by himself. But the sheriff wasn't there at the moment.

Abe had dragged a chair along the boardwalk and taken a seat where he could watch the inside of the jailhouse and still see his livery stable.

Zac wasn't sure if he had anything worth saying to Zaborski, but he had just the one question.

"I know you broke jail. Know it without anyone

telling me. That's the only way you could be here. I expect Trig's gone to send off a couple of wires, so we'll know the truth soon enough. But I have just one question. Did any harm come to Sheriff Broadly in your jail break?

Zaborski had nothing to say. At the question, he turned his head towards the back wall. One of the others volunteered.

"No, he wasn't there. Night man was tied up but not hurt."

"Thank you," responded Zac. "Dawkins is the name, is it not?"

The prisoner simply nodded, looking glum.

Stepping back into the sunshine, he met Trig returning from the telegraph office.

"Well, for a man who wasn't sure he wanted to be sheriff, you seem to have taken hold of the job well enough. Although I might say, that move of yours could have backfired if you were facing real gunmen.

"Those fellas are thieves. They're not really murderers. If the real thing comes along one of these days, you need to be cautious. Be ready to shoot. But, anyway, thanks for the help. It probably saved a lot of foolish hurt."

Trig, grinning as usual, responded, "Well, old buddy, I learned everything I know about bad guys from you."

Zac walked away silently thanking God that he hadn't been forced into using the Henry again.

CHAPTER FORTY-EIGHT

Zac lazed around the Wayward for a couple of days. He even took a siesta one afternoon. Although he really had nothing else to do, he still found the afternoon sleep to be a waste of time. It was doubtful if he would repeat it.

He finally saddled up and rode to town, intent on having some private time with Nancy. He shaved and took a soak in the creek before heading out.

He had been feeling quite well since his time with Moody, followed by the three days in the back country. No nightmares had bothered his sleep. He had seen no troubling visions, heard no pleading voices.

He wasn't foolish enough to believe he was totally healed. There was too much water under the bridge for that to be true. The hurts and trauma of war were too deep. He feared the memories would return from time to time, haunting him. But perhaps they wouldn't be so overpowering as they had been.

Now that he had found the strength and

determination to pray, he found further resolve to continue the practice. If God was truly offering him redemption, why be reluctant to receive it?

He had no clear idea what his future would look like. Did Nancy play a part in it? How would he decide that? How would she decide? Or had she already decided?

After a slow hour of riding, with his thoughts bouncing in every direction, he thought he had better make some kind of a decision. Las Vegas was coming into sight. He would soon be talking to the lady herself.

**

On his way to stable his horse, he rode past the jailhouse. Stationed outside, in two barrel backed chairs, looking for all the world like guards, were Consuela and Nancy.

He grinned as he pulled the animal to a halt in front of the ladies.

"I take it the town has hired you two to watch over the new sheriff."

Nancy smiled and responded, "Hired on for no pay, as Trig might express it. No, it's not like that. What you're looking at here is two women with little enough to take up their time. I was out for a walk and saw Consuela sitting here. She brought some lunch down for the sheriff. She looked lonely, so here I sit, comforting her in her distress."

Both women laughed, as if whatever the distress was, it wasn't too serious.

"What are you doing in town?"

Why was Zac, a grown and mature man, a

man of experience, nervous, and troubled by the question? He asked himself this even as he said, "I thought you and I might go for a short ride. That is, if Consuela can handle her own distress."

Consuela flashed a knowing look at the questioner.

"*Si.* I can be somewhere else."

As she strode across the road Nancy said, "My gelding is with Abe. I'll get him."

Swinging down and tying his ride to the rail. Zac said, "I'll do it. I want to talk to Abe for a minute anyway."

Within ten minutes the two were riding side by side towards the outskirts of town. Zac slid the Henry into the saddle scabbard, something he seldom did.

As they passed the small church, they saw a wagon pulled up at the side door. Curious, Nancy turned her gelding that way. Getting closer she could see both Moody and Sarah standing behind the wagon, examining something in the box. On the wagon seat was a young girl and an older girl, a pretty and well-dressed girl. Nancy knew immediately who they were. She turned to Zac.

"Abner Sallow and his daughter, Summer. The other girl is Toby Drummond's girl. GG ranch. Her name is Honey. She and Abner have become close the past couple of summers. She purchases all the garden produce for the GG, from Abner. One thing has led to another, as it so often does, and they've been spending a lot of time together. You know what I mean?"

Zac decided that was a question best left unanswered.

They rode close enough to peer down into the wagon box. Nancy greeted both girls by name.

Abner welcomed them with a smile and said, "Getting near the end of the season. Mostly root crops left now, but they're good this year. Carrots, beets, turnips, a few late potatoes. Lots of ear corn. Got some peppers but I've still got a lot to learn about the growing of them. Eggs and a few pounds of cheese. Butter if you need it.

"I'll have some smoked and cured side meat in a week or so. A few hams."

Nancy admired the work of the young gardener and turned to Zac.

"Do you need anything for the ranch, Zac?"

"Next time you're out that way, ask Alejandra show you her garden. If I was to bring anything back to the ranch, she'd be so insulted she may never get over it."

The riders hung around the wagon for just another couple of minutes before they said their goodbyes and pointed their animals south.

***

On a small grassy slope beside a slow-moving stream, they spread the ground sheet Zac had tied behind his saddle. The horses were turned loose. Neither would wander far from their owner.

Seated comfortably, Nancy cast a gentle eye at Zac, knowing just enough about his situation to be careful in her approach. And waiting for him to take the lead.

They were sitting in the full sunlight, but the fall day was slightly cool, with a few greyish clouds scattered across the blue.

Zac tossed a couple of pebbles at the water, not caring where they landed. He pulled a mature grass stem, studied the ripe seed pods on top, and stuck it in the corner of his mouth.

"I'm still studying on why, Nancy, but I've been feeling that I need to tell you some things. I enjoy your company. But I'm not sure if I'm courting you or just sitting by a stream on a sunny afternoon. I have no real idea if you welcome my presence or not. I'm sure you'll let me know by and by.

"I don't really know how I feel or what the future may hold. I'm not even sure what I want it to hold. I watched those men riding off north a few days ago and it was all I could do to keep myself from running for my horse and hollering for them to wait for me.

"Other days, I laze away the time on the Wayward, happy to be alone and hoping no one comes by. I'm sure people that study these things, if there are such people, would call me unstable. And at my age, that's not how it should be."

***

Needing to say something important but still thinking it through, Zac reached for another couple of pebbles. Nancy held her peace while Zac worked it out.

***

"Some days. No, most days, I'm more or less content. Happy with my own thoughts and my own company.

Other days, often when the weather closes in and I'm sitting by the fire hearing the pound of the rain on the ramada roof, I get lonesome. I didn't really understand, until I found myself in this position, that being alone and being lonesome are not the same thing.

"I don't really have much to do. I've thought of bringing in a herd of decent cattle. I have the land for it. And it would provide a continuing reason for getting up in the morning. Might keep me closer to home too.

"And I don't know where any of this talk is leading. Maybe it's not leading anywhere."

Nancy gently laid her hand on top of Zac's hand. She tipped her head so that she could look up into his face. She had admired his vitality ever since she met him. Now, looking into his strong face, studying his clear, blue eyes, she wondered, although she knew just a bit.

What had those eyes seen? What did that mind hold? What had those ears heard? As far as that goes, what had this hand done? This hand she was holding so gently.

She had some idea of the answers, for she had seen some things too. But not nearly as much as Zac.

"I believe, Zac, that there is much in my life that is similar to yours. I too, get lonely from time to time. I, too, have my memories. But I don't have the option of riding off. Sometimes I envy the men who can.

"Please understand and believe me when I tell you that Moody would never break a confidence. But much of your experience is public knowledge.

I know just a bit about your family and what happened. The horrors and bitterness of the war is common knowledge and, although I only saw it from a distance, I am not totally unknowing on that subject.

"I know you fight your memories. I don't have to be told that. Your silences and the remoteness you sink into from time to time make that plain. I fight my memories too, but probably in a different way from you.

"I guess the question is, Zac, should two people, no longer really young, and both a little bit broken inside, come together and share those struggles. Or are we better sharing them apart. Accepting our lives as they are? I'm not real sure."

***

A full three minutes of silence went past before Zac spoke again. Finally, he said what was really on his mind.

"Nancy, I'm not blind and I'm not totally unaware. You are a beautiful and desirable woman. I've tried to think this through since I first saw you on that train platform up in Pueblo. Is it fair to saddle someone like you with the troubles that seem to follow me? I don't have an answer for that question."

Nancy lifted her hand from Zac's hand and raised it to his cheek. With just a slight pressure she turned his head until they could look directly at each other.

"Perhaps that's not your decision to make, my good man. Perhaps that's a question that should be left to the woman who would be involved in the matter.

"In any case, it's also possible that you're overthinking the whole thing. Remember back. When you were courting Maddy. Did you think it all through or did you listen more to your heart? Did you need all the answers, or did you trust that you could sort out the future together, as it came to you?"

Zac's answer was silence.

Nancy waited just a few seconds before she continued.

"Zac. I have come to care much for you. But I confess that's my heart talking. My head knew all along that if we were to ever have this conversation, there were a couple of things I would have to tell you about."

When Zac still made no response, she continued.

"I'm not exactly who you probably think I am, Zac. It's true, I'm a Texas ranch girl. I know something of cattle and horses. I'm a good cook and a medium good housekeeper, although I would usually rather be outside with the stock.

"But I haven't spent all my time on the ranch. When the call came and the boys were signing up, I wanted to do something. Dad held me back, saying the whole thing wouldn't last long. The boys would be back home in no time. I'm sure they were saying the same up north.

"Well, of course, it didn't turn out that way. Finally, I defied the folks and left to help. To do something. I had no idea what that would be, but I was sure there must be something a strong ranch girl could do.

"It turned out that I was correct. I rode into a supply camp well behind the lines. An officer advised that I could make myself useful at the hospital not too far away.

"The whole idea of nursing is pretty new, but there were a few girls who had a little bit of training. Enough to sometimes help the doctors, although most doctors resented their presence.

"More acceptable to the doctors were the helper girls. We were sometimes called attendants. That is, we attended to the needs of the wounded men, after the doctors had done what they could. That's where I found myself fitting in. We changed bandages and made beds. We did mountains of laundry, although there were also women hired for that purpose.

"We served meals and fed men who couldn't feed themselves. We cleaned men who were so badly wounded that they couldn't clean themselves.

"The most difficult part of the job was watching men die. I've held too many men's hands who spent their last moments alone with me.

"I've heard them cry out in pain. I've listened as they called for their mothers or their fathers or their sweethearts. I've prayed with them. I've wept with them, and over them, as I closed their eyes for the last time.

"I've seen some things, Zac. And from time to time I also have a nightmare."

***

Zac nodded his head several times as if he was processing all the information Nancy had just shared. He finally showed her a small, lopsided smile.

"May I come courting you then?"

Nancy laughed out loud.

"You may not know it yet, but you've been courting me for the past hour. And I'm happy for that. I hope you won't change your mind after I tell you one more thing."

"Do you have to? If you can live with my past I for sure can live with yours."

It was Nancy's turn to nod her head.

"Yes. Well, I pray that will be true. But you must listen for just another short story. You see, as is common in life, a man meets a woman and the two are attracted to each other.

"I was very drawn to a young fellow that I spent a lot of time with as his wounds were healing. He had taken three shots. The wounds were horrible, disfiguring, but not life threatening. He was a gentle soul. He should not have been in uniform. He should have been a storekeeper or a bookkeeper or some such.

"As he was able to walk again, I spent hours helping him regain his strength. We walked together around and around the yard, one slow step after another until he was fully recovered. As soon as that happened, he was sent back into action. He didn't last three days. And that time he didn't need a doctor. I wept for him as for no other."

This time Zac reached for her hand.

"There's many stories like that. I relive them sometimes at night. I'm very sorry you had to experience that kind of hurt."

Nancy gripped his hand tightly as if she was afraid he might get away.

"That's not the whole of the story, Zac. And I've got to tell you the rest to be fair to you, and to myself.

"You see, Zac. It was not unusual for people to convince themselves they could be dead tomorrow. Grab today. That was the approach. I didn't really believe that but still, there were so many dying all around us. When Terry was ordered back to the front, well…

"I'm perhaps not quite the woman you think I am. Not quite the fair maiden…"

Zac gripped her hand so tightly she was afraid he might crush it. He spoke with his old authority, leaving no room for disagreement.

"Stop right there. I want to hear no more. What's past is past. Many things happened in that old war. I lay no unrealistic expectations on you. I've never given such things a moment's thought. Nor will I ever. It's done and ended. Leave it lay."

***

For some reason, unknown even to herself, Nancy rested her head against Zac's chest and wept. It was as if she had laid down a dreadful burden, a weight she had been carrying far too long. To have Zac accept her as she was, stilled the secret fears she had stored up inside herself.

It seemed perfectly natural for Zac to wrap his arms around her and hold her tight.

For just a flash of time, he thought how comforting it would have been over the years to have someone to hold. Or someone to hold him. He wondered if Nancy harbored the same thoughts.

***

An hour later they were in their saddles and slowly walking back towards town. Zac looked over at Nancy with a genuine smile.

"Am I truly courting you now?"

"Oh yes, you most certainly are."

"Well then, I'm real anxious to find out where all of this is taking us."

Nancy just smiled in return.

CHAPTER FORTY-NINE

Several weeks later, the sixteen-year-old kid who liked to hang around the livery stable rode, yelling and whooping, into the yard of the Wayward Ranch, his floppy hat brim pushed back by the rushing wind. Only the stampede string, held firmly beneath his chin, kept the cheap imitation Stetson from flying off. His eyes were distended in excitement. His horse was nearly collapsing with fatigue. With the last of his strained voice the kid started hollering for Zac.

Zac ran from the small stable with Amado close on his heels. The kid was working the reins callously in an attempt to pull the unreasoning animal to a halt. Both Zac and Amado rushed towards the chaotic scene, reaching out for something; a dangling rein, a bridle strap, anything to bring the horse under control. The badly abused beast shied from Zac and turned right into Amado's hands. The young man was lucky enough to grab a bridle strap with one hand. As the horse continued to run, he flung his other arm over the sweat-soaked neck and hung on. His feet were lifted completely off the ground, but he managed to pull the horse in a circle while speaking soothing words into its ear. Within a few seconds, Amado had the exhausted animal somewhat calmed down, although it still threatened to break out into a run at any time. The fatigued animal's chest was heaving, while he blew foam and mucus from mouth and nose.

Amado jerked the reins out of the kid's hands. As soon as Amado got ahold of the leathers, Zac rushed to the side of the weary horse. The gelding was still prancing in excitement when Zac reached up with one powerful fist and yanked the kid out of the saddle. He landed on the ground with a thump hard enough to force the wind from his lungs. Without mercy, Zac pulled him to his feet.

With a firm grip on the kid's small bicep, and with his anger nearing the boiling point, Zac shook the young man until his teeth were ready to rattle. As if he had lost all internal strength, the kid's head was flopping back and forth, out of control. He managed to squeeze out a few halting cries as the punishment proceeded.

The kid had been warned over and over what would happen if he ever ran an animal half to death again. At sixteen, he should have been old enough to do a man's work. He was certainly old enough to know something of horses. But all the warnings of the past hadn't been taken to heart.

Amado was walking the still excited horse in slow circles while he continued to stroke its neck and talk soothing words. He kept his eye on Zac's activities all the while.

Alejandra, Amado's mother, heard the kid's cries

even through the closed door of her little house. She ran out, fearing what she might find. There were many ways for a man to get hurt on a ranch and she always worried about both her son and Zac, their benefactor. She watched Zac for just a few seconds and then started shouting, "No. no. No more. *"Parada. Parada."*

Amado picked up his mother's alarm and ran to Zac, leaving the horse to its own resources.

Amado had great respect for Zac, his employer and protector, mingled with considerable fear. He had never gone against the man's wishes before. But now, driven on by his mother's cry, plus the screams of the kid, he ran to Zac. Catching Zac's arm, Amado cried out, "No, *Señor* Zac. It is enough. Stop, *Mi amigo."*

Zac attempted for just a moment, to pull free from Amado's hand but the young man was strong. Holding a firm grip, Amado again said, "It is enough. Enough for today, Mr. Zac."

Zac finally let go of the kid, allowing him to slump to the ground, rolling into a ball, his knees tucked under his chin. He didn't cry, although he had every reason to.

Seeing there was no need of her ministrations, Alejandra turned and retreated to the house.

Amado had gone back to the horse. Zac joined him. The animal was standing with his head hung low and with his front legs splayed in weariness. Zac lifted the fender and stirrup and released the girth. He gave the saddle a push and it plummeted onto the ground. Without looking at Amado, but watching every move the animal made, he said, "Drop everything else you were doing and care for this horse. Soak the saddle blanket and give the poor beast a good cooling wash after you let him drink. Just a bit. He can have more water later. Rub his legs down with liniment and keep an eye on him for the next couple of hours."

Zac walked back to where the culprit was now sitting up. He stared into the kid's fear-filled eyes with a look that made the boy shudder again and look at the ground.

This was not the first time the young man had run the legs off a horse. Zac had no mercy for anyone who would abuse any animal in such a way.

"Look at me."

There was a terrible force behind the demand.

Slowly the young man lifted his eyes. With trembling lips, he held the look, afraid of what this man might do if he looked away.

"Now, you obviously came with a message from town. I doubt it was worth killing a horse over. But now you'd best spill it."

The kid gulped and tried to find words that he could push through his dried-out throat. After a couple of false starts he haltingly said, "The bank. Down to town. Robbed. Banker shot. Still alive, last I heard. The sheriff. Mr. Trig. He's off chasing the robbers. Miss Nancy, she ran to the livery. Asked Abe if someone could come here. She's afraid for Mr. Trig. Thought you should know."

"Anything else?"

"No, sir. Except Abe, he thought you might want to know real soon."

"What's your name, kid?"

"Dean, sir."

"Alright, Dean, I appreciate getting the message,

but you've been warned before. To run a horse like that is just plain stupid and thoughtless. Cruel. You ever do that again I'll give you a real whopping. Not just a little warning like this here today.

"Now you sit in the shade for a while and then you walk back to town. Amado will keep the horse here. And every step you take on the walk back, you think about that poor beast and what you did to it. Do you understand?"

"I understand."

Zac doubted that he really understood but he walked away, saying no more.

CHAPTER FIFTY

The first time Zac's cavalry troop was ordered into the field on a moment's notice, the bugle woke him from a sound sleep. He leapt to his feet, shaking sleep from his foggy mind and within seconds had the saddle on his war horse. There was no time to roll his bed nor care for his kit. He rode into battle with all his supplies still lying where he had slept.

After the battle, when what was left of his troop returned to the previous bivouac area, he discovered that the fighting had raged over the ground he had slept on the night before. The cannon shot and hoof marks in the churned-up grass and mud hid any sign of his kit or bedroll.

There were shreds of bedding and smashed and broken canteens and camp supplies scattered everywhere. He took the incident as a lesson to be learned. From that day on, before settling in for the night, his belongings were gathered together and secured. He never again lost his kit.

Even on his own ranch, he had kept a pack ready to tie behind his saddle when speed was important.

Speed was important now.

Rushing to the tack room he picked up his big stockman's saddle and carried it to his cavalry gelding. He had never named the horse. When someone mentioned that fact recently, he had responded that it was a bit late to fuss over something the horse didn't seem to be worried about.

With the saddle snugged down, he returned to the tack room. Tied and laced neatly together was his field kit, packed and ready. Two oversized saddle bags held the necessities of camping life: coffee, a small cooking pot, matches, dried beans and a few other food items, including a can of preserved peaches and some jerky, which would seemingly last forever without spoiling. In a leather sack was a good supply of .44 ammunition that would fit both his Henry and his belt gun. Tied across the top of the bags rode a neatly packed bedroll, covered with an oiled canvas ground sheet. Inside the bedroll was a warm shirt and a few other items of clean clothing. Tied on the outside of the bedroll was his easily accessible rain slicker.

His spare canteen, which would be tied to the kit, was empty. He carried it, and the one he would hang from the saddle horn over to the pump. He took but a couple of minutes to fill the two containers and carry them back to his gelding. Together, all the provisions wouldn't make for high living, but the kit would mean food and a bit of comfort on a cold or wet night. In dire circumstances, it could mean life or death.

With the kit firmly tied in place, Zac led the gelding out of the barn. He never allowed anyone to sit a saddle inside the small building.

Amado followed him to the door. The kid was sitting on the ground in the shade beside the corral. He was hunched over, back to the stable wall, avoiding eye contact with anyone.

Amado said, "So you go to Mr. Trig? But you are to get married *mañana*."

Zac made a couple of final adjustments to the rigging and then stepped into the saddle.

"Yes. Well, it seems the wedding might be delayed for a day or two."

Amado crossed himself. With a sad and serious look on his face he studied this man who had earned his respect over the past couple of years. He and his mother had prayed that he would be freed from the call to further duty, and potential violence, but it seemed their prayer hadn't been answered.

"*Ir con Dios* Mr. Zac. Go with God. I pray for you and for Mr. Trig."

Zac nodded and touched his hat brim. "Take care of that horse. I've told the kid he has to walk back to town so's he'll have time to think. Don't you be letting him take a horse. Next time you're going in you could take the animal back to Abe. Otherwise just keep it here. I'm hoping to be back soon."

With that he turned to the town trail and kicked the gelding into a slow trot.

CHAPTER FIFTY-ONE

Zac rode directly to the sheriff's office. Pop Hennessey, the mayor of Las Vegas, New Mexico, was sitting in a chair on the boardwalk, holding a double barrel shotgun. Beside him were Consuela, Sheriff Trig's young wife, and Nancy, who had intended to become Mrs. Zac Trimbell the next day.

As he often did, Abe was standing close by, where he could keep an eye on both the sheriff's office and his own livery stable.

When Abe wasn't shoeing a horse or cleaning a stall, he was seldom seen without a weapon of some sort. He seemed to have a wide variety at his disposal, all secreted in his small office and living quarters at the front of the stable. In this instance he was cradling a Henry .44, nearly an exact match to Zac's, except it was a few years newer.

The look of relief on their faces told Zac that they had been waiting for him. Abe was the first to speak.

"The kid get out there alright?"

"He got there. Nearly killed your horse. Amado's seeing to the animal. The kid's walking back."

Abe knew there was more to the tale, but he decided to await another time.

Nancy got to her feet and stepped to Zac's side, reaching up to the saddle, laying her hand on his.

"Oh, Zac. I'm so sorry. I was so looking forward to becoming Mrs. Zac Trimbell tomorrow. I know you'll want to go after Trig, so we'll just have to have the ceremony when you get back. But you be sure to get back. You hear? Married men, or nearly married men, either one, shouldn't be taking risks. You go do what has to be done, but you keep your head down. And don't forget that there's a woman who loves you very much waiting for you."

Zac nodded in his usual way.

"I'll remember. And I'll be as careful as possible. We can hope that this will be the last such matter that will come my way."

Nancy hoped so too but, she had no confidence in that hope. Zac seemed to have a compelling drive to be where others needed help.

He looked over at Abe again and then to the mayor.

"What can you tell me? How many raided the bank? Did anyone recognize them? Which way did they go? Did Trig gather a posse?"

The mayor glanced at Abe. When the livery man didn't speak Pop Hennessey told what he knew.

"Seems there were three in the gang, although there may have been another standing lookout. Telegrapher, he says there was a stranger holding a rifle down past his office. Seemed to be sitting where he could study Main Street and a bit of the road out of town. Must have been on lookout. There was no more sign of the fella, after the raid.

"Anyway, there were for sure three at the bank. All masked. They grabbed the loot the teller shoved their way, about a thousand, by the teller's estimate. Then for some reason one of them turned to McLaren, the manager, and shot him. Stupid. No need for it. McLaren wasn't armed and was offering no threat.

"They ran outside and mounted their horses and were gone. Of course, that shot woke the town. Trig ran out of the office, but them thieves were riding off the other way, already out of range for a handgun. Seems they knew the roads around town. They were out of sight behind the buildings, in back of the bank, before anyone could get organized. Escaped without a shot being fired from the town."

Zac soaked in this information before asking again, "Which way did they go? Or did anyone see what happened once they reached the crossroads? And who rode with Trig?"

"He is alone, my Trig. No one know which way he go. He ask for no help. He take guns, get on horse and he gone."

Consuela had been stoically controlled up until that moment. She and Trig had been married for only a few months. She had obviously been silently thinking grim thoughts about her beloved husband. The beautiful young lady spoke excellent English until she got excited. When that happened the old speech and mannerisms from her native Spanish started showing through her school learning.

Nancy went back to sit beside Consuela. She took Consuela's hand in hers and held it, comforting the worried young bride. Nancy aimed a pleading look at Zac.

"It's already been several hours, Zac. I don't want you to go but I know you're going to. So, it would be best if you went quickly. Perhaps you can see some sign of running horses along the trail, to direct your path. We will be praying for you and Trig.

"You might tell Trig, when you find him, that banker McLaren said to just let it go. The thieves didn't get enough money to risk a life over. He was genuinely concerned when he heard of Trig running off like he did.

Doc says McLaren will recover just fine and there's was so little money lost.

"You go and find Trig and bring him back. His work is here in town, not running all over the territory."

With another nod, Zac turned the gelding, toed it into a trot and headed towards the crossroads.

There had been almost no other traffic since the holdup. The easily read signs in the thick dust of the road showed several horses running close together. They pointed south, headed towards Santa Fe. But that made no sense to Zac. Running to another populated area didn't seem reasonable. They might do that in a few days, but not right after the holdup. With the telegraph, one town would wire another town and a posse would be waiting for the fugitives when they arrived.

Zac was sure the bank robbers would find somewhere to lay low, hoping the searchers would give it up.

Between the two friends, Trig was the far better tracker. Zac would just have to do the best he could if the trail became dimmer. He rode along at an easy trot, watching for any changes in the hoof marks. Sure enough, in less than five miles the tracks turned off the Santa Fe trail, hard to the west, leaving the established road and heading into rougher, higher territory.

For the first half mile after leaving the road the horses had been kept at a run. There was little difference between the tracks on the Santa Fe road and the ones Zac was now following.

Soon the tracks showed that the riders had spread out. On the hard, gravelly desert floor the indentations were shallower. That was somewhat compensated for by the disturbed growth and the kicked aside pebbles. But that each man had begun picking his own trail through the cactus and scrub was a concern to Zac. He couldn't follow them all. He would have to choose. If he followed the wrong one, and the rider managed to elude him he would have wasted time, perhaps hours, in a fruitless search. Going back to pick up a new track would allow the thieves to gain even more distance.

In this mix of tracks and timing would be Trig's hoof marks. Trig would not miss so obvious a turn from the established road. Zac wondered where his friend was and how close he was following the fugitives. Almost at random, he chose a set of prints and followed them carefully, hoping not to lose them.

Zac finally slowed to a walk, following the tracks until they faded away on a rocky section. He had to dismount and lead the gelding slowly as he searched for evidence of the rider leaving the slab rock. He lost time but finally he spotted a low growing bit of brush, broken off at the ground and bent over, stepped on and pressed into the desert floor. The broken stem was white, showing no aging since the break. A careful study a few feet ahead of the broken stem showed a clear hoof mark. And then another. And another.

Zac remounted and followed. As much as he was not an expert tracker, the escaping thief was an even more inept at hiding his trail. Before long Zac was able to see more broken branches. Crushed leaves and shoe scrapes on flat rocks, led him on. The trail came and went, over the space of several miles.

The land was becoming rougher and steeper, as it sloped up to the higher country. Zac stopped and scanned the way forward. The rough country the tracks were pointed at was almost like a big bowl, perhaps a quarter mile wide at its opening, narrowing to just a few hundred yards at the back wall.

The bowl nestled into the rock walls that extended to both the left and right. The edges of the bowl were vertical rock cliffs.

Studying both sides, Zac was doubtful if a man could find foot holds enough to scale the rock. Certainly, no horse could be taken out that way. And no one in his right mind was going to abandon his riding animal in this country unless they had somehow managed to corral other mounts somewhere over that rim.

The rear wall of the rocky bowl was less steep than the sides but still no easy climb. At its base, the bowl appeared to dip down behind the irregular crest that was showing ahead. How far it dipped,

Zac could only guess. There had to be water in there somewhere. A seep, or perhaps ground water the tree roots were able to wind their way into. This was indicated by the presence of cottonwood trees and a couple of pines, hard against the back wall. Judging by the angle of growth formed by the branches, the bowl would be perhaps fifteen feet lower than the surrounding area. Maybe even twenty feet.

There was a good chance the thieves had chosen this place as a safe hideout until the search was called off. In any case, there had not been time enough to ride further on exhausted horses. The men had to be in that bowl somewhere. And Trig would be somewhere nearby.

Afraid of sky-lining himself, Zac stepped off the horse, preparing to walk from that point. He first pulled his Colt, checking the loads and looking for dust or twigs that might have found their way into the mechanism during the ride through the shrubbery. He then replaced it and slipped the leather loop over the hammer, holding the gun in place.

With the reins in one hand and his Henry in the other, he stepped forward. There was little chance of hiding the sound of steel shoes on rock, but the heavy growth prevented him from finding a rock-free passage. He kept to a slow, careful pace. Finally, the land opened up enough that Zac was able to lead the gelding off the bedrock and onto the hard-packed clay and gravel.

Noon had come and gone. It was now late afternoon. Zac had not bothered considering food, or even coffee, as much as he was a man who loved his coffee. He didn't really care about the bank thieves. But he cared very much about his friend, Trig. Food could wait.

He was now walking directly into the lowering sun. It wouldn't be long before the sun would dip below the back rim. Until that happened, he tipped his hat brim down for shade, but he still had to squint to protect his eyes in the brightness.

Ahead he could more clearly see the brush covered ridge. He no longer bothered looking for a trail. There was simply nowhere else the thieves could go. They had to be in that hollow. Did the ridge outline the hollow beyond? He couldn't tell.

He couldn't ride here without showing himself well above his surroundings. He would have to find a place to leave the horse. A quick search showed a small copse of bush. A couple of pinyon pine and a small tree he couldn't name had somehow found sustenance in the poor soil. He led the gelding to the shade of the trees, slipped the bridle off, replacing it with a halter and tying him with a light rope he carried for the purpose. There was no water, but the gelding would be able to nip off some of the hard, desert grass or perhaps browse a little on the bush.

Moving carefully ahead on foot, Zac thought he saw an opening off to the right. Easing himself as soundlessly as possible through the hard and brittle desert growth, he made his way to the opening. Again, he thought of Trig, who could move like a ghost while on a search.

A slow, careful half hour had him approaching the crest of what he was thinking must be the ridge around the hollow. After a cautious study of the ground, looking for snakes or other uninviting wildlife, he eased down to his knees. Wanting to keep the Henry pointed ahead and ready, he did a one hand, one elbow, crawl. It was slow but he didn't have far to go. As he reached the crest, he removed his hat and lay full out on his stomach, wiggling upwards until he could peer over the crest. The view was still marred by the growth, but he was able to confirm that there was no way out of the bowl, except the way the fugitives went in. Not that he could see, in any case.

Rising to his knees, while keeping his head below the crest of the surrounding growth, he studied the hollow. The growth prevented him from seeing much. He looked for Trig but there was no sign of the lawman. Finally, he spotted just a whiff of smoke at the base of the back wall. It was only slight, and difficult to see as it rose through the branches of a small cottonwood, but it was sure enough smoke. He guessed the bank robbers had let their desire for coffee overcome any fears they held. That would be an indication that they were unaware the sheriff was on their trail, or even anywhere near. There was no odor of cooking meat.

For a half hour Zac studied the bowl, looking for signs of movement and a path to the bottom. The only movement continued to be the greyish-white smoke that gently rose, waving in the slight breeze. He could see no easy or soundless way to approach the fire, or the men who must be hunkered around it. Clearly, the men had ridden down the south wall as they entered the area. He was closer to the north wall. If he could get over to their already broken path without being seen, perhaps he could follow it to the bottom.

Zac slid back a few feet, still lying on his stomach. He was about to roll over so he could sit up and put his hat back on to protect himself from the blazing, early fall sun, when a hand touched his shoulder. Zac nearly jumped out of his boots. He had heard no sound.

A voice whispered, "What are you doing here, Boss? You're supposed to be at home scrubbing behind your ears, getting yourself rigged out for a wedding."

Zac didn't need to turn around to know his friend was grinning from ear to ear.

Zac took a deep breath and exhaled it.

"You could get yourself shot sneaking up on someone like that."

"Not if they didn't know I was there."

"How did you know where I was?"

"Why, Boss, the noise you made clambering in here made me think the circus was come to town. Or maybe a brass band celebrating something or other. I watched you ride in. Watched you tie up the gelding. Followed your path to here. The top of every bush you crawled past was waving like a flag on the fourth of July. A blind man could have followed you."

Zac, knowing Trig was undoubtedly correct, made no further comment, except to ask, "You got a plan?"

Trig was slow in answering. Both men slid down the gentle slope, far enough to be able to sit up without exposing their heads above the brush cover.

CHAPTER FIFTY-TWO

The two men sat under the filtering shade of a large desert bush. Zac reached for his canteen. Trig followed his example. After they had each taken a liberal drink, swishing the water around in their mouths before swallowing, Trig laid out his plan.

"There's four of them. They separated back a few miles but came together right before they rode into the hollow. It's pretty clear they had this spot pegged out. They wouldn't ride all this way without they knew where they were going.

"They bunched up and rode together down the south wall. Left a trail a child could follow. Now they've boxed themselves in. I'm guessing these ain't the smartest cookies you're ever apt to meet.

"Don't look like they're going anywhere this night. I can smell coffee but no food. Must be making do with cold jerky, or some such. I have no idea what they have in mind. There's just nowhere at all to go from that hollow except back up here. I've studied every inch of those walls with my army glass. There ain't no way out except up and

340 | REG QUIST

over. That don't hardly seem likely. I figure they're hoping any chase will have moved on towards Santa Fe by this time and they'll be safe to ride out in the morning.

"I figure to disappoint them. Just haven't quite decided if I should do it now or wait till morning."

The two men sat looking at each other. Before Trig had accepted the sheriff's job a few months before, Trig had always stepped back, leaving Zac as the unquestioned leader when the two men were together. No matter where they went, or with whom, the lead duty always gravitated towards Zac. Now, without saying so, Trig was hoping to gain from Zac's wisdom on the matter before them.

Zac offered, "Long night. We could take turns sleeping and watching. But what if they decide to pull out in the dark of midnight and we're sleeping far from the trail they choose? Might be, they could slip past us or force us into another running chase."

Again, both men sat silently while Trig considered Zac's words. And then Zac remembered what Pop Hennessey had said.

"McLaren's shot up a bit but he's going to pull through. He sent a message for you. Said there isn't much money involved. To just let it go. Not worth risking your life over a few dollars."

Trig studied Zac, trying for his unspoked opinion. He finally made up his own mind.

"You know, my old daddy, back east, back in the piney woods, he mentioned something like that a time or two. Something about a man putting his hand to the plow and then looking back, not being fit for service. Seems to me he heard that somewhere.

"Now, I'm new to this job, Boss. Still got a lot to learn. But I've taken on the job and taken the town's wages. I figure I've got it to do.

"You mind advising me on how big a crime has to be before the law takes notice? Just a few dollars stolen is alright? A thousand stolen? Two thousand? Ten thousand? Where's the limit that divides mischief from a real crime. I maybe should have cleared that up before I took the job.

"What about a shooting? One shooting okay? What about two or three shootings? Or do I only do my job if someone dies? Or is it all just boys will be boys? Can you tell me how that all works?"

Zac studied the younger man, liking what he saw. He didn't figure Trig really need an answer to his questions.

"So, what's your plan?"

"Beyond thinking I'd like to have those fellas disarmed, tied securely and pulled tight to a cactus for the night, I'm not exactly sure. Oh, I know what I plan to do. I'm just not exactly sure on the timing.

"Taking them just before dawn makes some sense. But the two of us and our horses ain't going to get into that camp without we make more than enough noise to waken our quarry. Not if we go in fast, is what I mean to say. That will almost for sure result in more shooting than I'm comfortable with. I'd kind of like to avoid that.

"You might remember that I was shot that one time. Over south and west of here. Can't say as I really enjoyed that experience."

Zac figured he could make a suggestion without stomping on his friend's toes.

"I always pack a few lengths of light rope along. I

could go back to my kit and get it. If I was to make my way as quietly as possible down one side and you did the same on the other, we might get into the camp before any of them could see us. Even if they hear the noise, they won't be able to see us clearly. When we're both in position I can draw their attention. While they're taking cover, looking towards me, you can get the drop on them from the other side. With any luck at all there should be no need to draw blood."

Trig seemed to be considering this. Grinning, knowing exactly what Zac had in mind by 'drawing their attention', he asked, "When did you figure to do this?"

"Well, the sun's dropped behind the ridge. It's not nearly so light as it was a half hour ago. Anything stopping you from being ready just as soon I get that rope?"

"Nope. I'll make my way back to the other side and start down. You stay close to that shaded wall over here and keep low. There's a pretty good chance they won't see you. As to hearing you, well…"

Zac was familiar with Trig's habit of covering his words with a grin. He was grinning now.

***

Trig waited while Zac went for the rope. He returned within ten minutes. Handing the rope to Trig he said, "You keep this with you. I'll try to hold those boys still while you secure them. You'll need to cut that rope up some. Don't worry about it. It's easily replaced."

With that short message Zac eased off to the

right, working his way towards the rock wall.

Trig disappeared. He was there and then he wasn't. Zac, looking back, shook his head in wonder, and started for the north wall.

Along the wall where Zac was crouching, he saw a few larger trees. Bushy, but not tall. They hadn't been visible from his previous position. They would make his crawl much easier, hiding his movements. The darkening sky was also in his favor, but he would have to move quickly to avoid finding himself in full dark. As he got closer, he could hear the men talking, although he couldn't make out the words. He could tell by the tone of a couple of the voices that there was disagreement in the camp. He wondered what that was all about.

Four horses were staked out on Trig's side of the hollow. The young sheriff might be able to slide into position without disturbing the animals. Zac was pretty sure he wouldn't have been able to.

Fifteen minutes of careful crawling and crouch-walking took Zac right to the edge of the camp. He figured Trig would have gotten there by that time and would be waiting. Three of the four thieves were looking into the fire. They would see very little for the first few seconds after turning away. The fourth man was facing Trig's side of the hollow. Zac figured the situation was as good as he could have hoped for.

Easing to the left, away from the rock wall, so Trig would not be in his line of fire, Zac knew his position was as good as it was ever going to be. He stood up and leveled the Henry at the men. Squeezing the trigger from a waist-high position, he put his first shot into the fire, knocking the coffee pot into the lap of one of the seated thieves. The man screamed in surprise and pain from the scalding coffee.

After years of practice shooting from that position, Zac seldom missed. He could shoot one handed off his gelding almost as well as he could standing firmly on the ground. He did love his Henry. That first shot and the scattered ash and fire brands had the men diving for cover. But the only cover was desert shrubbery, which did a poor job of hiding them. The trees growing along the wall were too slender to provide much help.

Altering his aim from the campfire to the rock wall above the men's heads, down to the rough ground within a few inches of a man's face, and then back to the rock wall, Zac laid on shot after shot. Fragments flew off the rock wall. Pebbles and dirt shot up from the ground. The almost continuous roar of gunfire terrified the thieves. With .44 shells seeming to land everywhere they turned, they finally huddled on the ground. Two of the men were holding their arms wrapped around their heads. The gunfire continued until Zac had squeezed the trigger a dozen times. That still left him a couple of available shots in the Henry, in case the men somehow found a way to fight back. He also had his revolver.

The men had received some cuts and scrapes from the rock and pebble ricochets, but Zac had shot no one.

The horses were plunging and tossing their heads in fear. Two of them had pulled their picket pins and run off into the brush, dragging the rope and pins behind them. Zac figured it wouldn't be long before they would be tangled around something. There was little danger of losing them.

Into the echoing quiet following the shooting, Trig stepped up to the men. He had not bothered pulling his own Colt. His carbine was back at the top of the slight grade, leaning on a bush. He wasn't as handy with the carbine as Zac was with his. The coil of rope was held loosely from his left hand, his right hand free to do some shooting if that became necessary.

"Alright, men. Turn on your stomachs and lie still. Stretch your arms out in front of you. Any other moves will be your last."

The men, apparently content to have survived the onslaught of lead and stone chips, complied.

Zac stepped close enough to see the camp clearly. Trig went from man to man, lifting their belt guns and tossing them aside, into a small pile. Knives and any other weapons he found, followed the guns.

"Put your hands behind you."

The thieves, already sure what was going to happen, obeyed.

It was a matter of only a couple of minutes until the men were securely tied.

"Alright, you sweethearts, turn over and sit up."

Trig had studied the available trees and picked out the most likely ones for tying the men overnight. He walked up and kicked one man on the bottom of his boot.

"Alright, you first. Back yourself up to that pine and sit there. Kick off your boots."

The thief objected loudly to taking off his boots but finally he kicked one toe into the ankle of the other boot and slid it off. The second boot followed. Trig untied the thief's hands and retied them behind the tree. The man looked hatred at him the entire time.

Within a quarter hour, all four men were secured to trees, with their boots off.

Zac had gone for the horses. When he returned, he watered his own and Trig's before staking them out.

Zac had started noticing the signs of water as he was crouched down on the north wall. For several feet out from the wall, the desert growth, and the small trees, were showing signs of adequate ground water. Now, at the bottom he could see the small seep and the pool it ran into. The pool didn't look natural. Someone, sometime in the past had dug it out. The seep and the collected water would keep a small camp like this one going for a good amount of time.

Trig emptied the ammunition from all the weapons, including the thieves' saddle guns, and dumped it into one of his own saddlebags. He then made a pile of the guns and knives.

Zac built up the fire and put his own coffee pot on. He and Trig would make do with some jerky and dried crackers for their evening meal. But they definitely wanted coffee.

As Zac had predicted, it was a long night. The crooks sagged against their bindings, unable to find any comfort. Trig finally tired of their complaining. With a warning of the dire consequences of any more moaning or whining, the men settled in. They probably didn't sleep but at least they were quiet.

Zac and Trig took turns sleeping and guarding.

When the faintest notion of dawn finally began pushing the darkness away, replacing it with a hazy light, Zac tapped Trig's boot with the barrel of the Henry. Trig opened his eyes immediately.

"Coffee's ready. You get yourself one and then I'll put out the fire."

The four stiff and uncomfortable thieves looked on hopefully. Finally, one dared to ask, "What about us?"

Trig looked at him with no sympathy at all.

"Yes. What about you? You remember this night and the hundreds more nights you're going to spend behind bars. and the hungry and thirsty ride you're about to make. That'll give you time enough to examine your way of life, and all the trouble you put me through."

Zac led the horses, one at a time, to water. Trig then threw the saddles on, with each man advising which saddle went on which horse. Trig shoved the empty carbines into the scabbards. There was no other way to carry them.

The men were untied, one by one, allowed to care for their morning needs, scoop up a mouthful of water from the seep and were then tied to their saddles.

By late afternoon that same day, the six tired, hungry, and thirsty men rode slowly into Las Vegas. A shout from someone sitting on the boardwalk drew a large crowd of gawkers from the stores and saloons. A couple of kids ran beside the horses, whooping and hollering. One boy picked up a dry horse apple and threw it at one of the thieves. A hard look and a pointed finger from Trig prevented a repeat of that action.

Mayor Hennessey and Abe were holding down the chairs on the boardwalk in front of the sheriff's office when the group pulled up to the hitchrail.

"You been here ever since I left?"

Pop Hennessey laughed.

"Not quite, Sheriff. We've been taking turns though. Us and a couple of others. I see you bagged your quarry."

Trig turned to look at the droop-headed men tied to their saddle horns.

"Found the thieves. Found the money."

He stiffly stepped down from the saddle, stretching the kinks out of his body.

Zac stepped down slowly and carefully. His old hip injury was blazing up a storm of misery. Hours in the saddle, followed by a night on the desert floor, followed by more hours in the saddle, were more than a man with a poorly healed wound could expect to call enjoyable.

The hip had been bothering him in recent weeks. He figured the ride to El Paso might have been more than what was good for him.

***

With the thieves in jail and fed, and with Abe caring for the horses, Trig went home to bed. Zac borrowed a fresh horse from Abe and set out for the Wayward Ranch. First though, he rode past the church to talk with his friend, Pastor Moody.

Moody saw him coming and opened the door.

"You still in one piece?"

"Seems like it."

"Too tired and out of sorts to enjoy a wedding

this evening though, I'm guessing."

"I wasn't aware I was supposed to enjoy it."

"Well, perhaps it's just the ladies who enjoy it."

"Nancy here?"

A new voice, coming from the adjacent room, broke into this conversation of comments and half asked questions.

"I'm here. And I'm ever so happy to see you. I don't see any visible wounds or blood so would I be correct to guess that it went well?"

"No chase or arrest really goes well, but this one went as well as most. No injuries. No deaths. Just awful tired. I'm heading to the ranch. I only wanted to let you know that I'm back. I'm sorry about the wedding plans."

"It's alright. Sometimes things happen. I wouldn't want to make a habit of things like this though. Anyway, you go home, get some sleep and be back in here by noon tomorrow. I haven't asked Moody yet but I'm pretty sure he would have no objection to holding a Sunday afternoon wedding. But it would all be kind of pointless if you weren't here and taking part."

Zac thought the conversation was on a downhill slide. He was too tired and hungry for it. He nodded his head, tipped his hat, and rode to the chili house. He was only a few minutes putting away a big bowl of chili, along with four slices of still warm, homemade bread slathered with butter, washed down with coffee. A one-hour ride took him home. He turned the horse over to Amado, brushed off any talk, and headed to bed.

As he walked to the house he thought, 'no deaths and no injuries or blood spilled'.

There would be no serious challenges to his storehouse of nightmares.

CHAPTER FIFTY-THREE

Sunday morning Zac slept a bit past his usual time, but he was still out of bed while the sun was just pushing aside the dark of night. He had started attending church the past few weeks, but he would let that go for this one day.

Wrapping himself in a blanket and grabbing up a towel, he slipped into a pair of low moccasins and headed for the bathing hole. The air was cold. The water would be colder. But he had been cold before.

In any case, heating water enough on the kitchen stove for a bath was seeming like a lot of wasted time and work, when the creek delivered an endless supply of water.

When he returned to the house a half hour later, Alejandra was there, making breakfast. She watched him walk through the door with his hair still wet and dripping. He was shivering with cold.

"It is cold this morning. Maybe you crazy, you go to creek. Get sick from cold."

"You just could be right on that."

He offered no more response as he passed

through the big kitchen on his way to get dressed.

After drying off and dressing he returned to the kitchen. He took down the wash pan, dipped hot water from the stove reservoir and lathered up for a shave. Alejandra placed a cup of hot coffee within reach for him. With the shave completing his personal preparation for the day, dressed in the best suit he owned, he wiped his boots with a wet cloth, and sat down for breakfast. He skipped his usual trip to the barn and corral, leaving the day's small amount of work to Amado, who had just returned a few days earlier from his trip back north, back to the old homelands.

Alejandra placed his loaded plate before him and refilled the coffee cup.

"You all cleaned up. You go back to town?"

"Yes. Nancy talked Moody into doing the honors for the wedding this afternoon. I would like it if you and Amado would drive in."

"We come."

After a few moments of silence Alejandra turned from the stove and looked pleadingly at Zac.

"Nancy come to ranch now. You want Amado and me to go away?"

Zac was taken back by the question. Such a thing had never crossed his mind.

"Why would you think that?"

"This be Nancy's house after wedding. Nancy's job to cook for her husband."

"You have known for weeks that we were to be married. If you were worried, why did you not talk to me before?"

Alejandra noisily drew a pot from among the dishes and cutlery in the soapy wash water, poured some rinse water over it and set it down on the warm stove top to dry. Looking on, Zac thought the woman might be close to tears. He wasn't sure what to say that would assure her of her position on the Wayward Ranch. In her culture there was little room for a wife who didn't provide for her man. A second woman in the kitchen could be a problem. Of course, Alejandra had her own kitchen in the old bunk house but she had always preferred the bigger facilities in the main house.

As Zac was sorting this out in his mind, the door opened and Amado came in, setting a pail of freshly drawn milk on the counter. He was ready for his breakfast. He began telling Zac about the morning's work with the horses, as he was washing his hands, when he sensed that something more than cooking and dishwashing was happening in the kitchen. He stopped talking and studied his mother, then turned to Zac with an unasked question on his lips.

When Zac offered no information, he turned back towards his mother, asking, *"¿Qué pasa?"* "What is wrong?"

With that, serious tears started streaming down the woman's face. Feeling helpless, Amado turned again to Zac.

Zac, embarrassed by the tears and feeling a bit helpless himself said, "Your mother is afraid that after the wedding Nancy will run the two of you off the place. No such thought ever entered my mind. I can't imagine Nancy having that thought either. Your mother may have less cooking and cleaning to do but you are both still welcome to stay. She and Nancy will have to work a couple of things out, but this is your home for as long as you wish. You need to try to convince her of that."

There followed a back and forth exchange of rapid Spanish. Zac picked up bits and pieces, but for the most part he was still trying to sort out one word when that word had already been pushed aside by a half dozen others.

Amado finally took his seat at the table with a small grin and hunched shoulders.

"Mother will be alright. She didn't say anything before, so I had no way of knowing that she was worried."

He repeated, "She will be alright."

Alejandra turned from the stove just enough to drop Amado's breakfast plate onto the table before him, before turning quickly back to her dish washing. She didn't make eye contact with Zac. Her eyes were swollen, and the remnant of a tear hung on her one cheek. Amado ate his breakfast in silence.

Zac explained about the changed wedding plans to Amado. Then, figuring to leave mother and son to themselves, pulled on a jacket and opened the door. Amado found him a half hour later, fussing over his cavalry gelding.

"Are you riding to the wedding or will you take the wagon?"

"I'll be leaving the wagon for you and your mother. I'm not sure what time Nancy has things arranged for so you had best get the team ready and be underway so's you can be at the church right after lunch. Perhaps you should take some food with you. You could eat along the way. Tie Abe's livery horse behind the wagon and bring him along.

"I'll ride in, but Abe is shining up his buggy for

Nancy and me. We'll come out here in the buggy after the wedding. Appreciate it if you could trail my gelding back with you when you come."

"*Si*, Mr. Zac. I will do that."

***

At three p.m. sharp, Pastor Moody Thomlinson stepped out of the small pastor's study at the back of the church hall and made his way to the platform. Behind him walked Zac and his friend Trig, who would stand with him during the ceremony.

Honey Drummond, the young daughter of Toby and Mrs. Drummond, of the GG Ranch, sat at the piano. She had played a short collection of pieces while the folks were filing in for the ceremony.

As Zac approached the front of the platform, he managed to get enough self-control to glance out at the visitors. He was amazed to see the small building was packed, wall to wall, with several men standing across the back and down each side. The ladies had been given the seats. He saw faces he recognized but also several he couldn't place. The big entry doors had been closed, in spite of the warm fall day.

Following a sharp knock on the door, Pop Hennessey, acting as self-appointed doorman and official greeter, made a great show of turning the big latch and pulling the door open. Honey started into a special piece that Nancy had found the music for. She was a long way from a professional pianist, but no one really cared.

A radiant Nancy, dressed in the finest clothing she could purchase in the small town, entered on the arm of her sister, Mrs. Pastor Tomlinson. As the visitors stood, they slowly walked, arm in arm down the narrow isle.

Although Nancy really required no help, Zac stepped down the two stairs and took his bride by the elbow. Sarah Tomlinson stopped at the base of the steps while the bride and groom rose to the stage. Honey ended the piano piece with a series of dramatic chords.

After clearing his throat, Pastor Moody greeted the gathered witnesses, and then Zac and Nancy.

"Thank you all for coming. Please be seated."

Turning to the couple before him he said, "Isaac and Nancy, we are here today to witness the two of you becoming one in the eyes of God and all mankind."

Lifting his eyes to his wife, who had remained standing at the base of the steps, he said, "Who is giving this woman to be wed?"

Sarah, who at first had argued for an explanation as to why a woman was filling that traditional male roll, finally gave in to Nancy's insistence and simply said, "As her sister, and only relative present, and on behalf of our father, I do."

Then she stepped up to the platform and again took her place beside Nancy.

The ceremony proceeded smoothly, with Nancy, her arm linked through Zac's, seemingly taking in every word, although there was no way to know what she was thinking about.

Was it the young soldier she had nursed back to health? Was it the many years of single loneliness, hoping to meet that special man? Or was her mind cleared of the past? Perhaps she was truly thinking only of the present and the future.

Zac's cluttered and deeply hurt and damaged mind wandered as Moody was explaining the responsibilities and privileges of marriage.

Very briefly, his mind, seemingly on its own, with no conscious effort, flipped back to that special day before the war, the first time he stood at an altar with a woman who was to become his wife. Silently, at least he hoped it was silently, he said, "Maddy?" Perhaps he had only thought the name. He wasn't sure.

Could he ever love another woman as he had loved Maddy? Could there ever be so precious a child as his beautiful Minnie?

He had thought through these things in the weeks before he had asked Nancy to marry him. There was a great need to push aside the doubts before he brought another woman into his life. There was an equally great need for him to face the past before he could truly look forward to the future.

The miserable truth was that Maddy was dead. His little girl was dead. He, Isaac, Zac Trimbell, was alone. Had been alone for years. There was no more Mr. and Mrs. Trimbell, as there had once been. The plans they had held, looking towards the future were as dead as his dear wife.

He had been alone all the years since the war. He had stood grieving at his loved ones' gravesides. He had grieved over the years to the point of despair. The loss, plus that dreadful war, had turned his mind and soul into a twisted mess.

Years before, as he was riding away from the small cemetery and from the old hometown, his friend and pastor had asked the question, "Is it still well with your soul?" He had carried the question with him everywhere he went.

And the answer to the question? Well, no, it wasn't well with his soul. Certainly not when Moody first asked. How could it be? The loss, the damage, was new and raw, tearing him apart.

What about the faith in God he had claimed all his life? Was the struggle too much? Had his faith been just another victim of the war? Many men had lost their faith during that horrible time. He had seen it happen. Seen anger and despair replace faith.

For other men, their faith had grown as they recognized in the savagery, the true nature of men's hearts. And along with the recognition of that fallen nature, the redemption offered by a loving God. But to enjoy that redemption a man has to be willing to see it and receive it. Zac knew this but he had been somehow reluctant to receive his redemption. It had always seemed almost like a giving in, as if he was to accept the losses without feeling anything. He found he couldn't do that. It was like his mind had retreated to a neutral place, neither moving forward nor backwards.

Sometimes God has to take a man to the woodpile, as many a country father had done with their sons That experience, even to the point of being dragged near to a small corner of hell, was not easy for Zac. But he would have to admit that he came out the other end of the experience as a changed man.

He knew that, as with all wounds, there were scars. Emotional scars. Mental scars. Spiritual scars. He would learn to live with the scars. And with Nancy, this good woman by his side, he, they, could move forward. His reluctance was gone. He would wait for his full redemption.

The service ended with the pronouncement that they, Isaac and Nancy were now one. When he was invited to kiss his bride he did so, gently, and lovingly.

He walked down the aisle, heading towards the visiting and congratulations that would be coming their way. The lunch the ladies had prepared would soon be spread on tables outside.

Now he and his bride would be heading together into this new life, this new experience. Zac approached the future with the answer to two questions in his mind. The first was yes, it is now well with my soul, or at least much better, and improving daily. The second was, again, yes, there was room for a new woman in my life.

Oh, it wouldn't be the same. There would only be one woman who claimed that first blush of love from him. There can only be one 'first'. But he was satisfied that however different it would be, Nancy was a good woman and would be a good wife. It was up to him to be a good husband. It wouldn't be first, but it could still be good.

And Nancy? He wondered what her thoughts were. She knew about his past and his struggles with depression and darkness. And still she had said 'yes' at the altar. He decided they were off to a good start.

***

A couple of hours after the wedding, Abe, cleaned

up, shaved and dressed better than Zac had ever seen him, drove his equally cleaned and shiny buggy to the church yard. Trig, appearing as if from nowhere, quietly walked to the buggy and placed two valises into the back. The few other things Nancy owned could be claimed at another time.

Zac and Nancy, tiring of all the talk, were thankful for Abe's timing and his consideration. Zac helped his bride into the buggy and then walked to the other side. Abe was standing, holding the horse steady. Zac stepped up to him with his outstretched hand.

"Thank you, my friend."

Abe simply nodded, lifted his hat to Nancy and walked back into the church yard. With a slight flick of the reins Zac put the buggy into motion. He didn't look back, but Nancy did, and with a wave of her hand offered her final thanks and farewell.

***

"Ready to go home, Mrs. Trimbell?"

"Oh yes. Home. That sounds so inviting, Mr. Trimbell."

IF YOU LIKE THIS,
CHECK OUT: MAC'S WAY

Raised in poverty in Missouri, Mac is determined to find a better life for himself and the girl who is still a vague vision in his mind. Work on the Santa Fe Trail, and on a Mississippi River boat give him a start, but the years of Civil War leave him broke and footloose in South Texas. There he discovers more cattle running loose than he ever knew existed. Teaming up with two ex-Federal soldiers, he sets out to gather his wealth, one head at a time.

While gathering and driving Longhorns, Mac and his friends meet an interesting collection of characters, including Margo. Mac and Margo and the crew learn about Longhorns, and life, from hard experience before they eventually head west. Outlaws and harrowing river crossings are just two of the challenges they face along their way.

AVAILABLE NOW

ABOUT THE AUTHOR

Reg Quist's pioneer heritage includes sod shacks, prairie fires, home births, and children's graves under the prairie sod, all working together in the lives of people creating their own space in a new land.

Quist's career choice took him into the construction world. From heavy industrial work, to construction camps in the remote northern bush, the author emulated his grandfathers, who were both builders, as well as pioneer farmers and ranchers.

Quist's writing career was late in pushing itself forward, remaining a hobby while family and career took precedence. Only in early retirement, was there time for more serious writing.

Ruminations from the Minivan

MUSINGS FROM A WORLD
GROWN LARGE, THEN SMALL

Includes a discussion guide for book groups

For my mother, who inspired me

For my daughters,
who helped me see the world in a grain of rice

And for Jeff,
who has always encouraged me to wear fuchsia

AUTHOR'S NOTE

Though this is a work of non-fiction, I've changed the names of some, but not all of the individuals mentioned in this book to preserve their privacy and their feelings.

The events depicted here are as I remember them and as I interpret them. With age comes an expanding waistline and a faulty memory. I apologize for any inadvertent errors or differences of opinion.

Thanks to the following publications for publishing selected chapters from this book:

Harvard Review (Number 28, 2005) – The Benefit of the Doubt

Brain, Child, the magazine for thinking mothers – Diane: Lessons for Another Milestone (Summer 2004)

Secrets & Confidences, the complicated truth about women's friendships (Seal Press 2004) – Dinosaur Friends

Fugue (Summer 2003) – Valentines

There is no way to know which fragments of the past will prove to be relevant in the future. Composing a life involves a continual re-imagining of the future and re-interpretation of the past to give meaning to the present.

Mary Catherine Bateson

CONTENTS

ME

THEM

HER

US

ME

JUNIOR OFFICER

The American is young and bearded, wearing the billowy pants, loose cotton shirt and sandals that are standard-issue for Western travelers in India. I am wearing a fuchsia skirt and matching shoulder-padded top with high heels, and a strand of freshwater pearls with matching earrings. We are probably around the same age—twenty-five—but the difference in the way we are dressed says everything. For months he has been traveling the world, spending most of his time in Uganda and then India. Something has happened to him along the way and I am the government official—the representative from "home"—who will help him figure out his next move.

The day before, he had jumped into the Arabian Sea, motive unclear. That night I had received a call from the proprietor of the Salvation Army hotel, a place popular with budget travelers. The young man was "talking crazy" and the hotelier feared he would destroy hotel property. I was the American Consulate duty officer that night, so the responsibility for "talking down" the young American fell to me.

We spoke for hours. He was ranting and distraught and I couldn't say for sure what the problem was. Still, I felt we had made a connection.

"Get some sleep," I said gently. "Come and see me at the Consulate tomorrow. We'll talk some more and everything will be okay."

I have to admit I was surprised that he had actually come. This confirmed to me that the connection I'd felt between us was obviously mutual.

We are walking side-by-side in circles, along the grounds of the American Consulate, like Buddhist monks circling a *stupa*. He'd come to the Consulate at my behest, but was reluctant to come inside. So instead we walk along the manicured lawn, passing the tennis court and the celebratory-looking bougainvillea and jacaranda, so bright and fragrant that they seem to mock the fact that anything could be wrong. A group of Consulate staff follows discreetly behind.

We walk, and we, or mostly I, talk. Sometimes he rants, sometimes he cries, expressing a jumble of feelings that are too complex for me to get to the bottom of.

I suggest that maybe he has been traveling long enough.

Maybe, I say, it is time for you to go home.

We make the same circuitous path over and over again, getting nowhere with our paces or our conversation. Finally I feel impatient. I decide we need to stop circling and head somewhere in a straight line. I stop to consider, my hand on the young man's shoulder.

Of course I could see it coming in my mind's eye but I didn't have enough time to react. We have stopped near a ledge overlooking a square pit. Nearby, there is scaffolding leading to the roof of a shed, which is being repaired. There are sawhorses and sparse, dry grass in the pit, a contrast to the lush and manicured grounds we had been walking.

In a split second I know what will happen and in a split second, it does. The American breaks free of me, runs along the ledge and climbs the scaffolding to the roof. Before I, or anyone, can stop him, he jumps into the pit, some fifty feet below.

He lies there, body crumpled. But his eyes are bright. For the first time since I have known him, he is completely calm.

Then, he speaks.

Whenever I think about roast turkey, I am reminded of India. Not that forty-odd years of turkey eating and cooking haven't produced their share of memorable experiences, starting with the bountiful Thanksgiving feasts for 100 guests, prepared by my mother while I was growing up. The first turkey I'd ever planned to cook myself was left uneaten in my Washington, DC apartment one bone-chilling Christmas, because the power had gone out, the pipes froze and we'd had to abandon the meal that I had planned to prepare for my boyfriend Tom, my mother and my stepfather and go out for Ethiopian food instead. The meal, just the idea of that meal, caused great discomfort for my stepfather, and I knew his marriage to my mother would not last.

I walked my husband through the steps of turkey-making once; I was seven months pregnant and on bed rest because of a placental abruption.

As he followed my directions for stuffing and basting the first and last turkey he would ever cook, Jeff teased that "the magic" was gone. Our baby turned out fine and so did the turkey and to this day he likes to rib me by proclaiming his turkey the best one we have ever shared.

I basted a turkey while hiding the early labor pains that plagued me while pregnant the second time around. They were, we realized, brought on by the stress of having both my mother and Jeff's mother spend Thanksgiving with us. I basted, then retreated to my bedroom to call the doctor, who feared another placental abruption. Again, the baby and the turkey both emerged unscathed, though our mothers asked us to never invite them over together again.

I've cooked turkeys in cabins, cooked turkeys single with an odd assortment of unattached friends who added quahogs and gumbo to the feast, and cooked turkeys while married, making two kinds of gravy (with giblets and without) and two kinds of cranberry sauce (fresh and canned with ridges) to satisfy the two families I had brought together.

Still, turkey mostly reminds me of India. Most Americans limit their roast turkey intake to one or two times a year. I have never eaten so much roast turkey in the course of a year as I did when I lived in India.

India, as everyone knows, is hot. Beastly hot. In fact it's the last place you would want to eat, much less roast, a turkey. The locals are smart enough to retreat into the coolness of their homes for long afternoon naps. The food they eat, with its symphony of spices and cooling accompanying yogurt-based *raitas,* is designed to combat against the heat and aid digestion by making you sweat.

I came to Bombay as a junior officer, or JO, at the American Consulate General after three months of Foreign Service training. The night I arrived from America, it was actually 3 a.m., I was driven past the Consulate, where the line snaked around the block and people were already camped out as if they were waiting to purchase Rolling Stones tickets. Soon I would be spending my days interviewing these people to determine whether, if I gave them a visa to America, they would ever come home.

India in 1986 was not the economic dynamo it is today and well-paying job opportunities were limited. Scores of talented Indian software engineers with degrees from the Indian Institute of Technology wanted MBAs from American universities. Others planned to take contracts working as computer programmers for American firms. These jobs were low-paid by U.S. standards, but lucrative by Indian ones. Indians knew how to live frugally in the U.S. so they could send a portion of their salary home to help the family.

This flight from India of its best and its brightest was known as the "brain drain." Why should they return? some asked. There is no opportunity for them here. But I had to ask them why and reject them if they couldn't come up with compelling ties to their native country, because U.S. immigration law presumes a person to be an intending immigrant unless he or she can prove otherwise. The concept of the global economy was still young and no one could fathom then that soon there would be a myriad of opportunities for talented young Indians; that any call to a customer service center would be routed to India; and that Indians would be handling Americans' billing inquiries, calling Americans with telemarketing offers, and evaluating Americans' X-rays and CT scans.

Non-immigrant visa (NIV) *wallah* was the first of my three rotations as a junior officer at the American Consulate in Bombay. India has many wallahs, a word loosely translated to designate occupation. *Tiffin* wallahs deliver lunches in stackable tin containers, known as tiffins, to city office workers. *Paan* wallahs make unique aromatic mixes of betel leaves, anise seeds, fennel and other herbs known as paan, which are the Indian equivalent of the after dinner mint. Some people, especially those from the Parsi community, have wallah last names, much as Americans are named Baker, Smith or Taylor. There are Moneywallahs and Rubbertirewallahs, and the favorite among my colleagues, Sodabottlewasherwallahs.

Visa wallah was the nickname for NIV "line officers" like me, who sat on a stool behind bulletproof glass and interrogated applicants about their intentions, delved into their bankbooks and finally rendered the decision that could be life-altering. No one wanted the dreaded 214 (b), which was a rejection on the grounds that the applicant could not demonstrate enduring ties to India. During the long wait for an interview, I'm told applicants would place bets on which officers were the easy touches. Like some early Indian version of a reality TV show, there would be a collective sharp intake of breath whenever an applicant was called to the window of a tough interviewer and muted cheers from the crowd if the visa was issued. They watched when one of us got up from our stool to use the bathroom or take a phone call, because this could alter the draw. But Indians are fatalistic by nature and accepted whatever came their way as karma.

Being a visa wallah made one especially sought after for invitations to parties and dinners. Indians love to curry favor and, much like a doctor, I was often asked to give professional advice in social settings, despite the fact that often people assumed that my male colleagues, even the other junior officers, had the real authority. I attended glittering parties with *Bollywood* movie stars, newspaper columnists and famous artists and architects and they were all interested in what I had to say.

"You look like a gazelle," flattered a famous actor who had played a starring role in the movie *Gandhi*.

I was a chubby girl from New Jersey, who was perhaps enjoying a swan-like renaissance. Still, this seemed to be stretching the truth.

"Goodnight, gazelle," he called out when the party was over.

I appreciated my popularity and the distractions from the busy workday. Coming to India had been bittersweet because I had left Tom, my long-term boyfriend, behind. Tom was the one who had wanted to join the Foreign Service in the first place and when it came time to take the written exam, I just went along for the ride. Perhaps my "nothing-to-lose" attitude made me more relaxed, because I passed the test and he didn't. Neither did any of our friends from our California international relations school. I eventually went on to pass the oral exam too, and found myself in a quandary. Couldn't he try again, I wondered (it had taken me and most people I knew two tries to pass the orals)? Couldn't he come with me and share the life I knew we would both enjoy? No, he couldn't. I had felt held back by him during our years of poverty in Washington, D.C.

We, and a group of our friends, had moved to D.C. after receiving degrees from the Monterey Institute of International Studies. They had all received Masters degrees, while I, several years younger, had just gotten my BA. We rolled into town ready to take Washington by storm. But the combination of coming from a little-known school on the West Coast, instead of an Ivy League institution, and the harsh economic realities of the 1982 recession, made it difficult to find jobs. Our Russian-speaking friends had some success, going to work for intelligence agencies, something we preferred not to do. I remember sitting on the roof of our apartment building being interrogated about a friend by a security officer from the agency where my friend hoped to work. The child of immigrants from a Soviet-bloc country, my friend was squeaky clean. Try as he might, the security officer couldn't find a character flaw or any potential weaknesses in my friend's loyalty to the United States and the capitalist way of life. Finally, he asked me in a resigned sort of way

"What about food? Did he have any strong likes or dislikes?"

I was resigned too, and anxious to get off the roof, so I decided to give the man what he had come for.

"Hmmm. Well, he didn't like anchovies," I said, after feigning serious consideration.

The security man jumped on this, pencil and notebook at the ready. Maybe this was the weak link.

"Did he actually say that or is it just an assumption on your part?"

I considered again.

"Whenever we ordered pizza, he said, 'No anchovies.'"

In D.C., I worked for a while as an unpaid intern at my New Jersey Congressman's office, answering constituent letters.

Once, I responded to a letter from the parents of a childhood schoolmate of mine, who were lobbying the Congressman to persuade the army to posthumously change my classmate's discharge from a dishonorable one to an honorable one. It seems he had died of a brain tumor, and the tumor may have been responsible for the behavior that led to his dischargeable offense. I remembered this boy, who had often stood in front of me when students were asked to line up alphabetically. He was always in trouble, always unable to control his body, always ridiculed. Perhaps all that time the tumor had been growing in his brain, taking over. I wrote back as the Congressman and said that we would see what we could do. Later the Congressman was forced to resign because of peripheral involvement in the now-forgotten Abscam financial scandal.

While I impersonated a Congressman, Tom stayed home, revising his résumé and sending in job applications. No one called him for an interview. Both of us reluctantly filled out applications for the CIA and were relieved that we weren't called back after the initial interview. So I eventually took a job as a clerk-typist in the personnel office at the Voice of America. My salary was $10,000 a year, not very respectable for a college graduate, but more than we had been living on. Tom borrowed money from my mother and took a bartending course. On hot D.C. summer nights we would sit as close to the window as possible in our overheated flat and I would quiz him on the ingredients to concoct a Pink Squirrel. He passed the bartending test, but he never became a bartender. Eventually, he, too, became a clerk-typist, his brilliant political scientist mind defeated by being a little fish in a very big pond full of very smart, very connected, very ambitious fish. After a few years in the safety of his new office, his talents began to be recognized and he was starting the slow, yet steady climb up the government promotion ladder.

Now, here we were, dividing up the shared belongings from our six years together. We were sad and anxious, but both of us were also excited to see what the next phase of our lives might bring, though we were careful not to show it. Lying in the bathtub in the evening during the months and weeks before my departure, I would read guidebooks about India. There hadn't been much of a selection and so I bought the two that were widely available, *The Lonely Planet Guide to India* and a British book entitled, *India in Luxury*. Depending on my mood, I would either read about ways to combat intestinal parasites or delve into tantalizing descriptions of the rooms in the luxurious palace hotels in the former Indian princely states. I longed to share these opposing impressions with Tom, but I had to keep my excitement in check. And as my departure day grew nearer and I would return home, arms sore from the many inoculations I was required to receive, I had to keep that to myself as well.

I was also finding it hard to leave Kitty, the black and white long-haired cat we had acquired together in Monterey. We'd carefully hidden her from the property manager of our house in Pebble Beach until she was discovered, we were evicted, and we moved to an apartment in a de-sanctified church in Pacific Grove. When we moved from California to Washington, D.C., Tom and I drove cross-country and slept in campgrounds, our belongings stuffed into a cargo carrier on top of my navy blue Chevy Citation hatchback. But I'd saved my money so that Kitty could take a direct flight to Washington some weeks later, where she joined us in the efficiency apartment we had rented in a dicey part of Capitol Hill. When our finances improved and we were able to move to a ground floor apartment in more upscale Glover Park, Kitty appreciated the backyard. Kitty and I had history together. I would be sad to leave her.

As the gut-wrenching reality of our impending separation approached, we tried not to dwell on it. But, we had been good friends for six years, so it was only natural that we would have conversations about what might happen "afterwards."

"No matter what, you'll keep Kitty, won't you?" I asked, as if I were ensuring the custody of a child.

Tom hesitated. "Well, what if I move to a place where I'm not allowed to have pets?" he stammered.

He had a point. It was his life he would be leading, not ours.

So Kitty came with me to India, via a two-day layover in New York, where I trained with immigration officers at JFK airport, and another two-day rest stopover in Frankfurt.

After that 3 a.m. drive by the American Consulate to see the line of hopefuls that awaited me, I was deposited at the Taj Mahal Hotel, where I would live for the two weeks it would take to get my apartment ready. I laid out food, water and a litter box for Kitty, hung the next day's clothes in the heavy armoire in the closet and fell into a deep sleep. The next morning I put out the Do Not Disturb sign and left strict instructions that no one was to enter my room while I was gone.

At breakfast in the hotel coffee shop, I rejected the continental menu in favor of the Indian one. As I maneuvered my burrito-like *idli sambar*, a tangy South Indian breakfast specialty, I surveyed the array of international faces and listened to the mélange of accents. I know it sounds clichéd, but I had to pinch myself to believe that this was really my life. The rest of the day was equally thrilling. I was introduced to the local staff of the Consulate: Pat, Parveen, Satish, Shammi and Santano. Their names and dress betrayed which of the many Indian communities they belonged to. We all went out to lunch to bid farewell to a departing American and I went crazy over the food. The table was laden with savory stews, pungent pickles and large puffed breads and I stuffed myself like a starving refugee. The mango *lassi* I washed my meal down with was thick and tart, too much really, after all that I had consumed, but lassis were familiar. I had drunk them at "Taste of the Town" festivals in Washington, D.C. Ordering one now, in India, felt like a bridge from my old life to my new one. I had always loved spicy food. When we traveled, my mother and I made a game of trying to find the most exotic and spicy cuisines. Now, here were the tastes of the town laid out before me. I belong here, I told myself, as I ladled another helping of *daal* onto my plate. A few days later, as I liberally helped myself to the snacks at the first of the many receptions I would be required to attend during my time in Bombay, I received a warning from a French colleague. "Be careful," she admonished. "You will get fat here. You have to control yourself."

After lunch I was taken to the outdoor market, where, as we navigated around open sewers and tried to avoid beggars, we bargained for knock-off cotton clothes. They were already dirt cheap by American standards, but the game was to get them for even cheaper. I had that momentary sense of guilt that you have when you come from a rich country and are negotiating down a price with someone whose family subsists on a dollar a day or less. This is the way the natives do it, I told myself. I don't want to stick out like a foolish American. I want to fit in.

Afterwards, we attended a farewell party for the departing American at the restaurant in my hotel. I stuffed myself again and then the jet lag kicked in. It was time to go to sleep, for tomorrow I would be expected to go to work.

I didn't see Kitty when I stumbled into my room, bloated and exhausted. I looked under the bed and in every nook and cranny, but she was nowhere to be found. The hotel was undergoing construction. Feeling somewhat foolish, I grabbed a bag of Little Friskies and wandered among the scaffolding near my room, calling her.

"Kitty, Kitty." My stage whisper was growing desperate.

I can't really have believed that she would simply emerge at the sound of the shaking bag of cat food. But there was nothing to do but try.

And so the doubts began.

I crept into bed and cried myself to sleep, unable now to be excited by the novelty of my life. Why did I come here? Why did I leave my boyfriend? What made me think I could lead a normal life in the Foreign Service? What will happen to me?

The next morning, when my handler from the Consulate called to see if I was ready to be picked up, I told him about Kitty. This set in motion a chain of events that made me realize the power of the U.S. government. Uniformed security guards were summoned to search my room, but even in their khaki efficiency they could not find Kitty. The housekeeping staff was questioned, but everyone denied having entered my room, which was disheveled enough for me to believe that it had not been cleaned. When I returned from work that afternoon, dejected and deflated, I was informed by the concierge that I would be asked to "identify cats." It seemed that during the day while I was away, the hotel staff had been dispatched to the alley outside the hotel to round up cats in the hopes that one of them would be the missing American Consulate Cat. And so I sat patiently and examined cat after scruffy Indian alley cat, while the hotel staff inquired in the lovely Indian-British lilt that would soon become familiar to me,

"Excuse me Madame. Is *this* your cat?"

But of course none of them were. In my less depressed moments I became confounded by the mystery. Where could she have gone? And how would a pampered American cat, one who had flown across the United States and had cat food served to her twice a day, be able to survive in India? Maybe she was excited and experiencing the same sense of wonder and uncertainty that I was. Maybe, like me, she was prepared to leave the security of her old life.

I got into bed and hardened my heart. You have nobody here but yourself, I told myself. No boyfriend, no family, and now, not even a cat. Adventure requires self-reliance. So get used to being your own emotional support system. You can't count on anyone else to do it for you.

And so I drifted into a sad and cynical sleep. I was not the excited fresh young woman of the day before, but someone whose enthusiasm was already being chipped away by experience.

I awoke to a pounce.

It was Kitty, ready to take her place beside me on the bed, just as she had always done at home. I cried grateful tears as I hugged her. Then I went back to sleep.

The next day, after the joyful news had spread, the khaki-clad security guards were again dispatched to search my room. We all wanted to clear up this mystery. Finally, one of them moved the heavy armoire in the closet. We had looked underneath this armoire, but there wasn't enough space for a cat to crawl under. But a look behind the armoire revealed a shelf-like ledge midway up its back. It was low enough for a scared cat to jump onto and hide. As if to confirm our hypothesis, Kitty later jumped onto the ledge while I was watching. Our days at the Taj Mahal Hotel soon fell into a predictable rhythm and I would find her waiting for me in my uncleaned room whenever I returned from work.

I left the hotel sooner than expected and was assigned to a temporary apartment while my permanent one was being readied. My colleagues took pity on me, especially when the news came, a few weeks after I arrived, that my father had died. Several times a week I was invited to dinner parties, where more often than not, I would be served roast turkey, from their supply of frozen American foodstuffs that were ordered quarterly from the American Embassy commissary in New Delhi. When I settled into my permanent home, I had some of these turkeys in my freezer too, along with blocks of cheddar cheese and hamburger buns. Beef, though not consumed by Hindus, was available if we wanted it. Many of these formerly familiar but now exotic items were popular with the American expatriate friends I had made from Meherabad, the ashram of devotees of Meher Baba, located in rural Ahmednagar, some 300 kilometers from Bombay. There, the faithful adhered to a strict regimen of vegetarian food, eschewing alcohol and sex. They annually held a Silence Day to commemorate their teacher, who they believed had been the living personification of God, and who had chosen not to speak for the forty years from his enlightenment until he "left his body."

When visa extensions and other business took the "Baba lovers," as they were known, to Bombay, they were happy to cut loose with a nice roast turkey. I was happy to cook and serve it to them. But I didn't feel like eating turkey anymore and began politely rejecting the dinner invitations from the American community. Bhagwan, the somber elderly Gujarati man I had hired to be my *bearer,* the Indian term for male household servant, wanted to cook for me from the repertoire of Western dishes he had learned to prepare during his years of service to expatriates. I preferred his *palaak paneer.* Soon I also stopped attending the weekly TGIF parties at Washington House, the apartment complex where most of my American colleagues lived and where Bombay's expatriate community gathered to play darts. And I no longer hung out at Breach Candy, the swim club adjacent to the American Consulate that was popular with expatriates and where, despite the Hindu prohibition against beef, you could get a decent hamburger with fries. I grew fat on Indian food, just as my French colleague had predicted. But I couldn't get enough of it. I lived for late night Indian dinner parties, where the food wasn't served until 10 p.m. and everyone stood around drinking scotch and gossiping. I dressed for these parties in intricate *shalwar kameezes*, traditional Indian dress consisting of a tunic, billowy drawstring trousers and a *dupatta*, or shawl. My toes were festooned with rings, my ankle adorned with a heavy silver ankle bracelet. I wore only one, I explained to the Indian staff at work, because that was the custom in America. No one had the heart to tell me that in India, the custom is to wear two, because a woman with only one ankle bracelet is a prostitute.

State Department training is extensive and tries to prepare you for every situation. I had been briefed on the different stages of expatriate living and recognized that my flirtation with Indian food and culture and rejection of American turkey was a normal step in figuring out how to accommodate the dual pressures of representing one's country while "doing as the Romans do."

"After an initial period of staying within your own community, it's normal to be fascinated by the dress and customs of the host country and to make local friends," said the State Department speaker from the Overseas Briefing Center, rather patronizingly I thought.

She was an "old-school" Foreign Service spouse with decades of experience and she described to us how she had tactfully managed a taste of the boiled bumblebees that were served to her in China. She recommended that we "ladies" purchase two sets of white dress gloves for our wardrobes: full length and three-quarter length. She impressed upon us the importance of owning a set of fish forks.

"Acceptance and appreciation of the local culture are useful for effectively representing American interests abroad."

"The danger," she added ominously, "is in 'going native.'"

The way she described it, it sounded like a set-up for something out of a Graham Greene novel. In practice, it usually translated to people not being able to forsake the safari suits, *Guayabara* shirts or *Kente* cloth that they had been able to wear abroad, once they returned to the U.S.

Shopping seemed to be an area where you could appreciate the local culture to your heart's content without risk of being criticized for going native, so I continued to go along with my colleagues on their weekend treasure hunts. I don't know why I thought it was important to own a carved wooden Gujarati rice sorter, but I bargained it down to a very good price. I couldn't know that, years later, it would be the perfect receptacle for my daughters' large collection of naked princess Barbie dolls and headless Kens. The sitar that I hunted to find, but never learned to play, has been lovingly displayed in every home I've lived in over the past twenty-five years, along with the hookah pipe that I have never smoked.

I took every opportunity to travel around India, my American dollars enabling me to stay in the lavish princely hotels and well-appointed Kashmiri houseboats I had read about in my Washington, DC bathtub. Once, when returning late from a trip, I noticed the door of Bhagwan's room just off the kitchen was ajar. He was always careful to keep his private life separate from his official one, bidding me farewell each night with a salute before retreating to his tiny living quarters. Tentatively I took a step into the room, where I spied him lying on his cot. I checked to be sure he was breathing.

The next morning I questioned him. At twenty-five, I still wasn't used to being mistress of the house and these "official" encounters made me nervous. Bhagwan, who must have been around sixty, played his role of my servant with amused tolerance. But he called me *Missy Baba*, Little Miss, instead of *Memsahib,* the proper name for the mistress of the house, and fussed over me when I stayed out too late or wasn't eating properly.

"Bhagwan," I ventured, "why was your door open when I came home last night?"

He looked embarrassed. "It is because of Kitty, Baba. Sometimes when you are away she taps on my door. I let her in and she sleeps with me."

I moved into my second rotation, as an immigrant visa officer, six months or so after arriving in Bombay. Immigrant visas, or IVs as they are known, are far more straightforward than non-immigrant visas. Most of the paperwork has already been handled in the United States and it is simply the consular officer's job to ensure that everything is in order. There were straightforward marriage visas and work visas and the occasional adoption. But although it was nice to have a break from the intensity of the NIV line, I found the work boring and I was far less popular at parties. Once, Gurumayi, the charismatic and beautiful leader of the nearby Ganeshpuri ashram, a favorite with international celebrities, came in to apply for an IV as a "Minister of Religion." She had successfully overcome a challenge from her brother for the leadership of their religious community and was now planning to reside part time among the glitterati in New York. When her visa was approved, she passed out Godiva chocolates in gratitude.

As a single person, I'd noticed a double standard in the anti-going native policy. Apparently it was okay for the single male officers to date local women, but it was not okay for single female officers to date local men. I heard stories of male JOs who had preceded me, who had married much-loved members of the local Indian staff at our Consulate and taken them away to their next posting abroad. Will, the other JO at the Consulate, was dating Renuka, a staff member at the British Deputy High Commission. Male Foreign Service Officer friends of mine all over the developing world had taken up with exotic local women and some later married them. But if an American female JO took up with a local man from a less prosperous country, she risked being accused of flaunting her loose morals and was the unspoken source of a sort of disgust from her countrymen for cavorting beneath her station. So some of us females took emotional refuge in our pets.

My one attempt to date an Indian photographer had ended awkwardly, with him chasing me around my apartment after drinking too many gin-and-mango juices. For weeks thereafter, he sent his photographs to me at work with his bad poetry inscribed on the back for all to see. There was no mistaking the disapproving looks I received.

I began hanging out with Europeans, primarily French speakers, in order to step out from the American community in an acceptable way. This had the side benefit of improving my French. One night, partying hard with Jacques, the doctor at the French Consulate, and his colleague Henri, we ended up in the pre-dawn hours on the grounds of the Taj Mahal Hotel. Jacques and Henri quickly stripped down and dove into the swimming pool. To maintain the free-spirited European persona I had adopted, I felt I had to follow suit, but I was embarrassed. So I quickly removed my shalwar kameez and hastily jumped into the closest area of the pool. Unfortunately I chose the shallow end, breaking my nose in four places. Jacques and Henri quickly whisked the bloody dripping me through the hotel lobby, where we were spotted by a U.S. Congressman, who had just arrived on the 3 a.m. flight.

As I sat miserable and embarrassed, waiting for Dr. Gupta to X-ray my nose, he seemed preoccupied.

"I want to know..." he began, as the X-ray machine began taking pictures. I noticed I had not been given a protective garment.

"I want to know," he continued, as I imagined the radiation surging into my body, "if you've been rejected for a visa, how much money is it necessary to deposit into your bank account to prove that you have strong enough ties to India so you can be approved?"

I hemmed and hawed and wished I could give him a satisfactory dollar figure so he would turn off the machine that might be preventing me from ever having children.

Later I awoke, alone and forgotten in the operating room of Breach Candy Hospital, where the broken pieces of my nose had been set. Like a dream sequence in a movie, I climbed off the gurney in my green hospital gown and wandered into the hospital hallway, trying to find someone who was responsible for me. No one seemed surprised at the sight of a barefoot foreigner in a hospital gown wandering down hallways alone. Finally, I located the room where my clothes were being kept, got dressed and went home.

For days afterwards I stayed there, my swollen nose throbbing with pain. I sought solace from *Midnight's Children*, Salman Rushdie's seminal book in which the protagonist, born at the hour of Indian independence, whose prominent nose is central to the book, struggles with questions of identity.

Bombay's air is pungent with the aroma of rotting food and urine and heat and dust. The streets are choked with exhaust spitting vehicles, which pollute the air and leave everyone with a persistent dry cough. A throng of humans weaves in and out among the cars and along the congested streets. It is loud, so very loud. If you walk along the beach in the mornings, you see rows of men squatting near the shore, their eyes pointed toward the horizon. When I first arrived, I thought they were meditating. Later, someone explained that they were defecating. After I learned this, it was impossible for me to consider swimming in the Arabian Sea ever again. I traveled to Varanasi, the holy city on the River Ganges, where the ashes of the dead are strewn into the river and carried away for eternity. Bhagwan had asked me to bring him back some holy "Ganga water." I returned with a vial of it and imagined he would place a drop of it on his forehead every day for the rest of his life. He solemnly accepted the vial, opened it and guzzled the polluted ash-ridden water, while I stared in amazement.

Often I sought refuge at the Taj Mahal Hotel, a quiet oasis in this city of nine million people, and a place which seemed to have figured out how to meld the best qualities of east and west. No matter when I entered, day or night, or for what purpose, I was always greeted by a smiling staff member, who would say with a beautiful Indian lilt, "Good evening Madame. And how is your cat?"

My final rotation at the Consulate was in the American Services section, where I issued passports, reported the births of American citizens, provided lists of lawyers and visited Americans who were hospitalized or imprisoned. Every week, it seemed, someone lost a passport or a wallet and needed our help. Often this happened in Goa, a favorite hippie destination where one American woman, who renamed herself Shanti Om, told me she was living in a "perpetual state of orgasm."

One night I was the Consulate duty officer responsible for taking after-hours calls. The phone rang and it was the proprietor of the Salvation Army hotel. There was an American there, a crazy American, and he wanted me to calm him down.

I recognized him. He was the same American who had jumped into the Arabian Sea earlier that day. We spoke for hours and he was ranting and distraught. I tried to reach out to him and I felt we had made a connection.

"Come and see me at the Consulate tomorrow," I told him. "We'll talk some more. Everything will be okay."

Once the mess has been cleaned up and the broken American has been taken away, I return to the Consulate, where the afternoon mail has arrived. There is a letter from Tom. He is getting married. He hopes I am having adventures in my new life and wishes me the best.

I go home and lie on my couch seeking comfort from the book *Golden Gate*. It is a book written entirely in verse by Vikram Seth, an Indian writer, and it traces the lives and the loves of a group of friends in San Francisco. I hang on to this book for dear life. Then I dress in my shalwar kameez and go out to dinner at the home of a young Indian lawyer and his wife. We eat and talk and then someone takes out a guitar and plays "Hotel California" and songs by Bread and America. It is a warm and nurturing evening, the kind of evening with good friends that I could expect to have at home after an especially bad day. To experience this warm familiarity in India is unexpected.

"Why is this turkey green?" Drew asks, as Bhagwan somberly serves it to him from the dinner party platter we are using for the last time. I am getting ready to leave India and Drew is the new JO who will replace me and will come to live in my apartment. I am trying to use up my food, including the last frozen turkey, which has sat untouched for almost a year, apparently somewhat worse for no wear.

I borrow a Polaroid camera to take the necessary visa and identification pictures for Kitty, who will fly directly to

Washington, D.C. a few weeks after I depart. I am taking a whirlwind trip to Europe and Hawaii before heading back to Washington, where I will spend a year learning Vietnamese in preparation for my next overseas assignment.

Bhagwan has a request.

"Baba," he asks, "will you please take a picture of me with Kitty?"

I take two of them and we each keep one.

I don't know what became of Bhagwan. Drew later wrote to me that he had fired him because he wasn't able to handle the pressures of the many official dinner parties Drew had thrown. When I returned to Bombay some years later, having left the Foreign Service and now part of an official trade delegation from Washington State, no one could tell me what happened to him.

I visited the American Consulate and was greeted by the familiar faces of Pat, Santano, and Parvin. They were excited to hear that I had left the Foreign Service and moved to Seattle, where I had gotten married and hoped to start a family. Parvin invited me to her house for dinner. Before leaving the Consulate to return to my hotel and get ready, I heard a voice and saw the face of someone I recognized but could not quite place. It was Ravi, the mailroom clerk who had been responsible for ensuring that Kitty got all the necessary documentation and was safely put on a plane to America. He was wearing a business suit and told me he had been promoted from the mailroom and worked as an assistant in the Commercial section of the Consulate.

I knew what he wanted to ask me even before he said it.

"Madame," he inquired, with a beautiful Indian lilt, "how is your cat?"

ANTICIPATION

I am standing on an antique navy blue captain's chair trying to reach a soup spoon, a bowl, a family-sized jar of Hellman's mayonnaise and a graceful, long-necked glass bottle of Heinz ketchup that all sit on the white Formica kitchen counter. It is dinnertime. I am around five years old and I have two jobs which make up my contribution to the family meal: setting the table and making Russian dressing for the salad. I take both of these tasks seriously. I am proud of my ability to fold the napkins into perfect diamonds, to determine when and whether we need steak or butter knives and to decide the size of the spoons that I will carefully place beside the knives. But my Russian dressing is the *pièce de résistance*. I think it was my father who initially explained to me the importance of mixing the correct proportions of mayonnaise and ketchup so that the dressing would have the appropriate balance of sweetness and tang—the perfect complement to the iceberg lettuce that is the only available green for salads in the mid-1960s.

Though war and political and social turmoil will always be what the decade is remembered for, the early and mid-sixties were an era of optimism, affluence and style. My parents, especially my mother, were influenced by the young couple who redefined the White House and the responsibilities of their generation as the decade began. Like the Kennedys, they listened to Broadway soundtracks, especially *Camelot*, which told of the brief reign of King Arthur and his Knights of the Round Table and became a symbol of the Kennedy Administration.

Jack Kennedy rekindled my mother's devotion to public service, which had been ignited during the self-sacrificing years of World War II and fueled during the McCarthy era. She was active in Democratic politics—a true Kennedy idealist—and ran our county election board. According to family lore, or at least the way I chose to interpret the sequence of events, I was conceived during the blizzard of 1961, when my parents were snowed in and my six-year-old brother had the mumps. My mother's gold-embossed invitation to the Kennedy inaugural— an inaugural she didn't get to attend—was framed and hanging prominently in our house. Nine months later, in September of 1961, I was born.

Standing on tip-toes on the chair, I use the spoon to reach deep into the mayonnaise jar and ladle the heaping mass into the bowl. When I am older and can appreciate the concept of advance planning, I will sometimes have the foresight to turn the ketchup bottle on its head so that I will have a ready supply when the time is right. But waiting for the ketchup is part of the thrill. Later, "Anticipation" will become famous as the theme song for Heinz ketchup. Few people will realize that the song was inspired by Carly Simon's first date with Cat Stevens.

If the bottle of ketchup is new, then after a shake or two, the thick, rich ruby-colored tomato goodness will slowly emerge from its mouth. More often than not however, getting the good stuff requires perseverance and patience, and the careful orchestration of two simultaneous maneuvers: shaking the bottle of ketchup with one hand while smacking its side with the other.

Like many upper middle class young matrons of the time, my mother embraced Jackie Kennedy's sense of style and reverence for things European. Jackie's taste guided my mother, as she set out to renovate and redecorate our house. It was a California-style redwood ranch—unusual in the small New Jersey town where we lived—so much so that it had been featured in an article in the local newspaper entitled, "Meet the Krupnicks," as if our house were our identity. Most houses in town were classic two-stories or the utilitarian split-levels that were popular with nuclear families. We were the only family I knew who lived all on one floor.

My parents took weekly trips to New York to find the precise furnishings they wanted. The custom-made kitchen cabinets, the captain's chairs and the base of the round dining table were all finished in matching antique navy blue. There were navy blue wine bottle labels on the kitchen wallpaper, which also featured clusters of burgundy and rich green grapes. There were chandeliers and Tiffany lamps, antique butcher block side tables and a powder blue Louis XVI formal dining room. The sunken living room was still empty, aside from two large French area rugs with patterns of roses snaking along a pale blue background. I'm sure my parents had exquisite plans for that room. But for my brother, my cousins and me, it was the ideal place to play indoor touch football or set up the tracks for our Hot Wheels cars.

I spent my days in the backseat of my mother's brown Fleetwood Cadillac accompanying her on errands. We went to the gas station, the bank, the post office, the architect and to countless suppliers of home renovation products. Years later, when I am a mother, shepherding my kids to play dates and dance classes in my dirty minivan and saving the errands for my alone time, I am struck by something I read in another mother's essay: "When we were kids we followed our parents around. Our generation of parents follows our kids around."

I remember sitting on rolls of new carpeting, walking on flooring samples and playing with key chains filled with Formica chips or wood paneling. As an adult, I have Proustian moments—when I smell freshly laid carpet or accompany my daughter's first-grade class to a Tiffany exhibit at our local art museum—that take me back to my parents' house and the sense of anticipation that surrounded me in my early childhood.

The renaissance underway in our household extended to food. No Sloppy Joes or Tuna Noodle Casserole with potato chips on top for us. My parents were epicures. At their dinner parties they served *Lobster fra Diabolo*, *paella,* and Bananas Foster—a flambé desert my mother had mastered after a trip to New Orleans. My father ate steak with *Béarnaise* sauce. Everyone else's father ate hamburger. He preferred Grey Poupon Dijon mustard to French's yellow. His favorite pre-dinner snack was radishes with a sprinkle of salt. My parents had sourdough bread flown in from San Francisco long before the era when the trans-continental shipment of food was commonplace. Their marriage was troubled, but their shared appreciation of fine food and décor kept them together.

When our family dined out, we children were encouraged to be adventurous. My brother ordered *escargots* and frog's legs as a matter of course. At three and four years old, I was a perfect lady, with white gloves and impeccable manners—something my mother never failed to remind me of, years later, when I insisted on dressing in ripped jeans, marijuana T-shirts and flannel shirts, no matter what the occasion. At restaurants we ordered lobster with drawn butter or lamb chops with dainty ribbons around the bone, served with dabs of mint jelly. I took these meals for granted, yet still I was thrilled that my parents allowed me to order blue cheese dressing with my salad, even though it cost an additional 25 cents.

Maybe the end of all that optimism can be traced to the advent of the short, squat Heinz "wide-mouth" ketchup jar, which became available a few years after I began my Russian-dressing making career. Though I preferred the gracefulness of the traditional vessel, I was a fan of the wide-mouth because it allowed me to concentrate on achieving the perfect mixture of ingredients without delay. With the wide-mouth, there was no anticipation, and perhaps this lessened the thrill of achieving a balance of culinary sensations. Either way, my Russian dressing was the best, everyone in my family agreed. In fact, it seemed to be the one universal point of agreement. It got me my father's attention, my usually scornful older brother's admiration and provided us with a rare Ozzie and Harriet type moment in our tense household.

By 1969, our country's optimism had been replaced with disillusionment and my parents' marriage was over. Too young to understand the larger political and social forces at play, the only way I could make sense of my parents' divorce was to attribute it to the things I knew set them apart from one another: she was a die-hard Democrat, he was a Nixon man through-and-through. Her favorite color was the blue that was featured in all the rooms of our house. He preferred yellow, which was nowhere to be found.

So the sunken living room was never completed and the continental meals that were my first solid foods became a thing of the past.

My mother eventually sold the house she and my father had so lovingly decorated. Our "Meet the Krupnicks" identity was eradicated. My brother, almost seven years older than I, lived sometimes with my father, sometimes on his own. My mother and I moved to a tacky furnished apartment near the shores of our town's eponymous lake, where we lived for the year-and-a-half it took her to find a new house. I remember standing in my mother's bedroom in 1974, trying to adjust the tracking of the cheap sliding glass doors that led onto the narrow concrete balcony when I heard that Mama Cass had choked to death while eating a ham sandwich.

After Camelot and her marriage ended, my mother needed something new to believe in. Different cooking equipment and ingredients began to appear, first in our lakeside apartment, and later in the hundred-year-old house she renovated by herself. Teriyaki chicken was the first Asian meal I can remember her cooking at home on special individual broiler pans she had bought expressly for that purpose. She served it, and almost everything else we now ate, with rice. Everyone else's family ate potatoes. My mother often came home laden with boxes of rice with exotic flavorings—curry and saffron that gave the rice an appealing vermilion or reddish gold tint. She served the rice with meat that had been marinating all day in fragrant herbs and spices. Her glass of wine rounded out the meal.

Around this time, travel books began to stack up beside the French blue armchair near the fireplace, where my mother did her evening reading. At night, munching on Brach's Chocolate Bridge Mix, with Italian arias blaring from her stereo, she would fantasize about the trips she planned to take.

We took these trips together during my early years of high school, visiting England and Holland, France and Italy. We drank tea and cappuccino and Chianti and Stella beer, ate *frites* and mussels and *riijstaffel* and real French onion soup and *saltimbocca* and pizza that bore no resemblance to the greasy, cheesy slices served by Italian immigrants in New Jersey. We saw museums and cathedrals and volcanic ruins and enjoyed the hairpin turns on the road that hugged the Amalfi coast. Who does she think she is, whispered the upper middle class women of our town, still a few years away from their own eventual divorces. Who cared what they whispered? She was having a hell of a time finding out.

Back home again, my mother finagled things so that I could study French at a local women's Catholic college during my high school day. I immersed myself in the writings of Baudelaire, Verlaine and Rimbaud, but it wasn't enough. So after more finagling, in the fall of 1978, I set off to spend my senior year of high school in Evian-les-Bains, France, a town in the Haute-Savoie region of the French alps that was the source of the mineral water just beginning to appear on the shelves of American supermarkets.

In France I got my first opportunity to try out my own reinvention. Though I missed my friends and Bruce Springsteen music, my anonymity allowed me to adopt the outward affectations that countless American students in Europe have taken on. When I wrote, I crossed my sevens and my Zs (though I never got so pretentious that I referred to Z as "Zed"). I wore oversized sweaters and tight jeans. I grew out my armpit and leg hair. I stopped showering every day.

In France, even the mundane was interesting. I suffered from *"la bronchite"* throughout the bitter, cold Savoyard winter. Instead of anesthetizing myself with Day-Glo red Sucrets and green Nyquil, as I would have at home, I was advised to suck on Vitamin C tablets and drink *infusions* of herbal tea. When it came time to blow my nose, I discovered that Europeans were not as profligate as Americans. Tissues came in small tightly wrapped packets instead of large boxes that invited you to reach in and take sheet after sheet.

Despite the sophisticated meals I had been exposed to as a child, the simple food I ate in France during lunch at the *lycée* or dinner at the home of my host family was so different that I tasted familiar ingredients in an entirely new way.

Bread was something you dipped into bowls of *café crème* or ate smeared with wedges of ripe and runny unprocessed cheese or sandwiched around squares of dark chocolate. Vegetables weren't over-boiled and slathered in butter or cheese sauce to hide their taste. They were alive, bathed in an exhilarating vinaigrette. Milk wasn't something you refrigerated that came in a carton stamped with an expiration date. It was thin and bluish and could be kept in the cupboard for months. Like many a female exchange student, I grew fat on *pâtisseries* and triangular bars of Toblerone chocolate, anticipating the taste of every new delicacy I encountered.

All around me, people were reinventing themselves. Though most of the French students at the Lycée Anna de Noailles kept their distance, our gang of Americans provided a community for some of the misfits. Bruce, half-French and half-American, liked to sing us Bob Dylan songs by candlelight. Fatima, my Algerian friend, confessed to me that even though she was a good student, she had been "tracked" to attend vocational classes, instead of the more rigorous academic ones, because she was not French-born. Like me, my compatriots were enjoying the freedom of being strangers in a strange land. Elisabeth, the first person I had ever met who spelled the name with a European "s," ran off with her Moroccan boyfriend and we never heard from her again. Karen, out from under the thumb of her domineering mother for the first time, had her hair permed into frizzy, unruly curls. Julie paired up with Jean-Claude. Kathy paired up with everyone.

I discovered myself through travel—taking weekend trips to Lausanne, Geneva, Annecy, Lyon and Paris and longer excursions through Provence, Austria and Switzerland. On Christmas Day I sat in a Swiss family's living room and counted the languages spoken by the assembled guests: English, French, Swiss German, Italian, Romansh, and Spanish, spoken by the Nicaraguan daughter-in-law of our hosts. In February I took the train from Paris to Poland, crossing the Iron Curtain to visit my grandfather's sister and family in Warsaw. I befriended a young East German schoolteacher, who was nothing like the

stereotypical Communist I'd seen in films, and who became my
pen-pal for several years.

When the school year came to an end, I bought a cherry
red two-month Eurail Pass and traveled by myself through
Scandinavia, meeting my mother for a few weeks in Denmark,
before heading home via Iceland. On trains and in youth
hostels, I met fellow backpackers from all over Europe,
Australia and Israel. We were an international youth corps
united by the "No Nukes" patches sewn onto our backpacks
and our curiosity about the world and its people. This was the
promise of our generation and I anticipated the great things we
would accomplish.

And then it was over, and it was time to return home to
New Jersey, where I was as much of a foreigner as I'd been in
France. No one could understand why I now wore clogs and
carried a backpack everywhere I went. I knew that I would have
to shave my body hair if I wanted to be accepted at the Jersey
Shore. The music I had pined for while in France wasn't popular
anymore. Now, it seemed, everyone was listening to the inane,
uncomplicated throbbing of Cheap Trick.

The one recognizable commodity that everyone seemed to
appreciate was my French student ID card, with my birthdate
written in the European fashion of day/month/year, which
to the untrained American eye made it look as if I had been
born on May 9. That summer—the summer before I turned
eighteen, the legal age to drink—my friends and I would
drink sweet, milky Toasted Almonds, Bocci Balls and Tootsie
Rolls in bars along the Jersey Shore, one of us usually barfing
afterwards from the door of our friend's tan VW Bug. When the
bouncer checked our IDs, and frowned at the strange specimen

I produced instead of the standard-issued New Jersey driver's license, my friends would respond with the catch-all phrase used by the Coneheads on Saturday Night Live to excuse their oddities: "She's from France!"

It was time for me to move on.

SITTING IN A PARK
IN PARIS, FRANCE...

There is a broken telephone across the *Pont de l'Alma*, not far from the Eiffel Tower, where you can make international calls for free. On early September evenings, after we have arrived in France, but before classes have begun, my new friends and I traipse across the bridge and line up outside the booth. When it is my turn, I speak to the French operator in my clearest accent.

"*C'est de la parte de qui?*" she asks, with a stereotypical high-pitched bell-like French voice, wanting to know who is making the call.

"*C'est de la parte d'Alison,*" I respond, proud of my accent.

"*AH-LEE-SUN?*" Her voice is nearly a shriek. "*AH-LEE-SUN MAH-KEN-ZEE?*"

Who knew that Peyton Place had been popular enough in France that twenty years later, French telephone operators would remember the name of the heroine?

The Allison MacKenzie exchange happens every time I call the U.S. Maybe I am speaking to the same operator each time; maybe there is a bevy of them who pass around a dog-eared copy of Peyton Place and form opinions about Americans based on the goings-on in 1950s small town New England.

After a few weeks, I tire of it. I also tire of making calls home. It is 1979. Cyberspace does not yet exist. There are no Internet cafes or international cell phones, and so most communication is conducted via the international postal service. You hand-write letters on tissue-thin, red, white and blue Aerogrammes, which take two weeks to reach their destination. It takes another two weeks for you to receive a reply. During that month, you have time to digest your experiences and to consider how you will describe them in your next missive home. You write letters in the heat of the moment. You write long, thoughtful, contemplative letters. You imagine the reaction when your words are read in familiar houses far away. You can't wait for the response.

Overseas phone calls are expensive and so are only for special occasions, such as birthdays, Mother's Day, or when you are just so homesick you need to hear the voice of someone who knew you and loved you before you decided to leave your comfort zone to explore the world. Picking up the phone anytime you want would leave you with nothing special for those times of intense emotion—no way to fill the aching hole within you when you are homesick and no way to fully convey the exhilaration you feel after tasting your first *pain au chocolat* or seeing your first Loire Valley chateau.

Unlike my experiences the previous year, as a high-school exchange student at a French *lycée* in a small town and as a solo traveler with a Eurail Pass, at the American College in Paris

(ACP), I don't have quite the same freedom to reinvent myself. Most of the students at the school are American and savvy enough to form opinions about each other based on where you come from, what your last name is and what your father does for a living. Some people have a vaguely famous or moneyed aura about them. The scions of the Fruehof Truck and Grieco sponge companies (companies I had never heard of) attend the school, as do an array of international mongrels with one American parent and one (step) parent from Europe or North Africa. There is at least one Middle Eastern prince, a Peruvian girl who bears a striking resemblance to Peru's most widely translated author and several well-heeled Iranian women.

Even if I want to pretend to be more intriguing, I can't, because there is someone from my New Jersey hometown at the school. By unspoken agreement we don't acknowledge this. Nor do we admit that, two years before, we had attended my high school junior prom together—me because I needed a date, him because he actually enjoyed going to proms. As I stood uncomfortably beside him, waiting to get our prom portrait taken, I looked at the sample photo the photographer had hung near the portrait area. There was my date, in a powder blue suit with a big bow tie, his hands expertly on the shoulder of the girl he had taken to last year's junior prom.

At ACP, we avoid one another. But he is always there in the background, just like he was in the sample prom picture. At first when I'm around him, I monitor my behavior, so that nothing outrageous will be reported back home. But as the year progresses and I begin to change, I want him to notice these changes, to prove that I am no longer the person I was. It never occurs to me to notice or ask whether he is changing too.

The mailroom is the center of activity at the school and here, all socio-economic and cultural distinctions fall away. The desire for communication is, after all, a great equalizer. You reach into your mail cubby with the same hopeful expression as someone from California, Kuwait, Peru or Iran. The cubbies are arranged alphabetically, so that status, money and country of origin are irrelevant.

Until I find an apartment and some roommates, I am staying at a hotel near the school. There are two English movies playing nearby—*Midnight Cowboy* and *Midnight Express.* The other Americans at the hotel and I are all homesick and desperate to hear English, so we watch these movies over and over again, but they don't make us feel better. How could they? One is a depressing portrayal of hustlers in the U.S., the other a depressing portrayal of an American drug smuggler left to languish in a Turkish prison. These movies are my first introduction to films that carry a message and have an artistic sensibility. They make me feel world-weary and knowing.

I find an apartment with Sarah and Robert, two other American hotel residents, and we settle in to make it our home. The building, located in the 16ᵗʰ *arrondissement,* near the Bois de Boulogne, feels authentically French, despite the fact that most of its inhabitants are foreigners—Tammy and Lisa upstairs, Eric and Kumi across the courtyard, Linda companionably nearby. I like emerging from the metro station and walking *home,* oblivious to the cold stares of the Parisian patrons at the *tabac* and the neighborhood *brasserie,* where Sarah once tried to order two eggs and was told by the disdainful French waiter that she had asked for twelve. Though we are living on student budgets, Sarah often splurges, coming into the apartment with her arms full of colorful flowers she has bought at the local *fleuriste*. We can't afford it, but shortly after we move in, we take a spur-of-the-moment weekend train trip to Brittany. We're thrilled when Sarah finds an extra 100 francs in her purse that enables us to eat, creating fuel to keep us warm on the impossibly cold French train. It's all very bohemian and fun. But as bright October darkens into dreary, rainy Parisian autumn, the news becomes as somber as the weather.

I am in London for the weekend with my friends Paul, John and Beth. We've had quite a time getting here—eating and drinking on the train with new Moroccan and British friends—and later vomiting on the boat that takes us across the English Channel. We visit Big Ben and Trafalgar Square; we scale the fence of the Kensington Gardens; we have a drink at the Hard Rock Café and, at my insistence, skip the other West End offerings and see a live performance of the *Rocky Horror Picture Show* instead.

Tired, but happy, we make our way back to Paris late on Sunday, November 4. In our travel-induced time warp we miss the news that has shocked the world. Fifty-two Americans have been taken hostage in Iran.

My friends and I assure each other that the situation will be resolved quickly because such acts of aggression do not happen to Americans. But it isn't resolved, quickly or otherwise. In fact, though we don't realize it at the time, this event will usher in a new age of anti-U.S. terrorism. In the years to come, hostage taking will become the favored act of political militants; making the aircraft hijackings between the United States and Cuba in the 1960s seem almost quaint.

There is a large Iranian population at our school and the hostage crisis creates tension and awkwardness, despite the fact that our Iranian students don't look anything like the bearded students who stormed the U.S. Embassy in Tehran. They are wealthy and Westernized and we realize that they and their parents are exiled supporters of the Shah, who fled the country after the Islamic Revolution in January. They are properly sympathetic to the U.S. hostage situation, which drags on. In turn, though the conversations hover around the superficial, when we talk to them, it is possible to gain insight into what it must feel like to have the values of your country become unrecognizable.

I take another whirlwind trip on-the-cheap with Sarah over Thanksgiving weekend—this time to Salamanca. The trip is fraught with adventure—our train is delayed several hours and when we finally arrive at the Spanish border, we have five hours to kill before the next train to Salamanca. Spanish train tracks are narrower than those of other European countries, so you can only enter Spain on a Spanish train. This is to provide security from Basque separatists—a new disenfranchised group for me to learn about. We sleep in a field overlooking the Pyrenees, and when we finally board our ice-cold train, we spend the trip getting drunk with our Portuguese compartment-mates and teaching them to play Go Fish.

Back at the American College in Paris, the students seem to have settled into the new, uncomfortable reality of the U.S.-Iran conflict. Then, around Christmas, we learn that the Soviet Union has invaded Afghanistan—an act President Jimmy Carter calls "the most serious threat to peace since the Second World War." I don't understand the ominous implications of his pronouncement, but I'm beginning to get a sense of the complexities of geopolitical interdependence.

Iran, Afghanistan. Like the art films, these countries are new to me. Learning about them, and about my own country's behind-the-scenes involvement with them, makes me feel world-weary and knowing and scared.

During a return visit home over Christmas break, I'm embarrassed by the jingoism that has taken hold in my country—the crude bumper stickers mocking "Ayatollah-Assahola;" the Ayatollah toilet paper on sale at novelty shops; and especially the bantam cock bravado I overhear again and again about how we are going to "kick Iran's ass," despite the fact that the embarrassing U.S. withdrawal from Vietnam had occurred only five years before and a resolute Communist Vietnam had gone on to invade neighboring Cambodia. I find the ubiquitous presence of yellow ribbons on trees and pinned on lapels a more hopeful gesture, reminiscent of the POW-MIA bracelets I, and countless others, had worn during the Vietnam War. Later, I learn that the yellow ribbons were the idea of the wife of hostage Bruce Laingen, who said she wanted "to give people something to do rather than throw dog food at Iranians."

I return to Paris. Because money is tight, Sarah has moved out of the apartment and taken a room in a suburban house, which she is expected to clean in exchange for board. Beth moves in with Robert and me. I'm not at ease with her the way I was with Sarah, so I avoid going home. Still, it's the hopeful beginning of a new year and a new decade and it feels like a fresh start. And by February there is something to be excited about. The students at ACP are glued to the television screen in the common room watching the Winter Olympics at Lake Placid. Everyone is happy that American skater Eric Heiden wins five individual gold medals. But we can't contain our excitement over the "Miracle on Ice," the triumphant defeat by the U.S. hockey team over their Soviet rivals. Although I'm not a hockey fan, being overseas makes it seem especially important to root for the "home team," so I cheer along with everyone else. The fervor of the cheers makes me realize that this is about more than just an underdog team coming from behind to vanquish a rival. These are relieved cheers. America is great again.

The next month President Carter announces that the U.S. will boycott the Moscow Summer Olympics because of the continued Soviet presence in Afghanistan.

"Boycott the Iranian New Year Celebration!" reads a sign displayed by one of the American students at our school (her mother is married to a Getty). She marches around shouting her slogan in front of the Iranian students of ACP, who don't say anything.

"Our American hostages didn't get to celebrate their New Year!"

The Persian community of Paris is planning a big New Year's celebration and parade. Like our school, the city of Paris, I'm beginning to notice, is a microcosm of the world. I notice expatriates everywhere: Algerians, West Africans, Vietnamese, Middle Easterners, Eastern Europeans, Latin Americans. People displaced because of political repression or the arbitrary colonial drawing of boundaries; or, like me, people displaced by choice because they are curious and want to be exposed to different points of view.

This is the Paris where the Ayatollah Khomeini resided in the years prior to the Islamic Revolution; the Paris where Ho Chi Minh refined his philosophy; the Paris my American forebears liberated; the Paris of Hemingway and Gertrude Stein and Van Gogh. People come here to see and be seen differently. Paris, the City of Light, is for many people, Paris, the City of Illumination.

It is April in Paris and one afternoon, filled with emotion, I am ready to call home. The broken pay phone across the *Pont de l'Alma* has long since been fixed, but I call home anyway.

I reach my mother just as she is waking up and share with her news that, because of the time difference, I have already known for several hours.

"Turn on the television," I say. "There was an attempt to rescue the hostages in Iran and it failed."

A hangdog depression descends on our school. America, once so righteous and invincible, doesn't seem omnipotent anymore. Would I feel differently, I wonder, if I were just a citizen of an ordinary country instead of a superpower? Would I have a healthier "you win some, you lose some" attitude?"

During Spring Break I travel with Beth, Robert, Lisa, Andrew and another John to Italy and Greece. We visit some Italian students we had met in Paris, who show us around Rome. We tour Venice and Pisa and then head to Brindisi, where we will take the ferry to Athens. We spend the night in a cockroach-infested flophouse and seek refuge the next morning in the pristine bathrooms of American Express, where another traveler has left a philosophical graffiti composition.

God is Love
Love is Blind
Stevie Wonder is Blind
Stevie Wonder is God

We take the night ferry to Crete and sing Stevie Wonder songs and Eagles songs and Beatles songs with the other student travelers on the boat. We have no common language except the English lyrics and familiar guitar chords of well-known music. Somehow this speaks volumes.

I'm back in Paris. In May, the U.S. government releases data showing that residents of the Love Canal, near Niagara Falls, suffered chromosome damage because of long-term exposure to toxins from a nearby industrial chemical landfill. My country feels corroded within and without.

I have spent the past two years traveling all over Europe, sightseeing and singing and eating and drinking with people from all over the world. The camaraderie has been unmistakable. But I am learning that we are all breathing invisible toxins and sometimes they build up until the damage is corrosive. No amount of invading, evacuating or boycotting will change that. But maybe I can learn how to make sense of it.

So I look at college catalogues via microfiche and find one with a picture on the cover of waves crashing onto a beach. The school's name indicates that it specializes in international studies. Without reading further, just like Joni Mitchell, I know where I am headed next.

...*California, California coming home*

I tell someone that I think of 1979 as the year when the world was forever altered.

"Couldn't you say that about any year?" is the response.

Maybe so.

I went to California and I studied International Relations and in my free time I drank Jack Daniels and played Risk, the game of strategic conquest, with my friends, laughing at the archaic country names on the board. These names would resurface in the coming years, as Walls and Iron Curtains came down and boundaries were redrawn. Hostages were released and more were taken. There would be a bigger, tougher American president who would restore America's sense of might, but it didn't feel so good after all. Someone would try to kill him, but not because of his politics.

I went to Washington, D.C. and became a diplomat. There were civil wars and political assassinations and refugees to contend with; Ayatollah jokes were replaced with Saddam jokes; towers came down; hostages were beheaded; and always and still, there are ribbons, symbols of hope for safe return.

Go to Paris, everyone told me. It will change your life.

I don't know whether it changed my life or whether life just changed. Was it my coming of age or my country's? It doesn't matter.

It was my moveable feast.

BENEFIT OF THE DOUBT

I am standing in the lobby of the former Majestic Hotel trying to make a break for it. At the hotel entrance, a throng of fans is waiting for my companions and me. They've been waiting there all day, ever since they broke away from the roped off area at the airport and began to chase us. Chase us on foot, chase us by bicycle, chase us on mopeds. They chased us as we left the decrepit airport and drove into town. They chased us as we passed billboards for state-run enterprises and posters with Soviet-style artwork celebrating the workers' struggle that look out of place in this tropical environment. They chased us as we attempted to enter the hotel. They chased us and they called out to us by name and tapped us on the shoulders, trying to hand us scraps of paper with names and numbers written on them. Now, hours after our arrival, we want to go to dinner. But if we leave by the front door we will be mobbed. We are ushered out of the hotel via the service entrance and manage to slip away to Maxim's, a nearby restaurant. We are given a private room. We enjoy a dinner of *crab farci*, while musicians serenade us with traditional songs of old Vietnam. Then I have a moment to digest what has happened. This is the closest I'll ever come to knowing how it feels to be a rock star, I think. Nobody has ever wanted me so much in my entire life.

It's December 1988. Twenty-seven years old, fresh from a year of intensive Vietnamese language training, I have arrived in the former South Vietnamese capital of Saigon, renamed Hồ Chí Minh City by the post-war Communist Vietnamese government. I am part of a team of U.S. government officials. Our mission is to interview and decide whether to grant visas to Amerasians (the wartime offspring of Vietnamese women and American men); former prisoners of Communist "re-education camps;" and beneficiaries of immigrant visa petitions filed by family members already in the United States. We do so as part of the Orderly Departure Program (ODP), which was created under an international agreement to stop the dangerous flow of "boat people," who had been risking their lives to flee Vietnam. The United States has had no diplomatic relations with the Socialist Republic of Vietnam since 1975, no Embassy where Vietnamese people can simply apply for a visa. The ODP makes it possible for qualified applicants to meet face-to-face with a U.S. government official in Vietnam. The alternative is to take their chances with escape, which, even if successful, could leave them languishing for years in one of the many overcrowded refugee camps of Southeast Asia.

For nearly four years, I will participate almost every month in these ten-day interview trips, which are physically exhausting and emotionally draining. Despite my extensive training and the fact that I have experience conducting visa interviews in India, the stakes are higher in Vietnam. As I find myself in the uncomfortable position of making decisions that will literally change another person's life, the responsibility to do the right thing, sometimes with very little to guide me, is daunting. Ultimately the guilt that I have not done enough, that nobody can ever do enough, that we are being asked to do too much, will take its toll on me.

My colleagues on the interview team include two other State Department Foreign Service officers. There's Bill, a mild-mannered pleasant man, who spent several years in Vietnam during the 1960s with VISTA. He has a Vietnamese wife, two Amerasian children, and has recently adopted a Thai daughter. He's the most popular of our group and is followed around constantly by an endless parade of Amerasians, many of whom call him "father" or "uncle" or simply "Mr. Bill." He makes time for all who stop him, stuffing the scraps of paper they hand him into his bulging pockets, promising to review their requests, take action on their cases. There's also Bob, a taciturn, lanky, bearded man, who seems unruffled by any perturbations, usually shrugging them off with a monosyllabic, "Well, what are you gonna do?" He spent time in Vietnam too, in the military, and also has a Vietnamese wife, an Amerasian child and two Vietnamese daughters that he and his wife adopted during the war. He comes across as tough and unapproachable and quirky. But he, too, accepts the scraps of paper that are handed to him.

In contrast to Bill and Bob are the officers from the Immigration and Naturalization Service (INS), most of whom have no previous connection to Vietnam and don't speak the language. Many have spent time in the U.S. working border patrol, and seem to have carried this mentality with them to

Vietnam. My initial impression is that they are xenophobic good ole boys, replete with cowboy boots and suitcases full of American snack food. They brush away the hangers-on who follow them. They don't accept any scraps of paper or requests for help.

I'm determined to fall somewhere in the middle. I bring no baggage to this assignment. I was a child during the Vietnam War. I have only the faintest memories of televised images of American soldiers in camouflage running through rice paddies, of anti-war demonstrations, Lyndon Johnson's announcement that he would not seek re-election, Kent State. By the time I came of age, the conventional wisdom was that U.S. military intervention in Vietnam was a mistake. I have no children in my life with Vietnamese features. I have never had to protect U.S. borders. So I think… I hope… I can remain unbiased.

In the year I'd spent in language training in Washington, D.C., I'd been determined to learn all I could about this country, about the war and about Vietnamese—a musical language with five different tones. In Vietnamese, the same word can be pronounced in different ways; each tone completely changes the word's meaning. As I reviewed case files at the ODP headquarters in Bangkok, I discovered similar shades of gray. I read interview notes about assumed identities, fake birth certificates, and fraudulent marriages. Sometimes the files contained few documents and even fewer interview notes— only the initials "BOD," for benefit of the doubt. Armed with all of this training and displaying that particular combination of arrogance and naïveté common among earnest people in their twenties, I've come to Vietnam determined to conduct thorough, fair and impartial interviews.

At breakfast the first morning I join my colleagues. They are all drinking coffee and have ordered bowls of hot water to go with the packets of Quaker instant oatmeal they have brought. I'd been warned to bring provisions, since acceptable food was hard to find, so I reluctantly follow suit. Anxious to be accepted by the team, I participate as they read each other the quiz questions from the back of the packets. I hate the taste of the oatmeal and am desperate for something more exotic. I attempt to glean from the wait staff what else might be available. Eventually, I discover they have papaya. I learn the Vietnamese word for papaya—*đu đủ*—the second syllable with a musical sounding rising and falling tone. Every morning, to the delight of the Vietnamese wait staff, I order đu đủ. Pretty soon I give up Quaker Oats altogether.

We drive to the interview site. It's a two-story open building with a courtyard, located behind the Hồ Chí Minh City branch office of the Ministry of Foreign Affairs. It's built in a spare, functional style, pale yellow with linoleum style patterned floors. The downstairs consists of two rooms, abuzz with busy Vietnamese workers sorting documents. Stairways at either end of the building lead upstairs, where the interview rooms are and where applicants are required to wait in a narrow hallway with large open windows that look out onto the courtyard below. There are far more applicants than there are chairs, so many of them are crowded on the floor or on the staircase, fanning themselves for relief from the heat of the searing Southeast Asian sun. Some are eating watermelon and spitting out the seeds, leaving them where they fall. Others are sleeping, no doubt resting from the long journey to get here from their villages in remote areas of Vietnam. Others scrutinize the faces of applicants as they exit interview rooms to see if they've been approved and to gauge their own chances of success if called into a particular room. The people greet me respectfully as I pass. "*Chào, cô,*" hello, miss, they say, heads slightly bowed. Some bold, older women, surprised to see a young woman on the interview team, smile broadly when they see me. They look directly into my eyes and say loudly "*Chào, cô!*" When I respond, "*Chào, bà,*" hello, ma'am, they nudge their companions with their elbows, amazed to hear me speak Vietnamese. They look at each other, and at me, and they grin, teeth stained red with betel nut juice. We all laugh.

Because of my inexperience, the interpreter I am assigned is Mrs. Xuyen, a fat, bossy, opinionated woman, rumored to have family connections—a husband and father-in-law with important government jobs. She immediately takes charge. She leads me to the interview room. It's sterile, with three rows of folding chairs for the applicants. Across from the chairs is the desk, with one chair behind it for the interviewer and a chair to its left for the interpreter. To me the room seems unwelcoming and intimidating. To the applicants, who've likely had to sit in many such rooms to get to this point, I doubt it makes much difference.

We settle down in our room. Mrs. Xuyen calls in the first family. They are asked to remain standing, raise their right hands and swear to tell the truth. Then they sit down, chairs scraping the floor, like fingernails on a chalkboard. The interview gets underway. It's a straightforward first case—a family going to join relatives in the U.S. The paperwork is in order, so there's not much to ask. I rifle through the papers in their file and struggle to think up some questions, to look like I'm in charge. But as she barks out her translations, Mrs. Xuyen conveys the impression that she has the upper hand. I don't like her approach, but I'm nervous and not comfortable with what I am doing. The family responds to each question, looking scared. I feel foolish and useless. This is this family's big moment with a U.S. government official, one that they have waited years for. Surely I can think of something to say. I push the file aside and address each family member in turn in Vietnamese, waving Mrs. Xuyen away as she tries to cut me off and translate my questions. "What did you do during the war?" I ask the father. "I was a soldier," he replies. "How much time did you spend in a re-education camp?" I ask. "Three years," he responds, without emotion. "What do you do now?" I continue. "I'm a tailor," he says. "How many children do you have?" I ask the mother. "Four," she replies. "When did your eldest son leave by boat?" I ask. "In 1982," she answers, looking pained. Next I address the three remaining children in turn. "How old are you?" "What grade are you in?" "Are you a good student?" By the time I ask this last question of the third child, the family has relaxed. The boy answers proudly, "Yes, I'm a good student!" His sisters look amused and dubious. They laugh and nudge each other. The interview is over. I tell the family with a smile they have been approved and offer congratulations. Mrs. Xuyen looks askance, the family looks pleased and I am feeling more confident.

And so it goes that first morning. I've been given the easiest cases, my colleagues checking with me from time to time to see how I am doing. At lunch time we go out for a bowl of *phở*, Vietnamese noodle soup, and I am chatting easily about the workload. When we return, it is decided that I am ready to try my hand at something more difficult. I am given my first Amerasian case.

Amerasians, the products of sexual relationships between U.S. servicemen and Vietnamese women, stood out in the otherwise homogenous society of Vietnam. Called "children of the dust," after the war, they were often hidden, their birth certificates and other documentation destroyed. Their existence was concealed to keep their families safe from persecution from Communist governmental officials and the local authorities, who kept tabs on the community. But in recent years—once it was announced that the U.S. government had agreed to allow unmarried Amerasians to resettle in the United States with blood or "foster families"—they'd enjoyed a new kind of notoriety. Now called "gold kids," they were seen as a ticket out of Vietnam. They range in age from mid-teens to almost thirty.

The most difficult aspect of these cases was also the most basic—determining whether the applicant was actually Amerasian. In the absence of any documentation and often with no birth mother present to tell the story of her relationship with an American soldier, sometimes all we had to go on was looks. In some cases it was easy. A girl, much larger than a small-boned Vietnamese, with dark skin, nappy hair and a deep timbre to her voice, would clearly be the product of a Vietnamese mother and a black American father. In other cases, it was harder to tell. So a purely subjective decision had to be made.

I sit in my interview room staring at the boy in front of me. He's here alone, with little documentation and no knowledge of his father. His mother is dead, he claims. After she died, he lived with distant relatives. They are not interested in joining him in the U.S. Does he look Amerasian? It's not obvious to me. The longer I stare at him, the harder it is not to focus on his individual features. I can no longer see his face as a whole. I am frustrated. I have nothing to go on. No evidence one way or another to help me make this crucial decision. Yet a simple yes or no from me will change this boy's life. I ask him to get up and follow me. I lead him out into the waiting area. We walk past the gaping applicants, who are pleased to have some excitement to break up the monotony of waiting. One by one, we visit the other interview rooms so I can consult with my colleagues. In front of the boy and the family being interviewed in that room, we discuss the boy's physical characteristics. "The eyes look round and seem to be a lighter shade of brown," one officer says. "I can't put my finger on it, but there's just something different about his face," another offers. "That kid is pure Vietnamese through and through. He's just weird looking!" says another. Seeking other opinions was common practice whenever we were stuck in the interview process. Eventually, I learned which interviewers to go to when my gut told me to approve a case; I learned which interviewers to approach when my gut told me to reject a case. Sometimes during a power outage, the light in the interview rooms would not be sufficient, so we would conduct our scrutiny in the waiting area in full view of the other applicants. Humiliating, yes. But for these Amerasian applicants, with nothing else in their favor, their looks were their only chance. BOD. Benefit of the doubt.

Hard as it sometimes was to establish the bona fide characteristics of an Amerasian, it was harder still to determine whether the people with him were his true family. Fraud was rampant. Poverty and desperation would sometimes lead the birth mother of an Amerasian to sell her child. She would sell him to people who would then pose as a caring foster family; all of them were under the mistaken belief that once the Amerasian arrived in the U.S. he could petition for his natural family to join him. People with no other viable means of leaving Vietnam would use every imaginable trick to tag along with an Amerasian. As a result, there were often cousins posing as siblings, newly acquired "stepfathers" and various other hangers-on. Later, when U.S. Amerasian legislation was amended to allow married Amerasians to bring their extended families, virtually no Amerasian appeared for an interview without a newly acquired spouse. To determine if the marriage was real I would separate the couple and find myself conducting an interrogation alone with a naïve, uneducated young country bumpkin Amerasian. "Do you sleep together under the same blankets?" I'd ask, using the classical Vietnamese term for sexual intercourse that I'd carefully been taught in language training. "Huh?" was the quizzical response. I tried again. "Do you make love?" "Huh?" And again. "Do you screw?" "HUH?" Finally my last ditch effort. "Do you fuck?" I asked. It was a word I'd learned by mistake when I used the wrong tone for the word enough. But it did the trick. The Amerasian flashed a look of recognition. Success at last.

With the absence of documentation, I would look for subjective signs of family life. Was there physical resemblance to the mother and half siblings? Any genuine affection? Sometimes there was no choice but to ask the family to leave the room and speak to the Amerasian alone. "You don't have to bring these people with you to America," I would say kindly, but firmly. "Do you have a real mother somewhere that you would rather bring?" Almost invariably the Amerasian would look shyly down at the floor and mumble unconvincingly, "No, this is my real family." No amount of prodding could get him to say more. Only once, in four years of interviewing, did an Amerasian confess to me that the foster family he'd brought to the interview was a fake.

Something seems amiss as soon as the family sits down to be interviewed. The foster family, a mother, father and several children, are smartly dressed and seem eager to tell me how they had cared for this Amerasian. The Amerasian sits apart from them, dressed in clothes that are tattered and dirty. He isn't given a chance to answer any of the questions I ask him. Finally, I ask the family to leave the room. I come around from behind my desk and sit down in one of the chairs next to the boy. "Is this your real family?" I ask gently. "No," he mumbles, "it's not." Instead of looking down at the floor he looks me in the eye. "My real mother is still alive and lives in the country. This family gave her money so they could come with me to America. But I want my mother to come with me." I nearly fall out of my chair. The boy goes on to say that the family had been cruel to him, that he is afraid they will not let him leave if they are rejected and only he is approved.

I can barely contain my rage, my desire for revenge on his behalf, on his mother's behalf, on behalf of the U.S. government. With the help of my interpreter, I explain that we will tell the family they are approved. But over the next few days when the documentation is completed and travel arrangements are made, only the Amerasian's papers will be processed. By the time the family gets wind of this, he will be safely under our protective wing, kept in the transit area with other families getting ready to travel. Once in the U.S., he will need to file the necessary papers for his mother to join him. I note all of this in the file. We call the family back into the room. As they enter, the boy and I look at each other. His gaze is pure and unfaltering. The family sits down noisily. I muster up all of my powers of self-control. I tell them they have been approved, but this time I don't smile, I don't offer congratulations. Their reaction seems cocky and triumphant. At that instant I hate them, though they are probably driven by desperation like so many others. I don't care. I hate them anyway. And I wish I could be there to see their faces the day they discover they will not be going to America after all.

The work is grueling, the caseload heavy. We are exhausted by the time we return to our hotel but a parade of hopefuls is usually waiting for us there. Often the lobby ends up serving as a makeshift waiting area, with the lucky few who have managed to talk their way inside, sitting and waiting to pounce on the first sympathetic American face they encounter, trying to advance their case. Meeting the criteria for resettlement to the U.S. was one hurdle. But an interview could not occur until the applicant had been granted an exit permit from the Vietnamese government and placed on one of their infamous interview lists. How this happened was often a mystery, and it varied from locality to locality, depending on the benevolence and efficiency of the local officials in charge of registration. As a result, families often languished for years, sometimes receiving no news of when they would be granted an interview. But if they were able to push their papers into the hands of a U.S. government official, who, in turn, would place it in front of the appropriate Vietnamese official, they could be spared falling into this black hole of oblivion and/or paying lots of bribe money.

How can you say no to someone who has been waiting and waiting for a chance? Like a predictable scene from a B-movie, a small, timid woman sits quietly waiting, her hands folded. You walk by, trying not to make eye contact. You just want to get to your room and wash away the dirt and the sweat and the fatigue that come from listening to scores of people tell you their life stories all day. She stands up and nervously walks toward you, calling faintly, "*Sin, cô,*" please, miss. How can you say no, even though you're dead tired, exhausted from trying on behalf of your government to right a series of wrongs that have been done to people, wrongs you had nothing to do with, that you were too young to understand at the time? So you take the scrap of paper with a name and case number that she pushes into your hand. You nod as she rushes to tell you the problem. Her family has been on an interview list for more than three years but has never been called for an interview. You tell her you'll look into the matter. Some days when you do this you feel like a savior. You imagine her delight when finally her family is interviewed as a result of your intervention. Other days it feels hopeless. Yes, you'll put the scrap of paper into the hands of the appropriate Vietnamese official. But you'll never really know what happens. With so many scraps of paper and such a large caseload, it becomes hard to keep track. It's easy to confuse one case, one life, with the many others that need your attention.

The hotel bar is our sanctuary. It is understood that no supplicants can approach us there. Located off the lobby, up three steps, it opens out onto a small patio with a view of the Saigon River. After work each day, my colleagues and I congregate in this bar. We drink weak Asian beer the color of the urine you piss once you've downed a few. We trade stories about our day, regaling each other with funny or unusual interview tales, indulging in black humor. But we don't talk about the larger issue—the subjectivity of our work. The there-but-for-the-grace-of-God-go-I element of it. How it feels to be one human being passing judgment on another.

Evenings, we walk the streets near our hotel. It's unusual to find Americans in Communist Vietnam. As a result, there's an uncomfortable mixture of tension, curiosity, surprise and friendliness that surrounds us. Everyone notices us and feels compelled to comment. Adorable, barefoot little kids in threadbare clothes selling gum, stamps and curios accompany us, chattering and joking with us as we walk. Bicycle rickshaw or *cyclo* drivers pedal by, calling out to us. The only other foreigners we see are the Russians, who have replaced the French and the Americans as imperialists in residence. Fat, unfashionably dressed, they have distrustful expressions on their faces when they spy us. The Vietnamese word for them is *Liên Xô*, which means Soviet. It's become a catch-all word for all foreigners though, and as we walk, sometimes I hear people calling out to us, "*Liên Xô, Liên Xô!*" I'm told the South Vietnamese don't like them, that they call them "Americans without dollars." The reappearance of real Americans seems to please and surprise the residents of the former Saigon, whose lives have been significantly altered since the Communists seized control of their city. During the war, these streets were filled with Americans fighting to preserve their freedoms and bolstering their economy in the process. Each time we explain to a local that we are indeed American, a happy expression crosses the person's face. Sometimes they say, "Welcome back!"

When I'm anywhere, even in my hotel room, it feels wrong not to be fully engaged in the experience, wrong to be off-duty, wrong not to savor every sight, every sound, every smell, and every taste. Vietnam offers everything I'd ever dreamed of in a Foreign Service assignment—political intrigue, uncertainty and adventure. I feel like a character in a Graham Greene novel. I'm the Quiet American, filled with good intentions, excited to be a part of the fledgling relationship between the United States and Communist Vietnam. I won't make the mistake of those who have gone before me—a failure to understand Vietnam's present in light of its past.

Being fully engaged at all times means I never completely relax during these trips. I prepare for them as if I am entering a monastery and will be leading the life of an ascetic. I pack only my oldest clothes, nothing of value except a short-wave radio, books about Vietnam, Vietnamese-English dictionaries. My only pleasure reading is the *New Yorker*. But even this incorporates a self-imposed discipline. I'd bring back issues of the *New Yorker* that had stacked up over the past six months. I'd force myself to read them from cover to cover. On each interview trip I required myself to advance through the stack by at least one month. I wonder now if my asceticism came partly from guilt: guilt that the people on whom I was passing judgment endured what for me was merely a textbook war; guilt that I didn't have the deep connection to Vietnam that some of my colleagues did; guilt that sometimes I got tired and wanted a break from these desperate people and their miserable lives; guilt because sometimes whether or not I liked a person determined whether I gave them BOD.

For them it was a life-altering event. For me it was just another day on the job:

The family walks into the room silently. The father, dignified, back ramrod straight, evidence of his years of military service. The mother, still beautiful in a composed way, the tiny lines on her face showing that she has endured hardships and has found the grace to deal with them. And the daughters—five of them—demurely feminine in their white áo dài, the Vietnamese national dress of pants and a tunic, long black hair flowing down their backs, hands together, heads respectfully bowed.

What a contrast to the other families crowded in the waiting area—loudly eating, spitting, gossiping, snoring.

In the interview room, the family stands at attention, raising their right hands as instructed and promising to tell the truth. The wife and daughters look at the father for permission to be seated. He, in turn, looks at my interpreter, who nods. They take their seats, careful to avoid the scraping of chairs.

Experienced now, it is usually at this moment in the interview that I assert control. I call each family member by name and ask a few questions in Vietnamese. This will show them, and my Vietnamese government-assigned interpreter, that I speak Vietnamese and can understand what is going on. I want everyone in the room to know that there will be no altering by the interpreter of the questions I ask or of the responses they give.

I call the father's name. He rises. I ask him about his years of military service and the time he spent in a re-education camp. There is no need for me to do this. All of the information I need to know is there, well documented, in the file that lies in front of me on the metal desk. But not to ask him would have cheated him somehow. After all, this is his moment, one he'd been waiting for during the years spent in the re-education camp, the years spent waiting for permission from the Vietnamese government to exit the country. After years of supporting the American presence in Vietnam and years being punished for having done so, he'd longed to tell his story to a U.S. government official, one who could appreciate what he'd been through, what his sacrifices had meant. What a disappointment it must be for him to tell his story to an inexperienced young American woman who was a child during the war.

Next I speak to the mother about the child in the U.S., their only son, who had escaped Vietnam by boat and later filed a visa petition to bring his family to join him. They call these people anchors—people who risked their lives in rickety overcrowded boats to anchor the family in the U.S. and send out a lifeline that would allow the rest to follow.

Then the daughters. I call each of them by name and ask a few questions about school. But my usual ice-breaking question, "Are you a good student?" doesn't elicit the usual smiles and nervous giggles from family members. In fact, I notice the entire family and my interpreter looking at me strangely after

I question the first girl. My interpreter tries to call the second girl's name for me but I lift a hand to stop him. This is, after all, their moment to be interviewed by a U.S. government official. They had spent enough time being interviewed by Vietnamese government hacks.

And so I continue, "Pink shit, how old are you?" "White shit, what grade are you in?" "Yellow shit, are you a good student?" and so on. There isn't any need to ask any questions, everything is in order in the file on the metal desk in front of me.

I was humiliated after they left, when my interpreter burst out laughing and told me that I'd gotten the Vietnamese tone wrong; humiliated that I had transformed the names of the lovely sisters, each named for a different colored chrysanthemum, into something far more mundane. Humiliated that this dignified family had struggled to suppress their laughter as I painstakingly spoke to each daughter. I was humiliated at first. Later, I smiled to myself. Maybe I couldn't give this dignified man and his long-suffering family the interview they'd been expecting, the one they deserved. But at least the moment when I transformed their lives was a memorable one.

Eventually, inevitably, I burned out. Little by little, I stopped being quite as naïve, quite as curious, quite as engaged. I stopped being quite as compassionate, quite as unbiased. I got tired. Tired of the caseload, which had reached 10,000 cases per month; tired of the fraud; tired of the policy changes that kept expanding the categories of people eligible to go to

America, even as economic opportunities increased in Vietnam and government restrictions loosened. I got tired, too, of the changes in Hồ Chí Minh City, which was becoming more and more like decadent wartime Saigon. The adorable little gum sellers I'd met on my first trip could now be found dancing in nightclubs, some of them prostitutes. The city got sleazier and tackier until finally I chose to spend my free time in my room, listening to my Walkman, reading books that had nothing to do with Vietnam, trying to shut out the place I'd once been so desperate to understand.

One day, in a fit of rage I screamed at a particularly unhelpful Vietnamese official who had refused to take action on a case that had been mishandled. I shouted at him that his government condoned fraud, fraud, fraud. I was banned from the country, only allowed to return to work once I had apologized to his boss while he practiced ping-pong.

And then it was over. After more than thirty interview trips, my assignment finally came to an end. I returned to Washington, took assignments involving other countries and eventually left the State Department. Vietnam—a place, an experience that had consumed me for so long, strangely just wasn't part of my life anymore.

In the years since I left Vietnam I've had the opportunity to reflect on the experience with the perspective that time and distance can give. I see both good and bad on my personal balance sheet. Some cases remain fresh in my mind. An Amerasian to whom I gave the benefit of the doubt is leading a happy and productive life in the U.S. and has named her daughter after me. An applicant I rejected, a wily new husband, twice the age of his fresh-faced young Amerasian wife, remains in Vietnam, as far as I know. His case was championed by an American journalist, who later wrote a book about her experiences in Vietnam. In it, she criticized me as a narrow-minded bureaucrat who tore apart this loving couple. How could we have seen their relationship so differently?

Though Vietnam touches my life only peripherally now, reminders of it crop up from time to time: when I go out to eat phở with my husband, whom I met in the bar of my Hồ Chí Minh City hotel; in the delighted giggles of my daughters, who loved to count in Vietnamese while swinging at the playground; on the rare occasions when I get a manicure at one of the many Vietnamese-owned nail salons in my city. I've taught English as a Second Language to Vietnamese families resettled in Seattle. I've even written a letter to ODP on behalf of one of them, whose daughter was not approved to come to the U.S. along with the rest of the family.

I almost never encounter any Amerasians, though, or maybe I do. In a multi-cultural society such as ours, they don't stick out the way they did in Vietnam. I wonder how it feels for them to blend in, to no longer have their features scrutinized. I wonder if they are happy here, if by coming to America they feel reunited with a part of themselves that had been missing. And I wonder if they are as relieved as I am to no longer be anybody's ticket to a better life.

THEM

THE CUISINART TRAVELER

When I was twenty, I kept a list of all the countries I had been to, with the expectation that I would see every country in the world before I died. This was not unreasonable. My early years pointed to a lifetime of exotic travel. By the time I'd started the list, I had visited twenty-one countries. I'd hitchhiked to the Arctic Circle, traveled by train from France to Poland, celebrated Icelandic Independence Day in Reykjavik, sniffed sulfur springs in Rotorua and tasted curry in Fiji. By age thirty I'd trekked in the Himalayas, snorkeled in the Great Barrier Reef, and sung karaoke in Saigon, Hong Kong and Tokyo. By thirty-five, it wasn't enough to visit every country once; I longed to see specific regions. I'd been to Vladivostok, but not St. Petersburg; Vientiane, but not the Plain of Jars; Bali, but not Sulawesi. When I was thirty-six, I explored the backwaters of Kerala. A few months later, I became pregnant with my first child. With the exception of a few forays to Canada, I haven't set foot outside of the United States in four-and-a-half years.

Tonight we will dine on Chicken with Preserved Lemons and Cracked Green Olives. I'll let the chicken stew in its tangy broth for hours and will serve it in a deep oval blue and orange ceramic platter. We will hold warm triangles of bread in our hands to pull the meat off the bones, letting the bread soak up the liquid, just like they do in Casablanca. For dessert there will be fresh figs with honey and mint tea.

I've never been to Casablanca. Or Samarkand or Isfahan or Addis Ababa or Dakar or Havana or Lima. But one look at my recipe box and you would think I'd just returned from some exotic locale where I'd spent days with village women learning to shape tortillas or sear chilis or shred green papaya. One look in my spice rack and you'd find *epizote*, Jamaican allspice, *garam masala*, *asafetida powder*, *achiote* and *berbere*. I'm still traveling, even though I haven't gotten any farther away from my Seattle kitchen than Jonesport, Maine. I'm still traveling—with my taste buds instead of my feet.

On nights when I'm at a loss for what to cook, we eat a simple stir-fry of spinach and tofu with garlic, sesame seeds and soy sauce, an embellishment of the stir-fried Chinese broccoli I ate every day for lunch in Vietnam. When we have guests for dinner and don't have time to experiment, we stick to our old standbys: *gai yang*, sticky rice and *som tum*; Jamaican jerk chicken with fried plantains and coconut rice; Malaysian chicken rice. All winter long, as an antidote to colds and flu, we soothe ourselves with Armenian chicken soup. I keep preserved lemons in my refrigerator, bamboo steamer baskets from Laos on top of the kitchen cabinets, candlenuts and *blachen* and *papadam* in the pantry.

A typical day goes as follows: at about 10 a.m., I survey the contents of my refrigerator and cupboards for potential ingredients. Maybe an article in one of my cooking magazines has made me decide to take a culinary trip to Armenia. Maybe I'm remembering the fiery taste of *sambal* prawns washed down with light, sweet beer. Maybe there's a chill in the air, and I wish I were in a cozy French bistro, eating roasted chicken, potato gratin, *haricots verts* and pear *clafoutis*.

After a domestic whirl of preschool, play dates at the park, reading stories, singing songs, filling sippy cups, and soothing hurts, we settle in at home. If I'm lucky, my daughters will play happily together, dressing in feather boas and tutus, having tea parties for their stuffed animals or watching a Winnie-the-Pooh video.

I retreat to the kitchen and pour myself a glass of *Sancerre* or *Muscadet* or *Syrah* and my voyage begins. I prepare spice pastes with my mortar and pestle. I chop *gai lan* or *galangal* or lemongrass. I caramelize onions. I soak rice noodles or cannellini beans. Soon, the kitchen is filled with the pungent aroma of chicken frying in coriander, cardamom, cinnamon and turmeric. Soon, something is bubbling heartily in the blue Le Creuset pot on my stove. There's a moment in cooking when you know you've gotten it right. That's the moment when I am transported to a food court in Singapore, a *souk* in Cairo, a *taverna* on Sifnos.

But it's a solo voyage, and a short one. By the time we sit down at the dinner table, the spell is broken. I become preoccupied with coaxing my daughters to take one more bite. I try to get a word in edgewise, so my husband and I can share the details of our day.

I am no longer an unencumbered mortar and pestle making my way through the world. I am a Cuisinart, with attachments that need to be fed. So I cook them food as American as apple pie, steaming the windows and filling the house with its aroma of tart cinnamon-spiced fruit. I cook them the soul-satisfying comfort foods that speak of children's drawings on the wall, a cat sleeping on the windowsill, of love and attachment and interdependence. I bake chocolate chip cookies and muffins bursting with blueberries, three-berry cobblers and macaroni and cheese. I make turkey and garlic mashed potatoes and slow-cooked vegetable bean soups and tuna melts. The first time I made my oldest daughter a grilled cheese sandwich—not a *croque-monsieur* or *panini*, but an honest-to-goodness, old-fashioned grilled cheese sandwich, cut in triangles with bright orange cheese spilling out the back and sides—I nearly wept from the sweetness of the experience. I cook these foods and my heart almost bursts with love.

Life is like bittersweet Belgian chocolate. For every path you take, for every choice you make, you wonder what might have been. I sometimes wonder when I'll be able to add to my list, now tattered and faded, of countries I have seen. Meanwhile, my older daughter complains about eating *Uzbeki pilau* the way some kids complain about pork chops. But she washes down her meals with *horchata* and *karkady*, craves moon cakes in the afternoon and sometimes eats *budin de calabaza* for a bedtime snack, instead of Teddy Grahams. Cooking has made it possible for me to continue down the path that I chose when I was young and independent and free.

I think about dieting sometimes. I could deal with the hunger—the physical hunger that is. But if Weight Watchers or the Zone or Dr. Atkins forced me to give up my epicurean voyages, I don't think I could stand the emotional hunger. At least not until I renew my passport.

TYPE A-

"So, are you doing...anything?" Jane asks me hesitantly when we run into each other at the preschool barbeque.

Jane has an important job with a non-profit organization that is trying to improve the health of impoverished people around the world. She takes numerous international trips. When she's in town, she swims laps three times a week at 6 a.m. at the local swimming pool. In the course of our catching up she tells me that she's taking a gymnastics class too. Twice a week after dinner she makes a half-hour commute, so she can swing on the uneven bars. There are family hikes, trips to Mexico. She makes a mean quiche. Jane is one of those people, I've decided, who lives life "full tilt boogie."

For as long as I can remember, and especially since the birth of my first daughter Melanie, people have been asking me to account for my time. When my maternity leave stretched from three months to six and later, when it became clear that I wasn't ever returning to my job, people, usually other women, wanted to know what my plans were.

It never felt like enough to respond:

"I'm staying at home raising my kids," so I always made sure I was doing something else redeeming—working as a volunteer teacher of English to refugees; trying to promote the use of renewable energy; taking writing classes.

Friends from my childless days, usually women, would say sympathetically,

"Before you know it, they'll be in school..." their voices trailing off hopefully, as if I were fulfilling a prison sentence and we were all counting the days until I would be eligible for parole.

But the loudest voice and the most persistent questions came from me. For years I had defined myself by international travel and by my career. When we had kids, I assumed Jeff and I would cobble together a fifty-fifty arrangement that gave us equal tastes of domesticity and professional satisfaction: both of us working part-time, both of us caring for the kids part-time. Interchangeable parts of a beautifully oiled machine.

Around the time we were contemplating having children, Jeff and I went hiking one Saturday on a well-populated trail. On our descent we stumbled upon a woman changing her infant's diaper in the middle of the dirt path.

"That'll be you someday," chuckled Jeff.

"What do you mean ME?" I retorted sharply. "It could just as easily be you!"

"It could," Jeff agreed, "but you'll probably be changing most of the diapers."

I didn't speak to him the rest of the way down the mountain and for a good part of the ride home.

I got pregnant and, despite the fact that I was working for an abusive boss, I asked for the minimum amount of maternity leave.

"Why don't you ask for the full six months?" Jeff wondered. "You can always go back early if you really want to."

"I'll want to," I assured him.

But after three months, I didn't want to go back. I didn't want to go back after four months or six months or even after the abusive boss was fired. I'd seen the local daycare offerings. And I wasn't interested in having a nanny in charge of my child.

It was Jeff who changed Melanie's first diaper—black, tar-like meconium from her first stool sticking to his fingers. It was Jeff who gave Melanie her first bath, while I cowered in the corner, upset by her cries. It was Jeff who was perfectly content to spend hours reading Winnie-the-Pooh poems. Jeff, who parented by instinct, while I checked everything in the parenting books first. When he had the opportunity to take Family Leave, after Maya was born, Jeff asked for the maximum three months off. Jeff wasn't conflicted. He wasn't going to want to go back to work early. Not a chance.

But Jeff didn't have to deal with the nagging questions. He didn't have to agonize over walking away from a career. I wondered if his identity was as wrapped up in his career as mine was.

"Would you feel like less of a man if you were a stay-at-home dad?" I asked him.

"I don't know," he answered honestly.

When Melanie was four months old, I applied for a job at Jane's organization. It was a demanding position that would have required me to travel internationally fifty percent of the time. At the same time, I was offered the opportunity to work part-time from home, compiling a directory of renewable energy companies.

"I'll support you in whatever you want to do," Jeff said gently, "but imagine how crazy our lives would be if we were both working full time and you were traveling fifty percent of the time."

Instead, I let my days take on a sweet pattern—music and tumbling classes, afternoons at the park or lying on the grass looking at clouds—until about 5 p.m. As any stay-at-home parent can tell you, that's the hour when you begin questioning your choices. You watch the clock with hawk-like intensity, waiting for relief. Even a five-minute delay in your partner's return can determine whether he receives a calm reception or is confronted by a screaming lunatic.

When people asked what I was doing, I got a variety of responses to my response. Men usually gave me a beatific smile, as if I was now elevated to iconic status, along with baseball and apple pie. But I noticed they didn't talk to me the same way they had when I was working and had an assumed familiarity with the outside world. Most of the women I'd known before I had children gave me the parole pep talk. And on the playgrounds and at baby tumbling classes, I heard a variety of comments:

"I would never go back to work, would you?"

"I wish I could stay home, but we need two incomes."

"I love my job but I'm always playing catch-up."

And, most often, "I wish I could find a way to work part-time."

We sized each other up; the way women do, comparing lifestyles instead of hairstyles or bodies. Looking to see if anyone else had uncovered the secret that would lead to a balanced life.

It would have been so much less confusing if I had been more driven towards professional accomplishment. But I've always had an ambivalent relationship with ambition.

"So, are you doing anything...worthwhile?" Ira Horowitz asked me, the summer of my triumphant return to Beacon Beach.

I'd arrived dressed in my new uniform: an Indian wrap skirt picked up during my travels to Fiji, Birkenstocks, dangling ethnic earrings, hair permed and blonde, my non-Jewish Californian boyfriend Tom in tow.

The last time I had seen Ira Horowitz, he was a lifeguard at this beach. He'd gone decidedly against type. The lifeguards I'd grown up with had been big and buff, a thick smear of zinc oxide permanently applied to their noses and lips. They sat high in their lifeguard towers, as bikinied high school girls sashayed by them. They were surfers and swimmers. They were the cool older guys—my brother's friends, my cousins' friends, the guys you secretly had crushes on, who made you swoon when they noticed you, even if it was just to give you a big brotherly punch in the arm.

Ira Horowitz was skinny, with self-described "big adenoids" that gave his voice the whiny sound of a perpetual post-nasal drip. All the years we were in school together, he'd been like the character of Arnold Horshak from the hit TV series *Welcome Back, Kotter.* Whenever the teacher asked a question, no matter how easy, Ira, who always sat in the front row, body taut, would raise himself up to his fullest height, arm ramrod straight in the air and yell, "Ooh, ooh, I know, I know!"

The rest of us resignedly kept quiet while the teachers, searching in vain for someone else to call on, finally let him speak.

I found this tiresome. In the "0 track" classes where we smart kids were placed, I grew tired of the desperation exhibited by Ira and the other Jewish boys who were slated to become doctors and lawyers. They peppered the front rows of the classrooms, Ira and Ari and Seth, their "ooh, oohs!" drowning out the voices of other students who wanted to have a turn. But the year I rebelled, and asked to be in a regular Social Studies class instead of the 0 track, I was equally frustrated. We spent the entire year it seemed to me, learning that *guano* was bat dung. So the following year, I returned to the fold.

I decided I would not follow the anticipated career path— attending an Ivy League school in Boston. I wanted to get away from all the smart Jewish kids responding to parental pressure, who would become forty-year-old doctors with bald spots, healthy bank accounts and pleasure boats. If I stayed with them, I was guaranteed that my voice would not be heard.

My mother was supportive, helping me rack up college credits through a combination of summer classes and college credit exams, sending me off to France for my senior year in high school, and getting the school district to grant me the five credits I needed to graduate, by designating that year abroad Advanced Placement French. She supported my choice to remain in France for another year, attending the American College in Paris, and cheered me on when I decided to complete my degree in California.

Now here I was, back on Beacon Beach, fresh from two years in France and two years at the Monterey Institute of

International Studies, jobless in Washington, D.C. with nothing but a non-Jewish boyfriend to show for my decision to leave the tribe. And here was Ira Horowitz, deeper-voiced and hairier now, in the throes of med school, following his life-plan to a T, asking me if it had all been worth it.

I wanted to have an answer for him, the way years later I wanted to have an answer for Jane. Shorthand—an easily recognizable accomplishment that would cause them to nod their heads with quiet understanding and approval. But I didn't know yet how it would all turn out. I didn't know that Tom and I would struggle with menial jobs for years until having no money and no career prospects would prove tiresome. I didn't know that on the day a group of us would go together to take the Foreign Service exam, only I would pass—the youngest of the group, the only one without a Masters degree. I didn't know that one day I would leave Tom and join the Foreign Service—thus throwing myself into a bigger pool, with bigger, smarter fish, all trying to be noticed.

The Foreign Service was an elite specialty corps within the U.S. government. There was the cachet of being one of a select group of people who had passed the Foreign Service written exam and an even more select group who had managed to pass the orals. There was an immediate *esprit de corps* instilled in our "A-100" training class. Our class slogan was "Diplomats Do it With Immmunity," the third "m" a mistake when we got the T-shirts printed, yet another feature that set us apart. There was the camaraderie of shared experiences at one "hardship" post after another, talk of intestinal parasites and malaria medication and the frustration of waiting for mail to arrive via diplomatic pouch. There was the innate understanding that can only be shared by people who pick up stakes and move every two to four years. There was the lingo and the way we rolled our eyes every time a new Administration came in, and the format for preparing briefing memos changed. Shortly after I left, my Foreign Service friends confided, "Madeline Albright likes to be briefed on 3 by 5 index cards. What a hassle it is to get those in the printer!"

I rolled my eyes conspiratorially, still part of the colony.

Did I belong? In some ways it was like reliving my high school experiences. There were the stars, on the "fast track," the people who sought high profile jobs, working until nine o'clock at night, and who routinely came in on weekends. In Washington I often felt it was a pissing contest to see who would stay at work the latest. I joked that there was only one day a year that the family men went home early—Halloween— when it was apparent that instructions had been issued from home:

"I don't care if there's a coup in your country, you better get home in time to take the kids trick or treating!"

There was another career track too, a less sexy one in which you could work regular hours and have some balance in your life. But I thought it would be like studying *guano* all over again— work in international narcotics, oceans and environment or God forbid the human rights bureau? Not on your life! Maybe the jobs would be interesting, the issues something I actually cared about. But I wasn't ready to declare myself on the slow path to success. I was seeking middle ground—a Type A- in a Type A world.

At some point it began to dawn on me that as a single female Foreign Service officer I was likely to become one of two possible stereotypes: the thin, brittle emotionless workaholic or the overweight vivacious type, wrapped in yards of ethnic material. So far, with my tendency to put on weight from a diet of rice and beer, and my penchant for Thai *mutmee* and silk, my future was becoming clear.

And then, while working in Vietnam, I met him—the man who would turn out to be my Jewish Prince Charming, though I wouldn't realize it for some time. He'd been sent to me by mutual friends from Bangkok. When I received his call, at the former Majestic Hotel in Hồ Chí Minh City, after a grueling day of visa interviews, I was immediately dismissive. Jeff Greenberg. He'd be just another smart, nerdy Jewish boy with all the answers. I had left those behind. But I invited him to meet my colleagues and me at the hotel bar, where, after consuming bottle after bottle of 33 brand beer, we headed into *Chợ Lớn,* the Chinese district, to celebrate *Tết,* the Lunar New Year.

Jeff and I were the only clear-headed ones, hours and much alcohol later, when, crammed into a van full of an international array of drunks, our eyes met. And again, at my apartment in Bangkok, a few months later, the night we thought there had been a coup in Cambodia. After my friend Ellie, who was the Embassy duty officer, was assured the coup was just a rumor, we dressed Jeff and Ellie's boyfriend Kim in pirate scarves and earrings and, at the urging of a visiting Canadian diplomat friend, drank shots of raspberry liqueur *flambé.* Later, the Canadian treated us to her imitation of Salvador Dali, which involved painting a mustache on her face and hanging upside down from the couch, with lit candles in her ears. The next morning, when Jeff helped me scrape the wax off my hardwood floor, I considered that maybe, just maybe, he warranted a second look.

There was no doubt; Jeff was different from the smart Jewish men I'd known before. He was handsome and athletic and had been raised in a series of small artist enclaves on the West Coast, by his Buddhist poet mother. I joked that he'd be very different if he were an "East Coast Jeff Greenberg," and imagined him, pushy and ambitious, maybe wearing horn-rimmed glasses. Jeff was different too, from the other travelers I had encountered in Asia. Known as "World Travelers," "W.T.'s" for short, and "*Wah-Tahs*" in Thai, they were skinny, from battling intestinal parasites, always looking for the cheapest accommodations to stretch their meager supply of *baht* or *rupees*, and didn't seem to have much in the way of life goals. At age twenty-eight, Jeff had "retired" from his job as an engineer, with money in the bank, and was spending a year-and-a-half traveling through Asia, considering his career options. He wanted to do something more meaningful in international development or public health. "*Wah Tah* with a Gold Card" I dubbed him. He described his years in Santa Barbara playing beverage cribbage, taking trips to Baja California, sailing his boat to Catalina Island and working until late into the night at his engineering job. I'd never encountered this particular combination of fun and drive. A Type A- in a Type B world.

When my tour of duty in Thailand and Vietnam came to an end, and it was time for me to return for an assignment at the State Department headquarters in Washington, D.C., I was nervous. So it was Jeff, now settled in Seattle, that I called from my apartment in Bangkok for reassurance. It was Jeff whom I visited first, when I reentered the United States after almost six years overseas, and Jeff that I called from my temporary apartment in Georgetown, down the hall from the exiled Haitian president, Jean-Bertrand Aristide.

"The women here all dress like dead birds!" I lamented.

A few days later a postcard arrived from Jeff. "WEAR FUCHSIA!" it said.

Early in our State Department training, a visiting speaker had advised the members of our A-100 class:

"Quit the Foreign Service after ten years. It shows you were smart enough to get in and smart enough to get out."

And so, nine-and-a-half years after I joined, I gave up my State Department career to move to Seattle and be with Jeff.

"Are you doing anything?" my Foreign Service friends want to know.

The ones who come to visit are envious that I get to gaze at snow-peaked mountains, take hikes through evergreen forests and dispense altogether with pantyhose. They look bloated and gray to me, as they complain about not making the promotion list this year, the difficulties they are having in bidding on their next assignment, the ridiculousness of having to re-print briefing memos because the required number of spaces a paragraph is to be indented has changed with a new Administration.

"I can retire in ten more years," they sigh, their eyes taking in the ferry boats meandering across the sparkling blue Puget Sound. "I'd like to move somewhere where I can be in touch with the outdoors…" their voices trail off. And then they talk about Barranquilla and Madrid and what it felt like to stand in Red Square the day the tanks rolled in. My mouth begins to water. I look around my living room, at the tattered silks, the sitar with missing strings, the statues of Hindu gods and goddesses whose limbs have broken off. These are the remnants of my Foreign Service career. I wonder what I am missing.

"I can't wait to see you when you become a Girl Scout mother," a friend remarks, after I describe my efforts to fill 100 Easter eggs with recycled toys for our annual Easter egg hunt. "You'll be intense when it comes time to sell those cookies."

And it's true that in many ways I'm a misfit in this Type B existence I've carved out for myself. My life is always ripe for improvement. On my refrigerator are notes to remind me to be a better parent, and lists of the vitamins and Omega 3 oils I should take every day. I keep track of my food intake. I try to increase the number of pushups I can do and the amount of miles I can run. I do timed writing practices for twenty minute each day. I do Kegel exercises while brushing my teeth for two minutes with my Sonicare electric toothbrush. But I do these things sporadically, and sometimes blow off all attempts at self-improvement and drink margaritas instead. In August, I add a new note to my refrigerator. "Slow Down."

I run into Jane one Sunday afternoon at the swimming pool.

"Are you doing anything?" she asks.

I tell her about long afternoons spent at the beach after preschool, about running in Discovery Park, about my writing and my first published works.

"I wish I could quit my job," she says quietly.

"Really?" I ask.

She laughs. "Oh, I don't know. Not really, I guess."

And before I know it, my parole is almost here. Melanie is heading off to kindergarten and Maya will spend more hours at preschool. Soon I'll have the chance to "do something."

So I experiment—trying to land some freelance writing jobs, joining the board of a non-profit international organization. It's hard making time for meetings and clearing my head of Mommy minutiae, so I can focus on other people's deadlines and budgets and program objectives.

It's been easy to blame my kids for my lack of career, just like I blame them for my flabby stomach. But the truth is, my career ambivalence, just like my spare tire, existed long before I became a mother. My temperament is the same as my blood type—A-.

At a board meeting, I confide to two women, whose kids are much older than mine, that I am overwhelmed, but excited at the prospect of intellectual stimulation.

"I feel as if I am re-entering the world," I admit.

"Welcome back," one of them says. "We've been waiting for you."

MINIVAN

When we bought it, I felt as if I were crossing some invisible line. Hurling down the slippery slope into mindless Suburbia. I'd read somewhere that once you start driving a minivan, you leave your public sexual persona behind. Men don't crane their necks to check out the babe driving the minivan. What if I turned into a 300-pound polyester-encased beast, screaming at the kids while stuffing my face with greasy French fries and corn dogs?

It's for windsurfing, I told my childless friends. Which was true. Our Subaru wagon could no longer accommodate Jeff's growing pile of windsurfing boards and booms and masts and sails, the stuffed animals and pop-up books and sand toys and diapers and wipes required to appease our toddler daughter on road trips, and the rattles and squeaky toys and infant-sized diapers that would be required for the new baby we were expecting.

We bought a Japanese one in "Sailfin Blue" with a pearl gray interior. We put matching blue Bavarian Surf foam pads on the roof racks, a Dillfish sailboard decal on the rear window. I told myself it looked cool.

Two-and-a-half years after the fact, here is a partial list of its contents: Front driver's seat: me, fortyish, often sleep deprived, dressed in jeans and a T-shirt. Front passenger seat: a purple Arctic Cooler snack pack with sippy cups, peanut butter and jelly sandwiches, cut up apples, pretzels; a writing notebook; a pile of library books. Middle right-hand passenger seat: Melanie, my preschool-aged daughter, in a car seat, clutching her favorite stuffed cat, rocks, a pinecone. The crumbs of her most recent snack are embedded in the car seat. The pouch in front of her seat is bulging with picture books. On the floor are discarded stuffed animals and books, sand that spilled from her shoes, a half-eaten cheese stick, and some pretzels. Middle left-hand passenger seat: Maya, toddler-aged daughter, in a car seat that is smeared with cheese, snuggling her favorite duck, a touch-and-feel book about puppies on her lap, more books in the pouch in front of her. Rear: seats removed. A stroller, a gym bag, a diaper bag, sand toys, a picnic blanket.

Here is a partial list of the books that have lain on the passenger seat beside me: *The Price of Motherhood: Why the Most Important Job in the World is Still the Least Valued; Creating A Life: Professional Women and the Quest for Children; Flux: Women on Sex, Work, Love, Kids and Life in A Half-Changed World; Life's Work: Confessions of an Unbalanced Mom; The Time Bind: When Work Becomes Home and Home Becomes Work; Mother Nature: A History of Mothers, Infants and Natural Selection; A Life's Work: On Becoming A Mother; The Mother Knot; Writing A Woman's Life.*

I wasn't meant to be a minivan-driving, stay-at-home mom. I'd married in my mid-thirties, had an exciting international

career. I thought my parenting experience w(
avant-garde.

"You work from home two days a week, I'll work from home two days a week and we'll have a nanny one day a week," I told Jeff, who seemed amenable.

In practice it didn't work out that way. He didn't have the kind of job that made it feasible to be away from the office. I didn't have the kind of emotional makeup that made it possible for me to travel 14,000 miles away from home or leave my kids with someone else for large chunks of the day. We didn't realize it's damn near impossible to "work from home" with kids underfoot.

The fights we have now come from someplace deep within us. No matter how minor the argument, it quickly escalates. No matter how trivial the subject, it quickly turns into a game of domestic Can You Top This? Each of us tries to prove we are working harder than the other in these traditional gender roles we've assumed. I accuse Jeff of wanting the early 1960s Total Woman: naked, wrapped in Saran Wrap, greeting him at the door with a dry martini, beautifully groomed children playing contentedly in the immaculate house, the scent of roasting meat and potatoes wafting in from the kitchen. I accuse him of this even though I know what he really wants is the same thing I want: more time—time with the kids, time for windsurfing, time for sex, time for sleep, time for the two of us and time for himself. And maybe a little of the 1960s fantasy too.

"What do you want?" he asks. "Tell me what you want to change and we'll do it."

The trouble is, I changed when I had children. I can never change back.

We watch a Chris Rock video. Chris Rock is lamenting the lack of respect given to fathers and husbands.

"Everybody's always talking about Mama. Make your Mama happy, make your Mama proud, look at all your Mama does for you. Nobody ever thinks about Daddy. Daddy goes off to work and slaves away and nobody ever says, "Thanks for the electricity, Daddy. It sure is easier to do my homework with all this light! Nobody ever thanks Daddy. What does Daddy get for all his hard work? I'll tell you what! The big piece of chicken."

We laugh together as the sketch unfolds, but our laughs have an edge.

Jeff and I keep having the same "who does more?" argument. Neither one of us can figure out how to stop ourselves. The next time we have leftover chicken for dinner, I make sure Jeff gets the biggest piece.

The girls and I are in the minivan driving to music class. We are singing, "I had a rooster and the rooster pleased me, I fed my rooster on the green berry tree." We crow like roosters, we meow like cats.

"The duck is coming next, Maya!" Melanie announces, in a big sisterly way.

As we drive, we admire the spring trees in bloom—the lacey pink cherry and plum blossoms, the finely sculpted pink and white tulip magnolias, the stately white apple trees. Melanie asks me endless questions. I dispense motherly wisdom, pleased to have this glimpse into the inner workings of her mind. At home, I'm often impatient, preoccupied with getting the kids dressed, cooking dinner, doing laundry, making phone calls. But in our minivan we have golden moments, moments that

Jeff rarely gets to have, moments when the rest of the world stops.

1968. My mother is driving us in our gray Cadillac one afternoon. We are bickering, my older brother teasing, me whining. With a herky-jerky motion she steers the car to the side of the road and stops.

"Jesus Christ!" she screams.

The stress-induced herpes simplex sore on her chin throbs red with emotion. We are stunned. My mother has always been a screamer—a chain-smoking, coffee-drinking screamer—but she's never done anything like this. We are used to tuning her out, but the sound waves of her "Jesus Christ!" reverberate through the air. My brother takes matters into his own hands.

"My son's not in, but I'll take a message," he says brightly.

It's quiet for a split second and then my mother starts to laugh. Not the laugh of a frazzled single mother—a hearty, appreciative laugh. My brother and I laugh too. The car starts up again and we continue on our way.

2001. It is 4:00 in the afternoon. Melanie, aged two, has refused to nap and she is throwing a tantrum. I can't calm her down, can't calm myself down, and can't calm down Maya, who is frightened by all of the screaming. In a rage, I drag all of us out of the house, to the minivan and strap the kids into their car seats. I turn on the radio and I start driving. I tune out the tantrum-still-in-progress coming from the backseat and turn up the front speakers. I drive to the beach. The tantrum eventually stops. Melanie falls asleep, exhausted from her outburst of emotion. Maya coos and looks out the window. I sit for a while and watch the boats on the water and the outline of the Olympic mountain range, then slowly, calmly drive home.

These are the darker moments of parenting, moments Jeff rarely gets to have, moments that leave me fragile and emotionally shaky, clutching my glass of wine as he walks in the door.

The first time I screamed at my kids—really screamed— that squelched-self-within-me-fighting-to-get-out-wellspring-of-patience-finally-run-dry-kind-of-scream—I remembered my mother. I remembered her screaming and all the things I vowed I wouldn't say or do when I became a mother. Many of the women I know have had these moments of reckoning, when they sounded just like their mothers and hated themselves for it. It isn't supposed to be this way. Things are different for us. We have playgroups and preschools and music classes and gym classes and telecommuting and double short lattes and health clubs and baby joggers and enlightened partners who actively participate in the parenting process. We know that hitting your kids is wrong, that validating their emotions is right. We give choices, and time-outs when the choices don't work. We aren't supposed to be screaming Jesus Christ.

We are in the minivan listening to "Baby Beluga." We reach a red traffic light. I pick up the spiral notebook lying on the passenger seat beside me. I set it against the steering wheel and I begin to write, slowly at first, then faster, as my thoughts take shape and the words begin to flow. The kids are engrossed in their books and the music. The light changes. I put the notebook down and drive to a major intersection. The light is green. I drive slowly, hoping it will change before I reach it. Red light. I put the notebook on the steering wheel and begin to write again.

To be a mother is to be constantly interrupted, to learn to accomplish more in a discretionary five minutes than many people accomplish in an hour. At home during their waking hours, the only time my kids let me do my own thing is if I'm cleaning. Somehow they have received the message that this is a worthy use of my time.

To be a father is to compartmentalize. When he walks out the door, Jeff leaves us behind and I doubt he gives us much thought as he goes about his day. When he returns, he and I find it hard to connect. Words come spilling out of me and collide with his hand, which he holds up to signal me to stop, slow down, give him a chance to re-enter our domain. I know he just wants to bask in the glow of his family and let go of his work preoccupations. But I've been interrupted all day.

Tuesday afternoon. I am driving alone in the minivan, car seats removed, on the way to yoga class. After yoga, I'll have a bowl of *phở*, then head to my writing class. By the end of the evening, I'll be physically soothed and mentally stimulated. Driving home, I'll glance at my class notes whenever I come to a stoplight. But when my foot is on the accelerator, I'll think about Melanie and Maya. How they have unleashed the creative voice inside me. How discovering the world through their eyes is more fascinating than any foreign culture I sought to know.

After reading all of those books that have lain on the passenger seat beside me, after living for a few years with the choices I've made, there is one thing that sticks with me. Years after she wrote the *Feminine Mystique*—years after bra burnings and Roe vs. Wade and the ERA—Betty Friedan was asked if she still believed in feminism.

"You can have it all," Betty Friedan said. "Just not all at the same time."

It's almost time to pick up Melanie from preschool. I get in the minivan and start driving, stopping to admire the mountains on this gorgeous crisp, clear day. Maya falls asleep. I turn off the motor, listen to jazz on the radio and let my mind go. I think about jogging this morning with Maya. We ran to our neighborhood fish ladder and watched migrating salmon jump high in the air. Maya pointed out the splashing fish and the diving seagulls and I taught her their names. On the way back we stopped for a latte and a cocoa, then slowly walked home together, picking daisies and petting dogs along the way.

I think about the writing I will do this afternoon while the girls nap. I jot down some ideas in my writing notebook. I fantasize about the year-long, round-the-world trip I want to take my family on when the girls are eight and ten. I'll spend these next seven years honing my writing skills and publishing essays and articles and then someone will give me a book contract to write about our travel experiences. I plan where we will go and the curriculum I will devise for the children.

The minutes tick by. Time to get Melanie. I start up the minivan and begin driving. I think about the preschool adventures Melanie will share with me and wonder which park we will go to this afternoon. I anticipate the Moroccan Chicken Smothered with Preserved Lemons and Cracked Green Olives that I will cook for dinner tonight. Jeff will be refreshed by the girls' squeals of delight when he walks in the door and by the soothing meal we will share. Later, we will lie contentedly in our bed and silently work together on the Sunday New York Times crossword puzzle.

Maybe it will all work out this way. Maybe it won't. Maybe there will be afternoon tantrums and no naps, so no time to cook. The kids will eat macaroni and cheese from a box and Jeff and I will forage from leftover refrigerator scraps. I'll never get anywhere with my writing and we'll never travel again and tonight Jeff and I will be too tired to do anything but fall into a deep desperate sleep. Maybe.

I can have it all. Just not all at the same time. Except in my minivan. When Jeff complains how dirty it is, I want him to understand that my minivan is the one place where all of my disparate selves come together. Mother, wife, writer, reader, thinker, traveler co-exist amidst the debris of my domestic life. In my minivan, I'm grateful I have choices. In my minivan, I recognize that there are no perfect lives, just perfect moments. In my minivan I don't have to let go of my dreams. I just have to dig them out from under the cheese sticks and the crumbs and remember they are there.

THE AGE OF INNOCENCE

In a toddlers' music class, a circle of mothers sings a song about the stars—a spiritual with a haunting melody. As we sing, our children take turns carefully placing felt stars just so on a black felt sky. They smile with surprise and delight as the stars take their rightful place in the universe. The children are aware of nothing but their sense of accomplishment and wonder. And during this sweet interlude we, their parents, can briefly forget that terrorists attacked the United States only hours before.

When something horrible happens, the primordial instinct to protect your children kicks in with vigor. I want to shield mine from frightening television images of the attacks on the World Trade Center and the Pentagon and keep them away from conversations about the evil forces that caused these things to happen. So we spend September 11 in strange oblivion, driving out to the suburbs to shop for school clothes, sharing a chocolate-covered graham cracker before heading home. My daughters don't know that I am trying to avoid driving on freeways and bridges that might be targets of future attacks. In the car, instead of taking turns listening to kids' music or mine, I bargain for brief snatches of the news, explaining that "something happened." Weeks later I will be surprised when my older daughter Melanie begins using this expression as a catch-all excuse for her mercurial behavior.

After the kids go to bed, I am finally able to digest the horrific details of the day. I wonder aloud to Jeff whether we should send Melanie to her first day of preschool the next morning. Though I expect no threat to our little corner of America, the thought of having her out of my sight—even for a few hours— is unnerving. At school orientation the week before, I'd gotten unexpectedly emotional when asked to sign forms releasing the school from liability should anything happen during field trips. Now that the unthinkable has occurred, I wonder why I was in such a hurry to send Melanie out from under my protective wing.

We decide to avoid disruption. Life is topsy-turvy enough and we don't know how to deal with the recent changes in Melanie. A summer trip to Maine to visit family has left her raw and clingy, prone to violent temper tantrums, refusing to sleep alone. She has decided to move from her crib to a bed, is potty training herself and is dealing with powerful feelings of jealousy, as her baby sister Maya becomes more active. And she is also starting preschool. In terms of the stress they produce, for a two-and-a-half-year-old these changes are akin to the adult concerns of death, divorce, moving and job change. Also, I read in my parenting books, this is the age when children begin to experience fear.

Fear. We try talking about it.

"Are you afraid to sleep alone in your room?" we ask, half hoping she will identify a monster under the bed that we can chase away.

Melanie professes no fear, but runs into our room crying each night, comforted only if one of us sleeps with her. During the day she begins to use the concept of fear freely, more to reflect a two-year-old's inner turmoil over impending independence and the power of choice, than to express real terror.

"Do you want a bagel for breakfast?" we ask.

"No, I'm afraid of bagels!" she responds.

The nighttime sleep disruption continues. So does her erratic behavior during the day. I feel suffocated by her neediness, exhausted by her emotional outbursts and my own emotional response to them. Finally, in desperation I call her pediatrician.

"Melanie is suffering from anxiety and needs you now more than ever," she tells me. "Make a nest on the floor of your room so she can be near you when she is upset at night."

Jeff rises to the occasion and lays out a double futon with soft yellow blankets. He adorns it with Melanie's favorite stuffed cats and an array of brightly colored picture books. I am not pleased.

"You've made too nice a nest!" I wail. "Now she'll NEVER sleep in her own room!"

Each night Melanie comes to our room and I begrudgingly go to sleep with her in the nest. Each day she demands bear hug after bear hug, usually when I am occupied with her baby sister. Sleep deprived and frustrated, feeling that I have nothing more to give, I wonder when her anxiety would be alleviated. When will things return to normal?

In the meantime, the country struggles to make sense of jets crashing into towers, bodies falling from the sky, huge numbers of missing people. I remain strangely numb. People want to speculate on the political motivation for the attacks but I, a former diplomat with experience in the Islamic world, don't want to talk about it. The newspapers are filled with the extraordinary details of how the plots were masterminded. I want to find answers in parenting books instead. As the days pass and a shocked country grieves, I shut out the turmoil in the world and become more and more consumed by the turmoil in my own home.

Finally, one morning I cry as I listen to a radio story about a hero of Flight 93, who left behind a wife and three-month-old daughter. Later, I speak with a friend in New York, the mother of two daughters roughly the same ages as mine. Then I realize why I have deliberately turned inward. My kids still have the luxury of innocence. Theirs don't, and neither do any of the children left without a parent as a result of these attacks. One day I will have to explain about murder and guns and evil and disease and divorce and the countless senseless human tragedies that can't be fixed. But not now. Not yet. I still have some time.

So I decide to embrace my ability to make Melanie's world a safe haven and concentrate on the things I can make better. Each night at bedtime I take her outside. We look up at the sky, identify the stars and I sing her the star song. When she cries in the middle of the night, I willingly snuggle up in the nest with her. During the day I am freer with bear hugs. I want to do all in my power to dispel any anxiety she feels and to forestall the inevitable—the wiping away of innocence as she learns to be afraid of bigger things, things I can't protect her from. It'll happen soon enough.

About a week after the attacks, when we go outside to sing the star song, there is a lone airplane in the evening sky— the first I have seen since September 11. For me it signifies so much—the horror that has occurred, the need for life to continue as normal. I wonder if I will ever look at an airplane the same way again.

But for Melanie these are just magical, twinkling lights. It is still too light to see any stars so I point at the airplane lights and sing:

Star shining, number, number one, number two, number three
Oh my, my, my, my
Oh my, my, my, my, my

As she burrows her head against my shoulder, Melanie doesn't realize that the stars are not out tonight. I am glad. And I wish I could believe in magic again too.

DINOSAUR FRIENDS

My three-year-old daughter Melanie was learning about friendship. How to make friends, how to keep them, what you can and cannot do with them. There are books about this for preschoolers, I'd discovered. There are books about almost everything for preschoolers. Every afternoon we'd snuggle up together on our red and blue Snoopy beanbag chair and read a book called *How to Be a Friend*. It featured a cast of green dinosaurs.

"What are those girlies doing?" Melanie asked, pointing to a smiling forest-green dinosaur with cornrows, holding hands with a gap-toothed, grinning chartreuse dinosaur with a pageboy.

"They're having fun playing together," I said.

"And what about that girl over there? What is she doing?" she asked about a scowling dinosaur.

"She's saying an unkind thing to that boy (olive green dinosaur in tears) and making him feel sad," I responded.

"And is that okay?" she asked, anticipating my response.

"No," I said in my best wise and all-knowing parental voice, "it's not okay."

We looked at each other and nodded.

At age forty, I was learning about friendship again too—how to make friends, how to keep them, what you can and cannot do with them. When I was younger, friends were mostly recreational. We went to movies and parties and dinners together and occasionally consoled one another about failed love affairs during marathon phone sessions. But now that I was married and at home raising children, friends were my lifeline, my connection to the outside world. I hadn't found any books with dinosaurs to guide me through the process of making this kind of friend.

I'd noticed since becoming a mother that my friendships with other women carried an emotional charge I hadn't experienced since junior high school. Maybe this had to do with hormones left over from pregnancy and lactation. I'd find myself telling near strangers on a playground intimate details of our household affairs at the drop of a hat. You can imagine the scene: Late morning, in a neighborhood park. A mother pushing her toddler in a swing makes eye contact with the mother standing next to her, also pushing a swinging toddler. Shyly, tentatively they make contact.

"How old is your daughter?"

"Fifteen months. Yours?"

"Seventeen months."

"When did she start walking?"

"About a month ago." The words come faster. "Now I can't get her to sit in her stroller. Sometimes we need to get somewhere in a hurry and I don't have time to let her walk. But she struggles when I try to put her in the stroller and I have to force her to sit down!"

"Oh, my daughter does that too! It's such a relief to hear that someone else is experiencing the same problem!"

The mothers look at each other, eyes shining, and they're off. Before you know it they will have exchanged anecdotes about sleep problems, feeding problems, frustrations with their husbands and maybe even talked about post-partum incontinence, leaking breasts and changes in sexual arousal. Maybe an intimate friendship will be born from this one morning of shared confidences. Maybe the women will never run into each other again. But no matter how things turn out, you can bet that both women will leave the park feeling better.

The early weeks and months of motherhood can be a lonely time, especially for women who've been working and don't have any close friends with children. During prenatal yoga and birthing classes, I'd been encouraged to share my feelings, both physical and emotional, with total strangers. Six months or so of sharing on a weekly basis and I was hooked, so I was relieved to learn that post-birth, I would be able join a community-sponsored moms' support group. I cringe now when I remember the time, not many months into our sessions, when we polled one another to find out who had regained full sensation in her breasts, and the time one woman confessed that she and her husband were having marital problems and were thinking of separating. But during that vulnerable, isolated period of new motherhood, those women were all I had. Those meeting were everything.

One day one of them called me up.

"My kid is driving me crazy and I'm going out of my fucking mind," she said.

"Mine is too!" I said, giddy to hear my frustration so eloquently articulated by someone else. Pleased that I was not the only one trapped at home feeling decidedly unmaternal.

So we went out to lunch. That rendezvous led to another, then another. Another woman from our group began joining us, and soon I had new friends. Several times a week, babes strapped to our bodies, we tooled all over town, sharing intimacies all the while.

Predictably, as motherhood took hold and these new relationships became more important, older friendships began slipping away. The friend with the jam-packed social life stopped calling with last minute invitations to fabulous cultural events because I was breast-feeding and couldn't be spontaneous. Unmarried, childless friends from my single days reduced their correspondence with me to an annual Christmas card. My college roommate stopped writing to me altogether. A single, male friend with whom I had been very close for several years cut me off without a word. Our last conversation had taken place just after the funeral of his father and my release from the hospital following a pregnancy complication. I sent him a birth announcement to let him know that everything had turned out all right for me. I don't know how things turned out for him; I never heard from him again.

These losses magnified other losses I was feeling—the loss of the spontaneous, independent me, who had traveled, had a successful international career, and wore decent clothes. If my old friendships ceased to exist, did that mean that the old me had also ceased to exist? I thought I had simply added the layers of wife and mother to my core being. Maybe my old friends couldn't find me underneath those layers.

Melanie started preschool. For two-and-a-half years we'd done everything together—mom's group, music classes, gym classes—and we shared a group of mothers and kids as our friends. Now for the first time, she was in a social situation without me—her first real opportunity to pick her own friends. She spurned her old companions. This worried me. Her teacher encouraged me not to worry.

"They don't like mixing friends," she reassured me. "At this age, they don't even like mixing different food items on their plate."

Melanie talked about the kids in her school with interest, but when I asked who her friends were, she'd say,

"Not anyone," sometimes adding, "Nobody likes me!"

This worried me even more.

Meanwhile, Annie, a woman I had thought of as a close friend, seemed distant. I didn't understand why. Over the summer, we'd played tennis together twice a week and had taken our kids to the same swim class every day for several weeks. We'd supported each other through difficult medical issues, commiserated about our weight and the lack of time for ourselves. But by October, Annie and I hadn't spoken for nearly two months, and although we were in the same weekly children's music class, we hadn't managed to get together afterwards. This silence, this lack of intimacy, was eating away at me. I wanted to know what was wrong.

After many sleepless nights I called her up and confronted her. She was defensive. She denied that anything had changed.

"If you were expecting me to call you twice a week to check in, then maybe we're not a good fit," she said.

" No," I said, "I wasn't expecting that." I confessed that I missed talking to her. I missed sharing the details of our lives. Eventually Annie admitted that she appreciated me as a "mama friend," someone to pass the time with as our kids played with musical instruments or learned to tumble. But she didn't want any more from me than that. I was devastated, wondering how I could have been so wrong in my assessment of the relationship. I felt vulnerable and stupid for sharing so much.

Melanie began coming home from school each day spinning dramatic tales involving a girl named Olivia and their conflicts over a stuffed cat that Melanie had named Splendora. I suggested we use drawings as a way to work through their difficulties.

"Should we draw me playing with Splendora?" Melanie asked.

I dutifully obliged.

"Now should we draw Olivia playing with Splendora?"

Once again I complied.

"And now should we draw me taking Splendora away from Olivia?" she said, her voice rising excitedly.

I gulped, but did as I was told.

"And should we draw Olivia crying?"

I saw the process through to its conclusion. Over the next several weeks we drew what seemed like hundreds of renditions of this scene. I refined the process along the way, as my parenting books had suggested.

"Should we draw you asking Olivia politely for a turn with Splendora?" Then, "Let's draw both of you smiling and playing together with Splendora."

One Sunday, at our neighborhood coffee shop, we ran into Olivia's parents. I told them their daughter had become a central figure in our household. I didn't go into details.

"Olivia has been talking about Melanie too," they said politely.

I smiled to myself. I wondered what they were not telling me.

I should have been pleased that Melanie chose this period to become enthralled with the dinosaur friends book. But I was still smarting from my recent rejection by Annie. I felt insecure, as I navigated my way through a sea of preschool moms, trying to make new friends. And I missed my original mom friends, whom I rarely saw now that our children were attending different preschools. Night after night as we read the dinosaur book, I was forced to relearn the rules of friendship: how to overcome your shyness and approach new people; how to make up if you've had a fight; how to find someone else to play with when interests diverge.

At home there was more and more talk of Olivia. Melanie told me that at school Olivia took Splendora away from her, that she wouldn't let Melanie sit next to her at circle time. But one day while I was talking on the phone, Melanie got excited.

Who was that, Mommy?" she asked eagerly. "Was that Olivia?"

Soon after, at a school party, we watched as Olivia, a bright-eyed little girl with long dark hair went bouncing down the hallway.

"She's running away from the school!" Melanie exclaimed gleefully, clearly in awe.

I could see it by the look on her face. Catfights notwithstanding, Melanie wanted to be Olivia's friend. Maybe I could help her take the first step. I knelt down so that we were at eye level.

"Should we invite Olivia over to our house to play?"

Melanie looked up at me with a half-smile.

"Yes," she whispered.

I was circling around some new potential friends myself— people with whom I had things in common other than being a parent, women who wouldn't think of me as just a "mama friend." At a preschool potluck dinner I talked to Carol and Daniel, the parents of one of Melanie's classmates. I could feel the hint of similar experiences, a complementary outlook on life. So I arranged the Seattle version of an adult play date: we met for coffee. We had not been together for more than five minutes before Carol and I began talking about our relationships with our mothers, while our husbands talked about kite boarding and our kids playing with dominoes. I began getting together with a single woman from my writing class. We compared notes about our writing, our travel adventures and our experiences with long-distance love affairs. I could see the potential these new friends had to enrich my life. Still unsure of the rules of friendship, however, I was careful not to reveal too much.

Olivia came over to play. She and Melanie were polite and careful with each other at first, each waiting to see what the other would do. First one girl, then the other donned a princess dress, a tiara, sparkly shoes. First one girl, then the other reached for a stuffed cat. As one of them declared a preference for something, the other would exclaim

"I like ballerinas too!"

Their eyes sparkled, as they discovered more and more common interests—princesses, cats, and the color pink. They realized they were kindred spirits.

But then they clashed. I found Melanie in tears in her bedroom, Olivia smiling triumphantly. The stuffed cat they had had trouble sharing sat between them.

Although it doesn't say so in the dinosaur book, vulnerability is at the heart of friendship. Maybe that's why some friendships can't be sustained over a lifetime. We want to forget our earlier, more vulnerable selves and anyone that reminds us of them. We don't want to compare ourselves to others who have achieved different milestones in life. We don't want to confront our insecurities. With each new friend you can reinvent yourself— or at least present your best self. Maybe that's why sharing is safer with strangers.

Two years have passed. Some of my friends from before I had Melanie have resurfaced. Some of my newer friends and I have let each other slip away. It's usually nothing personal— we're all busy, we're finding a little more time to pursue our own interests, and in some cases, we just don't need each other as much anymore. I've established a few new recreational friendships, just for me, ones that have nothing to do with kids. But it's hard to find time to maintain them.

Melanie, almost five, is the veteran of many play dates and has formed some strong friendships. My heart swells with pride when I see her march confidently onto a playground full of strangers and create an instant bond with another child, who, she will later assure me, is her new best friend. My heart aches for her the times she shrinks, shy and trembling, too nervous to join a familiar circle of singing children. We still spend much of our time with Melanie's friends and their mothers. I usually enjoy myself, pleased to have fallen in with a group of women struggling with the same compromises I do. But occasionally I grit my teeth and hope that Melanie's infatuation with a particular kid will fade, because I have nothing in common with that child's mother.

Recently, Melanie's three-year-old sister Maya has begun asking me to read her the dinosaur friends book. As we snuggle up and I introduce Maya to the joys and frustrations of friendship, I realize how much she has to learn and how far Melanie has come.

Soon Melanie will go to kindergarten and we will have to start all over, making new friends at a new school, perhaps losing our connection to the preschool families we've come to like so much. They say that when you're watching your children learn how to make friends, you relive all of your old anxieties about friendship. As it turns out, you get to experience plenty of new ones too.

VALENTINES

Around Valentine's Day I realized he was more than just another classmate—this boy with the big eyes, goofy smile and head that seemed too large for his three-year-old body.

Melanie and I were making valentines for her preschool Valentine's Day party, one for each kid in the class—twenty-eight valentines in all.

We began the project on a weekend, when we were all sick, housebound and bored. Jeff lay on the couch watching football. Maya crawled from room to room like an explorer, hands slapping the floor as she moved to warn us of her arrival. And Kitty, my twenty-one-year-old cat, in the last stages of kidney disease, occupied her usual spot on the corner of the couch—an inert black-and-white body propped up against a pillow, sleeping so deeply that I had to touch her to be sure she was still breathing.

I was relieved to find an activity that would keep us busy. I went to the art supply store to buy the materials we would need to create valentines—red, blue, purple and green glitter;

stickers; extra-large red envelopes for the oversized hearts we would cut out. I am not artistic by nature. But since having Melanie and Maya, I'd thrown myself into projects that reminded me of the magic and innocence of childhood.

Melanie and I could do this project together. I would cut out large hearts from pink, red, purple and white construction paper. Melanie would decorate them with glitter and stickers—cats, hearts, insects, flowers, jungle animals, birds—something to please everyone and give each valentine a personal touch.

We settled ourselves at the dining room table, supplies laid out in assembly-line fashion.

"Whose valentine should we make first?" I asked, looking over the list of kids in the class, trying to match faces to the names.

I wasn't surprised by her choice.

"Olivia!" she announced, naming the girl she'd talked about most since starting preschool.

Olivia had been Melanie's first friend. After months of hearing her complain that nobody liked her and she didn't like anybody I was pleased when she began playing with Olivia. But theirs was a tempestuous relationship, with tears and power struggles and I wasn't sure whether to encourage it. I cut out a white heart. Melanie chose some stickers and placed them on the heart, proclaiming, "Olivia likes dogs! She doesn't like cats! I like cats!"

I decided to forego my usual speech that it was okay for two people to like the same things at the same time. Instead I asked her what color glitter we should use.

"Red," she answered.

I made a glue design and gave her the red glitter to sprinkle on.

"Not bad, "I thought, admiring our handiwork. "Only twenty-seven more to go."

"Who should we do next?" I asked.

Her answer surprised me. "Sage!" she said, her face illuminated by her smile. "Let's do Sage because I like him!"

I racked my brains trying to remember what I knew about Sage. He'd been the Cat in the Hat at the school Halloween party. The red and white striped stovepipe hat made his large head look even bigger, but with his rakish features and sly sense of humor he was a pretty convincing live version of the Dr. Seuss original.

Melanie carefully chose the stickers and colored glitter for Sage's valentine. She lost interest in the project soon after that and I ended up making twenty-two of the valentines by myself the night before the party. But though her interest in the valentines waned, her interest in Sage did not. She came home from school each day telling stories about him. The initial attraction had occurred at snack time, when he did undisclosed things with his milk that made her laugh. He liked to say, "Pop Goes the Weasel, mmmmmm," which also amused her. Each time she talked about Sage, Melanie became radiant, as she recounted his exploits in a loud, cheerful voice.

In the preschool hallway, as we waited to pick up our Rainforest Dinosaurs from the Rainforest Room, I mentioned to Sage's mother Diane how much my daughter liked her son. Each afternoon we'd gotten into the habit of exchanging pleasantries while waiting for the preschool class to complete its final ritual. Huddled on the floor in a circle, the children pretended to be encased in dinosaur eggs. When it was time to leave, one by one, each child would crack out of the egg and run out of the classroom into the arms of a waiting parent. Diane said, "That's funny because he never mentions her."

She was a down-to-earth, practical looking type with short hair, usually dressed in an oversized T-shirt and sweatpants. I was a little disappointed that Melanie had not become a central figure in their household, as Sage had in ours. But observing Sage and Melanie at school in the weeks that followed, I could see that he liked her too. After cracking out of their dinosaur eggs and greeting us with hugs and kisses, Sage and Melanie would sometimes linger in the classroom, fondling Legos and chasing Maya down the hallway. They didn't talk much, but giggled a lot, circling each other like Spanish dancers engaged in an elaborate *habanera*. Soon Melanie began seeking out Sage as soon as she arrived at school, once rushing across the classroom to ask him if he liked coleslaw. Clearly a bond was forming. I suggested a play date.

He came over on a snowy day in early March. The night before I'd been like a nervous teenager getting ready for her first date. I encouraged Melanie to take a bath, cleaned the house with unusual thoroughness, and sang her to sleep with the promise of what tomorrow would bring, as lacy white snowflakes gently fell outside her window. Finally after school the next day they arrived—Sage, Diane and his baby sister Bryn, who was a few months younger than Maya. We spread out a feast of peanut butter and jelly sandwiches, sliced apples and milk. I waited to see what would happen next.

Like a first date, it was awkward. Melanie was overly eager, pressing her face close to Sage's, and thrusting books, balls, blocks, Legos, stuffed animals and dress-up clothes in front of him, desperate to get him to play with her. I cringed. I was afraid he would recoil from so much unsolicited attention. We sat down to eat lunch, but Melanie and Sage were not interested in food. The dining room was uncomfortably still.

Maya broke the silence by shouting, "No!" when I offered her some apple. "No" was a word she'd recently learned and enjoyed saying as noisily and as often as possible. Implacable no longer, Sage laughed, his face enveloped in a goofy grin.

"No!" he echoed, standing up and dancing around Maya's high chair.

She was delighted to find a partner in crime. "No!" she yelled, and began to chortle.

The duet continued, louder and louder. Melanie was crushed. She came to me, her head lowered, big brown puppy-dog eyes on the verge of tears.

"I don't like that he's playing with Maya," she whispered.

I hugged her and wondered how many more times through the years she would be upstaged by her impish, carrot-topped younger sister. Diane lured Sage back to the table with his favorite snack, fruit-flavored drinkable yogurt in iridescent colors—watermelon and chartreuse—packaged in skinny plastic tubes. Melanie's eyes widened. She had never seen yogurt of such vivid hue or with such an elaborate delivery system. Shyly, she asked for some and watched Sage to learn the most effective means of extracting the sweet nectar from its flower. Together they slowly lifted the tubes to their lips, meticulously squeezing the gloop to the top as if it were toothpaste. Then, simultaneously, they slurped—loud and long, heads slightly tilted back, as the deliciously sweet and creamy yogurt dripped into their mouths and languidly down their throats. At that moment they resembled junkies, just after the needle goes in, relaxed by the warm flow of the liquid high throbbing through their veins. Triumphantly their eyes met and they erupted in belly laughs. The ice was finally and completely broken.

The rest of the afternoon was a joyful mélange of activity. They played with balls, blocks, Legos, a pink feather boa, an Egyptian *fez* and then, with the unspoken instinct of long-time dancing partners, they raced upstairs to Melanie's bedroom and began jumping on her bed. Exhausted, they collapsed under her flowered bedspread and looked at books, then climbed down from the bed, ran out the door and disappeared into my bedroom. I discovered them in my bed, lying together under the covers reading more books, like a comfortable old married couple. The play date was a success.

After that, Melanie talked about Sage constantly, but with a new self-assurance. She blossomed, eager to go to school each day, self-confident and at ease around other people. I was surprised at the relief I felt. My sensitive, timid, aloof little girl was coming out of her shell.

Less than a week after our play date, Sage's body erupted in violent bruises. His own immune system had attacked his blood, causing it to be deficient in platelets. He would need a transfusion of platelets to build up the level in his blood stream, and careful monitoring for some months after that.

We visited him the day before he went to the hospital for the transfusion. Melanie was excited to bring him a gift—a glossy marine life sticker book filled with octopi, starfish, otters, and seals that he could amuse himself with during the hours he would have to sit still, as the enrichment for his blood dripped intravenously into his body. He had a shiner that made him look like a prizefighter—a pint-sized Jack Dempsey—but his spirits were steadfast, as if to say, "You should see the other guy!" Though we'd planned to drop off our gift and leave, we stayed for two hours. As they had at our house, Melanie and Sage navigated their way through piles of toys in the living room, the den, the basement, stopping to share a peanut butter sandwich, gargling mouthfuls of milk and giggling.

The next week at school was difficult. We knew not to expect Sage on Monday, the day of his transfusion. Melanie was grumpy that day when I picked her up—tantrum prone, impossible to please. On Wednesday, I reminded her excitedly that he would be there. He wasn't. And for the first time ever she clung to me when it was time to say goodbye, time for her to join the circle of children as they sang their good morning song.

"I need you, Mommy," she said, closing her eyes tightly and clutching me.

And so I sat with her that day and again on Friday morning, when Sage failed to appear. I held her in my arms and sang with the circle of children, "The more we get together, together, together, the more we get together the happier we'll be."

Sage never came back. News of him trickled in like drops of blood after a pinprick. His platelets were low, his red and white blood cell levels were low, and his bone marrow levels had dropped to next to nothing. He was in and out of the hospital. Doctors struggled to determine why his immune system had turned on his body and whether, given enough time, the blood would regenerate or he would eventually need a bone marrow transplant. In the meantime, he couldn't have visitors. As part of this wait-and-see period, his immune system would be medicinally suppressed to see what his blood would do. For Sage, the pain of enforced isolation—no contact with children his own age except for the sick ones in the hospital—could be as bad as the pain from the continual pricks of the needles that dripped the life-sustaining liquid into his body.

I thought a lot about pain then. Sage's pain, his mother's pain. As a mother you come to know every element of your child's body and spirit. You notice every new freckle, every bruise, every sadness.

"We water them with kisses," a friend of mine once said. "That's how they grow."

I wondered how it felt for Diane, this plain-spoken woman who gave the impression that she did not give in to excesses of emotion. How did it feel for her to hold her bruised and battered child, to want to water him with kisses, knowing that the slightest touch gone too hard could bruise him all over again. She'd once told me that she was more comfortable mothering a three-year-old than a baby.

"Babies cry and you don't always know why or what you can do about it. But a three-year-old can usually tell you what's wrong," she explained.

Now Sage's three-year-old body was telling her, something is wrong. Only no one knew for sure what to do about it.

Sage's pain, his mother's pain, Melanie's pain. Melanie kept her eyes clamped shut at preschool circle time and I wondered what she didn't want to see. She came home from school each day angry and agitated, complaining about Olivia with a ferocity that I hadn't heard once Sage became part of our lives, hitting and pushing and shouting at Maya, until I had to pry her away. Outside of school a new shyness overtook her. When she spoke to people other than her father and me, she whispered, and hid her face in my chest. I didn't know how to comfort her, how to bring her back from the island she had retreated to. I hadn't expected her to have to deal with loss so soon after opening herself up to love.

Sage's pain, his mother's pain, Melanie's pain, my pain. Even though this wasn't happening to us, every time I looked at Melanie and saw her vulnerability, I realized that it *was* happening to us. And my pain at her pain was palpable. No matter that there were other things that needed my attention— visiting in-laws and the imminent death of Kitty, whose body was slowly shutting down. I just couldn't dull the pain. Waking up in the middle of one night, I was seized with the notion that I had to do something; that if Melanie and I could create a project to reach out to Sage in the midst of his isolation, it would somehow ease everyone's pain.

I come from a long line of proactive women—the turkey-makers I call us—reminiscent of the Thanksgivings of my youth. I used to separate the world into two kinds of people: turkey-makers and turkey-eaters. Turkey-makers would rise at dawn and begin chopping the celery, onions and sausage for the stuffing. They would butter and spice the bird, while the turkey-eaters wandered in looking for coffee and wondering how to spend the hours until dinner. The turkey-makers didn't need to wonder. They would spend the day chopping, slicing, basting, mashing and stirring to create the magic of the Thanksgiving feast for all to enjoy. After the meal was eaten, the turkey-makers would return to the kitchen, roll up their sleeves and wash the dishes, while the turkey-eaters retreated to the living room to digest their dinners, watch football and wait for pie. For turkey-makers there is always something to contribute. Turkey-makers don't accept that there is nothing you can do.

So the next morning, just as we had with the valentines, we set ourselves up at the dining room table, supplies laid out in assembly-line fashion, Melanie, her grandmother—another turkey maker—and me. We were making a Sage Page—actually a series of pages, one for each letter of his name. We brought out our trusty art supplies and an assortment of magazines to identify and cut out objects using the letters of Sage's name. Just as she had with the valentines, Melanie lost interest in the project soon after it began. My mother-in-law and I continued—thrilled to find storks, salmon, salami and snow, alligators, apples, asparagus and artichokes, geese, gorillas, green beans and glitter, elephants, egrets, English muffins and eagles—which we carefully positioned on each page. I placed the Sage Page in a manila envelope. Melanie chose the festive magic markers I used to write Sage's name and address on it. For the next few days, whenever she seemed upset, together we would imagine Sage's reaction the day the Sage Page arrived in the mail.

Kitty was dying. She'd been a beauty in her day, with lush long black-and-white fur; the black draped over one shoulder like a strapless evening gown. I acquired her in college in California and brought her with me when I moved to Washington, D.C. to begin my career. She'd accompanied me to India, to Thailand and back home again and had had her share of adventures, including getting lost in the Taj Mahal Hotel. Once, when flying home solo, she missed her connection in Frankfurt and had to spend the night alone in the airport there. She got stuck in the heating duct at my friend Ivar's house when he took care of her while I was traveling. When we settled in Seattle and stopped traveling, her fur lost its luster. She began to resemble the tattered silk upholstery that covered the furniture and pillows I'd collected on my travels years before. Now Kitty was dying. Several months earlier, on a frosty November night, she had disappeared. She must have dragged herself off the couch, through the house, out the cat door, into the alley, somewhere. I discovered she was missing the next morning. I was unprepared for the wave of sadness that overtook me as I contemplated the loss of this sweet creature with whom I had lived longer than any human being. Trying to keep my tears in check, all that day and into the night, I hunted for Kitty, Maya strapped to my back, Melanie running in circles around me. At some point I stopped hunting for Kitty and hunted for her body instead, convinced that she had taken herself off to die in some quiet, dark, remote space, but I was unwilling to leave her there. When, later that evening, a neighbor brought Kitty home, alive but disoriented, I knew this had been a dress rehearsal. Jeff and I discussed how we would explain Kitty's death to Melanie, but we couldn't reach any conclusions. We didn't have a religious framework to fall back on—didn't believe in God or Heaven—so it felt hypocritical to promote these concepts. But to thrust the finality of death onto Melanie with no means of finding comfort seemed wrong too.

I spent hours sitting on the floor in The Secret Garden, our neighborhood children's bookstore, crying as I surveyed the selection of books that gently introduce children to death. I was most drawn to *Cat Heaven*, with its beautiful illustrations of happy cats lapping up milk and napping in Paradise. But it was hard to ignore the kind, elderly God, who walked among them, cats at his feet, a cat on his head. There were books that described the cycle of life using butterflies, a willow tree, a leaf named Freddy. There were books about the loss of grandparents, books about terminal illness, even a book that posed philosophical questions about the afterlife. I sat on the floor and thumbed through these books and cried. I cried for myself over the loss of Kitty. I cried for Sage and his family at the unexpected twist their lives had taken. I cried for Melanie's loss of innocence.

Frail, incontinent, unable to eat, Kitty had taken up residence in the bathroom, near the heating duct, where she lay in a soft, fuzzy, round blue cat bed with a bright red, blue and yellow checkered blanket to keep her warm. Each afternoon Melanie and Maya and Melanie's beloved, tattered stuffed cat Meowme would sit on the bathroom floor next to Kitty, as if they were visiting an elderly sick relative in the hospital. Melanie would pretend to read to Kitty from her favorite book, an Andy Warhol collection of cat sketches. Occasionally Maya crawled closer to the cat bed, leaned in and gave Kitty a kiss. As Kitty shifted in her bed, disturbing the blanket, Melanie would tenderly cover her up again. On the day that I knew would be Kitty's last, we stopped at a pet store to buy her a present. Melanie and I sniffed and fondled the selections, carefully making our choice—a red and blue catnip heart. When we got home, Melanie rushed into the bathroom and said, "Here you go Kitty, here's your heart! This will make you feel better!"

Melanie made Sage the favorite male character in every book she read, a central figure in every game she played. She talked about him constantly, even when I stopped bringing him up and starting setting up play dates with other kids. On Easter morning, she was filmed by a local TV station collecting glass blown shells that an artist had hidden at the beach near our house. That day, on the 5:30 news, as she discovered the hidden shells, Melanie announced to the news-watching public:

"This one is for me, and this one is for Sage..."

We continued to send Sage periodic offerings—a videotape of the Easter news clip, a book about tools, drawings and pictures and stickers. We wrapped these gifts as festively as we knew how, in bright yellow tissue paper, with vivid purple ribbons, topped with a sprinkling of gypsy red glitter.

We saw him once through the window of his house, leaning on the back of the couch looking out. The black eye had healed and his face was as smooth and clear as an angel's. He was pale, his flaxen hair, fair skin and brown eyes muted. It was as if he were part of the upholstery of the couch he was leaning on and had faded from sitting there day after day, exposed to the afternoon sun. He looked like he had recently had a haircut. The cropped hair made his large head appear smaller, more in proportion with his body. I watched him as he gazed out the window, before he saw me. I thought I detected a look of longing in his eyes. No longer dancing mischievously, they looked lonely. Poor sick little boy looking longingly out the window at the great wide world, which he could not go out in for fear of catching the germs that dwelled there. When he spied Melanie and me he smiled. Not his usual big goofy grin, but a quiet smile. I think he was pleased to see us. Melanie grinned and squirmed excitedly. She waved animatedly. He waved slowly, quietly back, like Queen Elizabeth greeting her subjects. He moved in slow motion, totally unlike the erratic bursts of energy you get from a three-year-old, all the time, except when you ask them to hurry. I wondered if the blood flowed differently through his veins now that it was depleted of its essential elements—the platelets, red and white blood cells and bone marrow that are essential to life. I imagined it moving like caramel, thick and languid through the little boy body. Melanie blew him a kiss and we turned to go our separate ways—him to the hospital to be poked and prodded, us to play in the warm spring sunshine.

That afternoon we went to Swanson's Nursery. I had decided to create a Kitty arbor in our garden. Together, Melanie and I would select and plant a special shrub and place a cat statue underneath it. I didn't intend to tell Melanie that Kitty's ashes would also be buried there, at least not yet. But I wanted her to know that the arbor would be a place to remember Kitty and find comfort. We wandered among the aromatic, flowering shrubs—*daphne odora, osmanthus, viburnum*, before selecting the one we would plant—*pieris japonica*, lily-of-the valley. We also looked at stone statues of cats—cats wearing opera glasses, cats with binoculars, cats licking their paws, sleeping cats, pouncing cats. I couldn't find just the right one so we left, stopping to buy an azalea that was almost ready to bloom for our neighbor

Mike, who was recovering from open-heart surgery. I hoped these things—the Sage offerings, Kitty's arbor, Mike's azalea—were connected in Melanie's consciousness the way they were in mine. These are the things we do for the creatures we care about, I wanted her to know. This is how we provide comfort when we can't control what is happening. This is part of loving.

I don't care what my kids choose to believe in as long as they become turkey- makers. I know that they will experience the full range of human emotion, pain included, and that I will need to let their innocence go. So, if along the way, I can provide them with some tangible coping skills, so much the better. I want them to know that sometimes some glue, glitter, construction paper, stickers and an oversized heart or two can help.

On a bright chilly Sunday morning with dark rains clouds threatening, the girls and Jeff played with our next-door neighbors while I buried the cedar box that contained Kitty's ashes next to the lily-of the-valley shrub Melanie and I had planted the week before. I spread a carpet of bark mulch over the area so you couldn't tell it had been disturbed. The air was redolent with the smell of cedar. I thought I should say some special words, have some sort of ceremony, but it felt forced. Instead, while my family played nearby, I drove to Swanson's, certain now of my choice. The rain clouds burst and it began to pour as I lay the smooth stone statue of the sleeping cat in its rightful spot, next to the lily-of-the valley shrub.

"Have a good rest, Kitty," I said. "It's good to know you'll always be nearby."

Melanie and I admired the cat statue from our living room window, as sheets of rain poured down. For the first time, she asked me,

"Where is Kitty?"

"Her body wore out and she left us," I told her. "But the Kitty arbor is a place we can go whenever we miss her and need to be close to her."

She looked at me and nodded, accepting what I had said without question. Then we went to Sage's house to bring him a grab bag of novelty toys—lizard soap, a bird whistle, a rubber monster head and his favorite, a bright orange rubber lobster that squeaked and bobbed up and down from a string. Sick with a cold, Melanie watched shyly from behind the screen door. Sage, who had just been released from the hospital, ran around his living room with the lobster bobbing up and down. Occasionally he stopped by the door so that he and Melanie could growl and make funny faces at each other. He looked like any normal kid except for the IV attachment taped to his arm. This time Melanie was the sick one, the one who couldn't come in to play, for fear of infecting him. We left Sage happily playing with his bobbing lobster and went home to our front yard. The rain had stopped. Together we walked to the Kitty arbor, kneeling down so Melanie could get a good look at the statue.

"Kitty's sleeping," she said in a hushed voice. "She's sleeping and I'm gonna pat her."

She leaned over and tenderly patted the cold, hard sleeping cat lying in the bark mulch. Then she rose and hand in hand we turned and walked into the house.

DIANE: LESSONS FOR
ANOTHER MILESTONE

At the Burke Museum of Natural History and Culture, I watch a group of four-year-olds stare intently at naked Barbie dolls, which lie on their backs on tables, surrounded by white strips of cloth. After a month of studying ancient Egypt, of learning about pyramids and hieroglyphics and the gods of the underworld, this preschool class has come to see an exhibit entitled "Reverent Remembrance: Honoring the Dead." They are learning different cultural interpretations of death. They are learning about religious ritual. They are learning about the importance of belonging to a community. The children ooh and aah over a 2,000 year-old Egyptian mummy encased in a sarcophagus painted with images from the *Book of the Dead*. They admire the Indonesian textiles which enshroud bodies on the island of Sulawesi, before they are buried in high tombs chiseled out of steep cliffs. They shiver with-fear at Oaxacan *calacas* and *calaveras*—the skeleton figures and decorated sugar skulls that commemorate the Mexican Day of the Dead. And now, to end their visit, they will wrap the Barbies into mummies so that the dolls can journey to the underworld, where they will live forever.

Nine months earlier, on a rainy February evening, we'd gotten the call. We hadn't heard from our longtime friends Craig and Diane for a while. In the busyness of life, six months had slipped by since our last communal breakfast. We hadn't received a Christmas card from them. I'd run out of Christmas cards before their name came up in the alphabet. I figured we were all too busy to notice.

"How are you?" I gushed. "We've been meaning to call you, but life has gotten so busy."

I babbled about preschool and Jeff's work and lack of sleep and time. When it was Craig's turn to speak he only gave one excuse:

"Diane was diagnosed with Stage 4 melanoma. The cancer has spread to her brain and her abdomen. They've told us to think in terms of remission, not recovery."

We're getting older and so they come more frequently now, those moments when the harsh realities of life take hold of you and won't let go. It used to be only our parents who got calls like this. It was our parents who were preoccupied with mortgages, insurance, the quality of the school system and caring for aging relatives. Now it is our turn.

Jeff and I had been on a predictable path of marriage, home ownership and raising children. Craig and Diane, who had always been ahead of us in achieving life's milestones, were often there to point the way—reassuring us about marriage and child-rearing—lending us maternity clothes, baby slings, toddler backpacks and outgrown toys once we'd taken the plunge. Now they were reaching another milestone before us. Now they would teach us how to deal with death.

Death had only come up once before since we'd had children. When our elderly cat Kitty died, I'd worried how to explain it to Melanie, who had just turned three. Jeff and I didn't follow any religion, so Melanie was unfamiliar with the rituals and ceremonies that different communities use to mark the beginning and the end of life. Our daughters had had no christenings or baptisms. They were not introduced in any church or synagogue as the newest member of the congregation. We had no community, religious or otherwise, to speak of. Our families were far away.

How different my children's experiences would be from mine as a child. Jeff's parents had rejected Judaism and all its trappings. He'd had a nomadic childhood, sometimes attending schools in three different states in one year. I lived in the same small town for my entire childhood, attending the same high school that my mother and grandfather had attended. In the semi-observant Jewish family in which I was raised, we relied on religious ritual for important occasions. We didn't attend synagogue on a regular basis or keep a kosher home. We didn't use Jewish theology to make sense of the universe. But whenever we had weddings, funerals or bar mitzvahs to commemorate, our extended family gathered before a rabbi. My mother was in charge of shepherding grandparents and great-grandparents to synagogues and cemeteries. Afterwards, everyone returned to our house, where my mother and her sisters provided bagels, lox, whitefish and chopped liver. They served coffee from a large silver urn that was only used on these occasions. I loved the familiar routine: the excitement of dressing up, of seeing distant cousins and favorite eccentric great aunts and uncles, the feel of the prayer books, the soothing hymns. I didn't understand the words I was chanting. It didn't matter. The ritual was comforting.

For my children it would be different. It had been years since I'd participated in a religious ceremony. Our wedding had been a small, secular gathering. When it came time to select someone to preside over the ceremony and guide us into our new life together, Jeff and I didn't know where to look. Finally, an older friend—Ellen, who was dying of cancer, introduced me to her friend Mary, a King County Superior Court judge. A kind of equation dictated my choice: If Mary was important to Ellen, and Ellen was important to me, then Mary could be important to me. The following year we gathered on Lummi Island, the small fishing community where Jeff felt most at home. Mary read the unadorned words we had written for a ceremony that Ellen was no longer alive to witness.

But now there were no more large family gatherings. Our families were scattered and only came together every few years. My grandparents were dead, and with them went the ties that bound my family together. My mother was estranged from her sisters. She was beginning to need care—emotional and financial. My brother wasn't offering to help. Like many of my age group, I was part of the "sandwich generation," caring for the generations above and below me.

"I'm tired of taking care of people," I told Jeff.

Where was the extended tapestry of family and community now that I needed it? Where was the large silver coffee urn?

In my twenties it had seemed like a good idea to question my participation in a religion that we only half-heartedly practiced and to move far away from my family so that I could choose my own beliefs. I moved out west, bleached my hair blonde and lost my New Jersey accent. I kept moving, landing in India and later Thailand, where I was happy to wander among Hindu and Buddhist temples and admire the beauty of religious icons and practices that were not my own. I let go of my tenuous connection to Judaism. I was certain, in the way that you are in your twenties, that I wouldn't raise my future children to follow any religion.

"I'll let them choose for themselves," I would say definitively.

Fifteen years later, when I had children and they needed answers, I discovered that three-year-olds aren't ready to choose. They need comfort. They need uncomplicated explanations. They need a support system. I began to understand why church and synagogue attendance increases after people have children. Parents want tools to help children make sense of the painful and uncontrollable aspects of life. They want guidance on how to provide answers to the unknowable. They want their children to feel that they aren't in it alone.

I bought a book called *The Tenth Good Thing About Barney*, in which a little boy whose cat has died is encouraged to think of the cat's ten best qualities. He can only think of nine—until his father reminds him of the tenth: the cat's body will return to the earth and help make things grow. We buried our cat in the yard next to a flowering shrub and marked the spot with a stone statue of a sleeping cat. I didn't talk about God or Heaven or tell our daughters that Kitty's ashes were buried there. For the time being, our children seemed satisfied. But I knew that eventually the questions would come.

When people give you bad news, the natural tendency is to shy away, to give them their privacy, let them retreat to the confines of immediate family and most intimate friends. We thought this would be particularly true of Craig and Diane, who had extended family in the area and were active in their Greek Orthodox Church. But Craig reached out even further. He began sending a series of emails updating us on Diane's condition, welcoming visitors, letting us know the importance of our thoughts and our prayers. In March he updated us on the Gamma Knife procedure used to treat Diane's brain tumors and of the tube that had been placed in her stomach to relieve her intestinal blockage. He encouraged us to write, to visit, to call. He ended his email by saying, "We are so grateful to our family and friends for your considerable outpouring of love." He would repeat this sentiment in every communication.

The last weekend in March, Craig hosted two work parties. We joined a sea of friends and family in mulching the yard, pruning shrubs, weeding and visiting Diane, who was holding court nearby.

"The doctors were pretty skeptical about my chances. They told me I wouldn't be able to eat solid food again," she said, the trademark mischievous glimmer in her eyes, "but I believe I'm going to beat this. I told them I plan on eating lamb for Easter."

Diane started eating. I started cooking, grateful to have something I could do for her. When she was able to eat a limited amount of foods, I baked her a key lime pie, and then another. When my neighbor Mike was diagnosed with cancer, I baked a pie for him too. And another one for my friend Greg, who was recovering from pneumonia. I didn't believe in God, but

I believed in the healing power of food. I made soups for the parents of newborns; feasts of Chicken with Preserved Lemons and Olives for the guests who graced our table; grilled cheese, and stews and blackberry cobblers for the ones I loved most of all. Despite my previous efforts at camouflage, I was turning into the proverbial Jewish mother. Food connected me to the people I loved.

"Eat," I would say, as I set steaming plates before my family. "Eat," I silently willed Diane and Mike, as I baked what would become known as "chemo lime pies." Diane's faith was steadfast. She was surprising her doctors. On Easter, she ate lamb.

In the spring, Jews celebrate Passover. When I was a child, my grandmother would hand out mimeographed scripts for us to use in reciting the Passover story. My grandfather, with his thick Austrian accent, reminded me of a vampire, as he opened the ceremony. His "Tonight is our Seder supper," had a similar cadence to "I love to suck your blood." We ate bitter horseradish and parsley dipped in salt, as we listened to the story of how Moses delivered the Jews to freedom. Every year, as the youngest child, I was invited to ask,

"Why is this night different from all others?"

And it seemed that every year, at precisely the moment when we poured a cup of wine for the prophet Elijah and opened the door to invite him in, my brother—black sheep of the family—would enter the house. Stoned and hungry, oblivious to the fact that this night was different, he would ask,

"What's to eat?" prompting hard jabs in the ribs for anyone unlucky enough to be seated next to scandal-loving Great-Grandma Celia.

When I'd graduated from college and was living with my non-Jewish boyfriend Tom, my grandmother surprised me with a bag that she urged me not to look at until I got home. I opened it and removed the contents one by one. I was infuriated. The bag contained Passover paraphernalia—a *Haggadah, matzoh*, and a copy of the mimeographed Seder script.

"She's not honoring my decision to give up Judaism, and to live with you," I told Tom.

I ripped up the Seder script. I threw away everything, except for the matzoh, which we ate smeared with butter and salt, the way I had as a child. I didn't speak to my grandmother again until six months later, as she lay dying. Visiting her for the last time, I still didn't acknowledge her gift. I didn't let myself understand that it had been her way of helping me keep tradition alive. I couldn't understand that it had been her way of helping me keep *her* alive. Five years later, in India, only one religious ceremony didn't intrigue me. I refused an invitation to a Passover Seder, hosted by a family of Iraqi Jews, angry to have them assume that just because I had been raised Jewish, Judaism was still a part of the me I had created.

Things change when you have children. Certainty is replaced with doubt. You become sentimental for people and experiences gone by. I could pass on stories, but my daughters would never taste my grandmother's Belgian toast or feed ducks at the lake with my grandfather. They would never be pinched on the cheek by a bevy of older relatives, guess which of Great-Uncle George's legs was the wooden one or hear my grandfather and my great-uncles George and Al play the violin after a holiday meal. So when Hanukkah came, I decided to make potato *latkes*—my grandmother's specialty. My friend Stacy offered to lend me a *menorah*. But that was too much.

"You're a gastronomic Jew!" she said ruefully.

I took the children to see the Festival of Lights exhibit at the Seattle Children's Museum and came home with a plan.

"We'll celebrate all of the festivals of light," I told Jeff.

He raised a dubious eyebrow. But it made sense. We'd lived in or traveled to most of the countries that celebrate these festivals.

"We can celebrate *Loy Krathong* and *Diwali* and *Santa Lucia* and Hanukkah and make them meaningful," I said, trying to convince myself as well as him.

The plan petered out.

The following year, Melanie determined our celebration. She asked for a menorah.

"Can we light the candles? Can you tell me the story of Hanukkah?" she asked.

I borrowed Stacy's menorah. Every night we lit candles. I told the story of Judah Maccabee, who led his people to freedom, and of the miracle that allowed the candles in the Temple of Jerusalem to burn for eight days, even though there was only enough oil for one day. And then I told her the story of Hanukkah—my Hanukkah. How my grandmother could never make enough latkes to satisfy us. Of playing *dreidel* on her kitchen floor and receiving bags of Hanukkah *gelt*. How soothing it felt to light the menorah on crisp, cold evenings and receive one small gift.

In July, Craig planned a surprise fortieth birthday party for Diane. I stood in my kitchen rolling out dough for Syrian cheese pies to bring to the party. I took walnut-sized pieces of dough and flattened them between my palms, then stuffed them with feta cheese, shaping each morsel into a pyramid. The work was soothing and methodical. But I was alone. I longed to be in a kitchen full of laughing, chattering women—aunties and grandmas and mothers passing on their technique, sisters and daughters bridling at the direction, but secretly pleased to be a part of the process.

At the party, Diane was surrounded by the same sea of friends and family, who were becoming familiar to us. Jeff and I marveled about how public she and Craig were about their ordeal. We knew that our tendency would be to hunker down, to hide away, to suffer privately and alone. But Craig and Diane seemed renewed by contact with their extended community.

I noticed Diane's Aunt Katie and an elderly Greek lady sampling my cheese pies. Later, in a different kitchen, this time surrounded by laughing, chattering women packing up leftovers, I received Katie's verdict.

"Did you make those?" She gestured to the empty serving plate. "They were good."

Diane traveled to Yellowstone with Craig and the kids. When she returned, the doctors discovered new tumors. She was in and out of the hospital. Craig asked us to keep her in our thoughts and our prayers, because the knowledge that so many people were praying for her gave Diane the strength to keep fighting. But I don't pray. I have nobody to pray to. Still, I would find myself alone in my kitchen, wishing with all my might:

"Please, let there be a miracle. Don't take this mother away from her children."

On *Yom Kippur,* the year I was seven, my older cousins Timmy and Bobby, who did not usually attend synagogue, accompanied me to the youth-led junior congregation services that were held in a small room upstairs from the sanctuary at Congregation *Ahavat Shalom*. Experienced teenaged boys, some recently *bar-mitzvahed*, led us in prayer. They handled the velvet-draped *torah* lovingly and familiarly and sang hymns in cracked adolescent voices.

"Ask them to say a prayer for Uncle Herb," my cousin Timmy whispered.

Uncle Herb had been ill and had gone into the hospital a few days before. "No," I whined.

"I'm too scared, you do it!"

But Timmy didn't know the boys who were leading the service. He was unfamiliar with the rhythm and the pace of the prayers and didn't know when it would be appropriate to slip in our prayer. A few days later, Uncle Herb died.

"It's your fault," Cousin Timmy hissed.

I imagined God, sitting down to write in His big book, the fortunes that would befall us in the coming year. When He got to the page where He determined who shall die, He waited for the prayer that never came. Then He lifted His pen and added one more name.

We planned to spend Labor Day weekend on Lummi Island with our friend Michael, who was visiting from London to introduce the Welsh-born woman he had married the previous summer. Craig and Diane and their children were supposed to be there too. But a few days before the trip, we got another call from Craig. Diane's condition had worsened. The doctors said it was only a matter of days. Jeff and I each held a phone receiver to our ear, as the tears poured down our faces. The next day, as Melanie and I listened to the deep soulful sounds of a cello concerto, she asked me why we had been crying. I told her that Diane was going to die.

"What are the ten good things about Diane?" she asked, referring to the book we hadn't looked at since Kitty had died over a year earlier.

I reminded her of Diane's long glossy black hair, the spirited twinkle in her eye, her cinnamon rolls and how she liked to stay in her pajamas, watching movies all day with her son Blake.

"But what's the tenth good thing about Diane, Mommy?"

This time she was ready for the answer.

"She will be buried in the earth and help make things grow."

We gathered on Lummi Island with the circle of friends that Diane had inaugurated me into years before. Jeff and Michael introduced the newest members of their family to reef-netting, an ancient Indian fishing technique that was part of their history with each other and with Craig. That evening, we all shared a meal of the salmon that had been caught earlier that day.

We were moved by the strength of our ties to old friends on Lummi Island. When we returned home, there was good news from Craig. Diane was still fighting. She had been discharged from the hospital and was starting a new round of chemotherapy.

She had been rejected as a candidate for hospice for refusing to acknowledge the need for "end-of-life" care.

In October, Melanie's preschool class began studying ancient Egypt. She was excited to share what she had learned about the Nile River, the Pyramids and the Sphinx. I visited her classroom to show the children pictures and artifacts from my travels in Egypt. We shared the Egyptian food I'd prepared—hibiscus juice, brown beans and the sweet succulent pudding called "Ali's Mother." We passed around a *fez,* a *scarab* and pictures from the tombs of the Pharaohs in the Valley of the Kings. I held up a papyrus painting and told the children what the ancient Egyptians believed about death:

"When a person died, his heart was removed and placed on a scale balanced with a divine feather. A heart that was heavy with sin would be consumed. Only the owners of hearts as light as the feather were allowed to continue on to eternal life in the underworld."

On the day that Diane died, I held my daughters in my arms, tears streaming down my face, and hugged them tight.

"Will Diane be a mummy?" Melanie asked. "Will she be put into a *sarcophagus?*" I explained about coffins and cemeteries. And then I told her what I believe: that no one knows for certain what happens after we die.

We sat together in a crowded pew in the sanctuary of the Church of the Assumption—Jeff and me and two old friends from Lummi Island. Father Dean rang bells alongside Diane's coffin. He chanted prayers in English, which were repeated in Greek, by a church elder.

"God, have mercy on your servant Diane, who is sleeping. Forgive her every transgression, in thought and in deed."

When the ceremony was over, he turned to the congregation. "Diane wanted to know about Heaven," he said. "I told her what I believe: Going to Heaven is like falling asleep on the couch in front of the television when you are a child. Your father picks you up in his strong arms and you awaken in the comfort of your own bed. Your Father will carry you to Heaven, Diane. And you will awaken in comfortable, familiar surroundings. I'm sure of it."

At that moment I envied him his certainty. I envied him his ability to provide comfort without question.

We left the sanctuary to attend the *makaria,* the traditional lunch of fish and rice that follows a Greek Orthodox funeral. Diane's children, Blake and Katie, moved comfortably through the crowd of familiar faces, playing with their cousins and enjoying pats on the cheek from elderly relatives, just as I had during the religious gatherings of my youth. At a cemetery on a hill, with sweeping views of the Cascade Mountains, Diane was laid to rest under an old sequoia tree, next to the poet Denise Levertov. We returned to Craig's house. We were together again—the community of people who had cared for this family throughout the year. We had all been given the opportunity to express our love for Diane and her family. They had given themselves the opportunity to receive it.

That evening, still dressed in our funeral clothes, Jeff and I took our daughters to see the Disney Princesses on Ice. Graceful skaters reenacted highlights of familiar fairy tales—each story a reminder of the power of believing, no matter how you choose to do it. As a spectacular finale, pale princesses lying deeply asleep, were kissed awake, one by one, by their handsome princes. The mesmerized children nodded; reassured that order had been restored to the universe. But my thoughts were of another pale, sleeping lady. One who will sleep for eternity beneath a stately sequoia tree. One whose children will never experience the joy and the certitude of seeing her kissed awake.

For Blake, Katie and Craig
And in memory of Diane Wright

HER

BIG TRUTH

We came together every Tuesday evening—a group of strangers with stories to share. At first they dribbled out tentatively:

"I could never be what my mother expected of me," confessed the slender, soft-spoken poet.

"I was swimming with my family in a motel pool when I first realized that I hated my mother," said the self-proclaimed "artsy" girl with multiple body piercings.

"I know why my father left my mother. She deserved to be left," said the actress.

Soon a comfort level was established. We were encouraged to speak freely here.

The middle-aged nurse told us:

"My mother grew a vegetable garden when I was a child. It was only later that I learned that she loved flowers, but had never allowed herself to grow them because they were impractical. I never knew you loved flowers, Mother. Why didn't you ever tell me?"

And the child of immigrants: "I pretended I inhabited a secret transformation machine that could transport me away from my parents."

The middle-aged Southerner, who described himself as "somewhat deranged," drawled:

"My family was like something straight out of Faulkner—complete with inbreeding, craziness and iced tea."

And finally, the quiet African-American woman, who always dressed in a long skirt and a hat:

"I used to stare at the wall while my mother beat me. I imagined I could hear the sound of wet paint drying. That is when God came to me and told me jokes."

I felt insecure when it was my turn to share my story—maybe because it had nothing to do with my parents. Instead it was a humorous portrayal of my obsessive efforts to plan my four-year-old daughter Melanie's birthday party. We were in a writing class, a memoir writing class, entitled "Big Truth Talking." The brochure promised we would learn to get to the heart of the stories we wanted to tell, to make the personal have universal meaning. In my story, I planned to explore some big themes: nostalgia, a child's emerging independence, and the complicated bond between mothers and daughters.

On the second Tuesday of class it was my turn to read an excerpt from "The Birthday Party":

It began innocently enough: A desire to make a child happy. A desire to teach her to receive, as well as to give. A birthday party. A fourth birthday party.

I went on to describe the horrors of toddler birthday parties—cakes, presents, goody bags; over-the-top parents who insist on making these parties a spectacle; kids amped up on sugar, throwing violent tantrums. And then:

One Tuesday afternoon, I took Melanie to Archie McPhee, our neighborhood novelty store, because I had decided that snow globes would make a timeless party favor. But I grimaced as I picked up the snow globes, one after another. Were they always this shoddy? Melanie saw no flaws. She was just as entranced by the falling snow and miniature scenes inside the plastic domes as I had been as a girl. She wanted us to buy these snow globes, but I said no. I'd said no earlier that day at Costco, when she'd wanted to buy the Disney book, "Princess Stories of Love and Longing," featuring excerpts from Snow White, Cinderella and Sleeping Beauty. I'd said no, trying to explain that the original, unabridged, un-dumbed-down fairy tales that I remembered from my childhood were superior. I promised to find them for her. "But I love this book," Melanie whispered, as she sadly turned the pages, gazing with love and longing at the plucky, longhaired princesses and handsome, brave, uncomplicated princes. I'd also said no at the video store, when she wanted to rent a video of Rapunzel, with a Barbie doll playing the lead role. Each time I said no, I also said trust me. I don't want you to settle for this. I want you to know that there is something better out there for you. There is something better and I will find it. And then you will know how beautiful and magical a thing can be.

It's already begun with Melanie and me: the eternal struggle between mothers and daughters, the struggle between parents and children. Once I was the sun and the moon and the stars to her. Now sometimes she tells me to go away. I was her filter from the outside world. Now, sometimes she says she would like to trade me in for a mother who will let her watch Rugrats. She watches Sleeping Beauty and Snow White and Cinderella, anything with a dead mother and a wicked stepmother. I know from reading Bruno Bettelheim's The Uses of

Enchantment that this is healthy. It is Melanie's way of dealing with her emerging independence. Still, I long for the sweet, uncomplicated days when she watched Winnie-the-Pooh.

"Nice use of detail. You really captured the craziness of toddler birthday parties," said the soccer mom.

The child of immigrants said, "I really like the way Melanie's voice comes through."

"Do you have any idea how controlling you sound?" Faulkner boy eyed me accusingly.

And the teacher,

"I had trouble deciding what this story is really about. I don't think it's about birthday parties at all," she hinted.

Oh, please. When did life turn into one giant therapy session? I had no deep, dark secrets to reveal because for the most part, I viewed life as a Scrabble game. You make the most of what you are given and don't whine about it, because each time you throw away your letters, you fall further behind. But I was beginning to notice, the way you do when you come across something for the first time and then stumble upon it everywhere, how often the adults around me blamed their parents for unhappy childhoods and crippled adulthoods. I mentioned this to a friend, who shared my nostalgia for vintage snow globes, and had started a collection of them for her son.

"I'm not sure it's worth the effort," I joked. "Twenty years from now, our kids will probably be telling horror stories about us."

And thus I hit upon the structure I would use for my story. I would alternate paragraphs describing my obsessive mothering with paragraphs describing other people's disappointment with their parents.

"Keep it simple," voices inside my head warned me, as I awoke in the predawn hours to plan the cookie-baking party I had decided we would have. Melanie had insisted she didn't want a birthday party. I thought she would be disappointed without one. Now we were expecting fifteen kids. I anticipated dividing them into three, rotating groups of five kids, making three different kinds of cookies. I could shuffle the groups every twenty minutes to make sure each child was in a group with Melanie, that no two kids were grouped together more than once, and that each child got to have all three tactile experiences. From three o'clock to six o'clock, I tested every combination of children. I did this another dawn and maybe one more before giving in to the realization that sheer numbers would not allow me to achieve my goal. When I started yawning in the early afternoons, Jeff guessed the reason for my lack of sleep. He called me obsessive. "You tend to get that way," he commented. "Especially when it comes to the children."

When I was nine months pregnant with Maya, my father-in-law came to stay with us so he could care for Melanie when I went into labor. For more than thirty years, he has stayed awake late into the night trying to work through his childhood with immigrant parents, who lived, isolated and unhappy, in Brooklyn. One night, too pregnant to sleep, I sat up with him. "My mother taught me to mistrust people," he said, his voice still bitter after so many years. "But you did better," I told him. "You were a good father and your children love you. Isn't that enough?" His eyes told me that it wasn't.

"Careful. You are attempting a very complicated structure," warned the teacher. "The two stories need to build together in intensity. What is the connective tissue that binds them?"

She gave us an assignment to unearth an old family photograph and write about it.

"Mine your memories," she advised. "It will help you get to the heart of the stories you want to tell."

One summer day, in 1964, a few months before my third birthday, my brother and I posed for pictures on the blacktop driveway behind our house. Over damp bathing suits we wore white sweatshirts with the slogan, "All the Way With LBJ" written in bold black letters. The photograph I have from that day preserves our innocent simple summer happiness. But my adult self knows there is more to it than that. Our country was in the midst of the Cold War, the Vietnam War. Despite the optimism of our sweatshirts, LBJ was only in the running because President Kennedy had been assassinated the year before.

One summer night, four years after the photograph was taken, my mother would tell me that my parents planned to divorce. She didn't know that instead of tears, I was trying to stifle giggles, as my brother stood outside my bedroom door making funny faces. He would eventually be sent away to military school and later to a mental institution, the 1960s precursor to the plush drug rehabilitation facilities of today. LBJ would decide not to go all the way. My father would go away, becoming a menacing figure whom I would never see again after the age of twelve.

Photographs are like snow globes. They preserve perfect moments with fleeting clarity. But shake things up a little and the pristine images become murky.

My mother called me her clone. My brother reminded her of my father. Whenever he committed a transgression, she would sigh,

"Just like a Krupnick."

But I, the golden child, seemed to have been born without any Krupnick DNA. Sometimes I would look at myself in the mirror searching for evidence of my father's genes. Did I have his smile? The shape of his face? His ears?

My mother and my brother are perpetually stuck like figures in a snow globe from 1968. In almost every conversation, my brother will throw out names that suggest half-remembered incidents, blaming my mother for them all. My mother will hint darkly,

"You don't know how I suffered."

My memories of that period are filtered through the lens of an eight-year-old: my mother, chain-smoking, frazzled and screaming; the first day of third grade, when we filled out information cards and I was embarrassed because I didn't know my father's address; my friend Lisa telling me that she couldn't spend the night at my house because my parents were divorced. Divorce was unusual then; my parents may have been the first in town to do it. Eventually Lisa's parents got divorced and so did everybody else's. Almost everybody I knew had a sibling with a drug problem. So many teenagers spent time in mental institutions in the late '60s and early '70s, that there is a whole genre of memoir devoted to the subject.

But I'm not sure everybody's father menaced them the way mine menaced me. I remember his face, one Mother's Day, purple and contorted with rage as he banged on the doors and the windows of our house with his fists to force me to emerge for our court-mandated Sunday visit, even though I told him I wanted to spend the day with my mother. I remember the threatening index card he sent me, care of the business office of the school I attended in Paris. I remember the crank calls that would come on rainy nights when I was visiting home, always beginning with the overwrought melody of "MacArthur Park," followed by snippets of the tapes he had made of my mother's phone conversations when they lived together in the early 1960s.

It would have been satisfying to ask him why. To confront him as an adult and say:

"What were you thinking? I was a child, for Chrissakes."

But he died before I had a chance to do that. So he is off the hook.

Yet, I have never asked my mother, who is very much alive, for her side of the story. I have never asked her why she gave up her youthful ambitions to be a journalist and left college at age nineteen to marry my father. Was it his green eyes that drew her in, or did he possess a compelling strength of character? I know that they shared a passion for the exquisite—we had that sunken living room and a formal dining room with Louis XVI furniture and they were epicures. So why haven't I asked my mother how two people who appreciated beauty so much could have let their relationship turn so ugly? Maybe because I think it would be the same story I heard throughout my childhood— she was innocent and a survivor, he was a Krupnick. But it can't be that simple. I know something about squelching your inner desire. I know something about the disappointment of a life not lived. I know something about adult passion and anger and wanting to hurt someone because they have hurt you.

It's time to finish my birthday party story for "Big Truth Talking." I don't want to fall prey to pop psychoanalysis and use the details of my childhood to explain my adult behavior, so I am struggling to reach a conclusion.

So many of us harboring so much resentment; so many ways to get things wrong. So much effort that goes into trying to get things right.

A birthday party is one pure act that parents can perform; one way to create a little bit of magic to commemorate a day that was magic for us. Four years ago, on this day, little one, you began to exist. And your very existence has changed me, changed my life in ways you may never understand. You will experience sorrow and pain and disappointment, sometimes because of me. But know this. I poured my heart and my soul into loving you. I did the best I could.

When I ask Melanie how she liked her birthday party, she responds with a four-year-old's unbridled enthusiasm, "It was the best day of my life!" She's already thinking about next year. So am I.

"Frankly, it's weak and it just doesn't work," the teacher tells me, when we meet for our end of class evaluation session.

"Clearly the kind of mother you are was shaped by the kind of parents you had. Why are you still holding back?"

I am humiliated by my inability to uncover the Big Truth so I put the story away for a year.

In the meantime, I continue to hear tales of parental disappointment:

"My four siblings and I were raised by nannies because my parents hated kids."

"When I was two, my mother put me in a taxi by myself and sent me across town to my father's house."

"I have no happy memories of my childhood; by the time I came along, my parents were tired of raising children, so I raised myself."

I take my daughters to the library. Every week we check out a different fairy tale—stories from France, China, Vietnam, the Philippines, Egypt, Mexico and the Aleutian Islands. Almost every story is a variation on the same theme—a child loses her mother, to death or abandonment or cruelty, and so she must strike out on her own to discover the strength that lies within her. As far as I can tell, there are no fairy tales that talk about what happens later. Is there ever reconciliation? Does the child come to appreciate that her parents planted the seeds of her strength?

I am having some success publishing memoirs about my experiences with motherhood. My mother is supportive. She doesn't even mind being portrayed in one of them as a screaming, chain-smoking bitch. But it's always been that way. She's been supportive of everything I do, making things happen for me, despite the stumbling blocks.

After my father and brother left us, my mother came into her own. She had developed a taste for travel, which she passed on to me. Evenings, she would sit by the fireplace in an overstuffed blue armchair, a stack of travel books by her side, as she planned our next destination. Dinners were exotic—curry, *paella* and "Fucking Foo Foo Chicken," my aunt's disparaging name for the *tandoori* chicken my mother had learned to cook.

When we traveled, it became a game for us to taste the most exotic cuisine we could find. Indonesian *rijsttafel* in Amsterdam, Burmese curry in New Zealand, *wichety grubs* in

Australia. My mother planted the seeds in me that would lead to a lifelong appreciation of travel and culinary exploration.

But my mother, tired of fighting a younger woman's battles, has made a series of rash choices over the past twenty years that have left her destitute and alone. I could hear the bitterness in her voice whenever I called her from thousands of miles away. The bitterness, the vulnerability and the walls she put up to protect herself and maintain control of her life. I couldn't get her to talk about the root causes of her problems or ways in which they could be resolved. As a result, our relationship became strained and superficial. Disappointed with her own life, she wanted to live vicariously through me. I felt suffocated and disappointed with her for what she had become.

So when my mother sends me a letter announcing she plans to move across the country to where I am living with my husband and children, my reaction is powerful.

No. Not here.

Jeff has noticed that when we argue, I am sensitive to the sound of raised voices.

"Don't scream at me," I say.

"I'm not screaming, I'm being emphatic," he counters.

I explain that I grew up with screaming, that I do not want screaming to be a part of the life I have made for myself.

When I find myself screaming at my children, I turn to parenting books for wisdom. On my refrigerator I hang snippets of advice so that I can stop myself in mid-scream. "Validate feelings." "Commenting on bad behavior only increases it." For the entire month of November there is only one reminder on the refrigerator. "Calm."

The response I write to my mother's request is a three-page scream. In the subsequent phone conversation, we both scream. There are some screaming emails and a three-page diatribe from her, which concludes: "I have searched my heart and soul and I cannot understand why you feel the way you do." Her letter makes me want to scream.

Instead, I read a book entitled *Non-Violent Communication*. Now the snippets of advice on the refrigerator have just as much to do with my mother as they do with my daughters. "Observe behavior, say how it makes you feel, express your needs." I write her another letter. I suggest we stop screaming. She does not respond.

We come together on two Saturdays—a group of strangers with stories to share. At first they dribble out tentatively:

"I resented my parents for giving me a name people made fun of," says the self-effacing bank loan officer.

Soon a comfort level is established.

"I used to be a person named Sandra," says the vivacious Californian, draped in an intricate Indian shawl. "I gave myself a new name, so I could bury the person whose parents caused her to suffer abuse and humiliation."

But this time not everyone's story is a variation on the same theme.

"I'm uncomfortable reading my story," the technical writer tells us. "I feel as if I haven't suffered enough."

"My mother had a special friend when I was a child. I never knew if he was her lover. Now I'm hoping that he was. She deserved some happiness," says the former terrorism expert.

One year later, another birthday party has come and gone. I took it easy this time and organized a joint swim party for Melanie and her friend Sage, who thankfully has recovered from his illness. His mother Diane and I put most of our effort into the cake—a chocolate sheet cake decorated with shells and starfish and a Barbie mermaid riding on top of a dinosaur. Yes, a Barbie. One afternoon, months earlier, Melanie had fixed her deep brown eyes on me and said quietly:

"Mom, could you learn to love Barbies as much as I do?"

So we accumulated a houseful of Barbies and some Disney fairy tale collections too, because I am learning that each generation needs to form its own interpretation of beauty. It helps to realize that the fairy tales I loved as a child were themselves handed down from generation to generation and culture to culture. The story of the girl who must break away from her mother in order to find herself has been told for centuries. Maybe the Big Truth is that the struggle to disentangle ourselves from our parents is universal.

I write my own stories in the hope that my daughters won't have to wonder why I made certain choices. I write my own stories so they can understand that things are never simply black and white.

My mother writes me another letter. She tells me she is moving to Panama. But she never gets there. I hear that she is in Colorado, in Italy, in Florida. She can't seem to settle and I can't seem to finish my story—to make all of the pieces come together in a Big Truth that I can make sense of.

There are months of silence peppered by angry stabs at communication. We both feel betrayed. We both feel tired.

And then it is birthday party time again.

I host a princess party for four-year-old Maya and three days later a ballet party for Melanie, who is now six. I adorn their cakes with rows of Sleeping Beauties and ballerinas.

A package arrives from my mother. It contains paper dolls and a message:

"Tell your girls that when I was a little girl, I used to line up my paper dolls on the piano and play with them for hours."

But before I can even tell them, my daughters have lined up their paper dolls against their fish tank. They play with them for hours.

A writing teacher once told me that at the end of a memoir, the reader needs a sense of conclusion. "But for the writer, the story is never finished," the teacher continued. "You live with it for the rest of your life."

US

RENEWAL

I'd been dreading it for months. For most people, renewing a driver's license is no big deal, merely one of those bureaucratic annoyances that must be endured every four or five years. Nothing would be required of me except to sit in a crowded Department of Licensing waiting room on a hot August afternoon, wait for my number to be called and get my picture taken. But I was feeling the pressure.

For a woman, more so than a man, a driver's license photo is a report card. Every four years it documents how she is managing the shift from girl to woman, from student to professional, from girlfriend to life-partner, from no-strings-attached to caretaker. A driver's license photo marks a woman's place in time, like the annual school photos of childhood. In our youth and beauty-obsessed culture, a driver's license shows how well a woman is holding up each time she assumes a new role.

The pictures on my last two Washington State driver's licenses had turned out beautifully, nothing like the stereotypical mug shots people joke about. They were better, in fact, than most photos of me, taken in more natural moments and with better lighting. Unlike people who shamefully produce their driver's license, I've always been proud to display mine. Often, far too often, the me it portrayed looked much better than the sallow, haphazard me that offered it up.

The first time I sat in the waiting room of the North Seattle branch of the Department of Licensing, I had just quit my career in the Foreign Service to move to Seattle and live with a man I'd never spent more than two weeks with. I should have looked worried. But in that driver's license picture I look carefree and adventurous, dressed in a shirt of Cambodian silk, acquired on the exotic travels from the life I had forsaken, excited to begin a new chapter of my life.

Four years later, I sat in that same waiting room, fondling that portrait of the glowing, unafraid me, wondering what clues my new picture would give about how I had weathered the changes in my life.

I was older now, with shorter hair, married to Jeff and at home full time with a baby. My traveling days were over. I was afraid that my new driver's license picture would make me look matronly and dull. But the laminated me that the clerk handed back did not disappoint. She looked settled. She looked fulfilled.

Now, four years later, I'd spent months worrying about my next renewal picture, unwilling to believe that I could be lucky a third time.

Jeff, who has no patience for vanity, rolled his eyes. Easy for him to do. Though he may have a few more gray hairs than he would prefer, at 41, he is in his Master of the Universe prime. I was about to turn 42, an age when the best actresses stop getting offered interesting film roles and start directing. I was a stay-at-home mother of two, who'd been out of the workforce for almost five years. I drove a minivan, for God's sake.

Would my new driver's license picture merely reflect the tired, over-40, caretaker me, or would other aspects of my life and personality manage to shine through? Would the new photograph capture the me who enjoyed writing, the me who had discovered the joy of long runs through the woods, alone, for once, with nothing but my thoughts, the me who stayed up late into the night reading to prevent Mommy brain atrophy?

All year, I'd been aware of this looming assessment of how well I was doing at finding balance in my life. In February I'd embarked on a diet and exercise regimen so that when renewal time rolled around, I'd be within the ten-pound acceptable range for lying about my weight. I studied my four-year-old picture, convinced that wearing brightly colored clothes and make-up was key. I timed my hair appointment with precision, so that the cut and color would be fresh, but not too fresh, come picture day. Though I was offered the chance to renew my driver's license for an additional year by mail, I declined. I was ready now. Who was to say I would be ready a year from now?

On D-day I ate carefully and went for a long run. Then I showered and donned the brightest shirt I could find—a fuchsia three-quarter sleeve boat-necked number—and added my trademark lavender eye shadow and pink lipstick.

The air was humid. The hairdryer and the long sleeve shirt made me sweat profusely, my hair sticking against my face in clumps. I considered aborting my mission, but I'd come too far to turn back now.

At the licensing center, I sat for an hour and a half in the cold, beige waiting room, watching number after number appear on the screen. I reflected on why this photo mattered so much. If looks are the outward manifestation of state of mind, then I wanted to be satisfied with what others and I saw. And so I disliked the little "pop quizzes'" that came up from time to time—getting weighed at the doctor's office, where everyone knows the scales are five pounds over, trying on bathing suits in a poorly lit department store dressing room, and renewing my driver's license.

When my number came up, I walked confidently up to the counter and flashed a bright smile. And when the clerk handed me my new license, I liked what I saw: a strong, healthy woman with a playful smile on her face, the first lines of wisdom forming around her eyes.

Five months later, on a bleak January morning, my wallet, address book and cell phone were stolen and along with them, my driver's license. I had no access to my bank or credit card accounts and only an aging passport to prove that I was me. This time there was no opportunity for vanity. I needed a new driver's license and I needed it now.

I expected the worst. It was winter. Instead of tanned and ruddy, my skin looked sallow and green. My face was careworn. I was emotionally depleted from dealing with my aging and difficult mother and from preparing Melanie for a series of invasive medical procedures she required to deal with a congenital urinary tract disorder. And so the theft unnerved me.

Jeff was out of town when it occurred. The thief had tracked my whereabouts and had called me, pretending to be a bank official, so that I would give him access to my accounts. I had spent hours on the phone with police, credit card and cell phone companies going over the day's events. Each time I needed to buy something, I'd had to write a check and produce my passport as identification. I could feel the disapproving and pitying stares of the people who were behind me in line and the salesclerks who painstakingly copied down my passport number. That night I couldn't sleep.

Though it seemed futile, I donned a pink sweater, the same lavender eye shadow and pink lipstick that I had worn on that hot August day.

As I stood in line to get a number in the crowded Department of Licensing office, a poster caught my eye.

"Lose your driver's license?" it said. "If you've been issued a driver's license within the past two years, you can apply for a replacement on line."

I want to say that it was simply the prospect of a long wait that made my decision. That vanity had nothing to do with it. And it's true that five minutes after I logged onto the Department of Licensing website, my application for a replacement license was processed. But the truth is, I wasn't ready to let go of that picture. I didn't want to believe that my confidence and strength were impermanent.

At 11:00 that night, the phone rang.

"Alison?" a voice boomed.

I sighed. I was getting used to talking to strangers.

"I found your driver's license downtown, lying by a gutter. I figured you might want it back."

My stolen driver's license found its way back to me a few days later, my smiling face and pink shirt peering out from under a deep crease in the laminate. The battered picture was a perfectly accurate portrayal of how I felt.

Over the next week, my identity came back to me, in dribs and drabs through the mail. Ten days later, when my pristine replacement driver's license arrived and the hassles of recreating my identity were fading into memory, I could feel the cares and the creases begin to leave my body. I knew that I could be as fresh and as radiant as the woman in that picture. There she was smiling back at me, reminding me that I was off the hook for another four years.

RENOVATION

I am on a ladder, on a cheerless rainy Saturday afternoon, painting the dining room ceiling. A pope is dying. As the world waits for him to take his last breath, on the radio, papal experts are describing the planned elaborate funeral ceremonies and the secretive selection process by which a new pope will be inaugurated. To fill the void until something changes, they provide highlights from the years of his leadership.

I am painting the dining room of my 1912 house alone. I want the new wall color to deepen the dark wood trim, which surrounds the bay windows and the entryway, and to enhance the Vietnamese silk paintings, the Korean and Burmese wooden chests, the Indian *papier-mâché* lamps and the antique sitar with which I have carefully decorated this room. I want the colors of this room to complement the caramel walls of the living room next door—a room that I had also painted alone, nine years earlier.

I am painting alone, but I do not live alone. I share this dining room with my husband and our two young daughters.

Melanie and Maya are unconcerned by the color of the walls. This is home to them—however I choose to decorate it—the only home they have ever known. Years from now they may be resistant if I try to change the color or the décor of this room, a room where they will return to eat holiday meals and bring prospective suitors.

But Jeff, who is old enough to voice an opinion, does not share my vision of how these walls should look. We follow the typical male-female dynamic, which dictates that the wife takes more interest in home décor than the husband, and has come into the marriage with nicer stuff. But there is more to it than that. I have made our house far more an extension of me than of him. The paintings and *objets d'art* that I have hung on the walls are the culmination of my life's accomplishments. I see them as my diplomas. When newcomers enter my house, they invariably ask about the origin of the bejeweled mirror or the wooden rice sorter, thus giving me the opportunity to say something about my life. I want the people who enter my house to understand how who I used to be shapes who I am today.

For Jeff, the choice of wall color is not so complicated. He is not, as I am—as most women I know are—always seeking improvement. He was satisfied with the contrast of the stark white dining room walls with the mahogany trim. When I painted the living room, he conceded and has learned to live with and even like the color of those walls, which he once dismissed as being the color of baby shit. But he couldn't stomach any of my color choices for the dining room, so I covered the sample areas of "Dusty Rose" and "Camel Back" with leftover paint that I had found in the garage. As a result, for nine years the dining room walls have been three different shades of cold white. This incompleteness has rankled me. No one else in my family has given it a second thought.

I drive to Home Depot to buy another gallon of paint. Obsessed as I am with interior color, outside is devoid of color. The Seattle rain has turned into a fine mist that disappears into a fog that the paint companies would be hard pressed to describe as anything other than "Dismal Gray." The somber music on the radio alerts me that the pope is dead. Historians comment on the highlights of this pope's tenure; he was the third longest ruling pope in history. This pope's history is my history, as it has coincided with my entire adult life. And so, back at home, as I take up my place on the ladder, crane my neck towards the ceiling and start on the second coat, I go back in time.

Twenty-seven years earlier, I had just begun my first extended overseas adventure. I was seventeen and living in Evian-les-Bains, France—famous for its mineral water—with an inhospitable French host family. During the summer, shortly before I had left home, Pope Paul VI had died. *Newsweek* and *Time* were filled with accounts of the adoring mobs that flocked to see his body, which was transported around Europe so that the faithful could say goodbye.

It was an unusually hot August. The Pope's farewell tour had to be cut short because the extreme heat was causing his unembalmed body to melt. My friends and I found this amusing. On *Saturday Night Live*, which we relied on to interpret the news, Father Guido Sarducci, SNL's purple-clad Special Correspondent to the Vatican, gave regular updates on the state of the pope's body. He described pope-related souvenirs that were for sale, among them, pope-on-a-rope soap.

Whatever the news source, it was impossible that summer of 1978 not to be aware that the Pope had died. And after the white smoke appeared over the Vatican, indicating that a successor had been chosen, much was made of the fact that the new pope had selected the name John Paul, to honor the two popes who had preceded him.

"*Le Pape est mort!*" shrieked Madame Rousseau on a September morning as I stood ironing in the kitchen of my French family's small apartment, which overlooked Lake Geneva.

We were home alone together. For the few weeks that I had lived with the Rousseau family, I had avoided Madame. She was harsh and judgmental with a mouth full of prominent teeth and her face made it no secret that she was disappointed by the sloppily dressed American exchange student who had come to live with her family. I felt warmth from her elderly husband, a quintessential Frenchman replete with beret and poodle. But he disappeared every morning with his dog Timi, probably in search of peace and quiet. Like her mother, their daughter Marie-France, for whom I was supposed to serve as a companion, wanted nothing to do with me. Her mouth was crowded with the same jumble of teeth as her mother's and a similar harshness was beginning to settle over her lithe seventeen-year-old body. She wore the same tight jeans and pullovers several days in a row, and seemed to have no interests apart from her boyfriend. Perhaps a chubby girl, who showered and changed clothes every day, didn't fit her image of what an American was supposed to be. After dutifully inviting me on a few outings with her friends, some of whom exhibited a wisp of curiosity about me, Marie-France and I settled into our separate lives. We barely acknowledged each other at school or at home.

On this hopeful morning, I had decided to make an effort to become friends with Madame. So instead of escaping the apartment after Marie-France went off with her friends and Monsieur Rousseau and Timi left for their morning walk, I ventured into the kitchen—the traditional gathering place for women of all generations and cultures.

"*Le Pape est mort!*" Madame Rousseau shrieked again, tears streaming down her face.

Though she was a devout Catholic, it seemed an excessive reaction for an event that had already occupied the world stage. Still, I was careful not to judge. Madame mistrusted me as a *juive*. In fact, I'd noticed that labels were important to her. I was the Jew, and her daughter-in-law, born and raised in France, was *la Polonaise* because of her Polish immigrant parents. Madame liked to know where she stood in relation to other people. So I decided not to dismiss what seemed to be genuine emotion and tried to understand her. Perhaps she thought that Jews were unaware of the Pope's death. Maybe she would explain what He had meant to her. Maybe I would gain insight into French Catholicism. Maybe she would invite me to accompany her to church.

"*Oui,*" I responded, in my best newly-arrived-in-France accent. "*Il est mort il y a une mois.*"

I was proud of my complex sentence structure. There could be no mistaking that I was aware that the Pope had died a month ago. So I was surprised that the look she gave me was withering.

"*Non! Le Pape vient de mourir.*"

Eventually I figured out that the new pope had died, just one month after being elected. The linguistic frustrations of trying to make me understand this had extinguished any hope I had of establishing a rapport with Madame. Had I persisted, or been more proficient in French, perhaps we could have discussed how she felt about the new pope, another Polonais. But the moment to reach a *rapport*, a word that needs no English translation, had passed. In the year I lived in her home, we never had another private conversation.

As the paint roller rhythmically moves along the dining room ceiling, I lament that twenty-seven years could have gone by so quickly. Where once I was on the brink of everything, I can no longer fool myself into thinking that I have all the time in the world. Now, when I visit my gynecologist, we talk about endings, not beginnings. I am no longer on the brink of menstruation or motherhood; I am on the brink of menopause. My aunt used to refer to this as "the changes." In our family going through "the changes" became a catch-all excuse for any extreme behavior exhibited by a woman of a certain age.

There has been an unmentioned level of tension in our house, perhaps because we are all going through our own form of "the changes." Jeff and I are getting older, our children are growing and perhaps we are outgrowing this home and these boxes we have placed ourselves in. I have felt some long-suppressed stirrings—a desire to dress up, to step out of the domestic domain. Jeff has surprised me by suggesting we move—that we find a new house with bigger spaces or maybe relocate to someplace rural. But I don't want to move. I want to finish the job I started nine years ago and make this house complete. The baby and toddler stages behind us, I want our family to settle into the groove of middle childhood and leave the combat conditions of toddler and babyhood behind.

I saw Pope Paul VI once, in the square at St. Peter's, waving from the window of his apartment, a year or so before he died. He was a balding little old man, dressed in a white gown, a tall, angular miter on his head. Thinking about it now, that image of the Pope reminds me of my daughters as toddlers playing dress-up—their semi-bald heads adorned with tiaras, and their short bodies encased in stiff, intricately decorated gowns.

For nine years the dining rooms walls have been three different shades of a very cold white. I have decided that nine years is long enough. In our years together, Jeff and I have been through far more serious challenges than trying to agree on a paint color. Nine years is almost an entire life chapter. It's time to get ready for the next one.

The ceiling is now a creamy, warm linen, but I want something more dramatic for the walls. I spackle holes and cracks and smooth away rough edges. I hang sample color squares and paint wide swaths of hue, asking everyone who enters our house to tell me whether they prefer "Shaker Beige," "Manchester Tan" or "Waterbury Cream." I apply masking tape. Finally I am ready to paint the walls. I paint them two coats of "Monterey White." The sample had looked like an interesting aged parchment, but on the walls the color is dull and disappointing. I am frustrated, but there is no point in being frustrated. There is nothing else to do but try again.

And then, in the middle of it all, Melanie breaks her leg and everything stops. Jeff and I are allied once again. The fold out couch in the den is piled high with books, DVD covers, Chinese checkers and playing cards. The dining room table is piled high with take-out food, the ladder pushed into a corner, the drop cloths and masking tape forgotten for now.

Because now there is nothing more important than the little girl who is hurting and her sister, who is feeling upstaged. We are at our best, Jeff and I, in situations like these. We share the same vision of how to make things better. I sleep in the den beside Melanie during those first difficult nights, applying ice packs to her swollen leg and singing songs and telling stories to cajole her back to sleep. During the day, while I try to rest or wander around the house in a sleep-induced fog, Jeff reads endless books to our daughters and they watch *Harry Potter* movies together. He brings me home enough Indian food to feed an army.

Slowly, life returns to normal. I replace the drop cloths, pull out the ladder and finish painting the walls. The woman in the paint store has taken my remaining gallon of "Monterey White" and transformed it. Now the walls are a warm shade of barley. Each time Jeff and the girls enter the room, they dutifully say,

"What a beautiful paint job," as I have trained them to do.

Though I had spent much of the time I was painting resentful of the fact that Jeff wasn't helping, now a smidgen of pride creeps in. I think I have set an example for all of us. I wanted this and I made it happen. And I didn't give up just because I didn't get it right the first time.

For a few more days the walls are devoid of ornamentation, but somehow it doesn't seem so important anymore. Then Jeff helps me re-hang the Thai silk tapestry, the wooden Indian window frame, and the puffin lithograph that I had bought when we traveled together to Maine. He makes sure he takes every opportunity to tell me how much he appreciates the

warm glow of the dining room, even though I'm pr
makes absolutely no difference to him.

On the ceiling of the Sistine Chapel is Michelangelo's famous fresco of God giving life to Adam. Underneath the restoration, you can still see the cracks that run through the painting, enhancing its timelessness and its endurance.

The walls of our house are teeming with life—the life I once lived and the life we all live together. The cracks in our walls remain visible like the cracks that will continue to show in Melanie's bone, even after it has healed. Old cracks will fade or be repaired and new ones will appear. The passage of time will bring changes—career changes and school changes. There will be unexpected telephone calls, cancer scares, misunderstandings and attempts at reconciliation. There will be plane trips, not only to exotic destinations, but also to hospital bedsides. There will be weddings and funerals and dance performances and satisfying meals among friends. Most important, there will be stories told around the dining room table, of experiences past and experiences we have shared. People's lives, like walls, are made up of layers of paint and varnish and holes and gashes and ornaments. They can be smooth and textured and sometimes rough around the edges. It is this buildup of living that gives people and their walls a unique patina. But there is always the opportunity for renewal by applying a fresh coat of paint.

ELASTIGIRL REFLECTS

My family and I are watching the film *The Incredibles*. Reassigned to an ordinary existence under the "Superhero Protection Program," Bob and Helen Parr are forced to relinquish their previous identities. Bob, formerly Mr. Incredible, is now an overweight insurance adjuster, beaten down by the banalities of his middle-class suburban life. He instinctively knows it is wrong to deny who he really is, so he looks for ways to subterfuge the bureaucracy and gets his jollies at night by appearing at crime scenes and secretly rescuing people in distress. But Helen, formerly Elastigirl, has chosen to put her past behind her. She spends much of her time vacuuming and reining in her family's powers. She dismisses Bob's protestations that they should be allowed to live to their full potential. So it is especially satisfying when Helen dons her power suit (roomier now, to accommodate the saddlebags and paunch of middle age), reclaims her inner power and inspires her family to save the world from disaster.

Four days later, I dig an old power suit out of the closet and set out to have my own adventure.

"Are you going to a funeral, Mommy?" asks five-year-old Melanie.

"No," I respond.

"Is somebody getting married?" three-year-old Maya wants to know.

"Nope, not that I know of," I say.

I lean forward conspiratorially and pull on my L'Eggs Sheer Energy Pantyhose, which I purchased the day before. I tell them I am going to a meeting "downtown."

"You see this, girls?" I ask, stretching the nude color nylon away from my calf.

They move closer and wait. They know that this is one of those moments in which I will give them another clue that unravels the mysteries of a woman's life. My words come out in a whisper:

"I used to be Elastigirl!"

Pantyhose: formerly the bane of my existence. Expensive, constraining, unimaginative, uncool. The accessory I often believed inhibits a woman's individuality in much the same way that a tie can inhibit a man.

Pantyhose: now the source of nostalgia. Strong, powerful, sexy, liberating. The elixir from which I summon my special powers.

Before I felt constrained by them, when they were the forbidden fruit that held the promise of experiences yet to be had, I dreamed of wearing pantyhose. What girl didn't long for the day when she would be liberated at last from years of Danskin tights and ushered into the world of women? Even our mothers still exhibited girlish delight over pantyhose. Invented in 1959, pantyhose didn't really hit the mass market until some time in the 1960s, so women were still reveling in the freedom from garter belts. Pantyhose, tampons, hand-held blow dryers = women's liberation.

I suppose it's inevitable that when you look back on your life, you can see a series of turning points. But sometimes you are aware of them, even as they are happening.

I am standing in the ladies' room of the Circle in the Square Theater in New York City, circa 1977, on a school trip to see a production of *As You Like It*. My feathered hair is perfectly blow-dried. I am wearing a brown and salmon checked gauze shirt, salmon colored gauchos and...pantyhose. I catch a glimpse of myself in the mirror and come back for another look. I admire myself from every angle. I am sixteen. I don't look like my usual chubby, lank-haired schoolgirl self.

"What would it be like to feel like this all the time?" I wonder, not dumpy and uncertain, but cool and confident and taut like my pantyhose.

It was years before I would find out.

I buried my pantyhose during those years of college experimentation—years of hairy legs and Birkenstocks, black tights and Indian wrap skirts, jeans, flannel shirts and backpacks. But when I graduated and it was time to get a job, I knew it was time to get out the pantyhose.

Remember the white ones that everyone wore in the 1980s? I traipsed through countless offices in Washington, D.C. looking like a candy striper in my white pantyhose and brightly colored dresses that were fine in California, where I had gone to college, but out of place in our nation's capital, where the women dressed like dead birds.

A degree, a splash of color, intelligence and some panache were clearly not enough. No matter what the job, before any interview could be granted, I was subjected to a typing test. Oh, the pressure to be able to type forty words per minute! I had a degree in international relations, was fluent in another language and was smart, savvy and well traveled and well read. None of it mattered. Even once, when I pointed out that there was a typo in the typing test, no one seemed to appreciate my eye for detail. This was women's liberation? For me pantyhose, like typing, were a means of keeping a woman in her place.

I am wearing my pantyhose in the government personnel office where I have been assigned as a receptionist. It's not what I was hoping for, but I try to make the best of it.

"Good Morning, Personnel, my I help you?" I say cheerily to the callers on my first morning.

My supervisor, dressed in a brown suit the color of dry and fallen leaves during the final days of autumn, takes me aside.

"We don't answer the phone with 'Good Morning.' We simply say 'Personnel, how may I help you?'"

So much pride and individuality to swallow during that, my first job out of college, waking up every morning with a sense of dread as I strained to get into my pantyhose. I'd delayed putting them on until October, which raised a few eyebrows among my superiors. Now, in mid-winter, they made my dresses cling to my legs, crackling with static electricity. Throughout the day, the women in my office would congregate in the supply room, lift up their dresses and liberally spray Static Guard to their thighs. I was the only white girl in the clerical pool. I knew I had earned their trust when the African-American secretaries let me in on their secret:

"Girl, you don't need to use Static Guard. See this wire hanger? Take it and rub it up and down your thighs and along your booty. That'll kill the cling!"

Even in the dead of winter, pants were frowned upon. So day after day I donned my pantyhose, trying desperately to keep them intact. At three dollars a pair, they were expensive for a person trying to repay student loans on a government clerk-typist salary.

I could never wear them more than once or twice before they developed obvious runs that could not be stopped by the clear nail polish I'd been advised to apply. After the first few times that my toes poked through and rubbed uncomfortably against my sensible pumps, I got smart and spent an extra fifty cents for pantyhose with reinforced toes. I added an extra dollar for the privilege of wearing control tops. But there was no such thing as a fully reinforced pair of pantyhose.

At night I would rinse my pantyhose in the sink with Woolite and hang them to dry. On cold winter mornings when the heat in my studio apartment had given out, they would still be wet. So I blow-dried them.

Once, I put them in the dryer with the rest of my laundry. It was a pleasure that morning to be able to don warm dry pantyhose. But the nylon had reacted negatively to the dryer's heat. For the rest of the day I could feel them shredding around my legs, leaving me with nothing more than an inadequate set of nylon stripes to keep me warm.

The solution to pantyhose preservation came in an Ann Landers column. In a response to a reader with a similar dilemma, Ann Landers suggested putting pantyhose in the freezer to strengthen the fibers. Each morning I reached into my freezer and pulled out an Egg (unprotected pantyhose, I'd discovered, had a tendency to stick to the accumulated freezer frost). With a chill on my legs, I set off to answer phones. In March as the spring thaw set in, I removed my pantyhose. Eyebrows were raised and there was still a slight chill in the early morning air. I didn't care. I was barelegged and free.

You get used to pantyhose, just like you learn to work around institutional constraints. Eventually I said goodbye to the clerical pool and got my big professional break.

There was no question now that I would be wearing pantyhose to work every day. The only question was which kind? Perhaps L'Eggs were too frivolous. Maybe "No Nonsense" would be more appropriate.

I had already abandoned white pantyhose in favor of "Nude." Now I branched out even further. With my sensible dark suits, I occasionally wore black or navy pantyhose, which I felt gave me the appropriate professional air. During the months of training for my new job, I scandalized the other new hires by being the first woman to wear pants. But for the most part I wore pantyhose. All year round.

When I gained some confidence and some seniority, I added hints of color—violet and gray and lighter blue to complement my power suits, which were themselves getting lighter. But was it my imagination or did some look at me askance? Because when you're a woman, even a woman in pantyhose, you always have to work a little bit harder to be taken seriously than the man in the rumpled suit next to you. Maybe colored pantyhose weren't worth the risk.

The women ahead of me on the career ladder—the ones who never strayed from pantyhose in tasteful flesh tones—seemed to be clear on which things were worth the risk. They worked hard, so hard that some of them were a threat to the men around them. Year, after year, as the men married and built families and continued to climb the career ladder, these pantyhose-clad women grew thin and brittle or fat and dumpy and devoted themselves single-mindedly to their work. No men. No children—unless they managed to adopt a daughter from China.

Those who did manage to "have it all" seemed harried and joyless, their days programmed to the minute: drop off kids; go to work; work out at lunch time; pick up kids; make dinner; clean up; put kids to bed; catch up on work reading; have sex with husband.

I didn't like the future I saw for myself. So I left it all behind to marry a man who encouraged me to wear fuchsia. But pantyhose were still part of my new life in a more casual city—a life that promised a different future. A future that looked something like this:

Your stomach is pushing outward, until it reverberates against the maternity pantyhose you are wearing to keep yourself professionally presentable.

It may have been pantyhose's tarty little cousins that got you here in the first place—silky, sexy, smooth, slinky black stockings affixed to your thighs with garter belts. You like the way they make you feel—daring, uninhibited, and powerful. But you also worry whether you are buying into a stereotype that encourages the objectification of women.

Why isn't pure and lovely naked flesh enough? You "Google" pantyhose and discover that the first ten hits are devoted to fetish websites. The power of pantyhose scares you.

Your baby is born and you put your pantyhose away for now, maybe forever. You trot them out for the occasional wedding or funeral and feel like a grown-up, a well put-together respectable wife and mother. "What would it be like to feel this way all the time?" you wonder, not sloppy and sleep-deprived, but cool and confident and taut like your pantyhose.

Your kids get older, you volunteer for things, you join boards and once in a while you get to wear pantyhose. You get a thrill when you remember that you once advised presidents and met with foreign heads of state in your pantyhose. You thought you had buried your past. But once in a while it rises to the surface.

You meet younger women who wear fishnets and tights with chunky-heeled, thigh-high boots. You guess none of them has ever been subjected to a typing test.

You want to buy black sparkly pantyhose to wear to a Christmas party. Money isn't as tight as it was twenty years ago, so you venture into the hosiery section of an upscale department store. The array of choices makes you dizzy. There are so many ways to be a woman.

I return from my downtown meeting with time to spare before I have to pick up my children from school. Ample time to return to my normal uniform of ripped jeans and a sweater. But I don't go home. I go to school and I hang around. I want as many people as possible to see me in my superhero costume.

"Wow, you sure look different!"

"You must have gone to work today, I've never seen you looking like that!"

"How can you wear those heels?"

I confess that it has been so long since I wore heels on a regular basis, that I almost slipped and fell on my ass while walking in the rain up a steep hill. The women all laugh in recognition and female solidarity. And for a moment I am back in the supply room rubbing my booty with a hanger, along with all the other women in their pantyhose.

Sometimes I think the two legs of a pair of pantyhose are the perfect expression of their duality: flexible, yet fragile; liberating, yet confining. And so when it is time for Elastigirl to reveal another of the clues that unravel the mysteries of a woman's life, this is what I will tell my daughters:

"You will spend a lifetime teetering between freedom and constraint. Sometimes you will be confused by your choices. Don't be afraid to try on different costumes, because life can have many different stages. Just be sure that whatever you are wearing, you are never left without a leg to stand on."

DREAMING OF ITALY

It all started with *crêpes* and Van Gogh, neither of which is Italian I realize, but bear with me, I'm getting to that.

Actually, it had all started years before, when, as a way to console myself over giving up a life of international travel, I concocted a plan: when Maya and Melanie turned eight and ten, we would take them on a round the world trip. Over the course of a year, we would introduce them to the great civilizations of the world. They would become familiar with classic works of art and architecture. They would understand the primitive forces behind music. They would appreciate the ways in which history, landscape and identity shape the fate of a community. They would learn that most other cultures are less obsessed with material things; that instead of grabbing a quick bite and a plastic toy at McDonald's, most people in the world take the time to sit down and eat real food, if they are fortunate enough to be able to eat at all.

In my fantasy, not only would my daughters understand the world in a way that their textbooks couldn't show them, but they would experience the same exhilaration that I do whenever my feet touch foreign soil or my taste buds encounter a new flavor.

But my girls were still young, so I would have to bide my time. I consoled myself with cooking, taking wild culinary expeditions. In the morning I would decide on my destination. In the afternoon, instead of plane tickets, I would purchase ingredients. By evening I would be in Turkey or Morocco, Russia or France. I convinced myself that this was enough... for now.

One Sunday morning in August, I had a date with Melanie. We were going to the Seattle Art Museum to see a Van Gogh exhibit. I was prepared to rush through the exhibit in deference to Melanie's five-year-old's attention span. But as we made our way through the crowded exhibition rooms, Melanie didn't seem to be in any hurry. I knelt down beside her.

"What kind of strokes did Van Gogh use to paint that tree?" I whispered. Melanie considered.

"Little slashes instead of the dots that he used to paint the flowers."

We admired Van Gogh's sunflowers, his portraits of peach trees and cherry trees and looked for the hints of lavender and ochre and gray in his painting of the gardens of the asylum at Saint Rémy. When we came upon a painting of a café terrace at night, I remembered what it felt like to while away the hours in a European café. Melanie leaned in closer to me and gazed at the painting.

We emerged from the exhibit with a book about Van Gogh and stumbled upon an outdoor *crêperie*. We had been reading a book about a traveling Parisian crêperie and just that morning I had promised to make crêpes. But the girls were throwing tantrums and we were running late and so the idea was abandoned. Now we had the chance to prolong the feeling that Van Gogh had inspired. As we munched our crêpe au citron, I confided to Melanie,

"This is the meaning of the word serendipity."

It occurred to me that serendipity had once described the way it felt to walk along the quaint cobble-stoned streets of an ancient village or to have a pleasant conversation with a local resident. Now, it described the unexpected joy of having my child delight in the same things that moved me.

We got home and I downloaded the words to Don McLean's song "Vincent." Our bedtime reading that night was the Van Gogh book. When it was time for them to close their eyes, I sang Maya and Melanie to sleep with images of Van Gogh's canvas and the starry night that inspired him.

The following weekend, Jeff departed for a boys' windsurfing trip to Maui. I was fine with it. We had discussed the trip over our anniversary dinner and had agreed that this was the kind of marriage we wanted: a marriage with space for both partners to do what intoxicated them. Windsurfing intoxicated Jeff. He never got enough. Though we tried to make time on most summer weekends, he was often constrained by the mercurial behavior of our children and our domestic obligations. This boys' trip would guarantee him a week of selfish windsurfing time. He promised he would return to us sated and rejuvenated.

I was intoxicated by travel. I never got enough. Before I became a mother, I traveled to and lived in dirty, difficult, remote locales. I'd had my share of intestinal parasites and cultural misunderstandings. I'd removed my shoes upon entry into temples, eaten with my right hand and never my left, and squatted over a wide array of holes in the ground. Jeff's travel experiences were similar to mine. So it was understandable that when he chose to humor my travel fantasies, he dreamed of faraway destinations and rigorous activities—the kinds of experiences we both used to enjoy. He suggested that one day we could take the kids trekking in Nepal or white water rafting in Costa Rica. But Maya and Melanie were only three and five. The few short treks we'd taken with them across the United States had been excruciating. Travel would have to wait.

When I'd brought up the idea of something tamer, such as renting a house in Tuscany, Jeff scoffed.

"Europe! We'll save that for when we're too old to really travel."

I knew what he meant. There was so much of the world left for us to explore, so why waste our time on the accessible and easy?

I told us both that I was fine with Jeff's trip to Hawaii, but in truth I also resented it. I would be taking care of the kids without a break while Jeff enjoyed freedom of a duration I had never known since becoming a mother. We had talked about possible quid pro quos for me: a trip to San Francisco, a weekend island getaway with old friends, but these trips would have to be squeezed into the margins of our busy lives. I wanted something long and exotic. I wanted something accessible and easy that I could share with my family. And so when Jeff set off on his trip, I began dreaming of Italy.

First came the salami. Everything Marcel Proust had to say about the power of food to trigger memory came crashing back the moment I took my first bite of salami. I'd been eyeing logs of salami and *soppressata* for weeks at the supermarket. They were provocatively displayed in wicker baskets next to jars of red and yellow fire-roasted peppers. I could swear I heard one of them whisper as I passed, "Eat me and you will be transported. You can run wild in a land of olive groves and *piazzas*."

I stopped to listen.

"Yes, yes, I used to do that," I silently responded to the salami. "I took hikes in the hills above Taormina and picnicked with a wedge of *provolone*, a bottle of *Frascati*, rustic bread and salami."

But that day, the salami did not make its way into my shopping cart.

When Melanie was a baby and I needed to fill the late afternoon hours before Jeff came home for dinner, I would pour myself a glass of *Chianti*, listen to the soaring voice of Andrea Bocelli and imagine that I was in an old stone villa with heavy brocade furniture and a pot of marinara sauce bubbling on the stove. I grew up listening to Puccini arias booming from my mother's stereo speakers. At the time it embarrassed me. Now I wonder whether she, too, was dreaming of Italy.

A few years ago, I watched an episode of *The Sopranos*, in which Carmela Soprano, the long-suffering wife, put on the same overproduced Bocelli album that I had been listening to and dreamed about having an affair with Fiorio, her mob-boss husband's Italian hit man.

"Oh my God," I thought. "I've become a caricature of the stereotypical repressed housewife!"

I put away the Bocelli album and reined in my fantasies. But now here I was talking to salami.

I went to Italy for the first time with my mother at the age of sixteen. In the company of our intrepid guide Renato, we hit all the usual tourist spots—the Sistine Chapel, St. Peter's, Pompeii. But when we got to Sicily, things changed. Enzo, a blond-haired, blue-eyed Neopolitan with a smooth demeanor, replaced Renato. The tone of our trip turned decidedly more sensual. My mother and Enzo flirted with each other and one day they arranged to meet for *cappuccino.* I stayed behind, inadvertently locked in our hotel room, which could only be unlocked from the outside, fingering a tiny turquoise mosaic pill box I had bought. I thought this box was the most exquisite treasure I had ever seen and I spent my hours in captivity admiring it. When my mother returned, she was radiant and light-hearted. Instead of being apologetic, she laughed good-naturedly at my misfortune. I think I understood then that I had been ushered into the world of grown-ups—a world of romance and beauty and appetites. A world of serendipity. After that my mother and I shared bottles of wine al fresco, delighting in the perfect marriage of wine and bread and cheese and cured meats—the balance of sweet and salty, of sharp and suave—the tastes of life.

I finally bought the salami in the interests of culinary exploration. We were invited to a potluck dinner party the night Jeff was to leave for Hawaii. I wanted to make something new. *Pasta salad con salami* sounded promising. Soon it would be my turn to bring snacks for soccer practice. Wouldn't the kids enjoy *Soppressata Cheese Sticks*? I've been a semi-vegetarian for almost 20 years, so I hadn't actually eaten salami for quite some time. But lately my appetite had been growing.

"I think I'm experiencing a return to pork," I told Jeff.

Eating salami would be a bold step in that direction. There was no telling where it could lead.

The pasta salad was good. At the party, a man named Eric eyed it appreciatively.

"Oh I love salami," he gushed.

I looked at him and wondered if there was a secret salami-loving society that I was on the verge of joining. We met up again later in front of the serving dish.

"Damn," said Eric. "Someone ate all of the salami out of the pasta salad."

Half of the log of salami was left in my refrigerator, just enough to make the cheese sticks. I put the kids to bed, poured myself a glass of *Pinot Grigio* and cut myself one small slice, then another.

The beginning of Jeff's week away was tough. Melanie and Maya each woke up crying in the middle of the night. They bickered with each other during the day. As anyone who has ever done a stint of solo parenting knows, you get through it because you have no choice. We went to the library and selected a book entitled *The Year I Didn't Go to School,* a true story about two sisters named Giselle and Chloe who lived for a year in Italy touring with their parents' traveling puppet show. To ease the tension we were all feeling, that night at dinner, as I dished up *cannellini con tonno,* and *broccoli con aglio e olio*, I suggested,

"Let's pretend we are eating dinner in Italy."

The girls warmed to the idea.

"I'll be Giselle and you be Chloe, Maya," Melanie directed.

"Who will you be, Mommy?" Maya asked.

"Mariana, la Mama," I responded with an Italian warble to my voice.

"We are in Firenze, dining in a *trattoria*. We have spent the day admiring Michelangelo's David and wandering through the *piazza*. The waiter approaches us and asks, '*Signorini*, how is your dinner?' '*Delicioso*,' we respond."

Melanie and Maya's eyes lit up at my flight of fancy. We talked some more about the adventures of Giselle and Chloe.

"How's your dinner, girls?" I asked.

"*Delicioso*," responded Melanie, even though she had barely touched the unfamiliar food on her plate.

"*Delicioso*," Maya echoed shyly.

The next afternoon we gathered at our friend Brannon's house to pick plums from a grove of overabundant fruit trees. It was raining. The kids whooped and hollered in the backyard as they filled bucket after bucket with purple exploding fruit. We parents huddled in the kitchen, sipping glasses of the *Chantepierre* that Sage's parents Rory and Diane had brought from their cousin's winery in Eastern Washington. We complained that we were tired, we were overdue for a vacation, but what sort of vacation can you have with kids?

"I've been dreaming of Italy," I confessed. "Wouldn't it be great to rent a villa together in Tuscany?"

Eyes lit up and appreciative murmurs emerged from the group:

"That sounds sooo nice!"

"I could get into that!"

"Count us in!"

My words came out in a rush:

"If we pooled our resources we could rent a large villa in the hills above Florence or Siena. Maybe we could even afford to bring a babysitter. We could take hikes in the hills, meander in village *piazzas* eating *gelato,* and buy our dinner provisions at the open air markets."

"I'd want to spend a lot of time in museums," Heather called out.

"And at vineyards!" shouted Rory.

On the drive home I sang every corny Dean Martin and Tony Bennett song I could think of: "Volare," "Arriverderci Roma," "Cella Luna Metza Mada," "That's Amore." I remembered learning "Funiculi Funicula" while viewing the remnants of a funicular carriage at the base of Mount Etna. Memories of long forgotten places came flooding back: the ruins of Pompeii; the Amalfi Coast, which I had seen with my mother; Pisa and Venice, where I had been with college friends during my year in Paris. These were some of my first overseas experiences and I had forgotten them. How could I have thought that Europe had nothing to offer my family? Europe had prepared me to explore the rest of the world.

When Jeff called from Hawaii that night, I listened to his description of his day of windsurfing. Then, I said casually, "By the way, we are going to Italy. We're renting a villa in Tuscany with our friends."

He laughed and changed the subject. So I brought it up again. And again.

"Enough about Italy!" he admonished me.

The call ended unsatisfactorily.

That night, I munched the rest of the salami and got on the Internet. At www.tuscanynow.com I found fulfillment that

I hadn't achieved during my conversation with Jeff. I knew I could be happy at *Vaggio Savernano*, a three-hundred-year-old farmhouse, southwest of Florence, with terracotta floors and a swimming pool with a view of the *Val d'Arno*. Or perhaps *Villa Raffentini*, a fifteenth century villa with a glass-enclosed loggia. I imagined soaking in a claw-footed bathtub in *Il Querceto*, or hiking to the monasteries and markets in close proximity to *La Treggiaia*. *Poggio Alto* would be a convenient distance from the wine center of Orvieto, but I might prefer staying in *Il Trebbio*, a small castle in the heart of the Chianti region.

I chewed my salami and calculated. Four families sharing a villa for a week in Tuscany, plus another week to sightsee around the rest of the country, hotels, car rental, airfare. We could do it...for $10,000.

Like many families raising young children with one stay-at-home partner, we have a tight budget. We'd noticed that the costs of maintaining our moderate but comfortable standard of living were rising higher than Jeff's salary. We were constantly looking for expenses to cut and money had become a source of tension between us. We had money built in for modest vacations, but we couldn't afford to splurge. Jeff had gone to Hawaii using frequent flier miles, sharing cheap accommodations with his buddies and living on bananas and beer. I knew that I had no business dreaming of Italy because we couldn't afford to go there. But I kept dreaming all the same.

It had been a long week and I was frazzled. The night before Jeff returned home, I was too tired to cook but not ready to leave my Italian fantasies behind. So Chloe, Giselle and Mariana ordered pizza. When the girls went to bed I fell asleep watching *A Room With a View*. Lucy Honeychurch was transformed by her visit to Tuscany. It could be that way for us, I was sure of it.

The next afternoon after Jeff returned, Brannon accompanied me to see a movie about two young lovers wandering the streets of a European city. The movie reawakened in me the now familiar ache. Afterwards, over a glass of wine and *bruschetta*, we discussed our Italian vacation. We agreed that neither of us could afford to do it. But how could we afford not to do it? It would be a lasting gift for our children. Perhaps more importantly, it would be a reminder to ourselves that you shouldn't have to give up the things you love for the people you love. There should be room for it all.

Subliminal reminders of Italy mocked me for the rest of the weekend, as Jeff and I struggled to reconnect. Everyone, it seemed, was dreaming of Italy. Fine Italian wines were advertised on sale, extra virgin olive oils and roasted peppers were on display at our neighborhood supermarket, the couples in the TV Viagra ads seemed to be frolicking in olive groves. I'm sure Jeff didn't notice, but as we ordered lattes at Caffè Fiore, our favorite neighborhood coffee shop, someone had the Sunday newspaper open to the travel section. In big bold letters I saw the words "ITALY: WHY NOT?" above a tantalizing list of airfares. Jeff and I sat down. It was time for us to talk.

When you've been married to someone for long enough you know what it takes to finally get to the heart of what is bothering you. I talked about Italy and eventually Jeff listened. I talked about the career and travel compromises I had made for our family. I talked about my fear that we never would manage to take a year off and travel the way I had imagined.

"Maybe we won't be able to swing it," I acknowledged. "If not, then we'll just have to make it work some other way. Italy would be a step in the right direction. I won't compromise on my desire to introduce our daughters to the world. I won't ever stop dreaming of Italy. Because if I stop dreaming of Italy, then I stop dreaming."

On Labor Day we had brunch on Lummi Island at the home of old friends. Three generations of family and friends ate and talked in a garden filled with wild flowers, just as Italian families do every Sunday. After we were done eating, Maya spied a rocking horse and climbed aboard.

"See you later, Daddy!" she shouted. "I'm going to Italy!"

At home, as the autumn chill hit the air, I cooked *pumpkin risotto, spaghetti bolognese* and *eggplant parmigiana* and decided that like a fine wine, my fantasies needed time to ferment.

One night, Jeff remarked in that dense way that husbands do,

"I've noticed a lot of things having to do with Italy lying around the house—magazine articles, catalogues of Tuscan villas and recipes."

Surprisingly, now when we discuss our budget, as an inducement to get us to save more, he mentions that overseas travel should be factored into our plans. In February he said, "I've noticed that airfares to Paris are cheap at the moment. Maybe you should take Melanie on a whirlwind trip."

Melanie and Maya have let us know that they have their own plans.

"Maya and I are going to China," Melanie announced recently. "You can come with us if you want to."

Foreign travel even plays a role in their bickering.

"I'm going to Italy with Mommy," Maya proclaims. "You can go to France all by yourself, Melanie!"

As for me, I'm still dreaming of Italy.

Something tells me we're halfway there.

INTERNATIONAL POTLUCK

Okay, so by now you get the picture. World traveling career gal chucks it all to get married and have babies. Suffers from work versus family conflict, longs to travel, uses exotic cooking as an escape.

Fast forward a few years and you'll see me sneaking bites of *baklava* with my friend Clea's Turkish lover Akif. We are comparing the taste of the three baklavas he has made: a traditional walnut one, as well as baklavas made with pistachios and almonds. Our friend Avram has also made baklava from his Sephardic Jewish father's recipe and we have to sample that one too before discretely dipping our fingers into Norwegian custard with sour cherry pudding. I have made *Satsivi*, a walnut pomegranate sauce traditionally served over chicken. It is eaten at parties in the former Soviet Union and, according to Claudia Roden's seminal work *The Book of Jewish Food: An Odyssey from Samarkand to Vilna to the Present Day,* which has become my favorite bedtime reading, it is especially beloved by the Jews of the Republic of Georgia. Akif takes a taste and, with a practiced palate, begins identifying the flavors.

"There's something so familiar about this," he comments. "I can taste coriander and cayenne. What else is in it?"

I tell Akif about the walnuts that give the dish its texture and the pomegranate molasses that gives it its sweet kick. We talk for a while about the universality of certain spices, of how complementary the tastes and aromas of foods from different regions can be.

I have landed in a community of like-minded international foodies at, of all places, an elementary school.

After the isolation of new motherhood and the awkwardness of learning to make new friends, I'd bonded with a number of parents at Small Faces, the preschool that Melanie and Maya each attended for three years. These friendships were cemented in the first year, the year that Sage got sick and a group of fledgling friends rallied around him. Four families had emerged as a core group, which remained even after Sage recovered from his illness. Since then, there had been countless play dates and potluck meals. Our kids got along and so did the parents. We shared a taste for fine wine and food, for spontaneous gatherings, no matter how dirty the hostess' house was. Together we celebrated birthdays and Halloween and New Year's Eve. Together we fantasized about renting a villa in Italy.

And then the inevitable split. The day the elementary school assignments came in the mail, Diane, Brannon, Heather and I were spending the day together at a Korean health spa celebrating Diane and Heather's fortieth birthdays. We soaked in tubs, sweated in the sauna, relaxed in the mud and jade rooms and doused ourselves with water infused with mugwort, a medicinal plant. When we got hungry, we walked across the heated floor to the Korean café, where we feasted on *bulgogi* and *bi bam bap*. On the drive home, not one, but two, carloads of young men turned to check us out.

It was a glorious day, but it was quickly ruined when we pulled up to Diane's house and her husband Rory spread the news. Everyone else's kids had either been assigned or waitlisted to the same school. Only Melanie would be attending Adams Elementary. I felt like Dorothy, after the Wizard of Oz has distributed gifts to the Scarecrow, Tin Man and Cowardly Lion and she is left empty-handed.

Jeff was visibly nervous when I walked into the house. When we had ranked our list of elementary school choices, he had wanted Adams at the top of our list. It was three blocks from our house, featured a unique arts-integrated curriculum and an ethnically diverse student body, due to its English as a Second Language program. Melanie would have the opportunity to connect with children of other cultures; something I had always hoped she would do, but had feared was impossible since we no longer traveled internationally. But I balked. All of our preschool friends were choosing schools closer to where they lived and I couldn't imagine leaving behind the comfortable support system I had spent years developing. Jeff wanted to know when I had started playing it so safe. Hadn't I been the one who had moved to a new country every two years? Hadn't I been the one who wanted to pick up stakes and travel around the world for a year? Then why would I want to deny Melanie the opportunity for an interesting education just because I was afraid to leave my friends?

In the end, I won the argument and Adams was placed last on our list of school choices. So it was particularly ironic that after all the debate, Melanie was assigned there anyway.

"We'll make it work," I told him in my best "Don't Cry for Me Argentina" voice.

Though we didn't know a soul at Adams and the first parent I met there was covered in tattoos from the neck down, things started out well. On the first day, Melanie informed me that she had made a friend named Samantha. The next day, she announced that she had decided to name our recently acquired iridescent blue Siamese Betta fish after her. The second week of school we invited all of the girls in Melanie's class and their mothers over for a princess tea party. Neighbors smiled at the parade of little girls decked out in gowns and tiaras walking to our house. Kindergarten was going swimmingly.

Standing on the playground waiting for the kids before the after-school bell rang, I would often find myself beside Lea, an ebullient Rwandan woman, whose daughter Natalie was in Melanie's class. Sometimes Pedro, a single father from Mexico, whose son was in fifth grade, joined us. We would exchange pleasantries about the weather or our children and Pedro would sometimes teach Maya some Spanish words. Eventually and inevitably we would find ourselves talking about food.

I had recently discovered *chilaquiles,* a Mexican comfort dish made up of layers of tortillas and beans, *queso blanco* and sometimes eggs. Lea talked about *fou-fou*, the ubiquitous African staple of mashed yams, used as a side dish with Groundnut Chicken Stew. Pedro waxed poetic about *tamales.*

"How do you like being at a school with such an ethnically diverse population?" I asked Pedro.

He replied morosely, "They never do anything for us."

Pedro's comment haunted me, the perennial turkey-maker. And so I came up with the idea of hosting an international potluck dinner at our school.

I'd been warned by seasoned mothers at the neighborhood parks to stay away from the PTA. "Once they get their hooks in you," they warned, "they'll never let you go."

The women on the Adams PTA board were all very tall and I am short. At night I had dreams about tall women coming after me, *Invasion of the Body Snatchers* with a PTA twist. I drew myself up to my full height and approached the tall women to suggest that instead of having the school's annual Thanksgiving potluck, we host an event that would celebrate the diversity of our student body and make everyone feel included. Instead of turkey, stuffing and potatoes, we would ask everyone to contribute a dish that was meaningful to them, either because it represented their cultural heritage, or because it was something their family enjoyed eating together.

In the weeks leading up to it, I was nervous about how the international potluck would turn out. I needn't have been. Four hundred people showed up. Dish after dish of mouthwatering food appeared on the overcrowded serving tables, handed out by the proud, beaming women who had prepared them. Africans and Indians and Mexicans and Puerto Ricans and Native Americans brought traditional celebratory foods. Hawaiians and Texans and Quebecois and New Englanders followed suit. Families who had traveled to Thailand or the Philippines brought their re-creation of the dishes they had discovered there. And the tamales... We couldn't get enough of them. As if by magic, new infusions of tamales would appear every time the serving dish was empty. Pedro and his friends were beaming.

By the end of the school year, I volunteered to serve on the PTA Nominating committee to choose representatives for next year's PTA board, and I approached anyone I had ever heard make an intelligent or constructive remark at the poorly attended PTA meetings to ask them to volunteer. Everyone was reluctant, everyone was busy, and everyone disliked meetings and politics.

"What about you?" they asked me. I made all of the usual excuses.

"I'll do it if you do it," Gus told me.

Sitting in my living room, drinking wine with Clea and Steve, whom I was trying to convince to be co-presidents, Steve asked me why I was so reluctant.

"I'm already a stereotypical minivan-driving, stay-at-home mom," I lamented. "Being on the PTA board would be the final nail in the coffin."

"This is your life now," Steve told me. "Get over it."

I had spent the previous year on the board of an international non-governmental organization and felt completely powerless. I dreaded the monthly meetings, at which nothing ever seemed to be decided, and was irritated by the lack of order and substance.

The PTA board was different. I created a new position that was right up my alley: Vice President for Outreach. Clea, who was the only person other than Jeff to have my cell phone number, would call ten times a day, excited by new ideas. We would brainstorm, come up with a course of action and implement it. Meetings were engaging, with a group of smart, dedicated people committed to the same cause. Wasn't this what I had been longing for in the early days of motherhood—intellectual stimulation, like-minded peers and the ability to accomplish goals? What a surprise to find it by serving on an elementary school PTA board.

We continued to see our Small Faces friends, getting together for ethnic dinners every month or so, and congregating over wine and pizza on Friday nights.

By first grade our circle widened further. Melanie was assigned to a different teacher than most of her friends. This time she felt shy about the change. So we worked hard to maintain contact with the old friends and become acquainted with new ones. Already her life, and by extension mine, was becoming a series of concentric circles of connection.

One day after school, Lea's car broke down. She and her daughters came over to my house and waited for her husband to pick them up. The house was uncharacteristically clean, due to a burst of activity from Jeff. I noticed Samantha the Fish, who had been hovering on the edge of death all morning, floating at the top of the tank. Four-year-old Maya was distraught. I scooped up the fish in a net and declared that we would have a funeral. We congregated in the bathroom, around a toilet that Jeff had freshened with electric blue toilet bowl cleaner, the same color as Samantha. I dropped the blue fish into the blue toilet water and we each took a turn remembering her before she was flushed away.

"She was a good fish."

"She was our first fish."

"She was a blue fish."

Maya was still crying as she leaned over the toilet to say goodbye. Lea was crying too. I was uncomfortable. Had this seemingly insignificant death of a fish in a Seattle neighborhood reawakened memories of the Rwanda genocide? No, Lea reassured me. It was Maya's grief that had moved her.

One afternoon, after we had known each other a while, I drank tea with Lea in her apartment. Moved beyond the usual conversation about kids and homework and food, Lea quietly told me how the Rwandan civil war had affected her family. She described herself, alone and frightened in the United States, waiting for the news that inevitably came. Her mother and one brother had been killed.

A month later, when Lea was preparing her dish for the international potluck, I asked her if she often cooked African food.

"When I lived in Africa, I didn't know how to cook because my mother did all the cooking. When I came here, I was homesick and missed my food. But after my mother was killed I realized I couldn't ask her how to make the dishes I had loved as a child. So I would imagine her in the kitchen, while I worked in my kitchen. I closed my eyes and tried to remember each thing she did. All of the dishes I make are created from memory; the memory of my mother."

The next week, I hosted the first formal meeting of a multi-cultural committee I had formed to build on the success of the international potluck. The group included Lea; Juan and Irma, a Mexican couple; Yvonne, of Mexican descent; Petra, a single mother of a bi-racial son; Himan, a woman from Eritrea, who almost never spoke but always smiled; and Akif, Clea's partner from Turkey.

Of course there was food—the universal icebreaker. I prepared *muhammara,* a Middle Eastern roast pepper and walnut dip with pita bread. Himan brought her homemade *injera* bread and a spinach stew. At first everyone was shy. But as we ate, smiles broke out and words began to flow and we talked about our plans for the second annual international potluck.

"We should have music!"

"We should have dancing!"

"We should make this an event to remember!"

The next time our group met, in October at Clea and Akif's house, the feast of offerings grew. Indian chickpea stew and daal from Clea and Akif, who were vegetarians; chicken ground nut stew from Lea; a loaf of special Mexican Day of the Dead bread from Yvonne.

"Traditionally you place a candle in the middle of the loaf of bread and everyone remembers someone they have lost," Yvonne explained.

We decided to try it. The bread lay on a tray on the floor with a lit candle inside. We were quiet for a few moments, as everyone retreated into his or her memories. I looked over at Lea. Tears were streaming down her face.

When we were finished, the children came into the room and blew out the candle, as if it were a birthday. Then they clamored for pieces of the fresh loaf of bread.

Our second international potluck was even more successful than the first, with table after table overflowing with food. The African and Asian dishes were the first to disappear, and the women who made them were draped in brightly colored cloth, proudly serving the eager guests. As we took our shift at the

Middle East/Europe table, Akif and I couldn't resist sneaking tastes of the food we were supposed to be serving.

Two months later I was in my kitchen cooking *bstilla,* a Moroccan chicken pie, for the annual birthday celebration we held each January for Melanie, Maya, Sage, and Brannon's son Nathan. I was looking forward to spending Saturday evening with Diane, Brannon, Heather and their families in the warm and familiar embrace of established friendship.

But I would be spending Sunday afternoon with my new friends, attending a memorial service for Akif, who had died unexpectedly a few days before. So while the chicken stewed in a bath of onions, saffron, ginger and cinnamon, I was baking a Sri Lankan Love Cake for him.

Love Cake is a rich and celebratory dish and a perfect example of the wonderful things that can be achieved when you allow yourself to be open to exploration. The recipe is thought to have its origins in sixteenth century Portuguese cuisine. When Portuguese spice traders traveled to the island once known as Ceylon, they discovered the native cardamom and cinnamon and incorporated these into the recipe. I had clipped this recipe from the newspaper five years earlier, but had never found the right opportunity to use it.

I imagined Akif, sinking his teeth into the Love Cake and identifying the flavors:

"Hmm... cashews, semolina. We Turks use semolina when we make *halwa,* which we eat at funerals and celebrations.

"Is that rosewater? The Indians and the Moroccans rely heavily on that.

"Cardamom, honey, cinnamon. I think every culture uses honey and cinnamon in its sweetest of dishes. They have traveled around the globe and back again, and are universally recognized as the tastes of celebration."

The next afternoon in the pouring rain, Lea, Himan and I piled into my minivan; the dishes we had prepared bounced companionably next to each other as we drove to Akif's memorial service. We weren't from different cultures anymore, we were from the same community, and today, we were three women, united in our grief.

I remember going out for Chinese food with my grandfather when I was a little girl. Family members would look on in horror as he piled his plate high with different dishes, some on top of one another, making no effort to separate the *egg foo young* from the *moo shu pork* or the Lobster Cantonese. He had lost his sense of taste, someone explained, and Grandpa liked to say that it was the result of a heroic baseball accident, which occurred as he slid onto second base, just in time to avoid being tagged out.

We protested. For the benefit of the rest of us, couldn't he keep the different foods separate?

"What does it matter?" he would shrug, enjoying the commingling of items on his plate into one warm, delicious community of food.

"It all goes into the same stomach."

FOR WHOM THE
BELLBIRD TOLLS

"HONK!"

My family and I are hiking to a waterfall in Monteverde, Costa Rica, when we hear it: a resounding squawk, followed by a screech that reminds us of a car with deteriorating brake pads. There is a bird in the vicinity, a big bird, and I am determined to find it. Throughout the hike, we watch and wait and listen and look high into the trees. But despite the fact that we hear the sound often, we don't find the "honk," our nickname for the bird my guidebooks later identify as the three-wattled bellbird.

We'd chosen Costa Rica for its ease and proximity to nature. Jeff and I hadn't taken an international trip together since Melanie was born, seven years earlier. Our domestic forays with two kids had been difficult and we worried that they would grow up to be uneasy travelers.

So we waited for the ideal opportunity to spring something big on them. Each year, we wondered whether it was time.

Each year, we concluded that finances were tight and behavior was still unpredictable.

Then friends of ours started dying and couples we knew were divorcing. We noticed that during our brief hours together in the evening, it was hard to connect. By the time we fit in our individual pursuits and chores on the weekends, there wasn't much time for togetherness. Suddenly, it seemed silly to wait any longer for the perfect moment to take a family trip.

The weeks prior to our departure had been busier than usual. The kids had contracted head lice, necessitating chemical shampoos, daily nit-picking sessions and a mountain of laundry. Because I was a stay-at-home mom, much of the tedium of lice management fell to me and I felt isolated and frazzled. On the third day of our lice quarantine, desperate to escape the house, I nearly burned it down by forgetting to turn off the stove, where the lice combs, tweezers and brushes were boiling. So by the time we reached Costa Rica's Lake Arenal, I was ready to unwind.

We awake to the moans of howler monkeys. We have to step carefully to avoid crushing parades of industrious leafcutter ants. An occasional flash of iridescent blue signals the presence of a morpho butterfly. Each morning, Jeff windsurfs and I read, as the girls frolic in the coconut palm-flanked swimming pool. But we come together each afternoon, eating papaya in the garden, hunting for the mother and baby monkeys in the trees above us, and watching lizards scurry by.

Our second day, we take a nature walk with Roberta, a long-time resident, who teaches us how to be still and watch and listen in the forest. As we listen to what we think is the sound of croaking frogs, she shushes us.

"That's a toucan," she says. "Let's see if we can find him!"

The kids are impatient. They prefer spontaneous encounters with wildlife, like the armadillo that appeared on the lawn at lunchtime. But though, like every mother, I am a master at multi-tasking, I come to love the required stillness in the forest, which is sometimes rewarded by the colorful flash of a beak or the swing of a tail.

On an early morning rafting trip we spy baby crocodiles lounging on the riverbank. Our oarsman knows just when to row towards shore, so we can see animals in their natural habitat. He also produces a tantalizing array of snacks. Whenever the kids complain, we say, "Have another pink wafer cookie," followed by, "Hey, look! There's an anteater up in that tree! Pineapple, anyone?" Flocks of snowy egrets perch in a tree, then fly off in a beautiful white mass. White-faced capuchin monkeys mock us from above. Lunch at a riverside restaurant cools us, as do the tropical fruit shakes. We sample different flavors with every meal and pass our drinks around the table.

Now that our eyes have begun to see, we head to the cloud forest. Since many of the animals are nocturnal, we decide to go for a night walk. It feels exotic and, as dark descends, a little dangerous, except for the fact that we are one of many groups of tourists being led through the refuge by walkie-talkie bearing guides. Our guide Marcos explains that during the day guides identify sleeping animals so that they will have a better chance of leading visitors to them at night. Staged and commercial perhaps, but thanks to Marcos, we see a sloth lazily reaching for leaves, a drowsy porcupine, and a tarantula wasp and later, two tarantulas and an innocent looking, though deadly, eyelash viper. Five-year-old Maya wants to see a kinkajou. Marcos says that a kinkajou-like animal had been spotted earlier in the trees near the parking lot. He consults on his walkie-talkie, and we all converge at the likeliest spot, but this time we are disappointed. It's a welcome reminder that despite the lack of spontaneity, we are not at the zoo.

The next day I am determined to see a "honk." We set off on a canopy walk, where for the first hour, the only sounds of wildlife we encounter are the whoops of adventurous tourists who fly by on the popular zip-line tours. The unique perspective of walking above the trees is striking as we climb higher and higher, but we want glimpses of the trees' inhabitants. We make our way over bridge number 4, where Marcos thought we'd be most likely to encounter the bellbird. We hear the now familiar honk-screech do-wap, but there is no bellbird to be seen.

Everyone is getting cranky and bored and this time it's up to us to use our eyes and ears without a guide. The HONK of the bellbird taunts us as we make our way across bridge number 5 and we half-heartedly scan the tops of the trees. Suddenly Jeff calls out,

"Look, there it is!"

On one of the few branches that is higher than we are, we spy an unassuming brown and white bird. Our binoculars reveal the three distinct black wattles hanging down from its chin. We get to watch the little bird with the big voice for several minutes before it flies away, perhaps to haunt some other tourists with its distinctive honk.

Back at our lodge, we are the portrait of family togetherness as we sit in our backyard in full view of the Arenal volcano and check for lice. The bellbirds honk pleasantly in the distance.

I should have been satisfied. But it is our last day in the cloud forest and we still haven't seen a quetzal.

We head to the Santa Elena reserve, where the ranger points out the most likely spot to find quetzals. The air is filled with the sound of birds chirping and I step assuredly onto the trail. I haven't gone more than twenty paces before I hear a rustling in the bushes. I turn in time to see a mammal emerging and call to my family. Then I remember that Santa Elena has a peccary that was brought to the reserve as a baby and is now tame. This wild pig is more feline than porcine, as it rubs its smelly body against my daughters, leaving large mud stains on their pants.

The peccary accompanies us on the entire hike, occasionally ducking into green thickets, then re-emerging with a snort, sending my daughters into spasms of laughter. I admonish them to quietly watch and wait, but they can't contain their amusement. Though there are probably dozens of quetzals, I don't see them, not one. As I reluctantly step off the trail in frustration, Jeff reminds me that we came to Costa Rica to enjoy its proximity to nature together. A family hike with the Costa Rican version of Wilbur the Pig fits the bill.

We will spend our final days at the beach swimming and combating newly hatched lice. Occasionally I'll hear the warble of an unfamiliar bird and my eyes will scan the trees for signs of life. When it is time to leave, Jeff points out a tree full of parrots. "I don't want to go home," says Maya, voicing our collective regret.

A week later we are back at home on our individual treadmills, and the responsibility for daily nit-picking sessions has once again fallen to me. I go for a run and grapple with how we can preserve our sense of togetherness. Then I hear a screech and catch the scarlet flash of a red-winged blackbird. We have all learned to see beyond the immediate. Now it's just a matter of remembering to use our eyes together.

THEN, THEY FOUND ME

Past is merely prologue, I tell my pre-adolescent daughters. On days when they are suffering the inevitable emotional bruises of childhood, they are comforted by stories of my perceived childhood suffering. I was a chubby New Jersey girl with a dysfunctional family and an off-the-radar social persona in a small town where, as I saw it, no one appreciated my interest in foreign languages and spicy foods and people were in-your-face and proud of it. "And you know," my stories often end, "I grew up and never saw any of those people again."

Actually, it wasn't that bad: just the usual childhood middle class, small town angst, often portrayed in books and movies. And yes, I did grow up and, as many of us do, I've lived a life of many chapters: California student, exchange student in France, world traveler, Foreign Service officer and later, wife, mother and writer, settling into a peaceful existence in the verdant northwestern corner of the country, where the natives are polite and healthy and nobody ever gets run over by a garbage truck.

Here I've found my inner swan, taking the best part of my origins and subsequent reinventions and melding these qualities into the grown-up version of me. Over the years I've had happy reunions with several people from the more interesting chapters of my life. Yet, hovering on the periphery of fifty, I'm still a little ashamed of my roots. So I keep my Jersey self hidden inside me (like the fat person that lurks within the body of the newly thin), only allowing it to emerge on special occasions, like when Bruce Springsteen played the Superbowl half-time show, or when I am loudly (and some say inappropriately) rooting for Maya's basketball team.

Then, they found me.

The first blast from the past came from my mother, a seventy-five-year-old web surfing enthusiast, who, for most of her life, had been the living embodiment of a social networking site. Though, predictably, she moved to Florida, she kept up with the doings in our New Jersey hometown, remembered her high school years fondly and even lunched with her former classmates once a month. She found, and later directed me to, the website for my upcoming thirtieth high school reunion. Like a cyber peeping Tom, I looked but didn't act.

A few weeks later, I received a call from one of my best friends from high school, whom I hadn't communicated with in twenty-five years. She still lived in Jersey, was going to be traveling in my neck of the woods, and wanted to get together.

Sitting in a neighborhood sports bar that I hadn't known existed, I cringed as her husband, a die-hard Philadelphia Eagles fan, screamed epithets at his team as the game went into unexpected overtime. Near another big screen TV, polite Seattle fans quietly cheered every small triumph of the beleaguered

Seahawks, making polite allowances for their flaws. It was like being with an embarrassing, yet lovable relative.

Later, we showed my kids our high school yearbooks and my friend filled me in on the lives of people I had forgotten existed: the stoner had become a Port-a-Potty millionaire, the jock was a doctor and several people seemed to have done quite well selling cars.

All of this made my past real to my kids and I decided it was good for them to meet people who had meant something to me and with whom I could still enjoy an easy rapport, despite distance, different politics and years gone by.

Then came Facebook.

Egged on to join by some Foreign Service friends who had posted some amusing old pictures, including one of me circa 1986 wielding a (fake) gun, I succumbed to Facebook after months of resisting. I lost my innocence in the traditional way of Facebook newbies, wasting several hours the first afternoon reading the profiles of my many (thanks for finding them, Facebook) friends, prompting me to announce in my first status update: "Alison is regretting that she joined Facebook because she finds it as addictive as crack cocaine."

Friends complained about the pressure to join Facebook, and relaxed in a sheepish, conspiratorial way when I admitted that I had joined too. Some justified it as a way to monitor their kids' on-line activities, which we all know is the equivalent of saying you read *Playboy* for the articles.

It was only a matter of time before high school caught up with me via Facebook. The affable senior class president (now a media professor in Wisconsin) contacted me, I responded and we became "friends." You know what happened next. Friend requests came in from one of the class reunion organizers (still a die-hard Yankees fan), the audio-visual nerd (now with a struggling indie-music record label) and a woman last seen sneaking off to make out with my cousin (she appears to have settled down. He denies it ever happened).

I settled into a comfortable routine with Facebook, checking my "wall" (an ironic name for something meant to break-down barriers) once in a while, learning how to set my filters, ignoring martini and Farmville requests and never getting around to writing 25 Random Things About Me.

Then he found me.

Actually, I found him first. I admit it, that first addict-like day, I didn't just react to the friend suggestions Facebook sent me; I went trolling for people I knew and, in the process, learned that a lot of other people that I had once pigeon-holed had happily reinvented themselves too and that some (the senior vice president at Warner Brothers) would be well within their rights to have the last laugh. Ira, Ari and Seth had indeed become doctors, but their lives seemed to be happily filled with the joys of family, ski vacations, music and baseball games and they had managed to maintain close ties with each other and many other friends from our hometown.

While searching for my niece, I found eighty or so Krupnicks, none of whom was familiar to me...except one.

The postage stamp-sized photo revealed the unmistakable hair and brow of my father, who had been deceased for more than twenty years. The name, hometown and birth date were familiar to me too.

Here was my half-brother, whose birth, when I was thirteen, coincided with my permanent estrangement from my father.

I clicked the page closed and enjoyed telling the story for a few days. Facebook had the power to literally raise the dead.

But then, after a few months, he found me.

The nuances of Facebook are perhaps more, well, nuanced then email. His approach was tentative. "Are you related to the Krupnicks in New Jersey?" My response, less so. "Yes, and I'm also related to you."

His mother was also dead. I felt a surprising tenderness for this man/child I'd never met. I'd heard from my older brother that he had not had an easy life, though he had the standard carefree Facebook photo.

"I'm your half-brother," he said, adding, "I hope it's okay that I contacted you."

I am the veteran of a three-year, pre-internet, long distance relationship, which happily led to marriage. My attempts to choose the right words and the right tone and to interpret what my new Facebook correspondent was feeling, reminded me of the emotionally charged "voice-reading" I used to engage in during long-distance telephone conversations with Jeff, long before there was Skype or texting. At least then I had something to go on. These exchanges were much harder to decipher.

"Strange way to find a half-sibling," I responded, trying not to betray the emotional turmoil I was feeling, "but nice to meet you. I hope you have had and are having a good life."

Unexpectedly, Facebook had opened up the possibility that I could gain answers to the questions I'd never been able to ask my father. Doubtful, since my half-brother had been twelve when our father died. Maybe my father, whose bitterness at my mother tainted his relationship with me, wasn't the same father he had known and I'd get to hear about his positive qualities. Maybe we would share a sense of regret and unfulfilled possibility, since we'd both "lost" our fathers at roughly the same age.

Was he feeling the same jumbled mix of emotions and, if so, what did he want from me? After all, we were strangers, with nothing in common but some genes and a last name that means Cold Barley Soup.

I guess I'll never find out, at least not via Facebook.

Because despite my carefully thought-out response, I never heard from my half-brother again.

Was I too casual, inadvertently putting up a wall between us with my breezy "have a nice life" sensibility? Maybe I wasn't casual enough and should have added him to my "friends" list, though to me that smacked of insincerity. Or maybe, as many do, he had widely cast his friendship net to see what he could catch and had moved on.

It makes a good story and it's one I've told often, most recently during a face-to-face encounter with a friend from Paris whom I hadn't seen for thirty years. The Internet brought us together, but I realize that only a human connection will keep us that way.

Marvin Gaye had it right. There ain't nothin' like the real thing. Funny how the music from your youth sometimes says it all.

HERO SANDWICH

On some level I always knew this day would come, though I'd hoped to avoid it. We'd settled into a happy groove. The kids were older; I'd had a steady, yet flexible corporate writing job for the past three years and managed to publish magazine articles and literary essays from time to time too. We'd been to Costa Rica, had taken a road trip through Mexico, and had traveled to the interior of British Columbia to see grizzly bears in the wild. I'd begun planning the trip to Turkey we would be taking to celebrate my fiftieth birthday.

But now, staring me in the face was this: my mother, alone and destitute, had been diagnosed with Stage 4 cancer.

She'd been living her own life too. We'd reached a careful stalemate, which involved superficial conversations, mostly about the kids. Each year she traveled to Hawaii to visit the grandkids and then great-grandkids and would stop in Seattle on the way home to visit us. The rest of the year she kept in touch with everyone from afar, staying involved with the details of our lives. But life in Florida was a struggle, so she put herself on the waiting list for senior citizen and low-income housing facilities in Hawaii, where my older brother had settled, so, though estranged from him, she could be near his family in a sunny place she loved.

But now, it's fallen to me, three thousand miles away, to support my mother, arranging for her treatment, housing, home health care support and emotional support. In the week since we've had the news, cancer has become an almost full-time job, piled on top of my responsibilities as a mother with a part-time job and a life full of commitments.

They say you don't know what you don't know. Little did I know that attempting to figure out her health care coverage would cause me to become unglued. Little did I know that every day, I would move one step forward and two steps back, yet still make time to bake birthday cakes and cupcakes for Maya and Melanie, whose birthdays fell during Week One of cancer, and for whom I wanted to keep things as normal as possible. Now, facing insomnia after a particularly frustrating day, I worry that Maya, who has been suspiciously scratching her head for weeks, is harboring a nest of lice in her thick, red curly hair. Lice (and cancer) is what happens when you're busy making other plans.

My mother dreads the nights, but I dread the days. The endless to-do list that is not doable at all because of incorrect information, insurance loopholes and the sheer overwhelmingness of it all. The constant phone calls and, buried beneath all that, the emotional toll of the news on my mother, me, my kids. It sneaks up on me, but frankly, I don't have time to deal with it.

I know I am luckier than many. I have a wonderful, supportive husband, I don't have to work full-time and I have an understanding boss. Many people, friends past and present, have stepped up to offer support, the karmic pay-off of my mother's lifetime of giving to others and maybe even a reward for some of the giving I've done too.

But here I am, a native English speaker, intelligent and healthy, with time on my hands. And I am kerflummoxed at trying to make sense of Medicare and Medicaid and to figure out what makes the most sense economically. How do people with bigger challenges in their lives manage this? There are blogs and articles and books on caring for aging parents and I read them in the pre-dawn hours when I am unable to sleep. They help, but they aren't enough.

After a while, I develop a game plan, though it has as many questions as answers.

Sometime in the next week, I will fly to Florida and bring my mother to Seattle for treatment at the Seattle Cancer Care Alliance. She is suffering so much pain and discomfort already that I am trying to arrange a Medical Mercy flight, but barring that, we will have to fly first class. I don't think the bigger seats, complimentary drinks and better food will be enough to anesthetize us during the five-hour flight. I'm not counting on the movie either.

In every other aspect, we are also flying blind. What will the doctors tell her about her prognosis? She's been led to believe there is hope, but I have been painted a bleaker picture. How will she manage the rigorous chemotherapy? I've read that chemo can make you so bone-crushingly tired that you can't even get up to wash your face. Not to mention the possible nausea, diarrhea, mouth sores, dry eyes, itchy hands and feet and compromised immune system that makes you vulnerable to infection.

We will apply for Medicaid in Washington State in the hopes that it will help cover the cost of an assisted living facility we've found, where I had to laugh when I noticed that one of the residents is named Mick Jaeger. In Seattle, my mother knows no one but me. What will it be like for her to be isolated and ill in such a place? Even if she has good days, it's hard to imagine my independent, younger-than-she-seems seventy-five-year-old mother enjoying group meals or the bingo games and weekly outings to the drug store that I was told are the highlight of the residents' lives.

So my germ-ridden family and I will be her portals to the outside world. Over the past week I've begun adjusting to the fact that I will soon become a caregiver again and will have to give up some control over my life. It's been hard so far to deal with all the logistics, but I've been able to take a break from cancer whenever I wanted, taking a run, hosting birthday parties, drinking wine with friends.

Soon, for me, every day will bring new, unavoidable responsibilities. And for my mother, every day will bring unavoidable struggles.

We will truly be up in the air, hoping for a safe landing.

I lie on an emergency room gurney the morning of the day I am supposed to fly to Florida, my guts churned up and spilling out of me in a blood red rage.

I've spent much of the three weeks since the diagnosis on the phone—arranging treatment, trying to figure out Medicare and Medicaid and determining where and how my mother will live once she begins chemotherapy.

Three weeks and now the house of cards threatens to tumble down. We are caught in a Kafkaesque situation. A bureaucrat has yet to enter essential information into my mother's Medicare account that is required before the Cancer Care Alliance will honor her appointment. I spend hours groveling on the phone with all the relevant parties, to no avail. I have a momentary feeling of hope when I speak to a Medicare supervisor named Charisma, but when I arrange a conference call between Medicare and the Cancer Care Alliance, I am at the mercy of a bland peon who cannot help me. She has never heard of Charisma.

So I try my mother's new drug plan provider. I find a helpful woman named Stephanie and I appeal to her sense of humanity. She rises to the challenge, enters emergency notes into various and sundry computer screens and takes the gutsy step of giving me her last name and her employee ID number. She tells me to call back on Thursday, and all should be rectified.

So, once my guts stop spilling out of my body, I take the plane to Florida and wake up Thursday morning ready to hear the good news. But when I call the insurance company, no one can find a record of my previous call. WHAT HAVE YOU DONE WITH STEPHANIE???? I want to scream, convinced she has been vaporized for being helpful. Finally, I am referred to The Center for Excellence, where I am told that excellence entails initiating a status request to the Customer Advocacy Center, which, if I am lucky, will call me with an update, while I am on the plane back to Seattle with my mom. Did you really think they would give me the phone number for the people who are supposed to be my advocates? There is no number, I am told ominously.

We get on the plane for Seattle and when we get off, Jeff can't pick us up at the airport. He has been on the phone for hours fighting with the insurance company and doesn't want to give up until the problem is resolved.

Thanks to his tenacity, by the end of Friday, we have the necessary information from the insurance company so that my mother can meet with the oncologist on Monday morning.

She is lying on my living room couch moaning in pain. I sit across from her and we have the first honest conversation we have had in years. I tell her the truth about her condition. She tells me she's not sure she can handle the treatment. I tell her I understand. And I realize, finally, that she belongs home with us.

ALOHA OE

In the end, it only took two weeks. Two weeks from the time I flew my mother from Florida to Seattle and realized she had to remain with us in our home, two weeks from the time we visited the oncologist at the Cancer Care Alliance and he told us there was nothing that could be done. Two weeks, in which she ensconced herself on my living room couch, until the day she fell down in the bathroom and we moved her to the hospital bed we'd set up in the TV room, the bed she had been avoiding because she knew she would not leave it alive. Two weeks for her to go through her checklist of goodbyes. Two weeks to right old wrongs and make peace with loved ones. Two weeks for me to finally ask the questions I had always wanted to ask, and to be ready to hear the answers.

It's been six months. On my wrist is the "Kaddish band" given to me by my brother the night before her funeral. He's wearing one too. His giving it to me, and both of us wearing this reminder of loss for the next year, is his way of making peace with my mother and our way of bonding with each other, despite the different choices we have made in our lives. Acknowledging that we can't change the past, but can shape our own future together, one based on mutual respect.

We gave her a beautiful death. Though I chafed at being housebound, just as I had when caring for babies, I cooked her *congee* and butterscotch pudding and served her medication in little Moroccan dishes. We created a Care Pages website, where we could post updates and she could receive outpourings of love from family and friends. We filled the house with friends and relatives from Hawaii, including my niece and nephew, who are the embodiment of unselfish love, and feasted on the foods she loved. After years of battling, she was finally able to surrender and envelop herself in love.

During her last day and night, we played her the music she loved—Hawaiian music, *Camelot*, an aria from *Madame Butterfly* and Hoagy Carmichael's "Stardust."

The next month we traveled to Hawaii for a memorial service.

On Kapalua beach, our extended family gathered in a circle, talked about what my mother had meant to us, and sang "Hawaii Aloha," a song she loved. Then children, grandchildren and various other family members paddled out to sea on surfboards, paddleboards, boogie boards and sailboards. Our regatta gathered in a circle. My eldest nephew scattered her ashes into the sea while the rest of us scattered flowers. My niece and daughters jumped off their boards and swam where her ashes had been scattered, like mermaids attending their queen. Those still ashore sang "Aloha Oe" (Farewell to Thee).

We paddled back to shore and had a food-laden party at my niece's house. Mom would have loved it.

Jeff, the girls and I spent the rest of the trip strengthening our relationships with my brother and his new girlfriend, with my sister-in-law, who had been like a daughter to my mother and a sister to me, with my niece and nephews and their partners and children.

At my brother's house, near the end of our trip, we looked at family photos he had gotten from my father, which I hadn't seen since I was a child. Later, after I have made the Russian dressing for our dinner, the first time I have done so in many years, he tells me I have gotten the proportions just right.

For all of my resistance to Judaism, I take comfort in the fact that Jews believe we live on through our family and our descendents—through their memories of us, the ways we influence them and through our deeds.

Not long before she died, my mother and I sat alone together in the dark and talked. No single Big Truth emerged, but a series of small ones did.

"Now do you understand me?" she asked.

The story is never over. I will live with it for the rest of my life.

And it will live on in my daughters.

MY GRANDMOTHER'S THIGHS

One day, while sitting on the toilet,
I looked down and was shocked to see
My grandmother's thighs.
Not just my grandmother's thighs,
But those of my great-grandmother,
My aunts and great-aunts and my mother,
Once she'd given up chain-smoking
And began to fill out.

I remember those thighs best
During summers at Beacon Beach,
Spilling strongly and unashamedly
Out of sturdy one-piece bathing suits,
Varicose veins glowing in the sun.
No beach cover-ups for these thighs!
They existed proudly alongside
Aesthetically more pleasing neighbors,
Tanned, smooth, shapely thighs

That stuck unsubstantially out of bikinis.
The contrast was like that of stiletto heels
And sturdy winter boots.
From a child's height, the thighs
Were what you saw first
As you peered trustingly up
At grandma or auntie or mommy,
Waiting for them to dispense juice from the cooler,
Provide money for ice cream,
Or give you the go-ahead to return to the water,
Your thirty minute waiting period after eating
Finally at an end.

They were like buoys on the sand,
Attached to the ever-vigilant woman
Who watched you swim,
And you knew that they would propel her to rescue you,
Should you be trapped
In the jaws of the angry, churning Atlantic Ocean.

At the end of the day
They peeked out from under
The shower stall and later the locker,
Before being covered up again by flowered *schmatas*,
Encasing the women who led us to the car
Carrying bundles of blankets and coolers and bags,
The thighs supporting them
And their burdens
Like trustworthy yaks on a Himalayan trek.

I will never love my thighs
And will continue to run, bike and tone them into submission.
I will resent my genes for passing on to me such beasts
And will always cover them up at the beach
With exotic sarongs that say, "No! I am not like those women.
I am different. I have traveled.
I have done things!"

But I will also hope
That once in a while my daughters will get a glimpse of them
And experience the same sense of trust that I had.
I want them to know that I will always be there.
I want them to be aware of the strength
Of the women from whom they are descended.
But mostly I want them to be blessed with
Their father's thighs.

EPILOGUE

My thirteen-year-old daughter Melanie is excited at the prospect of getting her driver's license in two-and-a-half years.

"I wonder what my first car will be," she gushes.

Without skipping a beat, I reply.

"A 2000 Toyota Sienna minivan."

"In Sailfin Blue?" she asks, resigned.

"Yup."

My time as a minivan-driving mom with an identity crisis is coming to an end. Melanie and Maya will remain at home with Jeff and me for less than the lifespan of a guinea pig.

I'm fifty now. I'll be getting a new driver's license next year and, when I do, the new picture will document how I am managing the transition to menopause, with daughters who are just beginning the journey to womanhood.

We went to Turkey for my fiftieth birthday and stopped en route in Paris, a city I hadn't visited in more than thirty years. As we meandered down narrow Left Bank streets and ordered pâtisseries in neighborhood cafes, my French and my sense of exhilaration came pouring out of me, as if no time had passed.

At a cave hotel in Cappadocia, I encountered a vivacious thirtyish single female Foreign Service officer, on holiday from a hardship posting in Iraq. I could have introduced myself to her. We could have shared war stories and I could have told her how my story turned out, but I didn't. Her story is still unfolding.

I have remained Facebook friends with many of my classmates from New Jersey, none of whom I ever expect to see again. But when my mother died, their outpouring of condolences touched me. As the months have turned into years, they have begun losing their parents too. The collective sharing of this universal milestone with people from my past has proven more comforting that I would have expected.

I've begun exploring loss and other mid-life issues in a blog called "Slice of Mid-Life" (www.sliceofmidlife.com), and have appreciated being connected to and learning from a large community of people who are grappling with many of the same issues as I am.

As I write this, it is the second anniversary of my mother's death. We will commemorate it by burning a *Yartzheit* memorial candle for twenty-four hours and eating her rendition of *Buccatini al Ragù*.

Meanwhile, I am editing this book and my daughters are hearing some of these stories for the first time.

I hope it provides them some answers to questions they may not yet realize they will have, and is a source of comfort and clarity whenever they need it.

A DISCUSSION GUIDE
FOR BOOK GROUPS

1. The author's actions in India and Vietnam altered other people's lives. Have you ever been in a position of authority that affected other people? Can you describe a situation that was impacted by your youthful hubris and/ or naïveté?

2. What is your most memorable experience of culture shock?

3. Which foods have you missed most when traveling overseas? Have you added any international foods to your repertoire?

4. Describe your first experience in another country.

5. When she was in Paris, the author was exposed to a mélange of cultures and an array of political developments

that made her decide to study international relations. Is there a particular experience or a particular person that led to your career choice?

6. What, if anything, did you give up when you had children? How did you compensate for this loss?

7. The author describes her career ambivalence before and after having children. Have you struggled with where you should be on your chosen career path? Have you made a dramatic career change?

8. How has becoming a parent changed your relationship with your spouse? How has it changed the way you feel about yourself?

9. How has your relationship with your mother changed, as you've gotten older? Do you see yourself becoming more like her?

10. The author made peace with her mother at the end of her mother's life. Have you had, or do you wish you could have had, an experience of reconciliation with someone you loved?

ACKNOWLEDGEMENTS

For years on our refrigerator, we kept a Get Out of Jail Free Card, Good for a Reading by Adam Gopnik, placed there by my husband Jeff. *Paris to the Moon* came out in 2000, when I was the mother of a toddler and soon-to-be-mother of a new baby and the way I viewed the world was already in the process of transformation. I'm not sure whether Gopnik or one of his reviewers said it first, but his writing is about seeing the world in a grain of sand. As my world seemingly got smaller, thanks to Adam Gopnik, I was able to appreciate that just because your world shrinks, your worldview doesn't have to.

Having kids is a great way to make friends and I'm so thankful for the supportive group of buddies we've accumulated over the years, who are always ready to go out for coffee or celebrate Cinco de Mayo with us, no matter what date we pick.

Thanks especially to Diane, Carolyn and Steve for riding the wave of parenthood with me and for answering the phone when it mattered. Thanks to the members of my book group and Mother-Daughter book group for great conversations and insights into the female mind at various ages.

You can't spit in Seattle (not that anyone would) without hitting a coffee shop or a writer in a coffee shop. The writers, editors and writing teachers I have known over the years have supported me. I am especially pleased that, thanks to the Ballard Writers Collective, I get to be part of a creative community without having to leave my neighborhood. Special thanks to Peggy Sturdivant for creating the group and to Ingrid Ricks, Jennifer D. Munro and Wendy Hinman for encouraging me to finish this book.

My sister-in-law Denise is a dedicated proofreader and an excellent driver. I thank her for being my first fan.

When I married Jeff, I married into a family that has given me so much more than great earrings, and into a warm community of reef net fishermen and women and other friends associated with Lummi Island.

To far-flung friends and family, thanks for staying in touch on Facebook. My Hawaii ohana has taught me about unselfish love. My big brother Mike has shown me that it is possible to remain smart and savvy as you get older, and still have the energy to catch Bruce Springsteen multiple times on one tour.

To readers of my blog, Slice of Mid-Life, thanks for your comments and your support.

Jeff and I frequently remind each other not to sweat the small stuff, but, like most people, we get caught up in the frenzy of family life and don't always follow our own advice. In *The Woman at the Washington Zoo: Writings on Politics, Family and Fate*, a collection of essays by Marjorie Williams, who died of cancer at age 47, Williams reflects on what you do when you find out you only have a short time left with your family: lead as normal a life as possible, only with more pancakes.

Thank you, Jeff, Mel and Maya for a pancake-filled life with all the trimmings.